The Misfit Bride

Books by

PEGGY TROTTER

Year of Jubilee
Reviving Jules

~Unchained Souls Series~
The Secret Things
The Secret Storm

~Society of Outcasts~
The Misfit Bride
The Lowborn Lady (12/1/21)
The Spellbound Schoolmarm (6/1/22)

The Misfit Bride

Society of Outcasts
Book One

PEGGY TROTTER

The Misfit Bride
© 2021 Peggy Trotter

Visit the author's website at: www.peggytrotter.com

Published by Ransomed-Ever-After Books

This novel is a work of fiction. Names, characters, businesses, places, events, and incidents are either the products of the author's imagination or used in a fictitious manner. Any resemblance to actual persons, living or dead, or actual events is purely coincidental.

First Edition, 2021
ISBN 0578876302
ISBN 978-0-578-87630-6
Library of Congress Control Number: 2021905057
Printed in Seattle, WA, United States of America

All Scriptures used with this work are from the King James Version (KJV).

Cover Illustration © 2021 by Zanne Davis
Edited by Nancy Clark

No one abides as a member of the Society of Outcasts.

For, to God there are no misfits, only those who thirst to be

Redeemed.

"And Jesus put forth his hand, and touched him, saying, I will; be thou clean. And immediately his leprosy was cleansed."

Matthew 8:3

"For I will restore health to you, and your wounds I will heal, declares the Lord, because they have called you an outcast…"

Jeremiah 30:1

Chapter One

It was exhausting being a mannequin head. And painful to boot.

Cora Taggart's bent back ached, her chin digging into the wirework dressmaker's form. Adjusting her bonnet, she glanced back. Bolts of cloth spewed from various cubbyholes. Why hadn't she crouched behind those shelves? Poor choice slipping through the curtain into the window display. Yet there'd been no time to search for a better spot. She froze, unblinking, as two ladies breezed past the window.

"Ill-bred little thing." Widow woman Pearl Dixon's voice drifted from the counter. And then a sniff. "Only not little. Overly tallish is more the truth. Miss Too-Tall Taggart nearly steps on most of the men folk."

Cora clenched. Too-Tall Taggart. Holy tarnation, she hated that moniker.

"Och, Pearl, 'tis not kind what ye say. What a bonny lass she is," Miss McGarlee's Irish Quaker voice interrupted. Oh, the spunk of the woman defending her touched Cora's heart. "Crocheted the scarf in ma window with its fancy stitch, she did."

Cora's gaze shifted to the wooden milliner's head below her. That very scarf lay nestled around the dummy's neck. The mental image of the ginger-haired spinster gesturing toward the window forced a whispered plea. *Please don't let them draw the curtain aside.*

Parting with the soft yellow scarf had wrenched her heart a bit. Being nineteen, she had to earn some sort of wage. And there weren't many opportunities in New Albany, Indiana, to do so. In these modern times of 1853, earning her own spending money proved difficult. But the scarf would bring a good price.

She sucked in a deep lungful of air tinged with fresh linen and something like the underside of her four-poster bed. Her throat tickled, and she struggled not to cough. Thankfully, no footsteps approached. Perhaps she'd avoided disaster.

The widow snorted. "Bonny? Cheeky is what I've overheard, walking around muttering to herself."

Cheeky? The muttering, maybe, but cheeky?

Eyeing more passing shoppers, Cora stilled. Once safe, she mouthed a verse in silent cadence. "Love your neighbor as yourself. Love your neighbor as yourself." She let her eyes slide closed and then whispered an addendum, "Even when you want to poke them with a finely sharpened stick."

Best to distract her thoughts to avoid thinking about finding a poking device right quick. She stroked the sleeve of the full, rose dress hanging below her chin. Cotton batiste. Nice, light textile. She adored sewing with it—

"Gyrating with—what's it called, Elizabeth? The newfangled calisthenics only fit for men?"

"Baseball, I be—"

"That's it. Baseball. Rumors say she wears men's britches and runs rough and tumble with those brothers and nephews of hers. What suitor could tolerate that? Miss Too-Tall Taggart is nothing but a misfit."

Cora scratched her shin with the toe of her boot. So much for distraction. Glory hallelujah. Widow woman Dixon done picked her clean as a discarded Thanksgiving turkey carcass tossed in the chicken pen. Doggone baseball, anyhow. Why'd it have to be so entertaining?

And wearing britches? How Cora wished it were true. If she could convince her mother to allow pants instead of this confounded skirt, her base-stealing count might surpass her brother Miles's.

It'd be easier to quit playing if she weren't so adept at the modernized sport. And thanks to Levi's letters from New York, she knew all the rules. Good thing the widow had no knowledge of her treasured homemade leather glove and lemon peel baseball stuffed in her bottom dresser drawer. That wouldn't help her cause at all.

Miss McGarlee's voice cut in. "Misfit? I think not. No, indeed. And if the lass doesn't marry, what harm is done? There's worse ways to go through life, and I'm telling ye from a voice of experience. I've never regretted not marrying—"

"Look over there." The widow gasped. "Earl Jamison's just sauntered into Spizy's Tobaccy. And those amber colored bottles aren't filled with lemonade. Oh, Elizabeth, he'll soon be liquored up. When his mother finds out how he's spending his time, he'll lament ever setting foot in that sin-hole. Come along. We must be going. You understand, Maura? Let me know when you get some new parasols."

Scuffles indicated a hasty exit. Through the glass pane, Cora's eyes trailed the hefty widow dressed in a cape of Black Death. Petite and equally meek Elizabeth Rodgers, the bank president's wife, scurried in hot pursuit. They knifed toward Jamison's Coffee Shop.

Cora, now freed, massaged the back of her neck. She swiped the curtain aside and meandered to the counter. Miss McGarlee glared at the doorway, her face red, plump cheeks swollen. Her tiny fists poked deep into her ample waist.

"Ye will answer. Indeed ye will." The older woman shook a fist at the closed door, spun, and yelped. "Dear child, ye near killed me dead where I stand. Have ye been here long?"

"Long enough."

The proprietor's face fell, darkening the flush across her cheeks. "Och, 'tis such a mess."

The short woman dropped her gaze and repositioned the sawdust pincushion, the measuring tape, and the heavy scissors in much the same way a carnival hawker would swipe half walnut shells in a game of chance. Finally, the woman looked up. "Ye know how Pearl is. 'Twould never occur to her that a person's life is none o' her business."

The grin returned to the shopkeeper's face. She snorted, the Irish outweighing her Quaker side. "Old spinster, indeed. Lassie, I won't speculate on it another moment. But I will rehang the doorbell. Ye come to see the new cloth?"

"Yep." Cora set out after Miss McGarlee. She wound around another mannequin, fully dressed in a practical, brown Sunday dress with matching bonnet and reticule.

"Aye, let's see now. I wrote down the word." Her hand shuffled into a hidden pocket. "So odd ya' know. Azure. Some Frenched-up sort o' word. Might be ay-sure, or o-shore."

Cora tamped down a giggle. The seamstress constantly combined words into new ones. Thinking of this tugged her mind from the lash of the widow's words.

"Some queen's wearing it somewheres out there." The woman stopped beside a table and pulled a stunning blue bolt of cloth from under the sign of "newly arrived."

Incredible. The bluest of blue, with a hint of yellow. So bright it took Cora's breath.

"The ole shyster tried to foist ten bolts of ay-sher silk on me. 'Twould kill me right off, ye know, to pay for such finery. I wrangled him back to a couple bolts of polished cotton. Och, much more affordable to the common ladies."

Cora locked her loosened jaw as she fingered the shiny material. With the amount of shine on the fabric, who needed silk?

"Then that snake-salesman done accused me of putting curtains on the local ladies. Pshaw. He don't know how fine a seamstress you are, Miss Cora. Why, you could take a chewed-up wool sock and make a fine wedding dress. Even the widow knows that."

Miss McGarlee whipped the textile bolt from her and tottered back to the counter. Cora trailed the older woman's busy body back through the store. The proprietor chattered while spreading the material across the low table, measuring with quick, experienced hands.

Then she frowned. "What I'm a-thinking? Ye ought to take the whole bolt. I need more than one dress from this ay-zher. Once the ladies of New Albany get an eyeballful of yer creation, Lass, the rush will be on. Even them fancy ladies from downtown will stick their eyeballs in here. My shop will never have seen the like."

A laugh burst from Cora. A store full of eyeballs?

"And pay no mind to the widow." The red-head winked as she rewound the bolt and topped it with delicate white buttons and matching thread. "Yer the best catch in Indiana."

Sure, if Cora followed Jack up the beanstalk. Oh, her kingdom for some magic beans. Surely she'd be petite compared to a giant. Cora grasped the wrapped bundle from Miss McGarlee, forcing the silly notion away. "Yes, Ma'am. And I need a couple hanks of cotton yarn. I need to make Mama some more wash rags."

"Surely." She added the yarn to Cora's pile. "Don't even bother to pay. I'll take it out of your share when I sell that scarf. And make a few extree warsh rags, and I'll display them here. They sell fast."

Cora nodded and stuffed the yarn into the back of the package.

"One last thing. I fixed up some hard candies for that nephew of yours." Miss McGarlee pressed a small brown-wrapped bundle into Cora's free hand. "Don't them lads get into all sorta trouble? The good Lord done preserved him from the cows crushing him. Coulda done split his gourd instead o' his leg. He's a hero, 'tis what he is. Plain and simple."

A shiver danced down Cora's spine. The widow's words paled in comparison to her nephew's recent close encounter with death. "Thanks, Miss McGarlee. Jimmie will enjoy a little treat."

"You betcha. Now don't ye dwell on the widow's prediction, my lass. 'Twill come out in the wash."

Unless she happened to be a wet wool sweater shrinking in the hot sun, Cora doubted it. How she wished a good swish in hot water would shrink her six inches. Or maybe eight? With an inward sigh Cora nodded and headed for the door before she blurted her true feelings.

Fresh spring air greeted her through the soundless door, and she let out a low groan. Heaker Thomas, bearded blacksmith, paused on the wooden walkway and nodded a greeting. His big hand yanked the hat from his slightly balding head. Most women thought Mr. Thomas had a full head of hair. If only they had her point of view.

His weathered face remained solemn, but his eyes sparked with interest. "Howdy."

Cora bobbed a short nod, heat churning up her neck. Father had cornered Mr. Thomas last Sunday, and from the way they'd kept glancing her way, she feared they discussed some sort of courtship possibility. The man was nearly her father's age and had five children. Though it was a pure shame he'd lost his wife last year, Cora had no interest in becoming the next Mrs. Thomas.

Her heart sank. Plumb pathetic that the only man who'd ever expressed an interest in marrying her was twice her age. She scampered past him, feeling the heat of his gaze on the back of her neck.

The early spring wind whipped at Cora's skirt as she scurried to the next block near the physician's office. Hungering to be out of Heaker Thomas's eyesight, she cut into Kinderbrook's Stationery and Books. She might as well check for mail at the back counter. Between the widow and Mrs. Thomas, she could use a letter to brighten the day.

Harvey's pot-bellied stove poured out heat even though the temperature approached fifty. But there would be no complaint from her. Mama claimed Cora had the circulation of a ninety-year old anyway. She was constantly freezing near all the time. Or nearly, as her sister would be quick to correct.

Cora inhaled the distinct smell of paper mixed with burning wood as she settled against the counter. "Good morning, Mr. Harvey."

"Fine day indeed, Miss Cora. I mean, Miss Taggart." He shook his head, a topless brimmed hat revealing a sizeable bald spot. "You young ones grow up too fast."

Grow...up. Fee fie fo fum. That was an understatement. She glanced around the neat shop to keep from thinking of her height once more. Or her courting woes.

She didn't bother to alter Mr. Harvey's name. Mr. Kinderbrook didn't ring right in her head. There again, her reluctance to formalize his address made her feel like an old spinster set in her ways. Sigh...the word spinster seemed to be chasing her today. "Any mail for the Taggart family?"

"Must be your lucky day. Two for you. One, a right fancy envelope. President Pierce must need a vest and coat for his new term in office." He winked, drew a bundle tied with string from a small compartment, and handed it to her.

"I'll have to disappoint him. I specialize in women's attire." Her sister-in-law's neat script graced the first envelope. Too early to have become an aunt once more, so she shuffled it beneath the other. Her name and address beamed in showy calligraphy on the fine-grained stationery. "Who in the Sam Hill?"

Cora popped a hand over her mouth, eyes widening. Papa hated that phrase.

Mr. Harvey's brow rose. "Cora, Cora. You're a pistol."

"I'm sorry, Mr. Harvey. Really. Don't tell Papa."

He shrugged, twitching the broom-straw mustache. "You're secret's safe with me."

Cora nearly leaped to the door, biting her lips to keep any more improper phrases from tumbling out. Perhaps the widow had pegged her correctly as ill-bred.

She strode down the sidewalk, eyeing the surroundings for signs of the blacksmith. With the coast clear, her attention strayed to the envelope in her hand. Propriety demanded Mama and Papa read the letter first. Yet…where had it come from? Her finger swept over the fancy cursive. Never had her name been written with such an elaborate flourish.

At the end of the wooden walkway she paused. She should cross the dirt alleyway, mount the next set of steps, and continue to the physician's office. Instead, she skipped right, down the alleyway between the brick buildings.

Several horses, hips limp with relaxation, stood tethered to iron rings. Perfect. She scurried behind the last animal, a pony with attention-grabbing white blotches on red. It raised its head as she tucked behind him against the wall. The bricks, warmed by the sunshine, seemed to welcome her. She hunkered down in an awkward ball, balancing the larger package in her lap. The Pinto, one blue eye circled in white, nickered and reached out his muzzle.

"You're friendly." She patted his forelock. Might he be friendly enough to lend a hand? Or—in this case, a back?

She stood and with a quick glance over the animals' backs, she slid her extra envelope into the open saddle bag, and rested her big package on the horse's saddle. Then she returned to her dirty seat against the building. With shaky fingers, she lifted the flap of the elegant missive in her hand.

Out fell a sheet of expensive linen with gold heading. *Glenridge Estates, Lucas Place, Sixteen Hundred Locust and Thirteenth Street, St. Louis, Missouri.* The spotted pony repositioned his legs, jostling the fabric package. Yet, it stabilized, so Cora's eyes shifted back to the greeting. Seeing her name sent her heart jittering along her ribcage.

Greetings and salutations, dear niece, Cora Hope,

I pray this fresh season of spring has greeted you in good health. We have passed some time without communication, and I wish to remedy this very soon.

Your Uncle Calvin, your cousin Odette, and I invite you to visit us the beginning of May. It is our hope that you might stay for an extended period, perhaps even pass the entire summer in our company. Once a date is decided upon, we shall be able to accommodate you with an appropriate chaperone. Should you so desire to make this trip, please advise us as soon as you are able.

Cordially,

Josephine V. Glenridge, (Aunt Josephine

"Ahem."

Cora ripped the page from her nose and scrambled to stand. A shadow blocked the sun and two large hands gripped her elbows. In one smooth motion, she was on her feet. She brought her gaze up.

17

Up? There she encountered the bluest eyes she'd ever seen. Male. Just above eye level.

The air whooshed from her lungs. Dear heavens, had she really been sprawled in the dirt like some child at a game of marbles? Her face broiled. And it had nothing to do with the eager spring sun.

The feisty piebald shook, sending her brown parcel tumbling. The tall man shot out a hand, nabbed it, and turned to her with an elevated brow. "Yours, I presume?"

"Oh...my. Thank you." Excellent. A coherent, proper answer. A little breathy, but at least not some slangish minced oath exploding from her lips.

"My pleasure." He tipped his hat.

Jet black hair curled beneath the brim. Even if he'd been hatless, she couldn't have gazed upon the top of his head. He had a few inches on her. And dash it, a bit more handsome than Mr. Thomas. Younger, too. Now, here was a man who'd make a right fine suitor.

An indention dipped his left cheek as he pulled the other letter from the saddle bag. "I don't believe the postmaster left this for me."

Mortified, she stiffened into her full five-eleven height. "I apologize for using your horse as my correspondence desk."

A myriad of emotions raced across his features, but then his face flattened into obscurity. She couldn't help but admire the clash of his startling eye color against his sun-browned skin and dark hair. Yes, handsome. And tall. Very...tall. Hmmm. Lovely. His eyes narrowed. With a small gasp, she pulled back, yanking the package from his hands. She'd been gawking. At...him.

"Possum grease...oh. Pardon me. I need to go." She scurried from her warm spot against the bricks, gritting her teeth, both from the slip of the tongue and the dirt that most likely covered her backside.

"Don't forget this."

He held out the letter from the saddle bag. Her fair skin glowed hot as Mr. Harvey's pot-bellied stove. She imitated the widow's sniff to disperse her embarrassment. "Assuredly. Apologies again."

She snatched it and darted away. His laughter chased her. Cora's bones burned. As if she weren't humiliated enough from first, being caught squatting in the dirt and second, gawking at him like a four-year-old boy gapes at a new puppy. Now, he had the nerve to laugh at her mussed skirt.

Yet, it was hard to decipher if she were angrier at him or herself. What lady huddled behind horses in an alley? Simply more fodder for Widow Dixon's list of reasons why she would never catch the eye of a handsome young suitor. Or...a fetching blue-eyed cowboy.

She swiped her rear free of dust. What did it matter what he thought? The fact remained, such a man would never be interested in her. Too-Tall Taggart. Baseball playing, sit in the dirt Cora Hope Taggart.

And that was the whole rub. She was a misfit, destined to be joined to a man twice her age, and he, only interested for the sake of his children. Heaker Thomas was her one and only choice.

Yet, was a list of one a real choice? Or a lifetime sentence?

Chapter Two

T rigg couldn't stop the laugh that gurgled from his throat. Possum Grease? A hint of a smile quirked his lips. And using his Palouse horse as a correspondence desk? Not many young ladies he knew hunkered behind a smelly horse to peek at a letter. Most likely from a forbidden beau. Such a shame. He appreciated the blonde, green-eyed woman's beauty and stately form.

He shoved it away. Nothing but a distraction and he could ill afford that. Nope. The less he appeared in town, the better. Which was why he'd entered town on the northwest side. The path avoided downtown as much as possible. That and stopping by the best Swedish pastry shop his grandmother's maid had mentioned.

The sugar and cinnamon of the sticky bun he'd consumed in four bites still lingered on his tongue. Yet, it was time he put away everything sweet, both woman and bread, to continue his journey. He mounted his speckled horse and headed out the south side of the alley, avoiding the busy street.

Now, he had no choice but to head downtown. He guided the horse south toward the river, angling down the out of the way streets until he arrived on East Main Street. Mansions dotted the landscape. Gothic revival, Italianate. He paused in front of the huge gray mansion on his left, Romanesque in style, with corner turrets and budding maples framing the drive. The detailed wrought iron marched past the opulent home like well-trained lead soldiers. The double pointed towers on either side of the building bore much resemblance to raised human hands forbidding entry.

Much as he'd like to oblige the message, he clenched his jaw and urged his mount up the side drive to the back. Perhaps starting at the back door would squelch the disdain his presence was sure to fire up.

A young servant appeared from the carriage house. Right on time. Trigg nodded and the well-trained man took hold of the reins. Trigg wondered vaguely if the servant remembered him from his last visit.

"Morning." Trigg swung from the horse. "I've come to see the grandparents. I shouldn't be long."

The man's wide face registered no emotion. He merely bobbed his head and guided the horse to the hitching post near the garden.

The grandparents. Such a disparaging label. Not so much in the actual word. More in the tone it appeared both on his tongue and his thoughts. Trigg shrugged it off and climbed the steps to the back door. It opened after a couple of knocks to a puzzled African woman. Her eyes flared.

"Howdy. I'm here to see my grandparents."

She bugged her eyes at him. "Yes, sir. Come right in. Mostly callers come to the front door."

"I didn't think you'd mind, Miss Fibby."

"Oh no, Mister Trigg. You's always welcome. I'm sure the Missus will be plumb pleased to see you."

He stifled a snort. "Say, Miss Fibby, Bodine come this way?"

The woman glanced behind her with wide eyes and then leaned in. "Not that I recall. Some folks say he's chasing K'tucky liquor."

Before he could question her further, her heavy-set body scurried off into the innards of the muted, wood-paneled house. He stood in the large kitchen. Two other servants froze harder than horse tank water in January and stared at him from their spots at the stove and sink.

"Ladies." He pulled the hat from his head and they nodded. Like a rooster come to life after a mislaid chop, they dropped their eyes and bustled about the kitchen.

The place hadn't changed. A huge black stove, the sheen of oil making it glow, dominated the room. Butcher block counters surrounded it, while large pots of all shapes hung from hooks above. Dried herbs hung near the window bordered with bright yellow curtains. The floor was clean enough to lick. As always, perfectly manicured.

Miss Fibby appeared through the shadowed doorway. "She see you in just a minute, Mister Trigg. This here's Miss Ruth. She'll show you to the parlor."

Miss Fibby's portly form gave way to a delicate woman, with honey-colored skin. Miss Ruth kept her eyes on his Adam's apple as she spoke, her voice like cream.

"This way, please."

He followed the delicate maid through the labyrinth of shadowy, yet gleaming hallways until they entered a large room with high ceilings and equally high windows. A fire crackled in the fireplace amongst the pink floral walls. Windows let in a great deal of light, revealing the family crest on the far wall.

"You may have a seat, sir. Mrs. Graves will arrive shortly. May I take your hat?"

Her words came in perfectly cultured English. His mouth drew up tight as he handed her his hat. A new parlor maid, most likely an heir to a nearby plantation if her lineage could be revealed. But, instead she toiled as a lowly servant. His grandmother would have spared no expense to find this proper woman to greet the guests. She always demanded the best household help and spared no expense to obtain that goal. Yet another reason why Trigg never felt comfortable here.

With a heavy sigh, he sat down on a brown brocade sofa with a high back. Stiff matching chairs stood at attention at its flanks. He lifted his head to pore over the large painting hanging over the mantel.

So, they'd replaced the three-generation family scene with an earlier version. Convenient. Stifled any questions, or at least kept them to a minimum. Grandfather and Grandmother must have been just a few years older than he was right now. And mother looked about eight.

The adults' eyes were both cool and blasé. But the flash of adventure gleamed from his mother's. How the artist had managed to sneak in such a candid glimpse into his mother's personality and lived to paint another day was a miracle in itself.

Not even the drab olive green dress could drain away her exuberance. Though the black foil of his grandparents' formal wear balanced any impropriety. Must have been their burying clothes. He stifled a chuckle, and then shook his head. Mother had hated when he found humor in such things.

Heels clicked in the distance and Trigg stood. His grandmother flowed through the doorway to the right, full regalia in emerald, her face stretched tight into a long stiff mask.

She stopped a good ten feet from him and nodded. "Triggley, what a pleasant surprise."

Miss Stroud's charm school smacked him upside the head, but in his grandmother's gaze he gleaned the truth. He was an imposition.

She glided to one of the wing chairs and perched on the horsehair cushion, her chin guiding the way, assisted by the pinch of the snug bun at the nape of her neck. She lifted the silver bell on the small table and shook one perfect note. Miss Ruth materialized at the door.

"We'll take tea and scones."

Tea and what? Trigg had no time to ponder such things. The quaint maid bobbed a curtsy and disappeared.

Grandmother folded her gaunt hands in her lap and turned her boiling focus on him. "To what do I owe this pleasure?"

So, finishing school fled through the door with an unwanted guest. Ah, well, two could play at cat and mouse. "I'm fine, Grandmother. How are you?"

The slight rising of that pointed chin tightened her onion-skinned lips a smidge. She cut her gaze to the maid that drifted through the door. Silence swelled into an ominous presence as the brisk maid poured tea and distributed the flakey biscuits stuffed with jam and clotted cream onto small plates. Then she stood at attention, eyes lowered.

"That is all." Grandmother flicked her hand.

The girl evaporated from the room. Grandmother turned to steam him with her eyes. "I'll refer to my earlier question."

Trigg took a drink of tea. Sparring with her would solve nothing, even though it was quite tempting. "Fine. I'm looking for Bodine."

Her eyebrow rose. "And you thought he'd be here?"

Despite the tension, Trigg's lip twitched. "No, Grandmother. At least he wouldn't be here for long."

One dig.

"I'm quite startled you'd contemplate that your barbaric brother would be at this establishment. As you know, he's quite like your father."

Touché. A return thrust. And very true.

Trigg replaced the delicate cup to the tray and turned his eyes into the steely gray-blue ones of his grandmother's, so like his own. Fine. Down went the cards.

"Ivalee is missing."

Her rigid Victorian training concealed all except the paleness that stole over her face.

"She's followed Father."

The one swift blink before his grandmother looked away issued her confession of buried concern. However, she recovered and raised her cup, hands as sure as government taxes. "And what do you request I do of such circumstances?"

He crossed his arms and settled back. "Nothing, I reckon. But she is your youngest granddaughter."

Grandmother set the cup down with a rattle and turned her attention to him once more. "Your mother made her choice."

"So, you've no concern that Ivalee's alone, unchaperoned, and heading into a gold mining camp?"

She stood abruptly and whipped the silver bell from the table. "Take these dishes away."

The maid scurried to do her terse bidding. Trigg rose to his feet. Well, he'd known it'd be a short visit.

"I've not encountered Bodine since two summers past. As for Ivalee…" she shook her head. "I trust if anyone can unearth her, it would be you."

The tight set of her jaw indicated that perhaps she did care for her estranged family. Then again, it could be indigestion.

He rubbed his rough hands together. "Fine. I'll leave it at that."

With a grunt he spun and walked to the doorway.

"If you should desire lodging, I'm sure we could accommodate you for a few nights."

A few nights? That was nothing but crumbs of forced obligation. A feeble offering at best.

He snorted, "I'm not sure you have the room. Goodbye, Grandmother." He took his hat from the ready maid.

"Triggley."

The twitch in Grandmother's face gave him pause.

"Please...call again."

Suddenly she appeared tired. Old. Lonely. Perhaps her righteous stiffness was merely the bones that she hung regret on. After a long hard stare he replied, "I will."

❦

Cora hurried down the wooden sidewalk to Dr. Sokem's office. Most folks called him, Sawbones Sokems. At least that's what folks murmured behind his back. Rumors claimed his fondness for newfangled procedures boded unhealthy results for the patient. And many of the cemetery occupants might validate that sentiment. If they could talk. Surely, her young nephew required none of his untried tactics.

She swung through the office door and cut through a curtain hanging to the right. Eight-year-old Jimmie, buried in white on the corner cot, had his bandaged leg propped on a pillow. His cheeks tinged pink with the return of good health, the pallor of pain all but gone. Cora laid her packages down on a nearby metal table and stuffed the envelopes into her pocket.

"Hi." The boy's eyes had a glazy, dull glint.

Still under Sawbones's wicked pain-cutter. "Hi, yourself, Jimmie. You feeling better?"

He nodded, a swath of brown hair kissing his forehead. The child had somehow escaped the blond barrage of the Taggart family. Instead, he was the spitting image of his dark-haired father.

"Does your leg still hurt?"

A movement from beneath the sheets indicated a shrug. "I guess. It kinda aches a little."

"I got a letter from Aunt Beulah."

His eyes brightened.

"You want me to read it to you?"

At his nod she pulled the plain envelope from her pocket.

Dear Taggart family,

We're well this late winter and are looking forward to starting the planting. I hope the early spring finds you in good health. We miss you all so much.

Miles sends his love. Little Wiley is growing like a weed. He chatters most of the time now, copying every word he hears. He is such a joy to us.

We can hardly wait to make our family of three into a family of four. I've felt well, so that is a blessing. The doctor said the new one may arrive near Wiley's birthday.

We had two new calves arrive last month on the coldest of days. Both he-males, and Miles said that would figure after such an effort to get those two into the world. But we're still thankful for the new life on our farm.

The buds are beginning to swell here which makes us all anxious for warmer weather. I'm still boiling down maple syrup, as our maples were right generous this year.

Perhaps after the baby is born, we'll find a way to get over to visit, for we yearn to see everyone. I'll be anxiously looking forward to your letters. Tell everyone we said hello.

All our love,

Beulah Taggart

Jimmie's eyes had begun to close by the last line. Cora nudged him. His eyes snapped open. "Did you hear it all?"

"'Course." Despite his discomfort, he gave a weak grin.

"Just wondering because you were drifting off."

The brass clock on the table ticked off the seconds and his eyelids drifted downward again. "You want to know a secret, Jimmie Abel Breckinridge?"

His eyes snapped open. "Sure."

Glancing at the curtain, she pulled the other envelope from her pocket.

His eyes grew large. "What is that?"

She scraped her bottom lip with her teeth, not sure she should share. "An...invitation."

His brow puckered. "To where?"

29

"St. Louis."

Fatigue fought interest across his face. "St. Louis what?"

"Missouri."

"Oh. What's that mean?"

"It's another state. Like Indiana."

He nodded, growing less interested by the second. "Swell."

A grin plowed a furrow on Cora's face. "We have an aunt there."

"We do?"

"Well, it's your great aunt. Aunt Josephine. She's your grandma's sister. You know, my mom."

He nodded, obviously growing perplexed with the long explanation. "When's lunch?"

Cora chuckled. "I think you've got an hour or two."

"Where's Mama?"

Shutting down her fascination with the missive, she directed her attention to the small boy, so like her own brother, Miles, in personality. Perhaps that's why she'd always had a special place for him in her heart. "I think she's still at Pastor's house. She stopped by earlier."

Puzzlement skittered across his forehead. "She did?"

Cora laughed. "Yes. Oh, and Miss McGarlee sent along a sweet stick. But you'd better wait till after lunch"

Another gap-toothed smile shone from his sleepy face.

"I'll sit awhile with you." Cora leaned forward and whispered, "Maybe Sawbones will let you go home today."

"I hope so."

She adjusted the blanket and settled back into her chair. "How about I tell you a story about a brave boy who saved his brother from a crushing stampede of cows?"

His face grew solemn, and her heart squeezed at the dab of fear in his eyes. "No. I don't want to hear that one."

Cora stroked his freckled cheek. "Well, you were very brave heaving Roy over the fence. You saved his life, you know. Fine. A fresh, new story. This one is about a cowboy on the lonesome trail, facing down the rustlers to save his cattle."

Jimmie relaxed once more into the pillow.

She clasped his cool hand. "Once upon a time, there was a dark-haired cowboy with silver-blue eyes. He rode a spotted pony with one eye encircled with a patch of white."

His eyes drifted closed with a satisfied smirk on his face.

By the time she'd gotten to the exciting part where the rustlers swooped in, Jimmie puffed out little snores. She laid her head on the back of the stiff chair and let her words drift off into silence. She turned her head to the window, cracked ever so slightly for ventilation.

Poor Jimmie. Not only would he not remember much about the invitation she'd shared, but he surely wouldn't remember much about the mythical silver-eyed cowboy on the painted pony.

She, on the other hand, couldn't wipe his image from her mind.

Chapter Three

Trigg kicked dirt over the last of the coals. Body aches reprimanded him for choosing to sleep on the cold ground. Spring or not, the sun hadn't warmed the soil much. Perhaps he should have accepted the chilly reception of his grandmother. At least he would've slept upon a fine mattress with a hot fire on the hearth. Of course he'd be beholden, so cramps were the price of his pride.

He loaded his gear onto his horse. This was no time to contemplate his choice of last night's accommodations. He had to locate Bodine. On to his next lead. Louisville. Without more clues, it would be like searching for a needle in a haystack. But it was all he had, and he couldn't risk Miss Fibby's station to dig further. With Bodine's taste for bourbon, it did seem a likely trail.

He picked his way down the slope of the borrowed ground he'd used for his overnight stay and drifted toward Fifth Street near the Ohio River. The New Albany and Portland Ferry Company would oblige his trip. Given a couple coins that is. He'd search all six cities of the Falls Cities District if that's what he had to do. If Bodine had taken up abode here 'bouts, he'd find him.

However, after an afternoon of searching prosperous Portland for most of the day, Trigg was beginning to have doubts. He pulled his mount up at the Howe Stoones Saloon. The worn lumber nailed to the porch advertised its popularity with the working class.

Trigg passed over the weathered wood like so many before, creating a point of interest to the four characters throwing back mugs of liquor near the door. No top hats required here. Just sweat-lined, dusty broad-brims that partially hid a judgmental brow. And a smirk of unwelcome.

Not wasting one more thought on those rough characters, Trigg moseyed inside the darkened interior. One scan across the small square of space revealed no Bodine. He directed his boots to the counter, to a slightly interested pock-faced bartender.

"WhatcanIgetcha?" The man mumbled, planting a shot glass on the counter.

"Howdy. No drink." Trigg flipped two bits on the counter.

The scarred man's face ceased cranking on the tobacco in his cheek.

"You see a man today, big barreled, untrimmed black beard? Wears a dirty felt hat. He might have a couple of men with him."

"I seen lots of folks." He eyed the silver piece.

33

Trigg laid a hand over it. "And?"

He commenced chawing. "Ain't seen nobody but locals."

Figures. Trigg pulled his hand from the coin, shoved it toward the bartender. This had been an expensive journey. Gonna have to sell many a mule to make up for the bribes. He strode to the doors and slipped out. A guffaw burst from the group of men guarding the door. Trigg ignored them and beelined to his horse.

"Nice paint horse ya got there." One of the four inspectors stepped forward.

Trigg unknotted the leather reins from the oak bar. "Palouse."

The compact man leaned on the railing and wiped tobacco from his lips. "Injun horse."

Why couldn't Trigg nod and let the dust from his spotted pony's hooves season them? Because that derogatory slang name tightened his gullet, that's why.

"Nez Perce, actually." Why not start a fight? These fools were looking for one, and Trigg was dang ticked and frustrated from not finding Bodine. Still, one on four wasn't good odds, but his six-repeater, pocket rifle definitely helped to equalize any conflict.

"Uh-huh." Wired-up seemed to simmer. "All I heerd is Injun."

Trigg stepped away from his animal and pulled out the thirty-six caliber weapon, letting it hang at his side. "That so?"

The man straightened, the disdain in his eyes narrowing in uneasy respect. "But then, what do I know?"

The man melded into the silent group, and Trigg concealed his gun. Without another word he swung aboard his horse. He hung left at the intersection, not liking the four at his back. After

34

continuing on for several blocks, the river came in view, and he pulled up his mount.

He scraped the hat from his head in frustration. This was not a time to be making enemies. He punched the hat in his lap and the horse shifted. A crunch snagged his ears. That sound wasn't a hat maker's tag snugged in the interior flap.

He worked the corner of the brown butcher paper out of his hat and perused the plain signature at the bottom. *Fibby.* And from the looks of the neat cursive, details on how to find Bodine. A grin split Trigg's face. That clever woman deserved a cinnamon sticky bun. And his next time through, he'd see she got one.

Cora tailed her sister Aleena, close at her heels. She shouldn't have returned to Kinderbrook's to peruse the newly arrived novels after Jimmie had fallen asleep. The simmering expression on Aleena's face through the store window had surely shrunk her a few inches. Not that Cora wouldn't cotton up to a little shrinking.

The commanding thumps of Aleena's boots told Cora her sister intended to head out of the city and its busy nonsense as soon as possible. Aleena didn't care for the city. And the fact that Jimmie had been confined here had taken its toll on the family.

Cora flicked a gaze down the street where a grand house stood. Sure would be nice to live in such finery though. Passing time in a genteel manner. Reading the latest books, calling on other upper society friends. No farm chores. Just fancy balls and frills.

She supposed snobbery lay built in the very bricks of such places. Perhaps that superiority complex bled in deeper the longer a soul lived there. Like old Widow Dixon. Cora frowned, still stinging from the woman's words. And even closer to her own age, Rhapsody Hastings.

Horsefeathers, that woman was some missy. Gossip of Rhapsody jilting Cora's brother Miles still circulated town years after he'd married someone else. Widow Dixon herself probably still stirred that rumor. Cora harrumphed.

Aleena stopped and spun. "Did you say something?"

Caught. "Nope."

Aleena eyed her a moment, clenching the cheesecloth covered bucket handle. The smell of chicken and dumplings made Cora's belly growl. "The word, is no. Better yet, no ma'am. Did you retrieve the mail?"

Cora straightened. There. Now Aleena would have to look up a couple of inches. Take that for trying to boss a full-grown woman. "Yes. Of course."

Thankfully, Aleena turned and punished the wooden sidewalk once more with her sharp heels. "And?"

Well, luck had run out. "Two letters."

"I see."

Cora shoved her gloved hand into her pocket. *For once, Aleena, be content with—*

"From whom?"

Whom. Not who, like normal folk would say. But whom, like a professor of English at some hoity-toity college. Cora suspected it was Aleena's way of preserving her initial goal of becoming a schoolmarm. Until Abel had literally swept her from her intricately journaled plans.

Abel. If he hadn't gone off to the sawmill, these questions would be moot. From the moment Abel had burst into their family, he'd been Cora's hero, fending off Aleena's nosy intrusions. A dimple sank in her cheek. He'd presented her with her first baseball, dark leather, lemon peel with tight stitching. Much to Aleena's chagrin.

Her sister froze and pivoted again. "Cora Hope Taggart. I wish to get to Jimmie immediately. Do tell of the two letters we've received."

But currently, Abel wasn't here. Obviously. "One's from Beulah and Miles. And... the other one's from—"

"I declare."

Who would have thought Cora would be so pleased to see Widow Dixon? Fresh and puffed full of questions after grinding at the rumor mill. Cora side-stepped behind Aleena. Her sister swung to greet the widow and her shadow, Elizabeth.

"Hello, Mrs. Dixon, Mrs. Rogers. A pleasant day to you."

"To where has Abel wandered off?" Mrs. Dixon elevated her wiry brows, pulling the pale puffy skin into lines, her jawline melding into her swollen neck.

Ah, the widow never wasted time on pleasantries. Just poked the bear right off.

Aleena's chin rose a fraction. "He's about his business. And you? Have you completed your shopping yet?"

Snort. Mrs. Dixon didn't shop. Merely flitted about, stirring the gurgling caldron of gossip.

"Nearly. Why, Miss Cora. Haven't you grown into a fine young woman?"

The widow's hand gripped the buttoned front of her woolen coat, reminiscent of Napoleon Bonaparte. And she, too, had totally flip-flopped from her scathing remarks in the fabric shop this morning. Much like the blasted turncoat she imitated with her posture.

A scowl begged to grace Cora's face. *Just call me "Too-Tall Taggart" and be done with it.* But Cora managed a nod, relaxed her jaw muscles enough to press out a tiny smile, and bobbed a curtsy.

"Such a pretty face." Widow Dixon's gloved hand slid up to her tight lips. Her pointer finger rubbed an s to her chin, before her hand returned to grip the edge of her coat. Several blinks ensued. "Perhaps there is an Abel out there for you?"

Cora tugged her ears back with her facial muscles. An exercise she'd discovered as a child which moved her ears backward just ever so slightly. Kind of like a silent cat's hiss. She couldn't dare voice disapproval, so her childish game would have to do. After all, with a tone dripping in doubt, Widow Dixon made it plain what she really meant.

Such a shame. Pretty face, but much too tall.

"That's right, Mrs. Dixon." Her sister didn't pause a moment in the interchange. "Perhaps there's an Abel for you, too. You wouldn't have to spend so much time out and about with a man to care for."

The widow's eyes fluttered, and her lips gathered into a wrinkled rosette. "I beg your pardon? I buried my husband near on eight years ago, and none could replace him. I find it of bad taste to speak of such a thing, Aleena Breckinridge. I'll say good day to you."

A slight bit of air, compressed by laughter, leaked from Cora's lips. Aleena heard it and turned her head ever so slightly to silence it. "I beg your apologies, Mrs. Dixon. Good day to you, as well."

Black Death huffed off with her slightly grayer, thinner reflection right behind. A huge smile peeled open Cora's mouth as she turned to Aleena.

Her sister held a finger to her face. "Hush now."

"Wait. Aleena—"

But her elder commenced in stomping down the sidewalk. Cora scrambled to catch her.

"I find no pleasure in waylaying the town's old busybody." Aleena halted and faced Cora, fastening her green gaze on her. "But, always remember. Mentioning her dead husband will release you from any uncomfortable conversation. Is that understood?"

"I'm not a child, Aleena."

"Really?" Aleena's gaze swept over her. Then she held out a palm. "Give me the letters."

Defiance blossomed up Cora's spine. Always. She would always be considered a child. Ugh. "I just don't understand why no one trusts me in this family. I was going to tell you. It wasn't like it was some underground secret running about beneath our boots. Why I—"

Aleena swept the letters from her hands. "Stop mumbling."

"Tarnation, Aleena."

"Cora!"

One too far. Blame.

Aleena latched her fingers on Cora's arm and took off striding like a school mistress dragging a naughty child to the woodpile. Only Cora would more likely outdistance her sister's shorter steps. Not a word was said until they slipped into Sawbones Sokem's office. Durn, the place was empty. Her sister rotated in a flurry of infuriated skirts.

"This childish propensity of yours to voice inappropriate words and thoughts must stop." Aleena's usual beautiful face was marred with distaste, a deep furrow cutting through the center of her smooth forehead. "You're to never breathe that word again. Am I clear?"

Fine. Easier to agree. "Yes'm."

The respectful address suctioned some of the indignation from her sister, and Aleena brushed the rest of it off with her hands, like lint on the bodice of her dress. "We'll speak of it never."

A doubting grunt nearly made it past Cora's pursed lips. Oh, my, that would never do. Instead she kept her eyes on the floorboards and nodded demurely. Demurely. Why, that word should be ostracized from the dictionary.

"Mama?"

Jimmie's voice yanked Cora from her rebellion battle with Aleena and focused her on the most pressing matter. Getting her nephew home.

Aleena, too, pulled in her cannons and brushed the hanging sheet aside to the sunny room where her son lay. "I'm so sorry I've been detained for so long. Sister Virginia sent you some dumplings."

"Am I going home today?" Pain brought sincerity to the forefront of feisty Jimmie's gaze. He looked longingly at his mother, who surely hadn't been gone more than a few minutes.

"I believe so."

"I gotta get 'cause Cora says the doc really does have sawhorses."

Aleena turned a wuthering look on Cora.

Could he not have mentioned the cowboy rustler tale she'd spun earlier instead? "He'd wanted a story."

Had Aleena pulled her ears back in a hiss? Naw. Aleena was much too refined for such a maneuver. "Perhaps you could tell one that doesn't malign the local physician?"

"It is his nickname."

Fire flared in her older sister's eyes. Good thing she'd outgrown whuppings. In her younger days, about here is when she'd turn to run.

"If you want people to treat you as an adult, Cora Hope, begin acting like one." Aleena wasted no more time or breath on her and instead stepped to her son's bedside. The letters quickly disappeared into Aleena's pocket as she knelt on the floor to adjust Jimmie's blankets, crooning comfort while uncovering the dumplings.

Now, Cora would never get her hands on that letter. She stood for a few moments, but the two occupants had no interest in her. Poor Jimmie. So tired and needy after nearly three days here. Still, he could shovel in the dumplings. She stepped to the curtain.

"Don't wander far." Aleena's eyes were suddenly on her. Accusing. Displeased. Again.

Not trusting herself to speak without some blunder or sass, Cora stuck to a one-bob nod and slid through the opening. For a moment she stood, hating her circumstance. Aleena might put Widow Dixon in her place, but the widow had nailed her predicament to a tee. Pretty face, but undesirable in every other way.

Too-Tall Taggart said it all. Too tall to attract the attention of a young, available man. Too tall for courting and definitely too tall for marriage. Unless she resigned herself to a man like Heaker Thomas for the mere purpose of raising his young'uns.

Come to think of it, Cora was too much of a lot of things. Too old to be the baby of the family anymore and too sassy to be considered a grown up. And now her invitation would most likely disappear in the flurry of events. She opened the door and stood on the wooden walk and took a deep breath.

The northwest corner of New Albany buzzed with commerce, being the first signs of town on Boiling Springs Road. Horses and buggies jostled by, passersby in conversation, businessmen in bowlers.

Perhaps she needed somewhere new to spread her wings. To be her own person. To learn who she was and what she really wanted. Maybe this yearning was nothing more than to verify she needed to be here—where it always felt like home. Still, leaving Too-Tall Taggart behind would be a pleasure. Even if it were only for a short time.

Possum grease. That brought to mind the blue-eyed cowboy. Did he think her too tall or too childish? Even now her face burned to think of the impression she'd left. Not that it mattered. She would never see that drifter again. And besides, why would she dare think he'd be interested in her?

Abel appeared through the crowd of buggies in the high seat of the farm wagon. He raised a hand to hail her. She waved, relieved he'd cushion Aleena's disapproval on the journey back home.

Good. She could busy herself with Jimmie in the back. Perhaps Mother would listen once she returned. It was hard to wedge in a scrap of her mother's time with Grandmother ill. And there was something about the elderly woman's dying face that diminished all need in Cora.

Yet, St. Louis could be her chance to escape a forced marriage to a middle-aged man. How was yet to be seen. She would figure that out later. Right now there was only one thing she knew.

She had to get that letter.

Chapter Four

Mud splatted Trigg's trousers as the horses rushed by. Sure was blamed wet out here on Shippingport Island, just a stone's throw across a narrow channel from Louisville. Even now the bulky gray summer clouds threatened to up the quality of swill covering the dirt track. And the old racetrack appeared as shabby as great-grandma's gardening bonnet.

But this was where Fibby's note had directed him. He glanced about for Bodine's heavy-set form amongst the unwashed mob.

"Yep. Never been the same out heres since the '32 flood. Still, it's a place to while away the time. You been over to Big Jim Porter's tavern yet? He's got ten foot doors and a rifle longer than ol' grannie's turnip row. Ain't never seed nothing like it."

The old timer, firmly latched to Trigg's side, spat tobacco juice over the low bar of the racetrack. White billy-goat beards spewed out from each side of the old man's head beneath the beaten hat.

No one had to tell Trigg the ancient amusement area had fallen to the dogs. Gap-toothed groups of tattered men yammered over gambling bets and beat the battered fence sectioning off the track. Horses, one step above sway-backed nags, jostled around the far curve. Weeds overgrew the once entertaining mazes. Beyond, fused into a huge elm in a bubble of thick bark, the warped bar pavilion leaned precariously, collecting leaf debris and rubbish in the low spaces beneath the feet of the sparse crowd.

"You stick around awhile. You might run into the Kentucky Giant hisself. Believe it 'er not he used to be a jockey monkey. Yes sir, right here at Elm Tree Garden. 'Course, that be back in the golden days."

The codger let out a curdle of a laugh.

Trigg fixed a half grin on his face, seeing no humor in his words. Facing him brought the man's body odor to a peak like a face plant in a cow pie. Time to pump the gabby little fellow.

"Speaking of folks that hang around these parts, you see a big guy who looks like me, only with darker hair? He has a thick beard, fond of the spirits and horses."

The old man's light gray eyes took a Ferris wheel ride around, deep in thought. Even cocked his head and rasped his dirt encrusted fingers across his pock face sprinkled with wiry hairs. "Now that ya mention it, sure. Had a few other roughnecks with him?"

A cry went up around him, distracting the twitchy track rat. He waddled over to the group of gamblers and quickly exchanged some silver, chattering the whole time.

Trigg waved at him when the geezer stumbled away from the bookie. But the guy kept his head down. Great. More of his hard-earned money taking the form of bribery.

He cut through the crowd and sidelined the race sharp. The elder man jerked to a stop. "Here now."

Trigg held out two bits. "This man I asked you about. Where is he?"

"Huh? Oh, yeah. He wears out the tree." He flipped a thumb to the huge elm surrounded by the dilapidated wooden platform, still filled with people hocking their amusements. But his eyes stayed glued to Trigg's large coin. "I heer—d he had a nag to race."

"Has he been here long?"

Shifty eyes signified his greed for the coin. "A while, I reckon."

"You see him today?"

Weathered eyes went round. "Sure 'nuff."

It was tempting to head lock his scrawny neck until he'd pointed out Bodine. Hard to tell what was truth and what was a stretch.

The old man sported a toothless mouth. "Follow the liquor and yer gonna find him."

Well, that smacked true. Trigg shoved the coin at him. "Thanks."

Elbowing his way through a crowd ready for the next race, Trigg headed for the enormous elm on the far end of the park. He

46

stopped short as he approached the far curve of the infield. There stood Bodine, taking money from a group of men in ill-fitted clothes. A bear skin cape draped his back, making him look much more intimidating.

Trigg stepped in the circle, waiting for his big brother to stop chomping a hand-rolled cigar, his fingers flicking through a wad of bills. Oates and Burr stood tandem security on either side of him, like always. Bodine's eyes cut up and locked on his. A grin grew around the wadded end of the wrapped tobacco.

"Well, looky what the Ohio's washed up, boys." He catapulted out of a slouch and tossed his thick arm around Trigg's shoulders. "I knew you'd find me, Brother. I knew it."

He laid a rough knuckled fist against the side of Trigg's head and scrubbed.

Trigg pulled away. "Knock it off, Bo. Where've you been?"

A belt of thunder burst from the hefty man. A swift slap to Trigg's upper arm would have sent him tossing to the sod in earlier days, but now, it glanced off. A hardness fissured over Bo's handsome face.

"Ivalee waited for you. Now, she's gone."

Trigg dearly wanted to swipe the haughty blink out of his brother's eyes. "Git over here, little brother. Oates, Burr, take a walk."

His two cohorts swung away with bored expressions and moved off through the crowd.

"I'm a little busy here, Triggy. I could walk away with a good sum." Bodine squeezed the trapezius muscle on the far side of Trigg's neck.

To the onlookers, the show was just an arm of camaraderie, but Trigg knew the pinch of pain for what it was. Intimidation.

He went stiff, ignoring the pulse of pain down his back. "You promised her."

"Eight o'clock, Porter's Tavern, Portland canal." Bodine shoved from him and the gamblers enveloped him. Another race was starting.

Part of him wanted to pound his burly brother into the blades of the smashed, dying grass. And maybe he could at this point. Not that it would do any good. His two partners in the bounty-hunting game would soon return. Trigg may have thickened in muscle and age, but he couldn't pummel three of them.

He turned his back instead. Oh, he'd meet him all right. In the meantime, he'd circle the circumference, fixing his brother in his crosshairs. Bodine would answer to him. And then, he'd help track Ivalee.

Cora eyed her father. Green-eyed gentle man, a good five inches taller than herself. Those blasted height genes. Oops, those slippery minced oaths. The whole reason for this little interlude behind the woodshed. Literally. She plopped the axe head to the ground. The chopping block was usually her quiet contemplating kind of place. However, that was not to be today.

"You know how I feel about a gal chopping wood."

Dear Father. Always one to cast the disappointed aura, both vocal and in countenance. She supposed she should be grateful. Such a lovely father wasn't had by everyone. Sure and likely old widow whispered about her gentle upbringing as the reason she had such an outspoken disposition. A youthful, crusty spinster, that's what she'd be.

"I also heard tell you're taking liberties with muttering words that shouldn't be heard."

Aleena had been busy. Cora battled black thoughts as her father continued with his highlights of "good speech, good soul, good person, good citizen" monologue. In soothing tones. He reached out to slide a lock of her braided ponytail through his fingers, and pulled the ax from her hand.

"I'm sorry, Papa." And she was. Truly. Dagburn it—

"Let your brothers hack the wood. You…you know you have a special place in my heart, little Cora."

She sucked the breath to a stop in her windpipe. Little Cora. Even he didn't understand. She was no longer little anything.

"And your Mama and I are contemplating on that letter."

Again she nearly choked on the frozen breath in her windpipe. "Letter? From Beulah?"

Her father gave the crooked grin that looked so like Miles's. A swift longing, sharp and sure, squeezed her heart. Miles would understand if he were here. They were tight as last year's shoes.

How she longed to bump her knees against Miles's, leaning forward whispering furiously all the gone-wrongs in her world. He'd press his forehead against hers, his huge warm palm against her neck. How could he comfort her so with his sweet silence? A mystery Cora had no need to ponder. Only miss.

But her favorite brother wasn't here. She was grown and so was he. Most lasses her age had a couple of kids popped out by now, grubby fingers wrapped in mom's skirts, caterwauling about some sort.

"No, Girl. Your invitation from your Aunt Josephine."

Thoughts scattered like blackbirds at a gun blast. "My…invitation?"

Her father nodded.

"Oh." How could this be? She hadn't even found time to discuss it with her mother let alone work up a plan to get possession of the letter.

Papa parked his foot on her wood pile and rested a hand against his knee. "Your mama's been right busy. And right saddened. That's a burden in itself. She knows your grandma hasn't long, and it's such an overwhelming task to die. But she hasn't forgotten you."

What did one say to Papa who'd been steeped in wisdom a right long time? Besides, she still had a chance to make the trip. Why garble some nonsense that might make that flee from his mind?

"There's one other thing else we need to discuss." Her father tucked his hands in his pockets and stood tall. "You're grown and I have to think about your future. So, your mama and I decided to

PEGGY TROTTER

allow Heaker Thomas to come calling. And we want you to give him a chance."

Cora scrubbed a hand across her mouth to stifle any spicy terms that flew up her throat. So, that Sunday conversation had been about her. And Heaker Thomas? What in blazes would she talk to him about? "But Papa, he's...old."

A small rumble of laughter echoed from her father. "He is older, yes. But a fine Christian man."

"He's got five kids running about."

Papa merely bobbed his head as if this had no bearing on suitability. "Sure would be a good match with you so versed in young ones, thanks to your nieces and nephews."

He was serious. Completely serious. She pressed her mouth closed. "Papa, please...consider someone else."

Her father's eyes shone with a stubborn gleam she didn't often get to witness. But there it was, bright as sun in August. "There isn't anyone else, Cora."

Her throat seized like she'd been sucker-punched. It was one thing to think it herself. Even another to hear the widow draw up Cora's future in a few terse predictions. Yet, coming from her father, it burned like a cowboy's brand to her heart.

But she couldn't deny it. Total suitors for Cora, one. And the only one was Heaker Thomas, who'd already asked most every woman in the area to mother his daughters.

Papa sighed. "He didn't want to consider it at first, but I helped him see how you'd be good for the kids."

Scratch that. Suitors back at zero. When a father begged, it didn't count.

He leaned forward and squeezed her shoulder. "You're a good girl, Cora. I'm proud of you. Your mama is, too. Proud of the lady you've become and the help you've been. But you have to trust me. I'm doing what's best for you."

He walked off then, with her agape at the simple soliloquy. She let his words run through her mind several times as he grew smaller, approaching the house. Someday, she'd look back on this heart-to-heart talk with Papa and smile. He and Mama were proud of her. However, right now, the praise only resembled a spoon full of sugar to disguise the ugly truth. The ultimatum to accept an old man for a suitor. And even he was reluctant.

It grew dark as she stood there. Papa would now be sitting with Grandma, reading the Bible like normal. After all, his entire world hadn't tilted sideways like hers had. Mama would be in the kitchen wiping silent tears as she peeled tators. Then Everett would amble over to chop wood. Only she'd beaten him to it. How she wished she could ignore Papa's words and grab up the axe once more. She'd whack out another cord from the frustration frothing inside her.

After chores and lunch the next day, Cora meandered to Aleena's house to check on Jimmie. Maybe Abel would be around, which was almost as good as seeing Miles. Not quite. But almost. Maybe he could make sense with Papa.

She poked her head in the door of the house next door and tootle-ooed. No answer.

"Aleena."

Her sister appeared, flipping her apron and shushing. "Jimmie's asleep."

"Sorry." If Cora were smart, she'd pull her head out of the trapping stanchion of the door and the lintel and run for the hills. Instead she dutifully stepped inside. "You need any help?"

Aleena's brow puckered a moment, and then she raised a hand to fiddle with the cross that hung around her neck. "Did Papa talk to you?"

Cora nodded.

"Good. You need to settle down, and Mr. Thomas is just the man."

Even Aleena knew? Why should she be surprised? And, of course, she thought it a brilliant idea. She chose to bite a wad of the back of her lip.

"So be wise and obey him. It's for your own good." As if that settled it, Aleena spun to the door. "You may take the boys so Jimmie can sleep."

Cora followed her through the neat house to the kitchen. There Jasper and Roy sat at the table, faces pale and long. Little Maxwell sat in his high chair, applesauce goo covering his face, snuffling tears. From the previous sleepless night and courting nightmare that hung over her head, Cora wanted to plop in a seat and join the morose crowd.

"These two are banned from upstairs. They've woken Jimmie once with their quarreling. None of the elder cousins arrived to help keep them occupied, and Maxwell isn't much help unless he has a bowl of applesauce in front of him. I can't feed him that for another hour."

Cora tucked her hands behind her skirt. Nurse maid duties. Again. And with her new suitor waiting in the wings, it would never stop.

"Keep them occupied away from the barn. Maybe go find some spring flowers down in the lower field."

With a nod, Cora reached for a towel to sponge Maxwell off. At seven months, most of his food landed up his nose. Jasper and Roy rose and lined up in front of her like pupils on day one of school. Cora lifted the tike from the chair.

The four of them made a solemn trail through to the front door. Cora eased the screen closed. She patted Maxwell's back and waited until they were some distance from the house before initiating a conversation with the silent pair. Maybe it would lift her spirits as well as theirs.

"How was school, Jasp?"

The six-year-old shrugged, his blond hair, nearly white, shining in the sun.

"What about you, Roy? What did you do today?"

"Chores."

The snide reply of the three-year-old told Cora how that had gone. "How many eggs did you get this morning?"

"A bunch. I bwoke free."

Lands. Aleena probably birthed a calf over that. "Did you put plenty of straw in the basket like I told you?"

His snowy brows lowered into a pout. Probably hadn't used the basket at all.

"I hate chick—uns." Roy's arms crossed over his stout chest. "Dat bwack wooster pecked my weg."

Cora bit back a smile. "Jasp, maybe next time you could help Roy so he doesn't break any more eggs."

Jasper grunted. "I was at school. Besides, Roy always needs help."

Nothing truer spoken. Even if he was just weeks from his fourth birthday.

"Do not." Roy grunted back.

Even in bad moods the small boy constantly copied his older brothers. Cora stifled a giggle. "Think that old rooster will make a fine pot of dumplings?"

This drew a sidelong grin from the elder of the two blonds. The other—well, he was still sealed up like Fort McHenry.

"Roy?"

"What?" The boy stomped a few steps ahead.

"At the general store, I heard Mr. Callis mention his dog was having pups soon."

Like a wick turned high, he flared up bright and wheeled around. "She is? How many?"

"I don't rightly—"

"Can we see 'em? Wight now?"

Cora laughed. "No, Sugar Bun. They're not born yet."

The nickname brought back the brows of thunder to her nephew's face. "Don't call me dat. Dat's for babies. Wike Maxwell."

A laugh gurgled up. She might nanny more kids than anyone else in town, but they sure were the cutest bunch of tow-headed boys. She sobered. Soon she'd be mothering Heaker's daughters. "Okay. But you'll always be my sugar bun."

She dipped Maxwell low, and he burst forth a cute baby chortle. The boys ran ahead and picked up dirt clods as they veered off down the fence row. The two cotton-top boys flung their dirt balls at anything nearby, exclaiming over each burst of soil. From their reactions it was almost better than the Fourth of July fireworks.

Cora continued to bounce the baby on her hip as she went, getting a giggle each time. He found her pony tail without much effort, his tight fist yanking with glee. She grasped the hank of hair above his hand to save her scalp.

She strolled along, whispering a thankful prayer that Jimmie had snatched up Roy before being crushed. She only wished the older boy had made it through the fence as well before the jostling mob of cows had smashed his leg.

My, this is what it would be like raising up a passel of children. Dealing with their hurts, disappointments, and needs. Marrying Mr. Thomas would make her an instant mother of five girls, the smallest sickly-like. She'd be a…mother, full of responsibilities and a wife of a husband. A husband she didn't love.

Aleena had found and married the man of her heart, the traitor. Her other siblings, too. Yet she would be stuck marrying a strange, older man, someone who'd patted her head a few years back. Why wouldn't her parents allow her some say in her own future?

But she knew the answer. Even the widow knew. Cora was too tall and too odd. Too...everything. A misfit. Her eyes ached, longing to let her frustration drain down her face.

A noise caught her ear. From the eastern field came Evan's four kids, aged ten to three, picking their way over the unplowed field. Her other elder sister Mavis's two girls trailed them, nearly the same ages, and intermingled with the first bunch. The elders connected while the little ones fell to the rear. The sea of blond children drifted at a good pace toward them.

Succotash. Nine kids. Her own little school. Or baseball team. Cora blew out a mouthful of air. She bounced Maxwell airborne from her hip, and his opossum grip finally let go of her braid. The jabber of many young voices drifted to her ears. She knew what they would want to do. Play catch with her lemon peel ball, and then fuss and argue for the next turn.

She had to get away. Away from her family, Mr. Thomas, and Widow Dixon. St. Louis better show up in the cards real soon.

Chapter Five

Bodine scowled as Trigg settled on the bench across from his. The place was gloomy, dusty as a barn loft, but sported large windows. Light swept through the place only when a customer swaggered through the tall doors. And the old timer had been right. A huge rifle hung on the far wall in Porter's Tavern. Respect for his aged informant rose. Maybe the old man's info was worth the two bits. Trigg shifted his attention to his brother's smug face.

"Drink?" Bodine held up a jar of bourbon. He hadn't wasted any time.

"No."

"You're in the wrong city, little Brother."

"Ivalee. Remember? You promised you'd be back in Henderson." Trigg ignored Bodine's two lackeys leaning against the wall in deceptive casualness.

"Durn, Trigg. No 'how ya been, Bo? Business good, big Brother?' Nothing?"

Trigg swiped his upper lip to avoid chucking Bo beneath the chin. "Pleasantries aren't important at this point. You promised Ivalee you'd be home in six months. You broke your promise."

"She's a child. She'll get over it."

"No, she won't. She's gone."

Bodine's easy pace of imbibing slowed, and he screwed up one eye. "What do ya mean, gone?"

"She left to find Pa in Iowa."

"When?"

"A month back."

"With who?"

Temper boiled beneath Trigg's cheek bones. "With nobody, idiot."

The glass jar plunked to the scarred pine table, sloshing amber liquid over Bo's burly hand. "You saying she took off alone?"

"Nothing gets by you, does it?" Trigg returned his brother's glare.

"And you didn't stop her? Sounds like your fault, Brother."

And there it was. Bodine's flair for turning his every failure into someone else's responsibility.

"No. I looked for her for two weeks before coming to get you. I'd hoped you'd have some leads. You've been to the gold mines."

Bodine threw back his head and barked a laugh. "There ain't no gold mines in Iowa. Just a farmer saying he found a big fat nugget. All I got from that trip worth any value was a couple of spotted horses. One of which I gave you to rest yer sorry rear on. Besides, why are you worried? Ivalee can take care of herself."

Trigg rose and leaned forward on his hands, lowering his head near his brother's smug face. Oh, he remembered the generosity of his brother all right. He'd paid a pretty penny for that Nez Perce horse. And if Trigg remembered the story right, Bo's kickback for the other three horses he'd sold had been substantial. That was Bo. Always out to make a buck, even off his own kin. "Curse you, Bo. She's fifteen."

A grunt lit a snap of defiance in Bodine's eyes. "And smart as a cat."

Be right sweet to smack the smart aleck off his face. But then again, it wasn't just one on one. "Fact is, you made a promise and broke it. You're a tracker. Or so you claim."

His brother's eyes squinted. "Ain't got the time."

Trigg leaned closer. "She's our sister, Bo."

Bodine rose and stretched beneath the huge smelly bear skin. He downed the rest of the brew with a quick sling. "All right then. But you're coming with me."

"Of course." Trigg cocked a head toward the two lounging at the counter. "What about them?"

Bo's eyes took a lazy rove to his two cohorts before blinking a slow blink. "They go with me."

Not the best arrangement. Bo had grown hard hunting down criminals. Two lackeys without a family connection to soften their rough edges might hinder the journey. Only dollar signs danced in their eyes. Finding Ivalee might require more energy and perseverance than they were willing to give.

Bo intercepted Trigg's reluctance. "They don't go, I don't go."

He took a deep breath. Backed in a corner. "Fine. But you don't quit till we find her."

"Deal." He held out his hand.

Trigg couldn't stop the flare of distaste from crossing his face. What did he think? They were going to shake on it like some kind of horse-trading deal? This wasn't some plan to track an outlaw. "I'm not a kid anymore, Bo. And this isn't some bounty hunting, profit-turning adventure. This is Ivalee. You got it?"

An odd smile peeked its way through Bo's scruffy beard as he dropped his hand. "Sure, Trigg. It'll be like old times."

Old times? Bitterness rose in his throat. That did not bode well.

༺∞༻

Cora fluttered about her room. Actually fluttered. Who'd a thought she could flit about like some light butterfly? Especially when an unwanted courtship loomed in her future. No, she would deal with that situation somehow. Later. Right now, she was bound for St. Louis.

She held a fist to her lips and paused in the middle of the room. "Thank you, God." A grin split her face, and she tipped her head to the ceiling. Then she sobered and whispered beneath her breath. "And if it's not too much to ask…could you make this courting thing disappear?"

No harm in tagging on a new, very desperate request. Cora shook her head and focused on her father. After lunch, he'd taken her aside and told her of his and Mama's decision. No fanfare. Just a simple affirmation of her St. Louis trip and a date of arrival. She took a deep breath. This would be a journey of a lifetime.

More importantly, she'd escape the gossip of her budding spinsterhood. She twirled. Before long, she'd be rubbing elbows with the upper crust of the big city. The mere thought sent flutters to her mid-section. Cora pressed a hand to her stomach. My, perhaps she'd even meet a handsome stranger. Someone like the blue-eyed man who'd owned the spotted pony.

Then Mrs. Dixon would dine on her dire words of Cora's lonely future. She tucked away a wicked image of her flaunting to the widow. None of that. She had to curtail such revengeful thoughts. Yes, and her childish blurts. That would never do in high society.

"Time to get to business," she muttered.

She pulled out the small round box from beneath the cotton shifts in her bottom drawer. The discarded wooden spice box had her savings from the last three years. Her lungs emptied with excitement as she clutched the brown, tin-trimmed box. The faded label, Thyme, was splayed across the top. She couldn't have named it better herself.

She dumped the contents on her bed and fingered the bills and coins. Selling the shawls and dresses in Miss McGarlee's shop hadn't been the most profitable adventure, but living at home helped the money pile up.

Her breath snagged in her throat as she tossed down the last bit. Eleven dollars and fourteen cents. Cora's grin grew to full swing. In jubilation, she scooped up the treasure and funneled it into the wooden box and stowed it away.

The acceptance letter already penned by her father specified that her brother Bartholomew and his family would chaperone her. Then Eleanor and the children would stay at Miles's farm while she and Bartholomew continued to St. Louis.

She clasped her hands to her breast and fell backwards to the soft, feather-stuffed bed. A strange little quiver sent rivulets out from her chest. Cora recognized excitement, but fear jettisoned along with it. Her aunt and uncle were virtual strangers. What if her high society extended family didn't approve of her? She might be able to school herself into a genteel lady for a time, but she couldn't leave the "Too-Tall" home no matter how much she desired to do so.

Yes, just an inch shy of six foot, she was, without a doubt, too tall. But not married. And not courting. Not yet, anyway. Voices drifted to her ears through the screen at the window. Then a small pebble zinged off the sash.

"Cora."

She jerked from the bed, her pleasant reverie interrupted, and stomped to the window. A plethora of young nieces and nephews milled below her second story window with wide, expectant eyes.

"Stop throwing rocks. You'll break my window. Then Papa will tan your hide."

A few shrank away, but Loften and Hugh, the oldest boys of eleven and ten, refused to cower. Durn Hugh was a whiz with a baseball. He'd probably flung that rock.

"We wanna play baseball, Cora," Hugh called up.

Jennie, the eldest at thirteen, stepped up, her strawberry blonde hair matching Cora's in the sun. Terrible tomboy that one. 'Course, there wasn't a lot Cora could say about that. "Bring the ball. And the mitt."

A small fire ignited in Cora. She was nineteen after all. A grown-up. Why couldn't they be respectful and ask instead of demanding? Of course she knew the answer. She'd always been their playmate, from the time they'd been born. They thought of her like one of the kids.

Fine. It was time to separate from the children. "I don't have time now."

"Why not?" Jasper called up. The blond six-year-old had no concept of time.

"Because. I'm going to St. Louis. I've got a lot to do."

Hettie turned up her head of flaxen curls. "Please Cora? I gotta go home in a bit and watch Annabelle. Can't you play a little while?"

Even an eight-year-old had chores. Her sweet face was so hard to resist. Besides, once she left, she'd most likely miss her huge bunch of nieces and nephews . Her Double N Herd. A grin lit her face. How could she deny them? Which was exactly why they treated her like one of the group.

"Fine. But don't expect me to play all day." A cheer went up from the mob below and she hushed them. "I'll be down in a minute. Meet me at the far field."

They scampered off with muffled chatters, and Cora heaved a heavy sigh. Well, she'd counted her savings, but she had so much more to do. Her glance fell on the bright blue dress hanging from a peg on the far wall. It needed a hem and interfacing around the collar, but it would have to wait. She'd be using part of her precious savings on lamp oil again to get the creation done.

She bent and pulled the ball and homemade glove from under her bed and dusted it off. Quite surprising dust dared to settle, given its regular use. She shrugged and slung the lemon peel ball into the mitt until her hand stung. Maybe her city cousin would enjoy a game of pitch and catch. Likely not. Best leave it behind for the kids. Maybe.

Maybe not.

Trigg studied the crude leather map in front of him as Bodine pointed to each stop on the journey. A flurry of steam boat and stage coach rides seemed a waste of time.

He leaned away from the table and glanced around. The back corner at Porter's tavern kept them away from the majority of the noise in the place. Although early, the crowd was respectable.

"Why can't we just set off on horseback?" Trigg kept his voice even.

"Too slow." Bo barked.

How he wanted to shake that sneer from his brother's face. He was no greenhorn still wet behind the ears. "No. We could travel as the crow flies and be there much quicker. If we ride hard each day, we could hit the Iowa border on the banks of the Mississippi in a couple of weeks."

Bo shifted, alternately toggling his hand, drumming first his thumb and then his little finger on the stained table. "I got commitments, little brother. We're tracking outlaws even now."

Trigg stiffened his features to keep doubt from contorting his face. But something must have shown in his eyes.

"You don't believe me? Ask Oates or Burr. They'll tell you. We've been moving in on our quarry for the last couple of months. I won't stop now."

Trigg settled back. The question was, did he need Bo for this adventure? Unfortunately, yes. Bo had been the one to bring Pa the news of Iowa gold a year and a half back. Trigg owed him a bust in the jaw for that. But his brother did know the layout and Pa's whereabouts. "Fine."

"Deal."

Thankfully, Bodine didn't attempt another handshake.

"We've got a few more days here. We'll meet you at the crosshairs of Falling Run Creek and the Ohio Thursday night. Know where it is?"

"I can find it."

Bodine nodded and ceased his drumming to roll up the map. He secured it with a knotted bit of black horsehair. "From there we'll board the steamer the following morning. Got it?"

Trigg bobbed an acknowledgement.

"Good." Bo jerked his head at his two lackeys. They rose from the table.

He stood too. His brother nodded, shot him a salute, and the three drifted towards the exit. Trigg settled back on the bench, shaking his head. If Bo stiffed him and didn't show…well, he'd think on the punishment later.

Meanwhile, he'd post a letter to Roe. His younger brother had shouldered the responsibility of the farm in Trigg's absence. He deserved to know how long this could take. He and his sister Bliss couldn't keep things going forever. There was only so much a twenty and seventeen-year-old could do, even if Bliss could work like a man.

What a discombobulation. He grunted and stood once more, snatching his saddle bags from the bench. It wasn't fair to put his younger siblings in this position. Bo should've never promised to escort Ivalee to Pa. Even without knowledge of the place, Trigg knew it wasn't safe for a young girl to be amongst men infected with gold fever.

The leather saddle bag jutted into his neck. But the pain kept him from concentrating his anger on his older brother. What was done was done. Trigg stepped through the huge bar doors. He had two days to kill. Maybe he'd make his way back to starchy Grandmother Grave's estate. His feet hesitated near the worn steps.

The blonde girl's face from New Albany crossed his mind. She'd been tall, nearly eye to eye with him. He didn't know why he liked that, but he did. Wasn't hard to look at either with reddish-blonde hair peeping from her bonnet and her clear green eyes. Green as the meadow his mules grazed in. He grunted and drew some lounging patron's attention.

First, he'd thought about holing up at Grandmother's. Now daydreaming of a woman? He jerked up the back waist of his wool pants. Addled, that's what he was. Growing soft in the lap of luxury or gazing into the soft emerald irises of some gal wouldn't rescue Ivalee. No matter how much the willowy woman had captured his interest.

Nope. He'd camp near Falling Run Creek and wait for Thursday. Still…maybe he'd visit the north edge of town again. Once or twice. After all, breakfast at that Swedish pastry shop didn't sound too bad.

He slung the saddle bags behind the cantle and secured it, earning a disdainful glare from his horse. "Sorry, Buck. Meeting went sour."

Trigg swung up in the saddle and headed toward the wharf. Surely wouldn't cost much more to cross the Ohio than to hover here on Shippingport Island. He dug in his pocket and pulled out a half-dime. He hated wasting time. Ivalee would get farther and farther away.

The ferry boat lay ahead, loading passengers. He glanced at the Ohio River's muddy current. If it weren't for the fact that it was so wide and deep, he'd traverse it himself. He and Buck. But the currents were hungry, and he had no mood to wrestle himself and his valuable horse from the jaws of the greedy water.

The ferry driver nodded as he took Trigg's half dime and punched his finger toward an empty spot. Trigg dismounted and boarded. Completely addlepated to go to the other side of the river. He had a strange feeling that Bodine would need further prodding to meet him at Falling Run Creek. Then he'd be fifteen cents lighter in the pocket.

Yet, wide, green eyes tugged at him...

Chapter Six

Cora ran the flat tin skimmer just below the surface of the shallow milk pan. She held it aloft and let watery milk drip through the holes to separate the cream. Poor little piglets. There wouldn't be much fat left in their dinner tonight. With practiced hands, she transferred the cream to a nearby crock.

The cool breeze through the open kitchen window had quickened the cream's separation of the morning's milk offerings. Once she'd tended to all the shallow pans, she dumped the cream into the upright churn. Then she collected the leftover skim milk and added it to the pig slop bucket.

It was nice to be alone and have some time for her thoughts. Mama stitched a pillowcase pretty, as she called them, for a newly married couple from church. Papa, her brothers, and her older nephews plowed the spring fields while the rain held off.

She inserted the dasher and lid into the top and seated herself on a stool near the screen door. Up and down went the paddle, rolling back and forth with practiced hands. A sigh escaped her. With such a big batch, she'd be here for an hour or two.

Where were all the little people when you needed them? *Come butter, come.* Come nieces and nephews come. With your busy little hands. Cora couldn't help but chuckle to herself. They seemed to squeak in just when her tasks were finished. All morning she'd labored in the garden, raking and readying the beds, and not one child appeared. After she'd played ball with them all afternoon yesterday.

Not that it mattered. Every chore seemed to drag a hundred plows until Friday. The day she'd set foot on the steamer. The day she'd sail farther away from her reluctant suitor. Tomorrow, after baking, she'd head to town, run errands, and fetch the last of her necessities. She could probably pay for everything with the proceeds from the mountain of wash rags she'd crocheted. Miss McGarlee would be thrilled to get them. Which meant she'd have to sneak in and sneak out, being as Heaker Thomas's business lay straight across the street. At all costs, she'd dodge the blacksmith's shop like a quarantined house full of dysentery. Meeting up with Mr. Thomas would put a damper on the whole adventure.

She shoved thoughts of her possible intended aside and set her mind instead on her shopping expedition. Her carpet bag and trunk, packed near to bursting, would hardly hold much more. But maybe a couple new hairpins and new ribbons from Miss McGarlee's store. And those blasted white gloves for respectable ladies. Mama had insisted. Right after she'd allowed only one trunk and a carpetbag. Proper ladies wore gloves. And her aunt would expect it. Jitters chased through her stomach. Measuring up as a genteel lady might not be as easy as she'd hoped.

Her hands spun the dasher with an extra twirl. Surely she could manage. She'd had plenty of folks to study on. There was Widow Dixon. Elizabeth Rodgers, the widow's extra wagon wheel. And Rhapsody Hastings who'd thrown her brother over with a dismissive letter.

A few years ago, Cora had admired the young debutante so, thinking that someday Rhapsody would be her sister-in-law. But the high society girl had never taken a shine to her. Now, Cora supposed it didn't matter, other than cataloguing what little she'd gleaned of the cultured class's manners and polite civilities. Perhaps her small experience with Rhapsody would help Cora adjust to life in St. Louis.

Back to more pleasant thoughts. Filling her last-minute adventure list. Maybe her nieces Jennie and Claudia would accompany her to town and help select gloves. But if she invited them, then Hettie and Annabelle would beg to tag on, even though they were a bit too young. Which in turn would force three-year-old Salome to tag along with her older sisters as well. Then, Cora would feel sorry for Sallie, at four, and Bess, not quite two, because her sister-in-law Eleanor rarely let them join in with the others.

Yikes. Perhaps it would just be easier to go alone.

She'd see plenty of Sallie and Bess since Bartholomew and Eleanor were her chaperones. Already half the kids had expressed their unhappiness at missing an opportunity to visit their Aunt Beulah's and Uncle Miles's farm. Gracious, what a challenge to please eighteen nieces and nephews, fourteen that lived local.

The dasher grew stiffer, and she straightened her posture, pausing only a moment to sweep the escaped hair back from her forehead. She caught movement from her brother Everett's house on down the hill. Speak of the little devils. A lone figure approached. Probably Jennie. From this distance, the thirteen-year-old almost appeared a grown woman.

But as her niece drew nearer, the jack-rabbit slim shape gave away the fact that she was still just a child. Cora shivered at her height, praying she wouldn't grow anymore. Already she was up to her chin. She wouldn't wish her six-foot frame on anyone. Especially her dear nieces.

Jennie, blue calico dress a tad short, stepped on the porch and caught sight of her through the screen door. "Hi, Aunt Cora."

Such a forlorn tone. Poor thing must have been forced on some mission. "Well, howdy, Miss Jennie. And how's your day?"

The freckled girl shrugged. "Mama sent me to see if you needed help. You know, with your trip coming up and all."

Her eldest brother had sure married a thoughtful wife. Ada was always the first to lend a hand. Or in this instance, her children's hands.

"That's right neighborly of you. I'll give you a choice. You can either spin the dasher, or you can scrub sassafras roots in the sink."

73

Jennie cut a disdainful glance at the volume of roots in the tub. "Move over. I'll do the butter."

Cora gargled a grunt in her throat. Jennie may only be a young girl, but she knew how to latch onto the simpler tasks. Cora grabbed two tin buckets near the door on her way out. "I'll be back soon. Oh, and thanks, Jen."

The girl's thin shoulder hunched another wordless answer as she swiped the bonnet from her head, reluctance thick as a swarm of bees.

Despite her niece's gloominess, Cora swung out the door with joy singing in her heart. Jennie's sour attitude couldn't wash away her excitement. Neither would that courtship thing Papa was stirring up. Skipping the rest of the way to the hand pump, she settled the buckets on the boarded deck and grabbed the priming pail hanging from the spout.

"Psst."

Cora straightened, hand on hip. Now who lurked about? Seeing no one, she bent back at her task and poured the dingy water into the top of the pump.

"Up here."

She spun about, raising one hand to her forehead, and peered around, settling on Mama's apple tree some fifteen foot yonder. She strode forward, hands on hips, her eyes searching for the culprit. Sure enough, Jimmie's little three-year-old brother lay across one of the top branches, his foot fastened into the y of the tree.

"Roy Ulysses Breckinridge. If Grandma sees you up there, she'll be cutting a switch for your mama."

His little boy snickers greeted her ears. "I can get down 'for she sees me."

She didn't doubt that one bit. "You knock any of those blossoms off, and you'll be wishing you'd stayed up there."

His blue eyes blinked. "Aunt Beulah cwimbs trees."

Oh, that again. Aunt Beulah's early adventures of climbing trees had elevated to legend around the Taggart houses, and of course the Breckinridges and Garvins, whom the two older Taggart girls had married years ago.

"Get down from there and do it carefully."

Rustling noises emitted from the shivering treetop before his triumphant face appeared below, near the primary branching of the short tree. A wide grin split his button face. So much like Abel, at least in features and mischievousness, but blond as the clouds above.

"All right, Sugar Bun. Does your mama know where you are?"

"Shore she does." He gave a leap from the tree and landed in a heap. He rolled and popped back up, hitching up his wool knickers. "I'm checking on you."

That didn't sound quite right. "You know, your mama would skin your hide if you broke your leg. Jimmie's laid up already. She doesn't need two boys with broken bones."

"I won't fall."

"Roy, what's going on?"

He screwed up his whole face. "All wight. Woften, Hugh, and Jesse's farming wif Grandpa and Pa. Jimmie gotta way down on a-counts of his bwoken weg. Maxwell's asweep. Mama's taking a nap 'cause she's all tuckered out wif a house full of men. So, she told me to be quiet. So I am."

"You're not even home, Silly Pants."

He grinned, one eye nearly closed.

"Since you're being so cheeky, you can help me." Cora turned and made her way back to the pump.

"Wif what?"

"Water to clean the sassafras roots."

"Yum. Can I hab some tea, too?" He jumped up and down, rubbing his midsection.

"Maybe. If you're a good helper. Look what you did." She set her hands on her hips again. "You done made me lose my prime."

Roy whipped up the primer pail and sloshed in the last of it. "I can fix this fast. Watch me."

He leaped upon the long handle, set an impressive rhythm, and Cora filled all three buckets in a flash. "I guess you'll do. Come on."

She hung the primer pail back on the spigot and grabbed hold of both buckets, leaning toward the arm nearly being yanked off by Roy. It was quite a relief to set them on the porch. "Now, run in and bring out all the roots. They're in the sink tub."

"Yes, 'um."

Cora sat on the edge of the low porch and wrapped her skirt up around her ankles to keep the mosquitoes away.

"Get the brush, Roy," Jennie's voice had a superior edge to it.

Still, Cora was thankful. She'd forgotten to remind the little guy to grab that, too. The next couple of hours were spent scrubbing roots and cooking them down to syrup with a little molasses. Roy seemed right pleased with his sassafras tea. Pleased enough to skedaddle on home. Jennie followed him a ways, and then skirted to her own house, the slump of her shoulders eased by the tea.

Once Cora tossed the dirty water from her dish pan out the back door, she swung back into the kitchen. Mama had bellied up to the cutting board, chunking odd bits of smoked ham, adding them to the cast iron pot of softened beans.

"Butter done?"

"Yep."

"You take care of those roots the boys collected?"

Do you see them? Och, rude. And almost blurted. Her mother checked on her like an infant. "Yes, Mama."

"Good. Any help come to you?"

"Jennie and Roy." She snipped off the part of the boy's transgression into the apple tree.

Mama nodded, the swipe of her salt-and-pepper hair bobbing in rhythm above her ear. Her style was neatly coifed. She must have freshened up after her sit with the needle.

"How's Grandma?"

"Fair to middling"

So a good day. She must have gotten up and sat with Mama a few hours.

"You packed up?"

This time the impatient sigh slipped out, blame thing. Her mother shot a sharp look. "What's that about?"

Cora shrugged. "Sorry."

"Cora Hope Taggart, come clean."

Ah, the woman Aleena imitated so often. "I guess I'm impatient with all your questions."

Some of the starch left her mother's face. "And why so?"

"It makes me feel like a child."

Mama set the knife down and turned to her. "I suppose so. Reckon it's my way of pushing away the sadness at you parting."

Awash with a different emotion, Cora breathed, "Oh."

Her mother dabbed a pinky to the corner of her right eye. "You're my last one, Cora. My baby. And once you get back, you'll set to court."

Poof. And then there was that. Irritation swiped away the momentary melancholy.

Her mother grabbed a towel and wiped her hands. "Here. I've got something for you."

She scurried toward her metal recipe box on the high shelf next to the window. Cora hurried forward and lifted it down.

"Bless you, Child. The Lord did give you plenty of height." She opened the aged tin and shuffled through. At last a bit of stitching came to light, and Mama held it like a tender new chick. But it turned out to be nothing but a strip of feed sack with a ribbon threaded through. "Sit down a minute, Cora."

With a nod, Cora settled at the scarred table, and her mother sank to the nearest chair. "I know this may not mean much to you, but this was my mother's. She stitched it long ago. Even before she met your grandpa."

She pressed it into Cora's hand and only then did she get a good look at the dab of cloth. A bookmark, well worn, with a faded yellow ribbon threaded through the top lay in her palm. Cora glanced up into Mama's misty eyes.

"Oh, turn it over."

Cora acquiesced and discovered tiny stitching spelling out a Bible verse. Psalm 130: 5. *I wait for the Lord, my soul doth wait, and in his word do I hope.*

"It's lovely." What else could Cora say? Her mother was obviously moved to tears over the possession. The words rang sentimental, the verse a true axiom. But the stitching quite…amateurish.

Mama put her hand on hers. "It's where I conceived your middle name, Cora Hope. You see, your grandma nearly died from a wagon accident many years ago. She lost the sight in her left eye, and when she recovered, she always walked with a limp."

Cora nodded. Grandmother had often told the story.

"What you don't know is, her groom-to-be broke their engagement as she healed. Left her." Mama snapped her fingers. "Just like that. Near broke her heart. So she stitched this as she recovered. Both her wounds and her heart."

That explained the stitching. Cora studied the bookmark once more.

"Four years later came your grandpa, asking to court her. And at first, she was reluctant. Her heart had been shattered. But then, as she spent time with him, she realized that waiting hadn't been a bad thing. And, as you know, they fell in love." Mama gave a deep sigh. "Sentimental, I know. Now…it's your time."

Was she talking about the forced courtship?

Her mother wiped a tear with her towel. "You're going out there, into the world. St. Louis is so very far away. I feel like everything's changing too fast. Soon you'll be married. Though you're nineteen, it isn't easy to let you go."

That squish of emotion tightened a notch. "Mama?"

Her mother snatched her up for a quick hug and then flung both hands as if shooing the chickens from the porch. "It's fine. Just fine. If it's meant to be, it'll be."

Mama grabbed the knife and off she went. Cora turned to her duties of preparing the cornbread, expecting more questions. Yet, no more came.

Thursday. Finally. It'd rained last night making Trigg's camp on the ground down right uncomfortable. Getting up and stretching his bones had a double duty. He needed to dry off and get cleaned up. He searched through his saddle bags for a clean shirt. But he came up empty. He'd used his clean one last week.

He shook his head. Time to head to town. Buy a nice bath, have his clothes laundered, and get the last of his supplies. Bodine had better be here tonight. And it better not rain.

He climbed on Buck, and the horse showed his displeasure by bobbing his splotched head, shooting him the white of his one blue eye.

"Yeah, yeah, I get it. You're wet too." Trigg squeezed his boot-clad feet against the wide barrel of the animal's belly. "So let's get into town and fix it."

The horse set off, naturally guiding away from the mud of Falling Run Creek's inlet. Trigg set him north, toward the slope. Fine thing about this location. It wasn't far from a proper road. The High Street Bridge arched over the gurgling creek not far ahead. Before reaching the fringes of town and traffic, and to avoid appearing like a rat from the sewer, Trigg urged the horse up the low bank to the main thoroughfare.

He turned north, toward the area of the green-eyed girl and hadn't gone far when he located Carter's Barber Shop. Looked respectable enough. And the dark-skinned barber sitting near the door by the barber pole would be sure to give him a good price.

The thin man popped up from the dingy stool as Trigg tied his horse to the hitching post out front. Trigg tipped his hat. "Morning. Shave, bath, laundry."

"Yes, sah." The man nodded and held the door open. A two-seater, with a door to the right with a hand-sketched sign proclaiming "bath." Clean. Simple.

Two young boys appeared with buckets and whisked through the door with the sign.

"My horse could use some grooming as well. And oats."

"Ah, Lawdy, we gets you right set up." He motioned to one of the high barber seats and then mumbled to one of the boys. The young one took off towards Trigg's horse, and he saw no more as the barber eased him back in the chair.

"Cut and shave?"

Hmmm. Not a bad way to spend a few coins. "Sure."

He stared at the tin ceiling as the barber got busy, humming as he went. Trigg was conscious of the boys quietly traipsing in and out, toting buckets, but he ignored it. Right fine to lean back with a hot towel on his jaw and the scissors making history of the unkempt hank of hair.

The comb raked through one last time, before the man reappeared in his line of sight with a brush loaded with shaving cream. "Right booming city."

"Yes, sah. Biggest in da state of Indiana."

Trigg closed his eyes. "That right?"

"Yes, sah."

The straight razor raked across the rasp on his cheek. "I'm from Henderson, Kentucky myself."

"Uh-huh, uh-huh. Doin' business here?"

Trigg drew in a deep breath while the barber paused to wipe the foam from his razor. "You might say that."

The man wiped his face one last time and tilted his seat upright. Trigg ran a hand across the unfamiliar smooth jaw. Been awhile since he'd been so naked.

"Boys got your bath ready, sah." He opened the door and motioned him in.

"Right. Thanks." The door closed behind him. The room was small. Just big enough for the wooden half-barrel tub full of water frothing with steam. A table contained a clean shirt and pants. Now that was right neighborly.

Sinking down into the tub, guilt pangs stabbed at Trigg. Here he was soaking in the finer pleasantries of life while Ivalee…who knew what hardships she endured? Or worse yet, atrocities? He firmed his jaw. Tonight. He'd link up with his brother. And he'd find her.

One way or another. He would find her.

Chapter Seven

Cora tugged at the stiff gloves covering her hands as the blast of the steamer gave her a start. Bluebells, that scared near a month off her life. Abel stood next to her, tall and comforting while her brother, Bartholomew stood in the ticket office line. His wife, Eleanor, stood bouncing Bess while Sallie leaned into her delicate mother.

"I wish you were going," she whispered to her brother-in-law.

He winked and leaned down. "But not Aleena, right?"

She pressed her lips together and pulled a face. Never wise to voice that answer aloud.

"Nervous?"

She fingered the hanky and the bookmark she'd pinned inside her sleeve. One for crying and one for memories. "Yes."

Dare she say how anxious she was to be with Bartholomew? Eight years her senior, but eons separated in personality. Mama always said he could be British as proper as he was. Only a different proper than Aleena. She was like a Viking Pilgrim schoolmarm, as odd as that description was, and Bartholomew more of a quiet church mouse accountant. Glasses included. Round ones that beheld the world in a calm sort of detachment.

Oh, and Eleanor, who barely spoke two words. Shy as a colt and as petite as a meadow butterfly. And next to Cora, the jungle giraffe, Eleanor appeared so graceful. At least four-year-old Sallie would afford some entertainment, although more reserved in her mother's presence.

Bartholomew strode towards them. The smallest of the Taggart men, he stood just over five and a half feet. Cora towered over him by five inches. At least he wasn't bald. All the Taggart men had full heads of hair, mostly blond. But Bartholomew's was a light brown, cut full and thick. No facial hair, of course. He was much too finicky to allow a hair to sprout on his chin.

"Did you get them, Barth?"

He froze a few steps from her. "I'm sure I've told you, I prefer Bartholomew. Always have. Don't be difficult, Cora."

And she preferred nicknames, but no use making that point. "The tickets?"

Passing her, he lifted the paper stubs on his way to stand beside Eleanor as Bess pitched a squall.

Abel tugged on the back of her bonnet. "Don't pay no mind, Core. You'll get there sure enough."

True. Yet a tug of home sickness pulled at her insides already. Mother and Father had stayed home, along with the rest of the family. She'd said her goodbyes that morning under a family umbrella of prayer. The wharf would be crowded, the fields needed their attention, and Grandma couldn't be left. Abel had driven them to the teeming shoreline, and once he left, she'd be much on her own. Bartholomew had his family unit, and she, just an added responsibility.

"I'll miss you, Abel."

He grinned, and the hulking man gave her a side squeeze. "I'll miss you, Core. It'll be a mite different, I'm sure, but soak up all the world while you're there. Make the best of it always."

For the jokester he was, this seemed a tad too serious. And final. "I will."

"Shall." Abel snorted and winked as he mock corrected her.

She crossed her eyes and stuck the tip of her tongue out. But she sobered quick-like. It wouldn't do for Bartholomew to see her making silly faces.

The horn blasted again and Cora jumped. Abel grinned and motioned her to move with his head. Only then did she realize the sea of people drifting toward the steamer. *Lady Louisa* would soon loose her moorings and be off.

Abel boarded only long enough to handle her carpetbag. Thankfully the trunk was safely ensconced in the hold. Her brother-in-law gave another of his wide smiles, exposing the gap in his front teeth. He clicked his tongue and winked before turning and exiting the crowded gangplank.

"Cora." Her brother's impatient voice washed over her. "*Cora.*" She spun to find them on the already congested deck.

"Hurry along. Respectable company never resides on the bottom deck."

Oh, certainly not. A bevy of hogs squealed their way past her skirt, stemming any more smarty thoughts. She held her gloved hands high and tiptoed past the more unsavory occupants already setting up shop on the barrels and stacked pallets.

She grasped her long skirt to rattle up the steps behind Eleanor. But at the top she paused and let a gasp escape her throat. The sight of the river, the people, and the buildings with their toes nearly dipped in the Ohio caught her short. Never had life been so close. And real. What a vantage point on the second deck of the steamer.

"Cora. Move along, please."

Barth. Or rather Bartholomew. She supposed she'd been rude to cut him off still on the stairs. Tugging her eyes from the scene, she scurried after Eleanor, who'd found a bench to settle Sallie and Bess.

"Sorry."

"Completely understandable." He scooped little Bess from her mother while Cora settled next to Eleanor.

"Thank you both for coming and helping me get to St. Louis."

"We were most happy to chaperone you." He patted the teary-eyed child in his arms. "A welcome break for us."

Cora glanced at Eleanor who nodded but turned her head away.

Strange thing to say. Especially since he'd lived here all his life. Steps from his family. Strange indeed. She pulled her thoughts away and turned her eyes to peer between congregating people. It would be quite pleasant to watch the world drift by if not for the crowd.

Cora caught her breath and clenched the seat beneath her at the deafening horn blast. Durn, these gloves. She yanked her hands away to peer at them. A small splinter had embedded in the fingertip. Mother had said proper ladies wore them, and Aunt Josephine would expect her to be so adorned. But glory, these gloves were harder to maintain than keeping all her nieces and nephews combined. Her homemade leather mitt took a lot less attention. She worked the piece of wood free.

The steamer jerked causing her to recall the stories from her younger years of the explosion of the *Lucy Walker*. Ladies gloves, steamer explosions, yet she grinned. Abel's advice lay on her heart. Soak up life. Little did Abel know, she planned to jump right in. One last adventure before the...compulsory courtship.

Sallie's small hand crept beneath hers. Her wide face held a look of wonder. She squeezed the child's hand and shoved her father's unwanted martial arrangement to the back of her mind.

Oh, they were moving. Backing up. The loud rushing sound made her want to sprint to the back of the steamer to see the huge water wheel. But she held still, like a grown-up lady should, and even managed to hold her grin through the loud double toot of the horn.

She turned her head and pointed at the smoke pouring from the smoke stack. The expression on the girl's face made her laugh. Sallie tugged her hand towards the rail. At Bartholomew's nod, they wedged to the front, getting a grand view of the river and the deck below. A huge group of people waved from the gravel wharf below them. Cora waved harder than anyone at Abel's big form at the topmost section. He raised a hand.

The steamer navigated a turn and nothing but open water lay before them. With the morning sun at their backs, Cora looked from bank to bank, amazed at the breadth of the river. She inhaled the fresh spring air flavored with honeysuckle and lilac. Now, this was life.

Sallie gripped two spindles below the horizontal rail, drawing her gaze.

"It looks like you're in steamer jail."

The girl giggled but shot an uncertain glance back to her parents. Cora smoothed her hair, tightly braided for the trip, and leaned against the rail. The activity below caught her eye. Perhaps Bartholomew had been right about the bottom deck. Busy, filthy place, both man and beast. Best to be above—

Her breath snagged. One man near the left corner had a very memorable horse. An odd paint horse. With one eye encircled with white. Perhaps patient enough to be a writing desk? The tall man suddenly shifted and glanced up. Yep. Even shadowed beneath a well-used hat, his handsome face was much too familiar.

He raised his hat brim with his thumb and fixed his eyes on hers. Then, he nodded. The shivers of awareness chased up Cora's innards. She drummed up a shred of fury to tamp down the lure of his handsome face. He'd laughed at her after all. The scalawag.

Shamelessly embarrassed her. Even now, he stared longer than what was proper.

Still, her hot face exposed the thrill of seeing him again. His smile chased its way across the distance at her bold stare. There was no denying his fetching looks. And with his lanky, muscular form, he'd probably be very good at baseball.

She lifted her chin to rebuff him, studying the peculiar characters that seemed to be accompanying him. Two thinner, shorter men and one wide-shouldered man covered in a buffalo skin. Although she'd chosen a jacket this morning, the weather didn't seem chilly enough for such a heavy over-garment.

"Come away, Sallie. Let's sit back with your Mama and Papa." She pinched the child's sleeve and eased her from the rail. The less she saw of the tall, audacious stranger, the better.

Trigg pulled the saddle from Buck and tugged a curry comb from the saddlebags. Might as well make use of empty time. Bodine and his two lackeys sat on nearby stacked crates jawing on jerky.

"Give ya two bits to do the rest of the horses." Bodine's two buddies chuckled at his brother's words. "Or better yet, we'll get a darkie to do it for free."

This drew more chuckles from others on the crowded deck. Trigg ignored the anger that rose in his gut and turned his attention to his horse, thankful for the breeze that cooled his flushed neck.

He stroked the animal's hide in long easy motions. Dodging Bodine and his malevolent personality sounded like the best plan of action. Trigg's fist to Bodine's jaw was surely a quick way to break up this dubious alliance.

Better to think something else and be somewhere else. Like the second deck. He couldn't count how many times he'd been tempted to scout around for that pretty green-eyed girl one floor up. After all, at twenty-five, he was old enough to be settled down.

And he supposed he ought to be, but when the eldest takes off for parts unknown, someone had to keep the business going. With Pa's head in the clouds about prospecting, the responsibility had fallen to him at age seventeen, as the substitute elder.

Not that Bodine had been much good at raising mules. Pa had kept the business growing despite his oily palms. Trigg supposed he had his mother to thank for that. He cut his gaze to the balcony, but only chatting strangers rested against the rail. Leastwise, he had no time to pursue anyone, let alone a girl from round these parts. Made no sense. Nevertheless, she sure piqued his interest.

He ran a few hometown girls through his head. Constance. Nice gal. Funny laugh. Not much brains in her head. Yeah, no. Helen. Good dedicated church goer. Would definitely not launch a thousand ships. Especially with a wart that size smack dab on her eyebrow. Patience, lands no. Impatience, more like. Destined to become a seller of prunes with a face to match.

Nah. He had no time for such. But if he did, she'd be tall. Capable. And, of course, beautiful. Maybe feisty. A smile tugged at his mouth as he ran the brush down the horse's barrel. Perhaps

91

green-eyed. That image smacked right familiar. And maybe she stood on the second deck.

Buck turned his head and nudged him. Trigg blew out a flutter of air. "You're right, old friend. Ivalee comes first."

Still, a man could dream.

❦

A cough woke Trigg once more. He blinked, and the stars winked back. He grounded himself with the noise of the paddlewheel still churning and the hiss of steam escaping the boat engine behind him. The movement of the packet sent a continuing rush of chilly air, and he tugged the wool blanket tighter. Better to brave the cool night here than risk getting so close to the boiler.

Still, he wished away the night. The snores of men and the shuffles of beasts, not to mention the sensation of movement beneath the loaded pallet below him, made it difficult to settle deep into sleep.

He rolled over on the leather tarp covering several crates of Baltimore Oysters. Not the best bed, but the elevation kept him above the vile liquids on the floor. Bo and his two buddies, however, had been camped out on the deck against a couple of crates of Dr. Fetter's Botanic Medicines and Curatives.

Trigg threw a glance toward his brother's location but could only make out empty blankets. Strange. He sat up. Maybe they'd relocated to a comfier spot. He shrugged. Who cared? Not likely they'd jumped ship and swum ashore.

He lay down and shrugged his shoulders into the smelly canvas. No sense losing sleep over it now. With a deep breath, he cleared his mind and drifted off.

Light filtered through Trigg's eyelids, rousing him several hours later. Only then did he begin to notice the stirrings about him. He sat up and rubbed the sleep sand from his eyes. It had to be early. Wasn't even light proper.

A few of the old timers had a fire going in a sand pit frying up hard bread dunked in butter. The unappetizing meal made his belly growl. Lands, he really must be hungry for that hardtack to smell good.

He slid off his oyster pallet and meandered toward his dozing horse. A sour apple and jerky rested inside his saddlebag, and he yanked out the sorry offering. Grasping his canteen, he chugged a long drink. Bo and his buddies still snored in their bedrolls. By now, the animal liquid waste and spittle from the working men had ventured very close to their boots.

Trigg shook his head and turned away. Slowly, but surely the boat came alive. Tempting smells of breakfast drifted down from the salon upstairs. The men's raucous laughter showed their eagerness to be put ashore and continue their business.

Finally Bo rolled over and barked a deep cough. This roused the other two who sat up, disoriented. Most likely they'd shared a bottle or two of Kentucky's finest last night during their absence.

Trigg tapped Bo's boot, earning him his brother's scowl. "Best get up if you don't want to be soiled."

"Crimey's sake, Trigg, what're you—" Curses flew from the big man's mouth as the vile liquids sloshed across the floor. He scrambled up and yanked his wool blanket from the floor. The two idiots beside him did the same but not before a good slosh splashed against Burr's tattered leather boots.

Trigg shoved the remaining jerky into a pouch. The second deck was sounding better every moment.

Chapter Eight

C ora quickened her feet. How did her brother stride so fast with a young child in one hand and a huge carpet bag in the other? Even Eleanor trudged along, tugging Sallie behind her. And why hurry? For there appeared a hundred new things around them with every step. She so wished to soak in the new city of Evansville, but she had to keep her minute-minding brother in sight.

Exiting the steamer seemed much more of a rush than entering had been. Cora slipped her hand within the cuff of her sleeve. Hanky made a comforting pillow against her wrist, but the treasured stitching from Grandmother seemed...gone. River rats and snapping turtles. She'd lost it already. The one heirloom her mother had lovingly passed into her care. Cora choked and froze, glancing down amongst the trampling toes.

With a spin that set her cage crinoline tipping, she bustled back the way she'd come, eyes glued to the dirty wooden gangplank. People paid no mind to her and flowed in great numbers, making it difficult to make any headway.

"Excuse me, please." She shouldered her way through the crowd. "I've lost my—"

But it was useless to continue her protests, so she fell silent, battling the bubble of dread staining her insides with nausea. A huff of air found its way to her lungs.

A small scrap of white gleamed at her against the mud-smeared main deck. There it was. Thick boots and hooves bore down on the little bookmark, and she scurried to snatch it up.

As she dove to rescue her grandmother's treasure, a large hand reached down and grasped the wisp of material. She scuttled to a stop and straightened. Silver blue eyes topped with sardonic brows met her gaze. All words of appreciation died a quick death at her tonsils. *Him.*

"Looking for something?" His pause in the flowing crowd set up a buoy in the sea of scruffy men and gaggle of animals flowing around her on either side.

A pinch of outraged injustice tugged her brows together and popped open her mouth. Was he laughing at her? Again? Heat rose in her face. "I...I..."

A slow smile vined across his face. "Once more I rescue a damsel in distress."

"Dagnabbit!" She whacked a fist against her lips. The tall, handsome stranger drew back, eyes registering surprise.

"Such a strong word for such a fine lady."

Did his voice contain censure? A shaft of anger shuddered up her backbone until fury made her shake. She poked him hard in the chest. "Listen here, Sir. I hardly think I need to take correction from a rude, insufferable brute such as you!"

"Cora."

Her brother's tones seemed very near. And the disapproval in his voice was clear. She pivoted and pointed at the offending man. Bartholomew fought his way through the onslaught of animals and men, his face growing ever more like a ripe beet.

"So, it's Cora?" the objectionable goon next to her murmured.

Her head swiveled and she shot him a wuthering look. Was there no end of this humiliation? "It's quite disrespectful to use my given."

The blue-eyed man lifted one side of his mouth. Did he find this funny?

"My apologies, dear woman. My intent was never to offend you." He glanced down. "Beautiful work. Did you make this?"

Cora snatched the muddied bookmark from his hand. "That's none of your business."

"Cora." Her brother had arrived, face suffused with an angry flush. "We mustn't become separated. You're being quite childish to remain aboard."

"I'm afraid it's my fault."

Cora's objection to Bartholomew's accusation died on her lips. Her brother jerked back, recognizing the stranger as part of the conversation.

"I beg your pardon?" Her brother's outraged demeanor faded back into bookish.

"She'd dropped her bookmark, and I was merely returning it to her."

Her brother's brows descended as he looked up to greet the man. "And you are?"

The thick-muscled man stuck out a hand, thankfully clean, and gave an engaging smile. "Trigg. Trigg Gentry at your service."

Cora used her brother's hesitancy to study the man. Muscles of that size bespoke a life rife with physical work. Common laborer? Not likely with his proper manners and clean appearance. Not to mention a bear's size batch of confidence.

Her brother cleared his throat. "Yes, well, we appreciate your assistance on behalf of my sister. Now, if you will excuse us. Come, Cora."

She took that moment to sneak a peek at the stranger next to her. He beamed a crooked smile with one brow raised. Bartholomew took two steps among the now dwindling crowd and then turned to glare at her.

With a nod and a quick curtsy she pivoted to step to her brother's side. Bartholomew gave a sniff and set a swift pace through the animals and rough characters. Cora slowed her long steps and glanced back. The man with the buffalo skin, along with two scruffy companions, the same three from the night before, joined her blue-eyed stranger. Trigg Gentry saluted with a jaunty grin. She whipped her head away.

Her brother paused and gave a stern look. "Really, Cora. Consorting with such riff-raff."

Her mouth flew open. "I did no such thing. I dropped my bookmark. Grandmother Gusta stitched it herself—"

"A proper lady doesn't lose contact with her possessions."

Cora turned her head to the left so her brother would not see the roll of her eyes. That again. How much her brother was beginning to sound like Aleena. There was no sense in telling him she had pinned it into her sleeve. Or that she'd checked its location before they had started to disembark. No, clearly it was a case of childish behavior.

"Yes, Bartholomew." It was all she could do not to glaze the words in sarcasm. When her brother stopped to study her face, she knew he searched for proof of insincerity.

After a pregnant pause, he spoke. "Very well. Let's not allow it to happen again. Understood?"

She bobbed a nod. No use arguing.

They scurried up the muddy slope to a crowd of people dispersing. Eleanor's face looked as if she had her neck in a vise. Sallie had vomit all down the front of her new traveling dress, while Bess reared back in the throes of a screaming toddler fit.

Bartholomew rushed forward to aid his wife. He pulled the infant from her mother and plopped her in Cora's arms. The unwelcome smell of a dirty diaper hit her nostrils about the same time as the moisture pressed against her arm. She held the child away from her and lunged for Eleanor's carpet bag.

While the couple spoke in crisp whispers, Cora gathered the screaming child and a fresh diaper and supplies. Then, spying an empty bench on the side of the storage warehouse perched near the water's edge, she beelined towards it. With practiced hands, she cleaned up the child and wiped the tot's tears. By the time she had her cradled, happy in her arms, Bartholomew strutted stiffly on the narrow wooden walkway.

"Cora. You startled us again. Why must you disappear?"

"She needed a change—"

He drew the toddler from her. "Yes, well stay within eyesight. This is not a place for a wandering young lady with a baby."

Cora gathered up the messy diaper, wrapped it in a clean towel, and sealed it with a leather tie. When she dallied to do so, her brother froze.

"Cora, must you continue to delay us?"

"Shoot fire." Cora breathed as she quickened her steps to join her brother.

Sallie wore a clean, but rumpled dress even though her face glowed pale. Eleanor had her hand firmly planted in the child's hand. At least her sister-in-law appeared to have gathered her wits. Cora sent up a quick prayer for the lot of them.

She pulled her attention from her grumpy brother and his family for a moment to scan her surroundings. The river flowed silently at the base of the bank while a bevy of anchored steamships in various stages of loading or unloading passengers and stacked freight rested against the sandy shore. As she climbed the slope, a brick road appeared quite busy with conveyances and pedestrians.

Tall buildings, some as high as three stories, lay on the other side of the street.

Evansville had the appearance of a sizeable city. A lad hawking newspapers yelled nearby, but Bartholomew ignored him and strode to the corner of the block. A wagon pulled up alongside in the bustle and paused. Cora shuffled her carpetbag into her other hand before glancing to the passenger.

"Miles." Cora gasped.

He leaped from the farm wagon and waved to the driver, signaling him to stop. She raced into his waiting arms.

"Oh." Tears bit her eyelids and a longing rush swelled her chest. "I've missed you."

So, so much, but she left that unsaid. His laughter made her burrow against his shirt. She pulled away to study his face. The toothy smile and healthy face told Cora that life with Beulah not only suited him but blessed him. Miles stepped forward to give a bear hug to his brother, Bartholomew, who slapped an awkward hand on Miles's broad back.

"It's a pleasure to see you," Bartholomew nodded, his face slightly flushed. "I'm thankful to see a familiar face in this madness."

Miles threw back his head. "Why, Barth, I'd have thought this to be right up your alley."

Bartholomew sniffed, but gave a partial smile. Cora took note he didn't bother to correct his younger, yet larger brother on the informal nickname.

Clamping a hand on Bartholomew's shoulder, Miles smiled at Eleanor, Sallie, and Bess. "We best be getting to the stagecoach stop. You may be glad to see me, but we've a long row to hoe before we arrive at the farm."

Miles loaded their carpet bags into the back of the wagon. Then, he lifted Sallie aboard while Bartholomew assisted Eleanor to the back seat of the double bench wagon. By now the driver, dressed in stained clothes two sizes too big, had dismounted and lowered the tailgate. Cora clambered into the bed of the wagon and pulled Bess, who'd begun to fret, into her lap. Sallie settled against her.

"I wish I had tickets aboard the new railroad. That would have been quite an experience." Miles continued. "But, they're so expensive. We'll have to settle for riding the stagecoach. This all the luggage?"

Bartholomew shook his head, almost like a quiver. Miles motioned him down the long levee. Cora pointed to a shiny black coach pulled by two palomino horses amongst the jostling traffic. Sallie gasped in delight at the new sights. Bess forgot her distress and clapped her hands.

"Pretty."

Once the men returned, lugging the heavy trunks, they loaded them behind Cora, Sallie, and Bess for the short ride a few blocks up Main Street. Miles didn't stop for tickets but led them straight for the weathered Concord stagecoach. The scruffy coachmen made short work of pitching their luggage in the leather boot on the back and atop the monstrosity of a vehicle. Eleanor gave a little squeak as they flung her trunk up as well.

"Load up, load up. Last of the passengers to Princeton," the wiry man announced in a voice full of gravel. The man riding shotgun clambered aboard the box seat and gave a blast on a tin horn.

Bartholomew pushed her to the front. "Board Cora. We can't be left."

She stumbled up the floating steps only to nip her head on the top of the door. Blamed low thresholds. Once inside Jonah's whale, Cora had to shuffle to the back since the first two rows, more desirable locations with cushions, were already taken.

Collapsing on the simple board bench next to the window, she wondered how the six people following her would fit in such a space. While it was true that Sallie and Bess could easily occupy a lap, the room on the bench hardly left enough space for four grown adults.

Miles squished in beside her with a wide grin. "Gonna be interesting, huh?"

Her eyes flicked to Bartholomew behind him with his red face and clear disapproval written in caps across his brows. When she glanced back to Miles, he winked. Yes, her dear brother hadn't been gone so long that he'd forgotten Bartholomew's somber dislike for disorder.

Bartholomew settled next to Miles, tugging Bess onto his lap while Eleanor, face devoid of any color, squeezed into the seat against the far window. Bartholomew leaned forward and fixed a stare upon Cora. "Surely you could have chosen a more comforting arrangement."

Miles set his head back with a bark of laughter. "You could always sit on the roof."

Cora sat up a little straighter. No wonder Miles was her favorite brother. Always willing to set up a bulwark for her against the tide of disapproving family members. She settled back and shot Miles a grateful smile.

Bartholomew sniffed, patting the sweat beads on his forehead with a snowy hanky. "This is quite unacceptable. We're herded like cattle bound for the slaughter."

"Now, you can appreciate the company trying to make a little more profit, right Barth?"

A bit of a choking sound met Cora's ears, and since she could no longer see her smaller brother, she had to assume it came from him rather than Miles.

"Extra profit should never come at the expense of service," Bartholomew insisted.

"Maybe it's not extra."

Cora resisted a squirm of enjoyment. Miles may not be as bookish as Bartholomew, but he sure had a full ton of wisdom and a smattering of straight-forward honesty.

"Perhaps."

A childish whimper met her ears. She leaned forward to snatch Sallie who was struggling to move past her uncle's knees.

"I don't feel good." Sallie's voice was almost a sob.

"Come sit on my lap and look out the window," Cora offered.

With a pout, the tike clambered over Miles into her lap. Cora settled her forward, trying to ignore the smell of vomit. "If you get sick again, just lean out the window. Got it?"

The girl nodded. Bartholomew's head shot forward. "How undignified, Cora."

Cora went to speak, but Miles, her champion, beat her to the punch. "Better than a lap full, Barth."

"Humph." Bartholomew disappeared behind Miles's big body again.

The coach shimmied, tilting to the side. That coarse voice rang out again. "Hi-O."

Once more a long toot sounded from the horn of the man riding shotgun. The Concord lurched. Cora couldn't squelch the smile that popped to her lips. Only five hours and they would be at Miles's home. She'd get to see Beulah again and play with three-year-old Wiley, who according to Miles's letters, was the spitting image of himself with a cotton top and green eyes.

And with Beulah expecting a new one in the next month, her return trip from St. Louis would allow her to greet the new member of the family. She exhaled a happy sigh and even Sallie bounced in her lap. This trip was proving more fun than a rousing game of baseball.

❦

Trigg nudged his brother towards the steam ticket office across the busy street. "Forget something?"

Bodine merely grunted and ignored him.

"Whoa. Hold on." He tugged his brother to a stop. "Tickets, remember?"

"We don't need any. We're staying the night."

His brother and his two escorts towing the horses continued up the bank. Trigg raced to set up a stance in front of them. "What do you mean? We had this worked out. You said we'd turn in our tickets for a continuance to St. Louis."

Bodine's eyes narrowed. "Change of plans."

Trigg yanked him by the smelly buffalo wrap the side of the pathway. "This is not a time to track anyone but Ivalee."

With a shove Bo detached himself and straightened his garments. "Now look here—"

A yell lit the air behind them drawing Trigg's eyes. A man in a bowler hailed the nearest uniformed man aboard a chestnut gelding paused near the pathway. "I've been robbed. Robbed, I say. Aboard the *Lady Louisa*."

Chapter Nine

T he commotion of the theft caught his attention. Trigg stepped closer, pulling his bored horse with him. The constable dismounted and the man gestured wildly. Poor fellow. Pickpockets notoriously infested packets. And from the sounds of it, he'd been relieved of several hundred dollars. Others gathered, pointing and raising their voices. Sad state of affairs, it was, not to be able to trust one's traveling companions.

He spun and caught sight of his brother with his two buddies entering a three-story brick building with a stone banner above proclaiming "Richard Hotel." Speaking of not trusting, this was a perfect example.

How had they managed to cross the busy road in such a quick fashion? Lesson learned. *Don't take your eyes off Bodine.* Next thing he'd know, his ornery brother would be in Alaska as Trigg toed the banks of the Ohio. Besides, given their direction, Bo had plenty of explaining to do.

He glanced behind them, wondering briefly what had become of the feisty blonde, but only crowds of strangers struggled up the levee. Beyond, the dockworkers unloaded a wharf boat into the warehouse perched above the shallow water.

The uniformed constable dismounted his sleek mount and pulled a small pad of paper from his uniform pocket. The horse, well trained, froze into wood, stiff at attention. The desperate man in the bowler and sharp brown jacket described the events that led to the incident.

Trigg checked his own pocket to verify he hadn't lost his small amount of cash. Not much he could do to help the guy, but he thanked the Lord his stash was still secure. Besides, he was about to lose Bo again. He tugged his horse closer and navigated the haphazard traffic.

In the growing dusk, the silhouette of Beulah holding a toddler outlined the cabin's doorway. After the long uncomfortable stage ride and the bumpy trail to the farm, Cora wanted nothing more than to leap from the back of the wagon, race to the porch, and embrace her sister-in-law. She squelched the desire. A flat out dash to greet Beulah would only give Bartholomew another reason to consider her a child

Instead, she waited for the wagon to stop and aided Sallie from the back of the wagon. She grabbed up her carpet bag and sauntered behind the menfolk and Eleanor, exhaustion obvious from the droop of her thin shoulders. Hugs went around, and finally, Cora stepped up.

"Oh, Beulah," Cora breathed as she wrapped her arms around the petite woman with the huge belly. She didn't even have the decency to look flustered by her advanced pregnancy. Only happy and maybe a little tired, her auburn hair drawn back into a low bun. Yet her face radiated a cheerful welcome.

How close they had grown from corresponding. No longer was she just her sister-in-law, she had become a true friend. When they broke the embrace, a sparkle lit Beulah's dark eyes.

"I'm so glad you're here. I want you to know how precious your letters are to me. And this is my Wiley."

The cotton-topped toddler gave a shy smile and leaned into his mother. Cora beamed at him.

"Come in, come in." Beulah motioned everyone into the house.

The warmth of the snug space sent joyful shivers through Cora, and the smell of soup sent her tummy rumbling.

"We've a small place," Beulah began, "but there's room for everyone."

The small boy reached for his father, and Miles lifted him from Beulah's arms. "Yep. This is the main cabin. I built on two additional rooms. The boy's not quite big enough to be in his own room. But soon enough he will. And with the new one about to arrive, it may be the only way Wiley gets any sleep."

With a warm glance at his wife, he conspiratorially whispered the last part, "Or his Pa."

Beulah gave a shy laugh and her eyes danced with adoration. Cora inhaled a sigh and couldn't suppress the bubble of joy that foamed within her. Such marital bliss. It beamed from both of their faces. If only she could—

Just dreams in the clouds. The smile slid from her face as she gazed at the two couples conversing. She was too...oh, why go through it again? An outcast couldn't possibly expect that happily-ever-after. Papa would marry her off for convenience.

Marrying old Mr. Thomas was the best she could hope for. She'd end up looking after his five children while looking down on his balding head. A man in such desperate circumstances didn't much care if his woman was a few inches taller than he.

On the bright side, he was a good, sturdy, hardworking man. However, he didn't talk much and when he did, it didn't have much flair to it. He appeared about as interesting as the backside of an outhouse. A grin quirked at the side of Cora's mouth. But the really down side? She...didn't love him. Suddenly, any silly, internal humor fled.

"Cora, Mama tells me you've got yourself a good business going on through Miss McGarlee's sewing shop." Miles gave one of those grins accompanied by a slight narrowing of his eyes and a small head twist.

Miles knew her so well and, from that gleam in his eye, was probably curious at what thoughts occupied her brain. She straightened and ignored Miles's unasked question. "Well, not a business per se, but at least I manage to earn some spending money and squirrel away a bit of a nest egg."

"Oh, dear. I almost forgot." Beulah stood and waddled to the fireplace and brought down a paper. "This telegram scared us to death when it arrived. Sorry, Cora, but Miles read over it. Thankfully it was good news. It turns out Bartholomew won't have to accompany you to St. Louis after all."

Cora caught her breath as Beulah handed her the yellow scrap of paper. Bartholomew's brows descended into disapproval. Momentarily, she thought to hand it to him, but the missive clearly spelled out her name in the "to" line. The *St. Louis and Missouri River Telegraph Company* blared in black ink at the headline. Flipping the telegram over, she took a shaky breath and sank into the stiff kitchen chair.

Cora Taggart, meet our butler Dunkirk at the Evansville Wharf, April 12th for 2 p.m. departure. We are looking forward to your arrival.—Aunt Josephine

A grin vined across her face. Only a week away. "Oh, my."

"Let me see the missive." Bartholomew clamped his hand upon it before Cora had finished admiring the slip of paper. She tucked her hands beneath her as he adjusted his glasses to read.

"Preposterous. Escorted by a mere stranger? I think not." He crushed the scrap of paper into his pocket.

Hope sank like a hammer dropped into a lake. "But he's not a stranger. Aunt Josephine sent him."

"I'll not pass you off like some bread plate."

Cora squirmed in the chair, shutting off the blood to her fingers still tucked beneath her legs.

"Give it a chance, Barth. Aunt Josephine wouldn't send an unreliable person. Obviously this is a trusted servant. She is well off. I doubt she'd settle for less."

"Quite unsatisfactory. The timing doesn't fit the time schedule at all. No, not at all." Bartholomew crossed both his arms.

Beans and cornbread. Cora stilled her eyes from rolling with weighted strings. Everything with Bartholomew drifted toward poppycock, scones, and Earl Gray. Couldn't he for once relax a bit instead of being so tightly strung? He waxed so much like Aleena, she felt she'd gained yet another stern parent.

Miles gave a chuckle and slapped his knee. "Oh, Brother. You take the cake. If it makes you feel better, go with Cora and meet this chaperone. Perhaps it will put your mind at ease."

Beulah spread bowls about the table, and Cora jumped up to help.

"Such lack of foresight, I say." Bartholomew huffed.

Miles caught Cora's eye and winked, the corner of his mouth quirking up. She stifled an aggressive grin and concentrated instead on placing the spoons next to the bowls.

"If you all will seat yourselves at the table, I believe the soup is ready", Beulah announced.

Cora sat next to Beulah and tended Sallie on her right. Eleanor sat opposite beside Bartholomew with Bess in her lap. Miles led in prayer and the conversation drifted to farming.

Sallie, perched on a stack of books, kept Cora busy monitoring the child's soup bowl and water glass. Eleanor, like a specter from a Dickens's novel, remained silent and pale as she had been since entering the cabin.

The gist of conversation parleyed Miles against Bartholomew. First the farm work. Then the journey to St. Louis. Then the arrival of the railroads. And finally on to the Calvinism/Arminianism argument of old. One seemed always pushing the other, then retreating. Then a chuckle from Miles in acquiescence of their differing ways. The display reminded Cora of a sword swashbuckling tale of two pirates attempting to capture each other's ship.

The children grew cranky. Bess was nearly asleep upon Eleanor, so the two ladies ushered their tired offspring into the bedrooms. Cora rose and gathered dishes as the men leaned back with a good cup of tea. She grabbed the bucket by the door and slipped out.

Outside in the damp dusk, Cora breathed in a lungful of spring air tinted with the fragrance of apple blossoms. A moment alone. She paused in the center of the yard to listen to the stillness. A mourning dove wafted its soulful call, sending a wave of peace through her.

She fixed her eyes on the first star peeping out at the almost dark sky. A smile snuck out. "I'm here, Abel. I'm drinking in all of life. I miss you and everyone, but I know God's looking out for you all."

The night held her breathless. Her task tapped at her brain, and she soaked up the last of the absolute freshness of pausing from the world. With one last deep breath, she broke the spell and continued to the pump. The gushing water against her hands and into the bucket transported her back to her own yard. Here she was, fetching like always.

A giggle worked its way out. An odd sound among the quiet business of building night. She gave a small groan as she lifted the bucket, the pail handle cutting against the thick pad between her fingers and palm.

She meandered her way toward the house, rewarded by a slosh of water against her skirt that dripped down into her boot. A smile grew, as she tried to take in the wonder. On the cusp of a journey of a lifetime. Not even a wet boot, nor a mandatory marriage, could dampen that.

Trigg awoke to the flurry of skirts. He inhaled and rubbed a hand down his face. A swift gasp of air truly prodded his brain into consciousness. Cheap perfume drifted to his nose, and he opened his eyes to three women slipping out of their hotel door. Floozies. Great. Bodine and the two idiots hadn't wasted any time making themselves comfortable. Thankfully he'd been out since his head had hit the pillow.

He swung his feet to the floor. Snores lit up the air behind him. Sure. Staying up most of the night meant a body had to sleep sometime. It would probably be several hours before the three woke. Joining up with Bodine might not have been his best move ever.

He grabbed his boots from under the bed and yanked them on his feet. A good stretch standing up woke his muscles. He grabbed his shirt from the end of the bed and buttoned it up. Let the idiots sleep. He was hungry.

The leather hat crushed onto his head chased away the need for a comb, and he slipped through the door. He twisted the knob with a slow turn to avoid any noise. Not that he could awaken the three within anyway.

Once down the stairs, he headed for the saloon. But, when he arrived, the place was deserted. No breakfast here. He shrugged, turned, and pushed through the hotel's front door. The weak early sun greeted him through heavy clouds. A heavy mist trailed down the river's curve. Rain would put a damper on travel. He strode along the sidewalk.

The Verandah Restaurant and Liquors appeared open at the early hour, so Trigg shrugged inside. The smell of bacon slapped him in the face first off. Must be a good place. At least for breakfast. He stepped into the dank interior.

Simple wooden tables and chairs occupied the main dining area. A few customers were sprinkled about the place and a couple of weathered gents perched at the bar. A lazy-eyed bartender turned from the mirrored shelves littered with bottles of amber-colored liquid.

Trigg bellied up to the stool on the far right and nodded a greeting to the mustached man behind the counter. "Bacon, eggs, and a cup of coffee."

The man nodded and went to the batwings beyond the silver liquor cabinet. Trigg removed his hat and laid it on the seat next to him.

"Well, hi there, Sweetheart." A painted lady, face puffy, makeup skewed, picked up his hat and seated herself next to him. "You're getting an early start to your day."

He wondered if this woman had just slipped from his room. Hmmm. After an initial glance, Trigg focused on the mug the barkeep plopped in front of him.

"Got a big day planned?" The woman rubbed the brim of his hat and leaned forward to press herself against him. Her nasal voice was a touch too high and raked across his nerves.

He leaned back to avoid contact. "I reckon."

"Look at you with your big, strong muscles. You must work on the dock." She placed the hat on the counter in front of her and gave it a pat.

His plate arrived, eggs still sputtering and popping grease. He picked up his fork. "Nope."

"Steamboat captain?"

He filled his mouth with eggs and chewed. "Muleskinner."

"Really? How 'bout that? I hear it's quite lucrative."

Right big word for a faded flower to be using. He turned and gave her the once over. Some absurd smashed hat, feathers askew, drooped to the side of her head. Lipstick smeared. No doubt from the last conquest. Powdered makeup covered a bit of the dark circles beneath her eyes. He cleared his throat. "Actually. They're stubborn creatures. Won't give up. You work plum hard for any profit you get."

The hope dove in her eyes. Perhaps she wasn't as stubborn as he'd pegged her for. She stood and meandered across the room to settle next to a lone man with a furry beard. Too bad. She'd left before he could lecture her on finding a more respectable job. The woman was obviously not stupid.

He finished his meal, tossed the money on the counter, and nodded at the bartender. The volume of patrons and workers had doubled since he'd entered the place for breakfast. Evansville was coming alive. Once on the street, a steamboat blast greeted the morning as it chugged away down the Ohio.

With a whistle he swung through the Richard Hotel and hurried to the third floor. Time to move on. He shoved the door open to arouse the occupants inside. But there was no need. One didn't need to rouse the rumpled sheets. Bodine and his buddies were gone.

Chapter Ten

B y jove, those boys had simply disappeared. Like snow in August. He'd been up and down plumb every street that fed into the Ohio River and came up with nothing. Sycamore, Locust, Walnut, Chestnut, Cherry. Pretty much canvassed the tree streets. First, Second, Third on up to Sixth Street. He'd circled the huge Sherwood House Hotel, stopped at the Saddler &Co., the ticket office on First and Main, and stuck his head in nearly every grocery/dry goods store in the downtown area. The wide city area revealed nothing about where Bodine and the two idjits had disappeared to.

He headed toward the river down Locust Street and hit Water Street again. He stared out at the river. Sidewheelers outnumbered the sternwheelers three to one. But he didn't bother to count the busy traffic on the Ohio. His thoughts were on home. So close, yet so far.

That did it. With or without Bodine, he was headed home. With luck, he could get a ferry across and be home by afternoon. Then, once he checked on Bliss and Roe, he'd head out for Iowa on his own. He would pinpoint an exact location later. Somehow.

Trigg urged his horse through the heavy traffic on the road and cut through a space between two Sherwood House Carriages to the river bank on the left. He let out a breath. His mount's hooves cut through the sandy slope in quick order. The slower pace was definitely preferable to the busy street. Either way, he was heading home.

Cora slid the huge homemade ball glove on Wiley's small hand. "There ya go. Now you're the Knickerbocker's best fielder. Ready? I'll pitch you one."

Wiley worked his fingers inside the thick work glove and squeezed the leather pocket open and closed. Then he reared back, let go a giggle, and flung Cora's prized mitt into the air. It fell with a plop into the dust.

"Uh, oh." The tot leaned over to pick it up and scurry over to hand it to her. "Dirty."

She grinned. Yes, the obviousness of children. Perhaps it was more fun for a two-year-old to throw a mitt than have a catch. "Yes, you got it dirty, you mean ol' rascal."

He chortled in glee as he rushed to get away, and she swung him from the ground as he squealed. Cradling him and spinning all at the same time, Cora tickled him until he was out of breath. When they both came up for air, she caught sight of Sallie and Bess standing obediently near the cabin. Eleanor had admonished her not to get involved with the "rowdiness."

The yearning in the girls' eyes brought Cora rushing over to them. "Hide and seek?"

The small girls wrung their hands and glanced toward the quiet cabin.

"It's okay. We'll be careful." Cora took Bess by the hand, and Sallie grabbed her sister's. The guarded eagerness in the girls' faces smote Cora's heart. If she ever became a mama, she was going to let her kids get dirty. Dirt was fun.

She pressed the two girls to be the hiders while she and Wiley set their heads against the rippled bark of a cottonwood tree and counted to ten. She marveled how Wiley could already get past five. By the time, she left he would be able to count all the way to ten. Grabbing up the slobbering toddler, she spun and spotted Bess's white, potty-training gown. Even Wiley pointed with a giggle. "All right. Ready or not here we come."

Even from a long way off, Trigg drank in the sight of the farm. The huge clapboard two story house, expanded over time from a single room, to the log barns to the left. Mules dotted the landscape behind carefully mended fences. His finest crop of hardworking mules that would soon bring a good price down south. So all was well. He'd been traipsing about for near on a month and nothing had burned down or blown away. He grinned.

He hadn't bothered to stop in town but had headed straight south with a tad to the west. And there Bliss was, hoeing the garden, just like she oughta be. Pride rose in his chest. Poor kid had taken over all the mothering duties at the ripe age of thirteen. Now at seventeen, she stood a red-haired beauty, wiping sweat from her neck. She gave pause. Durn if she didn't recognize him even as this distance. Down flew the hoe and the figure hurried to the house.

By the time he'd drawn near, she appeared in a scurry, calling his name. He dismounted and she flew into his arms.

"Oh, Trigg, Trigg. You're back. And Ivalee..." She pushed from his brotherly embrace. "You didn't find her? Is she, I mean..."

Fear and dread mounted in her large brown eyes.

He grabbed her by the upper arms. "I don't know. Yet. I did find Bodine. Then I lost him. He's still a pistol."

She jerked back. "Bo ain't gonna help much, Trigg. I tried to tell you that—"

He put his arm around his sister and strolled forward. "Could ya save the motherly tongue-lashing until we reach the kitchen table, Sis? I've done passed lunch just trying to get here, and I'm powerful hungry."

She laughed, a light airy sound. "Sure. It's just Bo don't seem to be cut from the same cloth as the rest of us."

"Or he just don't care."

She grew still beneath his arm. Shucks, even in silence she reprimanded him. Finally she spoke. "I'm just glad you're home."

They hurried toward the house where Roe, his younger brother by five years, burst from the cabin with a huge smile across his face. The men were soon pounding each other's back in a manly hug.

"You back to stay? What about Ivalee?"

Trigg motioned to the house, and they all headed for the door.

Bliss wasted no time getting out cheese and bread and some leftover hog's belly from the larder. Roe seated himself next to his brother, scooting aside the ledger he'd clearly been working on.

Trigg motioned to the burgundy bound volume. "Everything working out okay?"

"Sure." Roe gave a huge smile. Even as a kid his smile was his most noticeable asset. Snagged girls near and far. "Just trying to cut a few expenses in case you needed more cash for the search."

That was Roe, ever the money manager. "I appreciate that. I'll need some if we can spare it. I may have to go on alone."

His sister edged toward the table. "But that's dangerous. I heard there's Indians."

Trigg nodded. "I reckon that's true."

Roe's brow creased. "You didn't find Bo?"

Bliss set a plate before him, and Trigg grabbed a wedge of cheese wrapped in bread. "I found him."

Trigg dropped his eyes to the cheese sandwich in his hand, but he could feel Roe's heated gaze.

"So he ain't helping. Like always."

At Roe's sullen words, Bliss scurried forward and seated herself. "I could come with you. I mean, Roe can run things here by himself, and he…"

Trigg threw the hard crust of bread to his plate. "No, Sis. Make sense. You really want me to tug you through Indian country? You think that's safe?"

She dropped her eyes.

"Okay. Here's my new plan. I'll stay around here a day or two and help out, get some more cash, and catch a steamer at Evansville and head for Iowa." He paused to peruse both their faces. "I'm telling you this, in case. I'll head to St. Louis, then changeover to Cedar Rapids. From there I'll try to determine the exact location of the gold strike."

Roe shoved his chair back and rose. "If there is any."

The three remained quiet. Roe had a tendency to speak what Bliss was loathe to utter aloud. Pa was half snake-oil salesman himself, and a horrible dreamer. "Well, if there is or if there isn't, that's not my concern. I'm going for Ivalee."

Bliss's hand flew to her throat. "What about Pa?"

Trigg shook his head. "I can't bring him back unless he's got a notion to. And that's not likely."

"So, we ain't gained nothing." Roe blew out a breath.

"Not yet." Trigg rose. "But we will."

"I wish Mama were here." Bliss breathed.

"Not me." Roe growled. "Pa would be making bad choices, just the same, hurting her over and over again. It killed her, you know."

"Roe."

"Just ain't no use hiding it, Bliss." Roe answered. "And Bo ain't no help neither. It's just the three of us."

"Four. Ivalee."

Roe hesitated before glancing at Trigg. "Sure. Ivalee."

Trigg took in his two siblings. Roe's doubt was thick as spring mud. He ran a hand down his bristly face. No matter. Maybe he wouldn't bring Ivalee home, but it sure wasn't gonna be due to not trying.

"Gertrude's about to foal," Roe tossed as his gaze went to the window.

Trigg nodded. "Wondered."

"Not sure she'll make it."

He glanced at his sister whose eyes softened with tears. Time to change the subject. He slapped Roe on the back. "Why don't you show me what's been going on around here."

His brother nodded, giving him a flash of his white teeth. "Sure,'nuff."

The two men exited out the back door.

Bartholomew gave the tidy servant a once over in the bright spring sunlight. Dressed neat as a pen, vest and pressed trousers the color of soot. The older man's hair tinged gray ever so slightly at his ears, the rest of his short black hair tucked beneath a hat. The man bowed, keeping his eyes low. Cora's brother glanced over the missive in his hand once more.

"Highly irregular," Bartholomew sputtered to himself.

Cora all but battened the hatches over her mouth. If she seemed too eager, Bartholomew would insist chaperoning her. If she could stay quiet a few moments longer...

"Very well," her brother clipped with a no-nonsense tone, looking toward the west as if he were conjuring each point of safety for her entire journey. "You must promise me to stay in the women's cabins until...Dunkirk comes for you. If you encounter any trouble, alert the captain at once. Captain Langhorn is the master of the ship. Be accompanied at all times. You will arrive on the third morning. Saturday. Am I clear?"

Cora bobbed her head, wishing ever so much to point to the tickets in Dunkirk's hands, where clearly, all of this information was posted. "Of course."

Amazing. She'd actually sounded demure. Well, almost.

"Fine." Bartholomew's eyes raked the older man once more. "No pish posh for her. She can be quite a handful. Clearly, she has more energy than sense a great deal of the time. You understand, my man?"

Cora rubbed her tongue against the top of her mouth not to spat at her brother. A handful? Pish Posh?

"Yes, sah." The well-trained servant touched a hand to his cap.

Evansville's after-lunch hubbub throbbed around them, everyone about their business in a brisk manner. Thank heavens for her brother's dislike of the city's ruckus. Bartholomew glanced around, distaste marring his handsome face, and then leaned forward to enclose Cora in an awkward hug. "Be on your best behavior. Don't think I won't learn of your misdeeds."

She nodded.

"And so, I shall let our aunt's man take care of loading the trunk. I have no desire to traipse into the mud today."

"Goodbye, Bartholomew. I'll be good. I promise."

He hesitated only a moment before nodding. Then he spun and the tail of his coat disappeared through the burgeoning traffic. The older man next to her motioned to a youth nearby to tote the large trunk to the boat. With a smile and a dancing light in her eyes, Cora swirled and beheld her solo adventure.

"It's Gertrude." Roe's voice brought Trigg out of consciousness.

He stumbled from his bunk in the boys' room and grabbed up his pants. "Coming."

Trigg headed to the parlor, led only by the light of the moon. A lantern appeared at his left. Bliss. Though her face remained in the shadows, he knew her thoughts. "It'll be fine."

She nodded and held the lantern for him to take. He followed Roe out to the barn. The big white mare labored on the straw, eyes distant. Trigg hurried to her head and rubbed her gray muzzle. He hadn't intended to breed her, the feisty thing, but she'd found her way into the breeding corral through a weak fence section. Now, she might give forth her last offspring.

"Shhh. Gertrude. Good girl."

The horse acknowledged him with the swirl of her eyes.

Roe positioned himself at the far end. "It don't look good."

One last pat and Trigg stepped over to investigate.

"She ain't got the strength. We'll have to pull her." Roe whispered.

"No. Only one foot is visible. The head is stuck. We've got to get her up."

"There's no way she can do that."

Trigg hurried to grab the leather harness. "Then we have to help her. That foal needs to drop back down and get into position. Otherwise, we've got two dead animals. Get a long rope."

They worked like frantic men, setting up a pulley system to support the mare from the beam over their head.

"I don't see how this is gonna work. We can't even get her up to wrap the leather around her."

Trigg ignored his brother and went to Gertrude's head. "Come on girl. Roe, be ready."

With a firm grasp on the mare's huge head, Trigg tugged her up from the floor. At first, nothing. Then the animal tried to set her hooves beneath her to rise. "Now."

Roe slipped the leathers beneath her before her bulk crashed to the ground once more. The old mare huffed in exhaustion.

"Let's hope the harness holds." He quickly attached the ropes to the two leather strips, one at her girth behind her front legs, and one across her flank near her back legs. "We need two mules. We can't pull her up by ourselves."

Roe ran through the open doorway past Bliss who stood like a frozen specter.

"Go back to the house."

She shook her head and meandered in, still dressed in a nightgown and bed jacket. "No. She won't die alone."

Once his brother returned, they hitched the two mules to the ropes. Sweat poured from Trigg's face despite the chilly air. He and Roe pulled the mules forward and the log building shuddered.

"Bliss, get out."

"She needs my help." She knelt in the straw next to the dazed creature. "Come, sweet Gertrude. You must. You must."

The brothers tugged on the mules again ,and they gave a mighty gargantuan pull.

"God, support the barn. Keep my sister safe," Trigg whispered.

Gertrude, as if waking from a dream, buried her hooves in the straw and strained.

"Now." Trigg shouted.

With one steady yank they lifted the big mare, and she struggled to put the knobby legs beneath her. One more steady pull and she was up, mostly hanging from the beam, but up. Trigg rushed beneath the rocking building. The foreleg had disappeared.

"Please, God, please." Bliss incanted a prayer at the mare's head.

Gertrude seemed to get footing but tottered.

"We can't hold her up forever," Roe hollered.

No, but maybe long enough. Trigg checked the location of the foal. He could feel two forefeet and finally, a nose. "Set her down."

Slowly they backed the two mules, and the mare eased to the ground.

"Did that do it? Did it?" Roe moved forward in a quiet rush.

Trigg panted. "We're about to see."

Chapter Eleven

The little gray mule danced about in tottering steps, its long ears flopping to and fro. Quite a beauty. Light gray johns brought higher prices. He even sported a bit of dapple across his back. But it would be moot if the mare didn't get herself upright. Gertrude appeared dead, eyes lolled back in her head.

"Got another mare to nurse him?"

"He needs his first milk."

Trigg gave a short snort. "He'll need any milk, period."

Bliss leaned forward and rubbed the mare's neck with fistfuls of straw, cooing as she went. Finally she pivoted a tearful face. "Help me. Please."

Both brothers stepped to help, rubbing the old mare as briskly as they dared. Behind Trigg the spindly mule approached to nibble on his ear. "Here now, Little John, get yourself back."

The tiny foal pranced a few fast trots, almost losing his footing in the process. Gertrude's ear flicked.

"Did you see that? She's alive. Come on, Girl." Bliss left off massaging the mare's neck and instead went to patting her face. Then the animal's head moved, eyes rebalancing themselves in her sockets. In a mighty herculean move, the horse planted her feet on straw and rose. Roe grasped her mid-barrel and lifted.

"Mind yourself. She could roll on you."

But she didn't. Instead the mare's eyes caught the youngster tottering about, and she seemed to gain strength. At last she was up, swaying, but gaining steadiness. The little foal pranced up with a happy tail, nose searching for his dinner.

"Should we prop her?" Roe threw his hands out to steady the wobbly mare.

"Nope. Nothing like a new baby to rejuvenate a new mama."

Bliss wiped happy tears. "She did it."

Trigg pointed a finger at the naughty mare. "Yep, she did. But she isn't doing it again. Got it?"

Gertrude's right eye gave a wink.

"Miss, oh, Miss!"

Cora ignored the call and settled against the railing, Dunkirk ever near. Mist swirled up from the water on this early April day. This packet was the *General Washington*. A typical sidewinder just like the one she'd ridden before. Which was a bit disappointing. She'd so looked forward to watching the water fall from the stern-wheelers. But certainly nothing to fret about, or pish posh about, whatever that meant. She grinned at Dunkirk who dropped his eyes and nodded.

"Miss." A woman about her age shouldered through to the rail. She gave a bright smile. "I believe you dropped this."

Cora looked to the woman's hand. That confounded bookmark. Ever escaping like some naughty toddler. "Oh, dear. Thank you so much. I can't seem to keep track of this bit of frippery."

Bartholomew would be so proud of her bandying about the fancy term. The dark-haired girl didn't seem to notice. "I'm Haleen Dunbar, and this—is my brother, Wilkinson."

She tugged a handsome young man to the forefront. He cut a fine figure in a nice suit, but his smile was as easy as the curls tumbling onto his forehead.

He bobbed his head. "Miss."

How fortuitous, as Aleena would say. Ready-made companions. She nodded. "I'm Cora Taggart, from New Albany."

The girl's grin widened. "How exciting. That seems terribly far away. Is it?"

Cora shrugged. "A bit."

"We're heading back home to St. Louis."

Her eyes grew wide. "That's where I'm going."

Cora's over-exuberance seemed to only draw the two rather than repel them. Dunkirk cleared his throat. Yes, yes. She mustn't be a handful. She reigned herself in. "Perhaps we could dine together."

The brown-eyed girl nodded. "That would be lovely. We will look for you in the dining salon later."

The two backed away with a wave and wove into the crowd on the upper deck. The ship's horn sounded and all but scared ten years off her life. She pressed a hand to her throat but couldn't stop the grin tugging at the corners of her mouth. The adventure had only just begun.

Trigg thundered down the gangplank, yanking Buck behind him. He couldn't be left. Gertrude's miracle had almost made him miss the steamer. He pressed forward onto the main deck and scooted into a small space next to a pallet of wool yarn and a huge pallet stamped "black tea." Not the best spot along the wall of the steamer, but it couldn't be helped. He'd have to stand, but at least he'd be shaded.

The ship gave a blast and Buck acknowledged it with a shake of his head. "Easy, Boy. More to come."

A burst of outrageous laughter accosted his ears. That did sound familiar. Too familiar. He lifted his head. Being the tallest man on this side of the boat had its advantages, but the source of the outlandish chortle stayed behind the corner. He'd be patient. If it was who he suspected, all the better to save a glance until the boat was underway.

The packet moved out onto the open water and increased its speed to a good clip. He pressed his back to the clapboard of the ship and crossed his arms. In less than two days he'd be at his destination.

The laughter burst out again. Trigg turned his head. Still, not visible. This was a small steamer. His brother couldn't run far. The object of his thoughts popped around the corner, still wrapped in the buffalo skin. A fat cigar stuck out from the corner of his mouth, a bottle of bourbon in his hand.

Bo stumbled as he approached. Drunk already? Or a continuation of last night's imbibing? His brother spotted him through bloodshot eyes. "Trigg. Come 'mere, you old dog."

His brother's hand clamped on his neck and yanked him forward. "Where ya been? Keeping the booty safe?"

Trigg elevated one brow. "Where have I been? Where have *you* been?"

"Doing business." His empty hand motioned to the pallet of tea. "Investing in merchandise, of course."

Now Trigg was truly confused. "Come again?"

His brother's two lackeys hushed Bo who seemed to be getting louder by the moment. "Yep, tea, pickles, molasses, even some tobaccy. Planning on making a huge profit up the river."

Ahhh…profit. Always money. So much like Pa. Forever looking out for the next money making scheme. "Ivalee?"

Bo cocked his head and spit. "Yeah, yeah, I'll make good on the girl."

Trigg caught sight of a golden watch fob on a shiny chain. Interesting. Thought for sure he'd drunk up his money from the track days ago. He leveled his eyes at Oates and Burr, but they shifted their gaze away. Something smelled like fish.

His huge brother slapped him on the shoulder. "We're heading up to the boiler deck with decent folks. Got a man seeing to our mounts. See ya later, Brother."

Trigg swallowed a retort. The three of them ambled to the stairway. Slippery as wet ice in the winter, he was. And he wasn't going away. So much for traveling alone. But if it meant locating Ivalee, he'd tolerate his obnoxious brother and his get-rich schemes. At least, for now.

Cora stared up at the bunk over her head. The ladies' cabin rocked gently in the pitch darkness, creaking with unfamiliar pops. The only light came beneath the door from the hallway lanterns. It was nearly impossible to sleep on the narrow, too short bunk. Especially when she wanted nothing more than to walk the deck in the moonlight.

The evening's dinner hour had been a disappointment. Due to the crowd, her seating arrangement had excluded her new friends. They'd waved but had to settle at a different table. And now, she was cloistered in the women's cabin with some fifty other women. Her friend, Haleen, snoozed softly across from her.

They'd whispered about escaping to the deck, but now it appeared her companion in crime had succumbed instead to the land of dreams. Cora gnawed the corner of her lip. It was a terrible habit. Much like her fondness for words slightly outside proper-company use.

Stay in the women's cabin... Bartholomew's exact words. Blast. Had she promised she would? She racked her brain. *Of course,* she'd replied, which really, was an answer to his last admonition about whether she knew of the steamer's Saturday arrival. The sighing of sleep about her smote her heart. Oh, why was she splitting hairs? Clearly she'd agreed to the last-minute dither her brother had blathered.

Even as this thought needled her conscience, she swung her legs to the floor, taking care not to bang her head on the bunk above. She would only step out for a moment. Cora breathed in small gasps, trying to keep her cot from creaking as she stood. It would be a long time before Bartholomew heard of her misdeed. Meanwhile, she would look at the stars from the packet's deck.

She squeezed through the narrow door into the corridor and froze. Tarnation. An outline of a man sitting in a chair greeted her. But with his shoulders lax, head back in sleep, she felt certain she could creep past him. Some guard. This was the very man who protected the ladies' cabins. Obviously fast asleep. She tiptoed sideways past the youth, his long legs a-sprawled, and slunk onto the back deck.

What a sight. Indeed, the sequined, dark sky cast a flickering replica on the black expanse of water, rippling with flecks of moonlight. The silhouetted tree line on either side framed a picture that could ignite any girl's romantic illusions. A twin cloud's silvery thread slipped across the waters, mirroring the one above. Breathtaking.

Her jaw juddered at the damp chill, and she rubbed her hands up and down her arms. Despite the cool temperature, the view enchanted her like no other. A small sound cooed from her lips. Worth every scrap of future guilt for disobeying Bartholomew.

A movement to the left captured her attention. A second gasp tore from her throat. But not from appreciation. From alarm. A shadowy figure leaned against the railing.

"Miss? Is everything all right?"

Those tones struck a chord of familiarity. A tall lanky figure rose to full height. Jumping catfishes. A witness to her misdeed.

"Ah, Miss Bookmark Cora."

"You!" It was *him*. Trigg Gentry. His name rose up too readily which made her jaw clench. In the faint light of night, he looked even taller. Not that it mattered. He may have rescued her bookmark, but that didn't excuse the laugh he'd had at her expense. And, he had used her given name. Without permission. Her chin tilted higher. "Miss Taggart, if you please."

"Nice to meet you, Miss Taggart. Officially, that is." His shadow nodded towards her.

He shifted back to the railing where the moon highlighted his handsome face. Despite her resolve, some of her exasperation with the man melted away. He cut quite a figure. She blinked, tempted like never before to linger.

Bartholomew would not approve of her traipsing about the deck at night. With a man. He would not approve at all. Yet, an electrifying shiver ran through her, whether from the cool spring air or the fact that she, Cora Taggart, stood on board a steamboat, alone with a handsome, tall man.

"Here, use my jacket."

"I...oh." She could hardly deny the comfort the heavy canvas brought as the coat settled across her shoulders. It smelled of hay and horses. Not an unpleasant smell. It reminded her of home. A tad bit more of her annoyance with the man evaporated. "Uh...thank you."

"I hope you're not seasick?"

"No, I...just needed fresh air." In a way. She tugged the lapels closer, the next words slipping out in a whisper. "And to see the stars."

A quiet laugh escaped her companion. A low pleasant rumbling. "Confession is good for the soul. Are you unaccompanied?"

Oh, my. Her experience with the opposite sex usually consisted of her trying to outrun them on the baseball field. Suddenly the water she swam in felt very deep and beyond her swimming capabilities. "I should get back to the cabin."

She whipped the jacket off and shoved it into his hands.

"Please stay."

His softly spoken plea snagged the breath in her throat and froze her. She should go. She should. But something inside her yearned to stay. Her voice came in a breathy sort of fashion. "I...shouldn't. Really. Bartholomew would be quite disappointed to learn that I've left the women's cabins. But as you can see, I ignored his instructions. As...as I frequently do, much to the disappointment of my family members, you know, so many misdeeds, pish posh, and all that..."

Her words drifted to a stop. Had she really just been blathering?

ço❀ç

Miss Taggart's whispered confession fell silent. But still, she stood there. Poised to run down the corridor. Yet, he'd managed to keep her from scurrying off like a timid bunny. "I won't tell if you don't."

Nervous laughter met his ears. "Promise?"

"Come back to the railing. We're missing quite a view."

She hesitated for several tics. Then Cora—Miss Taggart— relaxed and stepped forward. He held out the jacket, and she slipped her arms back inside the garment. A sigh rushed from her in a small puff of air. "Mr. Gentry, you're quite persuading."

"I do my best."

"It seems we keep crossing paths." Her voice grew a tad wispier.

"It seems."

She turned from the railing to face him. "You're not...following me, are you?"

He gave a low laugh. "As tempting as that sounds, no."

The woman took a step back. Perhaps he shouldn't have used the word tempting. Though, he could only be honest.

"But I saw you first in New Albany. Then...here?"

He leaned over the railing and clasped his hands. "As much as I enjoy rescuing your packages and bookmarks, I'm not tailing you. But, in truth, I am trailing someone. Namely, my wayward sister."

Her hands buried in the lapels of his coat—*his* coat. The moonlight carved out the delicate profile of her face. My, she was one beautiful woman. A tall, willowy strawberry blonde. He liked her height, he decided. Why, he wouldn't even have to bend over to kiss her.

"Is she lost?"

Trigg reined in his runaway thoughts and glanced back to the departing river. Too much daydreaming and staring would have her scurrying back down the hallway. He cleared his throat to focus himself. "In a matter of speaking. She ran off to find my father. The worst part is...she's alone."

"Oh." She stepped closer to the railing. "Perhaps it's not so bad. It's become more acceptable to—"

"She's fifteen."

Miss Taggart fell silent for a moment, fluttering those lashes in the dim light. "Oh, dear. She's...very young. I certainly hope you find her."

"Me, too." For a moment he wished away his circumstances. Getting to know Miss Taggart would be a pleasure indeed. He tugged his eyes from her, stifled anymore thoughts of kissing her, and set his gaze on the water. "So perhaps you can now understand my concern about whether you yourself were accompanied."

Her head dipped before she answered. "I am. My aunt's…servant is traveling with me."

"Good. I must agree with, uh, Bartholomew was it? A lady should be chaperoned in this day and age." His brother's image popped into his mind unbidden. "Immoral people are everywhere."

A bit of a snort popped from his companion. "Like on the back deck of a steamer?"

He couldn't help the laughter that tumbled from his mouth. She had a point and wasted no time expressing her opinion. He admired her spunk. "I am merely a lowly muleskinner searching for his sister."

"A muleskinner? In New Albany?"

"Kentucky."

"I see. So you…skin mules?"

He shook his head, trying to smother the chuckle that rose. "No. I raise mules and sell them. Well, my siblings and I. Plus, we grow our own hay and feed for the animals on the farm."

I guess that explains—" Her speech screeched to a halt.

"Explains what?"

"Uh…you being in this area?"

He touched her elbow to get her to turn to him. "That sounded more like a question than an explanation."

She shook her head. "I'm sorry. My mouth runs away with me sometimes. Most times, in fact. Anyway, I'm on my way to St. Louis."

Trigg narrowed his eyes at her quick directional change of conversation. "Is that right?"

"I'm going to stay with my aunt and uncle."

"Their house wasn't burnt in the great fire in forty-nine? They were tremendously lucky."

"I heard about the fire. And, of course," Miss Taggart cleared her throat and then whispered, "the sickness."

He nodded. Even as bold as his companion seemed to be, she balked at murmuring cholera epidemic.

"My aunt and uncle live in Lucas Place. I understand it's some ways from the river."

Ah. Lucas Place sounded much like an area where his grandmother would live. That explained a great deal. Rich folks. This tall, slender woman who moved like a fairy sprite came from money. Disappointment sunk deep in his gut. Miss Cora Taggart was simply above his station. Funny how she didn't strike him as a debutante. Not too many high-society ladies crouched behind a horse in an alley.

The sound of approaching footsteps earned a sharp intake of breath from his beautiful companion. Around the corner lumbered a huge shape with two smaller ones on his wings. Trigg recognized the profile before he opened his mouth. Bo's voice thundered in the dark, hushed surroundings.

"Now, who we got here?"

Miss Taggart leapt from the railing.

"She's a leggy one, ain't she boys?" Bo's grainy voice picked up some volume. "Why don't you introduce us, Trigg, old buddy?"

As booming laughter echoed across the back deck of the boat, Trigg found his jacket wadded in his hands. In a swirl of skirts, his chance meeting with this intriguing woman had come to an end.

Miss Taggart had vanished.

Chapter Twelve

Cots creaked, waking Cora from erratic sleep. Her long body just couldn't adjust to the tiny cot. Not to mention her unchaperoned meeting on the deck and the appearance of that frightening man in the buffalo skin. That was enough to keep her awake from excitement, trepidation, and…yes, guilt.

Would Dunkirk be able to tell she'd been gallivanting on the deck of the ship late at night? Unchaperoned? If so, would he mention it to her aunt? That was one sure way for her disobedience to get back to her family. She shoved the thought to the back of her mind when she caught sight of Haleen fastening her shoe laces.

She quickly smoothed her skirt and ran a comb through her hair. Rapid fingers rebraided the long swath. The object of her interest picked up a small carpetbag and headed toward the stairs.

"Haleen," Cora called over the hubbub of the women's cabin.

The girl stopped and glanced her way. Cora quickly finished her task, pinned up her hair, and put on her white bonnet. She grabbed her bag and hurried to catch up. "I thought you were going to leave me."

"Yes, miss. I'm sorry. I'm anxious to meet up with my brother."

They cornered the outer deck, the very place of Cora's tête-á-tête, and she hastened her steps to keep up with Haleen. "Oh, of course. I was hoping we all could have breakfast together. Please, Haleen, slow down."

Her companion stopped at the top of the steps. Then Haleen stepped aside to give way to the traffic of women flowing up the steps. "I'm not sure it's allowed."

Cora shook her head. Allowed? "Why would it not be?

Haleen's face lost its fresh openness and tightened. "Well, I mean. You being a lady with a servant, I assumed—"

A laugh popped from Cora, and she didn't bother to cover it. She grinned at Haleen. "I'm just a plain farmer's daughter."

Her new friend blinked. "But you have a traveling servant."

"He's not mine. My aunt sent him to fetch me."

Realization washed over Haleen's face. "Oh, I see."

"We'd better hurry, or we won't get a table."

Dunkirk materialized beside them with a brisk nod. He took the bag from her and clutched it along with the pink parasol Mother had made her buy. Both girls looked at one another and Cora pulled a face. Haleen relaxed and gave a small giggle.

Cora looped her arm in Haleen's. "To breakfast, Milady?"

Haleen gave a small smile. "To breakfast we go."

The crowd bottlenecked the door of the huge dining salon. Cora stepped back to allow some room but found a foot instead. She spun, an apology on her lips. The blue eyes that met hers were slightly quirked in amusement. Her breath dissolved in her throat.

"We meet again."

Trigg. Ahem, Mr. Gentry. Thunderation, that man had a knack for turning up in inopportune moments. *And opportune ones.* "Apologies, Mr. Gentry."

Daggum. From her lofty crow's nest, she should've had a fix on him. After all he stood taller than she. How he'd ended up right behind her was anyone's guess.

He inclined his head with a curve in his cheek. Though she'd never confess it, she rather enjoyed looking up into his blue eyes. For once. She looked up. Hardly ever did that happen. Certainly not with her future suitor.

"Good morning, Miss Taggart."

Haleen's mouth opened and then nudged Cora.

She covered a grunt. "This is my new friend, Haleen Dunbar from St. Louis. Trigg Gentry."

Her short companion bobbed a tight curtsy in the confines of the crowd. "Pleased to meet you."

A shy smile spread across Haleen's face, a flair of appreciation lighting her eyes. A tight knot settled in Cora's middle.

"Miss Dunbar."

Her friend shot him a beaming smile. "Perhaps you could—"

The crowd gave way and Cora gave Haleen a small push. "Hurry, we need to find your brother."

In the flurry, the women surged forth, and Trigg Gentry melted into the crowd. Well, not really. But at least her shorter companion had lost sight of him. She tightened her lips as she puzzled why that mattered.

Wilkinson stood at a table in the back, and Cora guided Haleen through the patrons. They were joined by two women, one with a lacy parasol, the other with a pale powdered face, accompanied by a man in a brown wool suit. The man seated the ladies and then tucked the napkin at his throat.

"Good morning, ladies," Wilkinson intoned as he assisted them both into their seats before taking a chair to Haleen's left. "I trust you both rested well."

Cora pulled her attention from the additional people at the table and nodded.

"Yes, I was exhausted. I think I must have fallen asleep the instant my head hit the pillow," Haleen said.

She had that right. Cora could attest to it. Which had left Cora tramping about the deck unescorted. Although, she had enjoyed her little encounter with Trigg, ahhh, Mr. Gentry. Bumblebees. Why was his formal name so hard to fix in her mind?

Anyway, she wasn't about to share her rendezvous with her new friend. Haleen's reaction to Trigg Gentry still rankled her insides like a bad case of heartburn.

"Miss Taggart, is it?" Wilkinson's brows rose above expressive brown eyes in his handsome face. An ebony curl flopped to his forehead as he leaned forward to speak.

Cora smiled. Haleen's brother was quite charming, but Cora couldn't help but compare him to the man whose coat she'd worn last night. And Wilkinson came up lacking. She feared at this point, every man would. "You may call me, Cora."

His face gave nothing away, but he cut his eyes to his sister.

"She is traveling with her aunt's servant, I believe."

A nice way to proclaim she wasn't some fancy lady-in-waiting, dripping in jewels. Several servants circulated the dining salons, holding plates brimming with food above their heads. One stopped at her place and laid a plate full of food before her. Although the ham and gravy seemed a little greasy, nothing like Mother would have fixed, Cora merely nodded her thanks. Seldom did she eat out. This was a luxury.

Her eyes flicked up and found Dunkirk nearby with his back against the wall. Did the man never eat? Entering her aunt's world of upper-class living was both thrilling and bewildering.

"Ah, I see." Wilkinson picked up his silverware to address his congealing goo of gravy. "From New Albany, correct?

A servant placed a cup of coffee next to her plate and disappeared before she had a chance to refuse it. Coffee had never been a favorite. Would Tri—Mr. Gentry decline the hot beverage? Or would he delight in its deep, rich taste? She gave a small sound of disgust which drew her companions' gazes. "Sorry. Something in my throat."

All right. No more thoughts of that tall...striking—no. Just no more thinking of that...man. She spooned four sugar cubes into the bitter brew. "Um, yes. You're correct. I live on a farm near there. And I believe you said you hailed from St. Louis?"

Aleena would be so proud of her proper English.

Both nodded and Haleen continued. "Yes, on Broadway. We've actually just returned from an uncle's funeral."

"Oh, I am so sorry."

Wilkinson wiped his mouth with a napkin. "A great uncle actually. We came as representatives of our family's condolences. Our parents couldn't attend. Mother is at home with our three younger siblings. Father is a piano tuner with Homer Phillips on North Fourth Street. Are you familiar?"

"No, I'm afraid not."

"He has quite an assortment of musical instruments as well as an extensive gallery of grand pianos."

Haleen cleared her throat and lowered her voice. "Mostly the items appeal to...well, more to the people at Lucas Place."

"Lucas Place?" My, the ham was cold, but she chewed and swallowed anyway. "Is that so? That's where my aunt lives."

Wilkinson dropped his biscuit in a puddle of gravy. "You don't say?"

"As a matter of fact, I haven't seen them since I was a wee child. I'm not even sure I would recognize her if I saw her."

Haleen's eyes grew wide. "How frightening."

"Oh, no. Not at all. She corresponds with my mother. Everything has been arranged. They're expecting me."

Cora took that moment to scan the interior. Blue eyes clashed with hers. Gee willikers, had he winked at her? Heat coursed up her throat as she tugged her attention from the man who seemed to continue haunting her thoughts. "They live on the sixteen hundredth block of Locust Street."

Haleen coughed into a napkin.

"Locust Street? I see." Wilkinson tugged at his shirt collar.

"Calvin and Josephine Glenridge. Do you know them?"

A choking noise emitted from Haleen, whose eyes bulged above the napkin at her mouth.

Cora popped up and pounded Haleen on the back. But the girl waved her off, and Cora returned to her seat. A servant brought a glass of water. Haleen sipped it, and her flushed face toned down a few degrees.

"I'm fine, really," her friend sputtered. "Just a cough, nothing serious."

A clatter behind them garnered the table's attention. A dropped plate. The noise startled the salon into silence for a few milliseconds.

Wilkinson arose. "If you'll excuse me. I have pressing tasks to attend. It was lovely dining with you, Miss Taggart. Excuse me, ladies."

Cora bobbed her head courteously and then eyed his plate, still half full of food, the unfortunate biscuit sodden with gravy. Odd.

"Wait for me, Wilkinson." Haleen paused for her brother to step back and pull out her chair. "I apologize, Cora. I usually write in my journal first thing in the morning. So sorry to abandon you, but it's so difficult to find a quiet moment on this boat. Perhaps we will meet up later?"

"Uhhh, yes, of course." Cora blinked, the pair scurrying away before she could even finish her reply. A servant arrived and swept the used plates from the table. The three at the opposite side of the table cast sympathetic smiles.

Brown suit shook his head. "Left all alone? Such a shame."

Why had they left so abruptly? Had she said something wrong? Again? Cora nodded and managed to finish off most of her food. It was difficult to eat feeling so unsettled. At last, she stood so abruptly, her napkin slid to the floor. "If you'll excuse me."

Dunkirk appeared at her side, toting that ridiculous parasol. She gave him a smile that threatened to slip and covered herself by reaching for the umbrella. "Just the thing, uh… Mr. Dunkirk, thank you."

She wove her way among the dining tables and stepped into the sun. When she floundered to open the cursed parasol, the butler stepped forward and opened in with a flourish.

"Thank you." She walked the deck until her face didn't feel quite so hot and then climbed the stairs to settle at the railing.

Trigg watched Miss Taggart's companions rush from the salon. Then, she herself rose a few minutes later and strode towards the exit, a servant in tow. He shoved the last of his meal into his mouth, excused himself, and headed for the doorway.

He hiked along the boiler deck and found her at the stern of the boat, watching the boiling wake smooth out. She struck a forlorn pose. He sidled up. "Missing home?"

She gasped at his arrival but shook her head. "Perhaps, but also puzzled."

"About?"

A small laugh burst from her. "About how skillful you are at sneaking up on me."

His lips twitched. "I doubt I take up much of your thoughts."

Her lips compressed, but a sparkle softened her eyes.

"I trust there is nothing amiss with your companions," he prodded as he leaned against the railing.

A stream of air left her lips. "I'm not really sure what is going on. I don't know if it is something I said, something I did or didn't do, or because I'm just...."

When she didn't finish, he grasped her elbow and turned her towards him. Perhaps he was taking liberties, but he had to know. "Just what?"

A squeal interrupted the conversation. A heavy-set woman, clad in a black cape, waddled their way. Behind her, a tiny mouse of a woman followed.

"Well, well, well. If it isn't New Albany's Miss Cora 'Too Tall' Taggart," the larger woman purred.

Breath almost hissed from the beautiful woman at his side. But Miss Taggart recovered quickly and dipped a quick curtsy. "Mrs. Dixon. How nice to see you."

Somehow, Trigg got the impression his companion wasn't in the least pleased to see her.

"And who is this strapping, young man? A beau perhaps? He certainly is tall enough, don't you think so, Elizabeth? A marriage for Miss Taggart after all?"

After all what? Trigg had no time to ponder this. Instead his mind circled around the name "Too Tall." He leaned forward with a nod and started to introduce himself, but Cora had already begun to sputter.

"Oh…dear, I mean, well, this is not—"

"Trigg Gentry at your service, Ma'am."

Mrs. Dixon gripped her coat with one hand and brought out a red fan with the other. With a bat of her eyes, she flipped the Japanese fan open with a flourish. She waved it toward Cora with a coy bounce of her eyebrows. "You've been holding out on us, Miss Taggart. Here I'd been hearing your father had finally convinced someone to court you, and you have this young man in your pocket. My, my, what a handsome one. And tall, of course since, well, you know, one of shorter stature would not be interested at all."

Cora blew up her bangs, her face the color of a glowing horseshoe fresh from the forge. He allowed Miss Taggart to stew a moment and shifted his attention back to the woman. "And who is this beside you?"

Mrs. Dixon dismissed her companion with a wave of her flamboyant fan. "That's just Mrs. Elizabeth Rogers. So, where are you two love birds going? Hmmm?"

Man, it got thick quick. "St. Louis, actually. You?"

"Oh my goodness. So are we. What a stroke of luck. And I just bet you're visiting with your Aunt Josephine? Why we'll be within a few blocks of you. Virginia and Robert Cantrell live on Fifth St." She fluttered the fan and leaned toward Trigg. "My husband, God rest his soul, and Robert were distant cousins."

"Yes, I am staying with my aunt, but we aren't—" Cora motioned to Trigg.

"But, I do believe Robert and Virginia are looking to purchase some property in Lucas Place near your aunt and uncle. Robert's quite successful, you know. He suffers from consumption, but you wouldn't be able to tell. So hardy and such a quick business mind."

Mrs. Dixon, decked completely in black, continued the saga of the Cantrells while Mrs. Rogers stood by, quite mum. She, wearing proper gray, was a mere wisp of a woman topped with a smallish hat of some sort. And netting.

Trigg turned his attention back to Mrs. Dixon, whose neck roll applauded her dramatic soliloquy. Poor Miss Taggart tried several times to jump into the fray, but the large woman had a complete monopoly on the conversation.

"I'm glad to see that you've taken up carrying a parasol. If you want to keep that tall, handsome man, you'll behave seemingly, rather than flit about with a ball in your hand. Lands sakes, I'd say so."

And if it were possible, Miss Taggart's cheeks tinged a deeper red. Like a boiler…about to blow.

Chapter Thirteen

Jumping junipers, Widow Dixon wouldn't stop yammering. How, why, or where had this woman boarded? It was as if she had materialized out of thin air just to haunt Cora. Not only did the woman have Mr. Gentry and her plumb married off, she was dropping every detail of her unmarriageable traits to the world. Where was Aleena when she needed her?

"But let's get back to you, Miss Cora. I thought sure you'd end up with Heaker Thomas. At least that's the way the wind blows." She stepped back and spread her hands like a star actress on stage. "I reckon he doesn't mind you're taller than he is, given he has five kids crawling all over the place like a nest of roaches. 'Twas a tragedy about his wife, though. I'm sure she must've done something horrible to die at such an early age. Tsk, tsk."

"Yes, such a terrible thing, but—"

Mrs. Dixon gasped as she noticed Dunkirk hovering nearby. "Is that your servant? Oh no. Silly me. Of course he'd be part of the Glenridge Estate. I had to sell three of mine off when my husband died. It was right tragic to learn how to run a household with just the remaining two. But I manage."

The woman paused enough to fetch a handkerchief and wipe her brow, a powerful end to an emotional performance. Cora cleared her throat. *Now is my chance to clear the air.* "Not to mention they are people rather than possessions. And while I've got your attention, I'd like to clarify—"

"Miss Cora. Are you insinuating I didn't care for my servants? How absurd. I fed and clothed them. They were quite well taken care of, I assure you."

Cora bristled. How dare she use such a condescending tone with her? She opened her mouth, but Trigg stepped forward. His hand upon her arm froze any words she'd begun to form.

"So delighted to meet you both, Mrs. Dixon, Mrs. Rogers. Perhaps we will meet up in St. Louis. Good day, ladies." And with that, Trigg pulled Cora to the staircase.

This man was quickly becoming her hero.

The next two days cruising the wild Ohio River first and then dove-tailing around Cairo into the Mississippi waterway proved to be both invigorating and frustrating for Trigg. He'd like nothing better than to continue basking in Cora's company. Meeting the beautiful blonde at the stern of the boat each night became the thing he most looked forward to with eager anticipation. Yet this slow mode of traveling kept Trigg from his duty. Above all else, he must locate Ivalee.

Both days he and Miss Taggart had been quite busy finding entertainment at the chess table, strolling to catch a breeze, and ducking about the boat to avoid both his brother and his lackeys and her wicked widow acquaintance. They'd laughed and dodged, finding solace, sun, and camaraderie on top hurricane deck. Never once had he thought he could find such friendship with a woman. As a matter of fact, such a familiarity had sprung up between them that he just couldn't think of her as Miss Taggart anymore. She was Cora—feisty, funny…irresistible. And he'd taken on the privilege of calling her by her first name tonight. Though she'd protested, he could tell she'd been rather pleased.

On this last night, he lay stretched out on his bunk. Trigg couldn't stop ruminating on Cora's tinkling laughter or the way her green eyes sparkled. He found her mischievous humor entertaining and much too charming. Way too charming, if he knew what was good for him. But that hadn't kept him away from her. He'd sought her out every chance he could.

At one point, having dodged the widow arch nemesis by charging up the stairs to the upper deck, Cora had spun near the railing, alight with laughter, trying to catch her breath. She carried no parasol, as usual, and her face glowed pink from the previous day's sunshine while they'd gallivanted about the ship. She'd cocked her head at him, an impish grin on her face. A flushed, wild, playful soul, alive with blossoming promise.

And…he stopped breathing.

Had he ever seen a more beautiful woman? Ever? A frozen image of her imprinted in his mind. One he would never forget. And he knew in that moment, he would never be the same.

She'd branded him with memories that would never fade. He fought against them with weakening strength. Her allure caught him in the most unexpected ways.

"I want to be…a thick , cotton dish cloth."

The woman said the oddest, most captivating things, and she'd announced this to him just a few hours ago as they'd whispered together in the dark, watching the water slip away. He'd laughed, fighting his delight with her, and muttered, "Strange ambitions."

Then she'd turned a gentle smile on him, her eyes aglow in the moonlight. A night nymph come to capture his heart.

"Not when you want to soak up the world."

He'd so wanted to kiss her. But he hadn't. He couldn't. Propriety stilled his hands. Instead he'd clenched the railing and nodded, yearning instead to soak in *her* presence.

Having Haleen and her brother Wilkinson served well as chaperones, though Trigg grabbed every chance he could to be alone with Cora. But tomorrow, it would end. He had to remember it was a nothing but a passing fancy. As much as he was drawn to the willowy blonde, he had a very important mission to complete. Ivalee must be found.

With gritted teeth he flipped to his side on the narrow bunk. The whole affair had been nothing but a distraction. And now he must focus on the task at hand.

Still, setting eyes on her at breakfast would be a welcome goodbye.

ఎఠ

Cora's smile widened as Trigg's muscular form made his way to their table. Haleen fluttered her lashes and adjusted the cameo nestled at the base of her neck. Frustration bubbled up at her new friend's obvious infatuation with the man who'd escorted Cora around the steamboat for the last two days.

Yet, Trigg had sought out Cora each night, to whisper future dreams and promises. She, not Haleen. He had been the one who'd tugged Cora inside the salon to cut themselves off from their ever-present companions to scurry onto the sunniest deck. Haleen despised the sun on her skin and happily kept herself tucked beneath her frothy parasol.

Cora took a deep breath to steady the breathless, shaky reaction as the tall, handsome man seated himself next to her. Silly, really. She had to keep a lid on this strange awareness that enveloped her every time he drew near. As if she could sense his presence. Such an ability could have come in handy growing up. But somehow, it only seemed to work for…Trigg.

Haleen leaned forward, her eyes alight with kittenish delight. "Good morning, Mr. Gentry. You're running a bit late for breakfast. But don't you worry. I've so much on my plate, if they short you, I'd be glad to share."

"Yeah, thanks." He turned a grin on Cora. "And good morning to you."

And Haleen was promptly dismissed, though that knowledge stirred up that runaway tingle, threatening to fluster Cora. Trigg raised that brow and tilted his head.

He'd called her Cora again late last night in their last secret rendezvous. Though she'd protested, he'd agreed to keep it between them. Yet, his bewitching grin told her of his temptation to blurt her given name once more. Right here. In proper company.

She stiffened into a conventional pose and dipped her head, though she was sure a spark of flippancy gleamed from her eyes. "Ah, Mr. Gentry. Lovely of you to join us."

Her prim address brought a smirk from Trigg, and she had to press her lips together to stem a giggle.

He lowered his voice and bent his head towards her. "I wouldn't miss the last morning to dine together for the world, Miss Dish Cloth."

Tea sputtered from Cora's mouth back into the cup pressed to her lips.

"I'm sorry." Haleen patted her mouth with a napkin. "Did you say…dish cloth?"

Trigg had settled back into his chair and schooled his features into innocence. He raised a hand and motioned to a waiter. "Of course not. I said Miss Taggart. And I can see I've failed to wish you good morning, Miss Dunbar."

Haleen flushed and fluttered her lashes to her cheeks, the strange greeting all but forgotten.

With a nod Trigg acknowledged Wilkinson. A plate arrived full of eggs, bacon, and toast. "I trust you slept well."

"Very well." Cora nodded, stemming a grin.

"I also."

"But the ship pitches so." Haleen reached for her cup. "I've hardly slept a wink the whole trip."

Tea almost spewed from Cora's mouth once again with much more power. She fumbled for a napkin and found it in Trigg's hand at her elbow.

"I think you'll need this."

"Any little thing disturbed me." Haleen continued. "I'm such a delicate sleeper."

Cora blotted the moisture at her lips. Her new friend hadn't even stirred the three nights Cora had crept from her bed.

Trigg winked at Cora. "I'm sorry to hear that."

Haleen continued, lauding them both of her gentle nature, taking milk in tepid tea and needing smelling salts for her vapors. Cora let the conversation flow about her, while memorizing Trigg's features. Soon they would part ways, and he would be merely part of a fond recollection. Those blue eyes and quick grin.

Oh, who was she fooling? She'd miss more than that. He'd just brazenly winked at her after all. He always seemed to be doing that. Charming her with his brassy humor, taking liberties he ought not, even flirting with her outright. Yet, he'd done nothing to malign her reputation.

She inhaled and let out a long, soft sigh which drew his gaze. Glory, it set her nerves prickling, bringing up goosebumps on her arms. He hadn't shaved this morning, and she hated to admit it but she found it enhanced his masculinity. As if the man needed anything else to draw her to him. She dropped her eyes, fearing he'd read her thoughts a little too accurately.

Wilkinson rose. "Well, we should be disembarking soon. I best see to the luggage."

"Yes. I suppose I should see to organizing my things as well," Haleen said. Wilkinson pulled out her chair and she stood. "Are you coming, Cora?"

"I'm already packed."

Dunkirk already toted her carpet bag and parasol, poor man. He'd been a faithful escort for the entire trip. Though she hated to see the man utilize his entire free time following her about and transporting her possessions, she was most grateful for his service.

"I'll see to her," Trigg said as he drew back her chair.

"It was so nice to have met you both." Cora grasped Haleen's hand and nodded to Wilkinson. "It's been a lovely adventure to share the journey with you."

"Yes, absolutely lovely." Haleen squeezed her hand, but shot a blushing smile at Trigg. Then she fixed her gaze on Cora. "Write to me."

They departed as Black Death crept closer. Oh, dear. Cara snatched up her reticule.

"Miss Taggart, Miss Taggart…"

Widow Dixon hailed her from two tables over. They were too near to risk a dodge and not be rude. Instead Cora planted a smile on her face and spun to face the woman. Trigg took her by the hand and placed it on his arm.

"Gracious, look at this couple," Widow Dixon gushed to Mrs. Rogers hot on her heels "Quite stately with such height. I've noticed you two flitting about the decks the last couple of days. You're hard to miss."

Here her brows rose before she continued with a flick of her hand. "Miss Taggart, where is the brother and sister couple who chaperones this match, hmmm? I believe their name is Dunbar, isn't that correct?"

"Yes, Mrs. Dixon. I believe so."

The elder woman sniffed, taking a full sweep of them both. "From St. Louis too, I believe. Well, since you have no one to accompany you about the ship, Elizabeth and I would be glad to stroll with you."

"Why that's a fine idea." Trigg's smile disarmed the bold woman for a moment.

Had the man gone mad? The last thing Cora needed was Mrs. Dixon quizzing her over every moment Cora and Trigg had spent together aboard the ship. Yet, Trigg's hand patted hers comfortingly.

"We were just going down to the main deck to feed my horse. He'd be right glad to meet you both. Perhaps you'd like to help curry his coat?"

Mrs. Dixon's eyes blinked as if in a convulsion for just a second. "The main deck? Why, that location's not fit for genteel ladies. Miss Taggart I'm surprised you'd agree to such a thing."

Cora swallowed before Aleena's advice whisked into her mind. "Now, Mrs. Dixon, you know I'm a farm girl, born and bred. Besides, if I recall, your husband was quite enamored with fine horseflesh. He probably quoted numerous times that noble people highly regard the life of their beasts."

Cora could have hugged Trigg when he jumped into the fray.

"I believe that's from Proverbs. A wise man, your husband."

The widow swelled like a squall on the horizon, jiggly neck skin quivering in outrage "How unbecoming to talk of my dead husband. He would have never stepped so low as to attend a common animal on the vulgar lower deck of a steamer."

Trigg cut in smoothly, "Ah, more the shame. But thank you for your kind offer. Good day."

He whirled Cora toward the back exit, his next words coming in a whisper. "Her husband's dead?"

"Yes, sorry. My sister says mentioning her husband changes the tide and allows one to escape her gossiping claws. And she was right. It worked like a charm."

"If we hurry, we can ascend to the hurricane deck. I doubt Mrs. Dixon would put out that much effort to climb the stairs or stand in the sun for the next topic of her interest."

"I thought we were going to the lower deck?"

He grinned. "I just remembered. I already fed Buck. I don't know how I forgot."

Cora stifled a giggle, her body alive with delicious tension starting where his hand rested on her fingers at his elbow. This man had allied with her to evade the clutches of that nattering widow woman—again. "Terrible memory you have."

Once a level up, they settled at the railing. Perfect for viewing the river. And the sun felt glorious. Cora took it all in, glancing back down the river.

A young boy exited the Texas house and Trigg hailed him. "How much longer till we dock?

The cherry-cheeked boy couldn't have been more than fourteen. His clothes were clean, but weathered. "Not much longer, sir. And just to warn ya, I'm fixing to blow the horn. We are coming up on Duncan's Island."

"An island? Where?" Cora shaded her eyes to cut the sunlight.

The boy stepped forward and pointed to the left. "Right about there. The captain says it's washing away since the dike was built on Bloody Island, but it's still there."

Sure enough. If Cora squinted and stared long enough, she could see a small body of land jutting out into the water. "Why are they eroding it?"

He shrugged, and jostled his feet as if in a hurry to exit. "St. Louis can't lose its river front, Ma'am."

Cora stifled the snort that rose in her throat. Ma'am? Perhaps she appeared so to him. Or perhaps he, too, assumed she and Trigg were a couple.

Trigg nodded. "I think I read about that. I believe they were even going to add another dike at the top of Bloody Island, but that was blocked by a land owner."

Cora turned to catch the boy's answer, but he had already scurried away. "I guess we are very close to the city, right?"

"I believe so."

She glanced back at the pilot house. Oh, dear, the horn. Clutching her reticule against herself with her arm, she covered her ears with her hands. The long blast still caused her to tense.

Once it passed, a shiver of anticipation snaked up her body. She was almost there. Trigg leaned forward, still straining to see what was ahead. She stared at his handsome face, raven hair and silver-blue eyes. Heaker Thomas didn't hold a candle to Trigg Gentry. And soon, he'd disappear into the crowd at the loading dock. Gone forever. Something large lodged in her throat.

"Thank you for your assistance and companionship, Mr. Gentry. You've been most helpful." Her words seemed stiff, much too formal after the intimate companionship they'd shared the last few days.

He nodded, with perhaps a bit of disappointment in his half smile. "Cora—Miss Taggart, although I would be honored to escort you to your final destination, I have my obligations to attend to."

My, how they had morphed into the extremities of politeness. She missed the familiarity. Never in her life had she felt more wanted, more admired, valued and less like a misfit. "If you are ever in New Albany..."

A dash of devilment rested in his eyes. "I'll be sure to check the alleys and keep my eyes peeled for bookmarks."

Blasted blush that heated her face. "It seems you've caught me in several...predicaments. I apologize."

"You've no need to apologize, although I am still quite curious about the ball Mrs. Dixon claimed you own. From the look on your face, I would say it's quite an interesting tale."

One he wouldn't hear of anytime soon. She left the railing to hide her face, but he fell into step next to her. She couldn't think about the parting with Trigg anymore. Instead she turned her thoughts to the butler. He trailed behind like a faithful hound, carrying her carpet bag.

The man seemed like a shadow with no real needs. But that surely couldn't be true. The conversation with Mrs. Dixon and her disregard for her servants still rankled. Cora paused and studied the elder black man. "Mr. Dunkirk, are you doing all right?"

His blank face remained emotionless, yet a touch of sparkle fired in his eyes. "Yes, Miss. Quite fine."

"My Aunt Josephine must love having you so much. I can't wait to see them."

A different light transformed his expression. Dunkirk did not seem to contain the same excitement.

"Ma'am, the horn." The young sailor leaned from the doorway.

"Oh, yes."

"Let's hurry to the main deck," Trigg said as he tucked her hand inside his elbow.

They had no sooner scurried to the boiler deck when the blamed thing blared once more. "I am so glad I am not a cabin boy. Or girl, I guess. Or anyone that works on a ship."

Trigg laughed as he weaved his way through the gathering crowds and found a shady spot to rest and wait. It would not be long now.

"Look." She pointed at the collection of buildings growing ever larger as they approached. The horn tooted a double note and another long blast. The landing at St. Louis bustled with activity. Cora's mouth gaped at the number of steamboats moored at the edge of the block and gravel landing. "Have you ever seen so many steamboats in one place? Oh, my. Look at all the buildings."

He grinned at her as he wove the two of them through the gathering crowd. The steamboat slowed, expertly weaving through the throng of other boats. The bank was narrow with the spring rise of the river, and the docked steamers seemed merged with the street traffic. The crush of watercraft threatened to impede the *General Washington's* landing, at least to Cora's thinking. There had to be nearly one-hundred steamers, flatboats, or packets moored or in the midst of departing or arriving.

The captain above, obviously not a novice, guided the cumbersome vessel through the horde and banked the boat on the narrow shore like gliding one's foot into a sock. Smooth and sure. A shout went up from the passengers as the gangplank was lowered.

She gave a small hop-skip, grinned, and turned to Trigg. "We're here."

He nodded. "We're here."

His less-than-enthused reply sucked out any excitement she'd experienced. Trigg would go on his way, and she would never see him again. That thought seemed to dim the whole purpose of the trip. "I hope you find your sister. And thank you again. You've been an....engaging companion."

He clasped her hand and brought it to his mouth. Having forgotten to don the bothersome gloves, his work-roughened palms sent a flame of fervor zinging up her arm. His bright blue eyes captured hers and sparked something unknown. Then his lips pressed against the sensitive skin on the back of her hand.

"The pleasure has been all mine."

She drew in a breath. Never had a man kissed her. Not even her hand. The funnel of exiting passengers grabbed at her. But she couldn't break the spell of his gaze. His Adam's apple bobbed and she gripped his hand. If only...but it was not to be. She loosened her grip and he reluctantly let her fingers go free. "Goodbye...Trigg."

His eyes came alive. "Cora, I—"

She spun, knowing she must go. Now. Cora couldn't dare expose the yearning heartache she knew shone in her eyes. Blinking, she focused navigating the last set of stairs. Dunkirk appeared just to her right. The movement of everyone separated her from Trigg, but she kept her eye out for him, and he did the same. It seemed they continued to speak without words across the heads of the crowd. Her heart wrenched.

He raised a hand and then wove away from the exit and disappeared amongst the goods on the main deck. Cora forced her eyes from where Trigg had disappeared to accompany Dunkirk who led her across the walkway and up the steep, stony bank toward a carriage.

The butler nodded at the driver of a swank phaeton and stowed the carpet bag in the back. She searched the throng for one last glimpse at her companion, but in the sea of people, freight, and buggies, even her height failed to give her a last glance at Trigg. With a sigh, she grasped Dunkirk's hand and stepped into the fancy buggy. She settled into the plush green velvet as her aunt's butler climbed up next to the driver.

How silly she was being. She barely knew the man. Best to keep her mind on why she had come in the first place. Certainly not to be enamored by a passing man. Enamored? My, Aleena's far-reaching influence on her vocabulary made her want to spout a giggle.

Yes. Just nonsense. She couldn't possibly have feelings for a man she'd only known for a few days. Still her breath shuddered up her throat in regret that she'd never lay eyes on his handsome face again or latch onto his mesmerizing blue eyes.

She shook it off. No more. Time to push it aside and concentrate on her journey. She settled back in her seat and watched the chaos of carriages vying for position on the busy street. Cora couldn't help but stick her head out and cast a long look at the tall buildings and the people on the concrete sidewalks. Yet, she couldn't help thinking her first sights of the big city certainly would be much more exciting with Trigg seated next to her.

The expanse of the buildings' heights took her breath. Gracious. She wasn't in New Albany anymore. The two servants talked lowly in the driver's seat. "How far is it, Mr. Dunkirk?"

"Not far, Miss."

Not far? She swept her head around to look through the back curtain, searching for a tall, dark-headed man with flashing blue eyes and a playful grin. A body well-versed in checkers and how to dodge an unpleasant adversary. One who knew how to make her laugh, who breathed her name in such a thrumming baritone that it stirred her like no other voice could. Somehow, she feared she'd left part of her heart behind.

But the crowd was a faceless jumble, and she felt far removed from the wharf already. From...Trigg. And the distance grew with every hoof beat, every turn of the carriage wheels.

Dunkirk was wrong. Her aunt's house was far. Much, much too far away.

Trigg handed the young boy a few coins and took possession of his horse. He'd done a fine job grooming and watching him. He ran a hand down Buck's speckled neck. Enough lollygagging with women, no matter the draw. Time was a wasting. Even as the thought flew through his mind, shame burned his insides. Cora was not a girl any man should fraternize with. She was the real deal.

He ran a hand through his hair. If not for Ivalee, he'd be planning what more he could do to get to know Cora a whole lot better. He gritted his teeth. What a fool he was. He heard of men becoming an idiot over the love of a woman, but this was pointless. Besides, love? Not hardly. But he'd sure wanted to plant his lips a little closer to her face.

But thoughts like that got him nowhere fast. Cora had gone on her way and Ivalee was still missing. Time to drop his fascination of the willowy blond and focus on the next leg of his journey.

Cranes elevated chunks of freight, men shouldered their wares, farmers curtailed their small herds, young boys scurried about, hauling smaller loads to waiting wagons. Bo's voice raised above the din on the bottom deck. Trigg searched the crowd for a familiar form cloaked in buffalo skin. There, below, his brother had collared a bevy of young boys who bore up his freight pallets.

With a grunt he stepped over to him. Staying with Bo had to be his dumbest decision ever. "Morning. How long before we set out?"

Bo's red eyes were a testament to his previous night's activities. His brother let out a gaggle of a laugh. "Dear brother. The day's barely begun. I've got business to tend first, and then off we go."

Right.

"St. Louis gets a university." A newsboy yelled as Trigg labored up the slope. "Get your news here!"

Trigg hailed the hawker and slipped a penny in his hand.

"Thanks, Mister."

St. Louis Daily Union. The bold titles splashed across the front page of the newspaper. *Seminary Comes to St. Louis. Cholera Outbreak Stalled. Newly Elected Mayor Fails to Reappoint Isaac Curtis as Chief Engineer. Miasmas at Fault for Typhoid Fever.* Trigg folded its pages and shoved it into his saddle bag. He'd have more time to peruse it later for any news on gold in Iowa. For now, he kept his eyes on Bo leading the entourage up the bank.

A ruckus caught his attention at the *General Washington* steamer. Another robbery apparently. Good thing he was already off. That would have delayed the departure for sure.

He scanned the buildings. The city had bounced back from the infamous fire of forty-nine. And from the volume of people, the population seemed to have rebounded from cholera, although from the headlines, more sickness could be on the horizon.

Bo, wreathed in smiles, hopped in the wagon seat next to the driver he'd procured. His two lackeys tumbled into the back alongside the cargo with their horses tied to the back. Trigg slung his leg over Buck and followed at a crawl through the streets of St. Louis. He'd tried to keep a tag on Cora, but he'd lost her once he'd descended the stairway to retrieve his horse on the lower deck.

Just as well. Ivalee had to remain his main focus. Although he'd say Bo didn't seem to share his view. They went west three blocks on Locust and turned right on Broadway and kept right on battling through traffic. This place would be easy to get lost in. Several blocks down, the driver stopped and pulled to the curb. A sign proclaimed John Leach and Co. Family Groceries and Dry Goods with the second "o" in "Goods" partially peeling off. That could either be the just the weather or an omen.

Trigg decided to dismount and pulled the newspaper from his pack rather than join the ranks of the three "businessmen" who entered the store. Hopefully, whatever they were doing would get done quick-like.

He opened the paper and laid it across the saddle of his mount, which brought a similar circumstance into his head. A grin brought a grunt. Cora's face and shapely form hunkered behind his horse caused him a moment's deadpan stare until he shrugged himself back to reality.

Trigg scanned the paper for interesting articles as Buck lowered his head and dropped his hip to nap, making Trigg's grin widen. But the smile fell from his face when he caught a small article in the back on the right-hand corner. *Gold in Iowa?* He scanned the two brief paragraphs. Perhaps his father had headed in that direction? Eldora, Iowa. Prospecting on the Iowa River.

Now all he had to do was light a fire under his stubborn brother. Not likely to happen soon. Well, this would be his brother's last chance. If Bo didn't grab hold of this idea, Trigg would branch out on his own. And right soon.

Chapter Fourteen

After blocks and blocks of head swivels, Cora felt the carriage slow. The green velvet tassels that trimmed the edge of the leather roof bobbed merrily, as if announcing the completion of the journey. Far beyond the reach of common store fronts sprang narrow opulent homes and row houses. Every blade of grass seemed manicured and each bush a work of art. A tall wrought iron fence surrounded one narrow home with huge columns, and a flat roof topped the three stories.

A small guard house stood to the right of the gate. A brown-skinned man stepped regally from the small enclosure and unlatched the gate. Cora whipped her head around to watch the man close and lock the gate as the carriage moved through the enclosure. The driveway continued next to the tall home and paused at the brick sidewalk leading to the burgundy front doors.

On either side of the massive double doors stood a lady and a man servant, hands clasped, as if standing guard over the mansion.

The light blue dress and apron contrasted nicely against the mahogany skin of the young girl. The small ivory hat perched at the crown of her head hid all of her swept-back hair. The man, dressed in black wool pants suspendered over a white shirt complimented with a matching blue bow tie, stood at attention.

Oh, my word. Would President Pierce step from the stately building? The thought stilled her legs, and good thing, too. Mother had reminded her before she left New Albany that manners would be undeniably necessary at Aunt Josephine's home. And one glowing example demanded she be assisted from a carriage. Leaping from the lavish carriage would not start the visit off on a positive note.

The phaeton halted and Cora gripped her hands in her lap as she waited. Dunkirk dismounted from the driver's seat, circled the vehicle, and opened the short little door.

Good gravy. How formal. She rose and clutched the butler's uplifted hand to navigate the hanging stairs. Once she arrived on solid ground, her squeezing stomach stabilized. Dunkirk reached for her carpet bag and indicated she should precede him.

She clutched her parasol and checked for the wayward bookmark in her sleeve. Satisfied that it had not strayed, she slowed her hurried pace. Ladies in this neighborhood would not scurry to the front door while calling, especially on one's kin. Her glance strayed left to the row houses across the street. So odd to live in such narrow, yet architecturally magnificent homes. Yet, no cost had been spared on the stonework nor the trim or fencing.

The man servant stepped forward from the door and assisted her climb to the immense porch, and it was all she could do not to gape up at the ceiling and the columns' ornate capitals.

"Miss Taggart?" The petite female servant nodded, curtsied, and lowered her eyes.

"Yes, Ma'am. I mean, yes, I am Miss Cora Taggart."

The small woman, her posture so stiff, seemed pulled erect by some invisible string. "Welcome to Glenridge Estates."

The man who'd aided her up the stairs stepped to the two huge doors bordered with sidelights and a transom, and whipped them open with a flourish. Cora paused for a moment with three sets of eyes on her. Her gaze traveled up. Ten windows just on the front. She wasn't sure her home had that many total.

"Miss?"

Oh, lands. She was a square peg bound for a round hole. Again. After a blink to gather her thoughts, she replied. "Yes, thank you."

Brushing through the huge doors didn't prepare her for the space within. A palate of yellow and white was everywhere in the two-story room. Stairs meandered up the right to an arched balcony, perfect for a Shakespearean play. Juliet would surely be able to spout a woeful, "wherefore art thou?" If only the balcony were on an outer wall. At least, if Cora remembered her studies.

The pale walls were covered with a golden pattern, so faint at this distance that Cora couldn't identify it. Some kind of fruit? Strawberries?

"Mrs. Glenridge will be here shortly. Please be seated."

As the young servant from the porch took her leave, Cora drew her eyes from the odd patterns and beheld the large room. The furniture huddled together in the center of the room facing a white, brick fireplace. A green patterned rug separated the seating. She settled on the edge of a gold settee and studied the plant that decorated the middle of the fine carpet. It bloomed with the same kind of fruit that graced the walls.

And now that she looked around, there were representations of this fruit everywhere. A huge statue of one stood between the windows. Smaller ones served as the candelabra bases resting on the mantel. Along the stairway wall stood a narrow side table topped with two lamps, both of which had glass bottoms shaped in the same spiked silhouette. The stately white grand piano at the back of the room sported a prickly strawberry vase of fresh flowers. Even the bottom post of the stairway sprouted the foreign fruit.

The sound of a door and feet clicking on marble tugged Cora away from puzzling over the unidentified shapes that peeked at her from every surface. A tall woman in a bright yellow dress sashayed into the room. Long, green feathers frothing from the top of her hat made the stately woman even taller, though not as tall as Cora herself.

But what grabbed Cora's undivided attention was the sight of the enormous gold prickly strawberry smack dab in the center of Aunt Josephine's cap. Cora bit the inside flesh of her mouth to stay the unladylike snort. Perhaps she wasn't the only odd bird of the family. Manners jerked Cora to her feet.

"Miss Taggart. Or should I say, Cora, my dear niece. Here at last." The woman tottered closer, grasped Cora's shoulders, and made kissing sounds as she cheeked each side of Cora's face.

Cora bobbed her head, trying to keep her eyes from the oversized strawberry on her aunt's head. "Yes, Ma'am."

The woman shook a finger. "No, no. I'm your Aunt Josephine. Address me as so. Please sit."

Cora nodded and resumed her perch on the gold horsehair settee. Aunt Josephine chose neither settee facing one another but one of the side chairs with a view of the fireplace sporting a low flame. The tiered flounces of her skirt seemed to applaud as the older woman took her throne. And the look she turned onto Cora embraced her much like that of a reigning monarch.

"Now, Cora. I am most pleased you've arrived. I have so many plans." Aunt Josephine took up a bell, of course shaped like none other than the odd fruit, and rang it. The same young servant from the porch appeared. "Lille, refreshments."

Cora glanced from the departing servant back to, oh flaming flowers, that hat.

Aunt Josephine reached up and stroked the strange thing. "Have I caught you admiring my pineapple chapeau? My glorious, new summer headdress. I had it specially made at my favorite millinery. I simply adore the fruit. As you can see, I use its image in my décor as well."

"It's very…unusual." Cora could barely voice it without a grin.

"The fruit of the aristocracy. Why, when I had my first taste, I simply demanded that your Uncle Calvin build a pinery to grow our own. And so we did. I'll be sure to give you the grand tour. But first we must plan the cotillion."

Caught by yet another unfamiliar word, Cora hesitated. "Co...Cotillion?"

"It is French for a formal ball, ma chérie."

A wave of uncertainty hit Cora. Pineapples, cotillions? Frenchy words? Her barely discernable Latin from grammar school would never keep up.

Aunt Josephine let out a tinkling laugh. "I see I've overwhelmed you a bit. No mind, ma chère. Let me take care of everything. I can see I am almost too late. If not for the horrible fire and sickness in St. Louis, you would have been here much sooner." She snapped her fingers. "Lyon."

When no one appeared, Aunt Josephine rang the pineapple bell with a flourish.

First Leel, and Lee-own? Such strange names and spoken with such an odd accent. The names sounded...foreign. Cora glanced at the velvet gold pineapples speckling the walls. She was indeed in a very foreign place.

Lyon appeared, the servant who'd helped Cora at the porch steps.

"Deliver Mademoiselle Taggart's trunk and trappings to the Musée du Louvre suite."

"Qui, Madame." Lyon bowed and then scurried away.

We? Mudom? Moosey d' Loova? The Louvre Museum? Was she supposed to remember that?

But her aunt's shrewd eyes were fastened on her. "The dressmaker should be here inside the hour. I suggest you rest, ma nièce."

Nee-es? Niece? At this rate, she would need a French to English translation book. Succotash, had she just said a dressmaker?

"I—"

"Ma douce fille, worry your little head about nothing. Odette will soon return, perhaps in time for the measuring. In the meantime, you'll want to settle in." The bell rang again. Her aunt spoke French to the little maid, Lille, and then turned a beaming smile on Cora. "Madame Gerard will be most pleased to stitch you a gown. Go on now."

Her aunt shooed her like a stray goat, which must have made her think of one more thing for she sputtered more French at the servant leading Cora up the stairs.

The servant moved quickly, and Cora stumbled up behind her, hoping her gait didn't reflect the days ahead.

৩০৫

Three stores later and Bo still hadn't lightened his load of merchandise much. That was it. He was done. Trigg stepped in front of his brother. "Listen, Bo. I don't have time to gallivant from one grocer to another hoping they'll give a good price on tea and tobacco. I'm heading out. Alone."

A beefy hand stopped Trigg as he spun around. Bo tugged him to the back of the wagon, away from his two buddies. "Trigg. Be reasonable. I'm doing this to fund our trip. I didn't want to tell you this before, but I know where they are."

"What?"

His burly brother nodded. "I got a letter."

"Why didn't you tell me this before?" Trigg oughta just box him. One time. Surely all the frustrations of this trip, and yes, childhood, could be resolved in one good punch.

Bo shrugged. "Didn't seem important. What's important is we're brothers. All for one and whatever such nonsense. We work together to get Ivalee and Pa back."

Trigg fought against the warmth that seeped through him. Bo, actually trying to connect with him. Being brotherly. He was right. It would be better if they worked together. If that were truly possible.

"But you're going to have to give me some time. I don't earn my money from the mule farm. I have to make do with what I can. And right now, it's selling these wares."

He stared at his brother. For the first time since he'd met up with him, Bo was making some sort of sense. Still, why hadn't he told him about this correspondence? "What did Pa say? Is Ivalee with him?"

Bo pounded his shoulder. "Now, don't you go worrying, little brother. All is well. We have plenty of time. And you'd better be practicing that "come home" speech, 'cause they're liking it up in Iowa."

Insane that he felt small when Bo walked away. Yet, he did. He shook his head. Nothing made sense. Did his brother really answer

182

his question? Was Ivalee with Pa? They liked Iowa? Where was this letter?

The wagon pulled out into the busy street, and Trigg had to sling his leg over Buck's back before he was swallowed in strangers. Trigg grunted a sigh. For now, it seemed he'd hitched his wagon to Bo, for good or bad.

By the end of the day, they sold most everything and ended up in a dumpy sort of boarding house on Market Street, a mere four blocks from the landing. H. Hudge House was painted in brown shaky letters to the left of the front door. The two-story house had seen its grander days. But the hefty woman at the door had a welcoming face and smelled of pie, so it made up for the shabby exterior.

"Now, y'all know I only have one room. And there's a passel of you. The room only has two small beds, but you might be able to scrape up a couple of cots from the carriage house." She waved a dishtowel towards the back door. "Given you're all boxed in one room, I'll lower my rate. But I have to consider you big old men eating your weight in my fried chicken. So, a dollar sixty is all I can offer."

Trigg opened his mouth to answer, but Bo beat him to it.

"That's fine, Mrs. Hudge. We're respectable businessmen. We'll give you no trouble."

The woman laughed a short laugh, her jowls bouncing. "Best not. Hocum's my most loyal boarder, and he looks out for me. And I feed him well. Top of the stairs, last door on the left. The necessary is out back."

The men moved through the parlor brimming with glass objects like a herd of flaming buffalo through a gun powder mill. Mrs. Hudge seemed right fond of the sparkly trinkets for they covered every surface. A gleaming grand piano tucked into a windowed alcove stood in stark contrast to the rest of the shabby interior.

Trigg headed out the back door to inspect the carriage house for the cots. With twilight approaching, he'd have to hurry. He found household wares in the upper loft. Most surely had been situated before the Revolutionary War. But he scraped back the spider webs and found two beds of solid construction. The twine peeled in a few spots, but most distressing was the length. They couldn't be more than five feet long.

It might be better to snug up on a few quilts than scrunch up on this thing. With a shrug, he grabbed a well-worn mallet from a rusted bucket on his way out. He might just need to firm up a few of the joints on these cots.

By the time he landed in the small room, Bo and his two friends were already reclining on the beds. His brother took up one by himself, and the other two lay opposite each other on the other small mattress.

Oates raised up, nearly pitching himself to the floor. "'Bout time you arrived. What do you call that?"

"Cots."

"I'll take them both."

He tugged them from Trigg's grip, leaving him only with the mallet. And boy, did he have an idea of what he'd like to do with that. Instead he turned back to the door. Perhaps a pallet on the floor was preferable, but then he'd most likely be stepped on. Actually the carriage house might be preferable.

He retraced his steps to the loft. Plenty of space, if one didn't mind the varmints. Spiders, mice, and such. He shook out another cot and then spotted a large trunk. Shrugging, he waltzed over and threw it open. A grin split his face. Old quilts filled the cedar-lined space. Now, if that didn't say welcome home, what did?

He pulled out a couple and meandered to a dusty mound of hay near the loft door. He spread them out. Yep. Fine bed. Oates could keep his old cots. He'd found his place. Now if only Ivalee could be located so easily.

Chapter Fifteen

F rench words flew about Cora's head as she concentrated on being immobile. Madame Gerard, quite petite beneath her duster cap, never seemed still and chirped like a bird with a passel of worms. Aunt Josephine clapped her hands several times, obviously delighted with either the way the fitting progressed or the opportunity to launch into French.

The sewing room on the second floor boasted a map of France on the wall behind the mirrors. Each dot had a city's name written nearby. A star emblazoned Paris as well, the *Arc de Triomphe* in the center of the display, all roads exiting out from the landmark. Other cities were stenciled in, Lille, Dunkirk, Lyon…weren't those the servants' names?

A jerk at her hem made Cora shift her attention to the three mirrors in front of her. Each showed a slightly different profile as the seamstress and maid scurried about her. She'd never seen such a panoramic view of herself at one time. Mercy, maps on the wall, servants named for French cities, luxury, sectioned mirrors. What sort of place had she stepped into?

"Zoo may steep down." Madame Gerard scurried over to make one last note on her sketchpad.

Cora tiptoed from the fitting platform with a sigh. Standing in her chemise and drawers in front of near strangers unnerved her. Lille appeared, toting Cora's cotton petticoat and dress. Cora gladly stepped into them.

"She is badly in need of—"

Her aunt's voice halted and then continued in French. Of all the times to wish grammar school had taught her French. Cora pushed her arms through the sleeves. Surely they spoke of corsets and hooped skirts. If only she'd known they would undress her like a child's doll a mere sixty minutes of arrival. She would have…well, she would have spent some extra of her savings and sewn a little fancier dress. Even the maid's clothing seemed to outclass her.

The two women continued to prattle as they stepped from the room. A flash of gray and black scooted by the women's feet. The thing cackled as it dashed. A chicken? Aunt Josephine motioned to Lille and spoke her code language.

The maid disappeared down the hallway after the speckled stray. Cora paused, looking down the long passageway, hoping to catch another glimpse at what she thought she saw.

Aunt Josephine swished toward her. "Cora? I think Odette may have arrived home."

No time to explore whether a hen had entered the second story. Cora copied her aunt and tried to glide down the stairway. There at the entrance stood a young woman, very much like the tintype her mother had at home, only older.

"Oh, Odette. I am so glad you've returned. Cora Hope, your cousin, mon fille."

Cora arrived on the bottom step. She towered over Odette in her pale tan dress.

Her cousin stood a moment blinking up at her. Then a proper curtsy. "Hello. How do you do?"

Well, at least it wasn't an air kiss to each cheek. Cora bobbed a greeting. "Fine, thank you."

"Odette. What a greeting for your long-lost cousin. Greet her properly, ma chère."

Cora's cousin's lips pinched ever so slightly. "Mother, la bise is quite out of vogue, even in France."

Lille appeared at the top of the stairway clutching a mottled black and gray hen.

"La Poulette! You have found her."

The maid strutted down the stairway, and Aunt Josephine met her at the landing where she took the chicken in her arms. "La Poulette, you naughty hen. You should stay on the bottom floor. Now you must be relegated to the hen house."

Her aunt scurried off down the hallway, muttering French to the speckled chicken under her arm, Lille hot on her heels. A tsk and a sigh from Odette drew Cora's attention. "Welcome to Glenridge Lunatic Asylum. You may check your llama at the door."

Odette whisked up the stairs. Now, that brought a trunkful of thoughts. Cora hesitated before climbing the stairway also, careful not to cause any echoes in the drawing room cavern below. She ventured down the hallway until she found an open door. Odette stood at the window, arms crossed.

"Odette?"

"Come in. And please, shut the door."

Cora did as her cousin bade her. Her eyes circled the room from the large *Arc de Triomphe* sculpture that encompassed an entire corner to the small velvet pink ones on the walls. The rosy brocade fabric covered the tall massive canopied bed in front of Cora. Beyond, several chairs covered in the same magenta fabric completed a small seating area.

Suddenly Odette spun, walked around the bed, and looked her up and down. "Well? Have you a seal in your pocket? Perhaps a kiwi in your bonnet?"

Cora fought a grin. "No. Not today."

Odette's perfect rosebud lips twitched. Then a smile appeared. "Refreshing."

Cora returned her scrutiny.

"Care to sit on a pink elephant?" Odette motioned to the chairs in the far corner.

Cora bobbed her head and perched on the overstuffed chair.

"I would ask how you liked your room, but I fear you hate it as much as I. After all, you have a replica of the *Mona Lisa*, the fake French Crown Jewels, and a near-naked Michelangelo statue in your Louvre Museum room." A giggle popped from her cousin, who turned blue eyes to the arched monstrosity between them. It reached clear to the tall ceiling.

The sculpture in her room *had* startled her. It was quite unnerving to have a larger-than-life human form staring at you in your very bedroom. But now, the famous *Rebellious Slave* reproduction now slumbered beneath an extra blanket she'd found. And would continue to snooze beneath its comforter as long as she occupied the room.

"Can you believe my mother actually commissioned a sculptor to construct this…thing." Odette flipped a hand to the replica of the *Arc de Triomphe* as she removed her tan bonnet. Her shimmering light brown hair was gathered below a lacey day cap. After a long moment her cousin gave a deep sigh. "I'm sorry. It's been a trying day. Mother and this Pineapple Cotillion has stomped on my last nerve."

Finally, a subject she could jump in with. "Yes, I was measured for a dress."

Odette's eyes popped wide. "Did you demand no pineapple fabric? Did you?"

"I…uh…well, it didn't seem necessary."

Her cousin's eyes slid closed, as she froze into a statue, much like the oversized sculpture in her room. Then a laugh burst from her cousin, the type of laugh that one couldn't stop. Cora giggled. And then snickered some more. The more she laughed, the harder Odette laughed. Her poor cousin could not seem to stop, her face flaming bright red. She clutched her abdomen and tears sprouted from her eyes. At last, she pulled a hanky from her sleeve and dabbed her eyes.

"You certainly have a point there." A few more snickers broke forth beneath Odette's handkerchief. "Cora Taggart. I must say that did much more good than the drive I took."

Odette fanned her face. "How rude I've been. Snide remarks, and I haven't inquired how your trip was."

"It was fine. But, I'd rather talk about this pineapple dress." Cora leaned forward. "I'd much prefer blue or green. Plain or maybe with a flounce?"

"That's right. Mother mentioned you sew. That's perfect. You can repair any damage. Don't worry. I'll tell Mother green." Odette leaned over, hand to her mouth, yet she whispered loudly," but prepare for some sort of leaf pattern."

Her cousin smiled, reached out and clutched her hand. "Thank the heavens, I think you might be normal. Excellent. I shall like having you here, Cousin Cora Taggart."

Normal? If only Odette knew…

Trigg emerged from the carriage house at early dawn, making a quick trip to the necessary where he passed Oates who grunted at him. The man looked a little worse for wear. The cots must not have agreed with him last night. Serves him right for stealing them.

Even from the steps at the back door, Trigg could smell bacon. His eyes swept the untidy back yard, wondering if even the birds' stomachs growled at the scent. Trigg wound his way from the back hallway and let his nose direct him towards the dining hall. A large walnut table boasted two long bench seats occupied with a smattering of men. Plenty of seating for everyone.

One large gentleman, whose nose resembled a pig snout, sat on the far corner. Trigg wondered if this were Mrs. Hudge's loyal lodger. What did she say his name was? Hoke...nope, Hocum. Hokey Hocum. Probably best, however, not to say that to his face unless a person just had a sadistic desire for sound pounding.

A narrow-shouldered man with a reddish mustache perched on the furthest end from Hocum. Smart guy. Two sizable men sat next to one another with their backs to him. But they weren't Oates and Burr. They also sat on the opposite end from the big brute. That left two middle spots on the far bench, the end chair, or the spot in front of Hocum. Trigg chose the last.

He nodded to the big man, but the bear only grunted. A tray of bacon sat between his plate and Hocum's. Well, he certainly wouldn't be the first to reach for a piece.

"Here we are." Mrs. Hudge bumped the kitchen door with her ample rump, cradling two large bowls in her hands. "Eggs and Gravy."

Everyone scrambled to stand. She set them in the center and surveyed the tabletop with chubby hands on her hips. "Oh. The biscuits. Where's my head?"

Trigg followed his table mates' lead and took a seat. They sat at attention while she scurried back to the kitchen. Again, everyone rose.

So, where was Bodine and the other two? Had they slept in? Left him, more likely.

"Here we be." In she burst again with a basket of biscuits and apple butter. "This can go there and that here. Good."

Mrs. Hudge bustled to sit at the head of the table with Hocum holding her chair. Trigg followed suit with the rest of the men, standing as they waited for their hostess to be seated, and then took their chairs once more.

Mrs. Hudge patted the pig-snouted man's hand on her right. "All right, Mr. Hocum. Would you bless the meal?"

In a voice of gravel, discombobulated into a rushed growl, Hocum prayed, "Come Lord Jesus be our guest, And let Thy food to us be blessed."

Everyone about the tabled mumbled "Amen." Trigg, still ruminating on Hocum's formal prayer, uttered amen last, late and noticeable, but no one said a word. They were too busy grabbing at food.

"Please pass the bowls, men. And where are your three friends this morning, Mr. Gentry?" Mrs. Hudge held the bacon plate at Hocum's elbow.

Trigg took the gravy bowl from the man on his left. He grabbed a hot bun and split it with his knife. "I'm not sure Mrs. Hudge. I'm afraid I spent my first night in the carriage house. I hope you don't mind."

"Not at all. Of course your rent will stay the same."

He cleared his throat over a mouthful of gravy. "Yes, Ma'am."

"Mr. Hooberstook, please send the egg plate. Remember, pass the dishes to the right so everyone can get a bite."

Trigg stifled a snicker, both for the name Hooberstook and the childhood rhyme. Red-mustache's lips blew out, his cheeks shaking at the faux pas, and quickly started the egg dish.

"Oh, where are my manners? Mr. Gentry, this is Mr. Gabriel Hocum."

The faithful and loyal. Trigg couldn't stop the elevation of his brows at "Gabriel." Hocum's, however, lowered a smidge. Hmmm. That completed his bulldog look.

"And then there's Mr. Egor Hooberstook, and on this side, Joe and John Smith."

The two men were identical. Round faces, bovine eyes. But surely no one would have such non-descript names? Trigg gave them the once over to knock out any dishonesty, but their big brown eyes seemed vacant enough. Not just of dishonesty.

"And this is Mr. Trigg Gentry. Absent from our table is Mr. Bodine Gentry, Mr. Bernie Oates, and Mr. Elmer Burr, our new tenants. Also, Mr. Hobart Whittaker is visiting his sister this morning and won't be dining with us. I think that's everyone."

Forks scraped plates. Surely small talk would not be required here.

Mrs. Hudge pressed a napkin into her lap. "'Tis such pleasant weather we're having. Beautiful spring."

Evidently, there would be small talk.

194

"Not too much flooding at the docks. The new mayor seems to have such good plans for the city, now that the dreadful cesspool debacle is done."

The only one to mutter an answer over a mouthful of food was Hocum. And he merely grunted. This did not seem to stop their hostess.

"My husband once contemplated running for mayor in '28, but William Carr Lane had the office fully under his control for years. Six years in a row to be exact. And nearly nine years later, he was elected for three more. By then, my dear departed husband had settled into the newspaper business. He was quite successful."

Trigg caught her eye and nodded since everyone else's gaze seldom left their plates.

"His first newspaper is framed in the parlor. *The St. Louis Sentinel.* The first headline: *City Consecrates First Cathedral West of the Mississippi.* Quite a beginning I'd say."

"Yes, Ma'am." And no charge for being the only one who bothered to give an answer. Grub was good. At least she could cook.

A noise at the door yielded Bo and his two buddies, looking a little worse for wear. Oates looked as if he'd stumbled out of a coffin. Pale-skinned, and definitely a bit hangdog.

Mrs. Hudge lowered her fork and stiffened. "You're late to breakfast, Sirs."

Trigg all but spit his coffee out. But Bo didn't have the decency to even acknowledge her reprimand. They seated themselves in the empty spots and started reaching for the grub.

"Excuse me, men." Mrs. Hudge's face pinched tight, but it didn't forestall the hungry men. The big woman jumped to her feet. "Stop!"

Hands froze in midair.

"You will not paw at the food. We will pass the dishes accordingly. And you will not be late to meals. Is that understood?"

Oates and Burr shrank back like boys with dunce caps, but Bodine turned a toothy grin at her. "Pardon your high-mightiness, but I'm a paying customer."

Trigg wished right then he wasn't sitting so close to Mrs. Hudge. Hocum stood, yanking the napkin from his throat. The man was even bigger upright. He and Bo would be a good match.

Mr. Hooberstook's red mustache trembled as he muttered, "Oh, dear, oh, dear."

"Mr. Bodine Gentry," Mrs. Hudge's usual cheery voice had lowered a pitch into softness, "You will be charged an additional five cents for your impertinent remark. Now, will you comply or should Mr. Hocum remove you from the premises?"

Bo stopped munching mid-chew. He eyed Hocum then flicked a glance around the table. "Reckon I'll be on time."

"Excellent." Mrs. Hudge seated herself and went back to eating.

Hocum, one cheek still stuffed with food, shot a death glare at Bodine before sitting. Trigg resumed his meal. Mrs. Hudge led with an iron whip. He stemmed a grin.

Oates snuffed out a sigh as he swallowed. His face resembled a turnip.

Then he stood and clutched his stomach. "Excuse me, Ma'am."

He raced from the room. Mrs. Hudge shook her head and sipped tea. Earl Grey, he could smell it. However, he was afraid there was a much different smell in the outhouse.

Trigg gritted his teeth. Oates had picked up something nasty. He hadn't even been in this city twenty-four hours. Trigg hoped it was merely a passing flu. Being in this city, known as a hothouse of disease, could be downright dangerous. And being in the same house, down right deadly.

Chapter Sixteen

P ineapples. All over her ball gown. Little tiny ones repeating in a nauseating pattern. Cora peeked up into the tri-fold mirror. And silk? Who in their right mind would make such a ghastly pattern in silk? At least the light green bodice that connected to the shoulders was plain. Madame Gerard flitted about the flounced skirt, fluffing and chirping French to Aunt Josephine. And at least she'd gotten flounces. And plenty of them. Perhaps that would hide the ugly pattern a bit?

Doggone. What was she going to do? Her cousin breezed through the door just then and froze, the horror plain on her face. She met Cora's eyes in the mirror.

"Mother, I asked for Cora's gown to be green which complements her eyes."

Aunt Josephine, her hat spouting real palm leaves which wrapped around her head, rose from the royal-blue brocade-encased chair. The same blue that echoed the French flag, frozen in a still-life wind flap, next to the map covering the entire wall behind her.

"And I took your advice. With her creamy skin and green eyes, this was the perfect choice."

"But—"

"Don't be a chore, ma fille. Cora is transfixed with the gown."

Transfixed. Not far from the truth. Horrified might explain it more truthfully.

"Mother—"

"Not now, chérie. Madame and I must work on the tablecloths for the cotillion. Lille, assist Cora. Come, Antoinette. We must plan."

Madame Gerard strutted from the room in Josephine's wake of palm leaves. Lille stepped forward to unbutton the tiny pearl buttons lining the back of the dress. No doubt to stop her quick get away from her reflection in the loathsome gown.

Odette sighed. "I knew this would happen."

Cora shrugged as the pert little maid slipped the sleeves down her arms. Cora puckered her lips. It was as if she were a child unable to dress herself. Her plain blue frock swathed her, fastened with utmost efficiency, and Lille stepped back, waiting for more instructions.

"It's fine. It is well made."

"It is not fine, it's—"

Cora flicked her eyes at the maid, demure and motionless. Like a lamp. A lamp with ears.

Odette rolled her eyes. "Come on. Let's go to my room. Lille, check on La Poulette or La Chèvre"

Before Cora could questions what a La Chèvre was, her cousin yanked her from the room, shuffled down the hall in her muted gray skirt waist and white blouse. Odette managed to shut the door before the dam burst.

"Unbelievable." Odette brought her hands down in a clench, her fingers curling like talons. "Every time. She manages to ruin everything. First the whole pineapple theme, then Albert, and now this."

Now spent, her cousin stomped to the window and slung the curtain aside. The light highlighted her cinnamon brown hair, fine clear skin, and petite form.

Cora gave a silent sigh. What did it matter if she wore pineapples? Her cousin was beautiful, even when stomping angry. And she wasn't nearly six-feet tall either. Odette would absorb all the attention of the room with her dainty figure.

"Albert?" Cora ventured at last.

"Him." She pointed across the street and down a few houses. "My mother's choice for my husband."

"You're getting married?"

"Not to him. But Mother thinks the Pineapple Cotillion would be the perfect occasion to announce our courtship."

Cora clenched her hands together, unsure what her cousin meant. "Aunt Josephine said the ball was my debutante presentation."

Odette crossed the floor and drew Cora's hands into her own. "I'm sorry. I'm not being a good cousin nor a good daughter. But I have to confide in someone. Can I trust you, Cora?"

Pineapple parts. What to say to that? Already she felt the constricting ties of her aunt's expectations. "I suppose so."

Odette took a deep breath and squeezed Cora's hands. "None of this is about either one of us. Do you know really why Mother has deemed it necessary to have a cotillion?"

Why did she feel so ignorant? Like a child who'd wandered into an adult conversation. How much easier it would be to snatch up her lemon peel baseball and mitt and have a game of catch. "Why?"

"The pineapples are about to be ripe."

And they were back to pineapples. Of all the things Cora expected Odette to say, this most certainly never occurred to her. "I don't...understand."

Her cousin dropped her hands, wandered to the bright fuchsia chair next to the replica of the *Arc de Triomphe* where she collapsed. "Exactly. No one does. Mother gallivants about with giant fruit on her head, toting a chicken while doting on the precious pineapple plants growing in the pinery. She plans her whole life around when the fruit ripens. She gives no care for the feelings of her only daughter or a visiting family member. I can't do it anymore."

A familiar yet unfamiliar sound drifted in from the hallway. Odette rose, stomped to the door, and swung the door open. There stood a brown and white spotted goat, chewing its cud.

"Baaaaaaa."

Odette motioned to the animal who tried to step past her. "See? My point exactly. Lille, get La Chèvre."

A shuffle indicated the maid had arrived and led the animal away. To where, Cora wouldn't begin to guess.

Her cousin closed the door with a soft click. "I want my life to be different. Refined, gentile. I want—never mind."

Again she collapsed on the chair, head down, examining her hands. Cora approached and took the other chair. "You want what?"

Her head came up, eyes shining with tears. "I have a secret beau."

Cora caught her breath.

With a nod, Odette laid one finger over her lips and directed her eyes to the door. Did Lille stand just beyond the oak wood? Or Aunt Josephine? No, she'd be much too occupied with Madame Gerard. Or the hen. Or perhaps the goat.

Odette's voice came much quieter. "He's a piano tuner. Well, his father is, and he assists him. He's proper, decorous. Of course, handsome. Funny. And he understands me."

"Then you should share with your mother."

The vapid stare Cora received let her know right quick that wasn't a stellar answer.

"He's working class. Not acceptable in my social circle." Her face grew dreamy. "But he's oh, so handsome."

Handsome. Hmmm. Her thoughts drifted from Odette and settled on Trigg and his tremendous blue eyes. Now, he was handsome. His eyes were so blue, she'd found herself gazing at him just to sample the deepness of their color. Surely both Albert and this mystery man of Odette's would never compare to Trigg.

A gasp slid through Odette's lips. "You have a beau, too."

Cora stiffened. "No…not really."

"Yes, you do. I saw you go all soft and wistful, the way I do when Wilkinson comes to tune the piano." Odette slapped a hand to her mouth.

"Wilkinson?" she took a deep breath. "I'm sorry, did you just say…Wilkinson?"

Bodine and Burr had disappeared into the guts of the downtown to finish transferring the rest of the wares. But Oates spent the better part of the day perfuming the john in the far portion of the back yard. Once more Oates stumbled past Trigg penning a letter home as he lay stretched out under a willow in front of the carriage house. Perhaps it had been God's providence that Oates had taken both cots.

Yet, if Trigg were honest, he didn't feel too well either. With a grunt, he packed up his gear and moseyed back to the carriage house. His stomach took a twist, and he hurried inside the barn.

Just at twilight, Trigg stared at the bottom of a rusted bucket, trying to head off the shivers with the extra quilts he'd found in the dusty trunk. Stomach emptied, he rolled over with a groan. Durn, had Oates given him the cholera?

His face pulsed with heat, and his throat seemed full of the same hay he rested on. Swallowing was near impossible with the scraping pain. He covered his head with the quilt and shivered himself into oblivion

"Mr. Gentry?"

Somewhere in a circus of rivers, ships, and faces both known and unknown, piano music intertwined, Trigg floated somewhere between sleep and consciousness. Light tugged at him when the blanket swished from his head.

"Hello?"

Trigg turned toward the voice. A young man's face hovered over him. A smile touched the corner of his visitor's mouth.

"Ah. Here you are. I'm Dr. Hendricks. Mrs. Hudge has been quite concerned about her politest border."

The man lifted the corner of his round glasses and Trigg continued to blink at him.

"What time is it?" Surely that croak couldn't be his voice?

"About eleven-thirty. When you didn't show up for breakfast, Mrs. Hudge insisted I check on you. Especially since she has another patient inside the house."

How could he have slept that long?

Dr. Hendricks pulled a stethoscope from his black bag. "Let me listen to your heart, Mr. Gentry."

"Trigg."

A smile lit the young doctor's face as his eyes went distant, listening through the instrument. With a small "hmmm" he nodded and returned the stethoscope to the bag.

"Have you had much loose stools?"

"No. Just vomiting."

"Mmm-umm. May I check your stomach?"

The cool air set Trigg to shivering as he shoved the quilt down. The doctor took his time gently pushing here and there. The roiling in Trigg's stomach started again, and he jerked toward his bucket, but it was nothing but dry heaves. The doctor handed him a hanky, and Trigg collapsed onto his pallet.

"Ahhh. Mr. Gentry—Trigg. Although you don't feel lucky at this very moment, you are indeed one blessed man. It's merely a touch of the stomach flu. I have some peppermint oil here that may be of some use. Also, I'll suggest Mrs. Hudge fix up some broth and chamomile tea for you as well. If you are in excessive pain, I have some strong elixirs for that as well."

"I just need sleep." Trigg managed to croak out.

"Indeed. But you also need hydration. I will let Mrs. Hudge know, and I will be back to check on you tomorrow."

All Trigg could do was nod. The man disappeared from his line of vision, and Trigg closed his eyes again. But sleep had drifted far from his grasp. He shivered and prayed the nausea away.

Some twenty minutes drifted by, and he pushed the blanket away. Vomiting or not, he had to visit the necessary and take care of Buck. He stumbled down the ladder, lugging a rusted bucket, and took care of both tasks, shivering and miserable. By the time he'd made it back up the ladder, he was spent.

However, on an overturned wooden box lay a tray of broth and tea. Neither sounded good, but if he were going to get better, he should try to ingest something. He downed nearly half the broth and a several sips of the tea. Once he'd managed that, he snuggled back into the quilts, tucking in the edges to keep in his own body heat.

Progressively, the sickness waned, and by the end of the week, Trigg was nearly back to regular form. Nearly. He'd lost a bit of weight and felt weak as watered-down tea. He eased out the barn door and took a lungful of fresh air.

"Ahhh. Just the patient I wanted to see." Dr. Hendricks strutted from the back door of Mrs. Hudge's home. A smile snaked across the man's face. "I see you're feeling better. Up and about."

"I reckon this is feeling better. Don't think I'll take on any tasks of much effort even so."

The doctor laughed and set his black bag on a barrel near the doorway. He eased out his stethoscope once more. "I believe my other patient is a few steps ahead of you. He put away his share of fried chicken last night according to Mrs. Hudge."

Trigg stood and allowed the doctor to listen to his heart. "Yes, your pulse is up a bit, but that is to be expected considering the wallop you took from that nasty bug."

"Thank you, Doc. What's the damages?"

He chuckled. "Mrs. Hudge has already taken care of it. She avoids anyone with a sickness and either calls me or Dr. Barnes as soon as a boarder shows signs. I'm sure you'll settle up when you pay your bill for her."

"Well, thanks, Doc."

He nodded, collected his bag, and gave a wave. "You take care now. Rest and drink plenty of fluids."

Trigg waved and headed for the back door. Right now, paying Mrs. Hudge extra for the doctor's attention was the last thing on his mind. The doc had him at fried chicken. He pulled the rusty latch and walked inside the house.

The dusty house smelled of heaven. By the time he'd made it to the dining room, he'd decided it was chicken dumplings. The same list of characters sat bullwhipped like young scallywags facing the wrath of a harsh schoolmaster. Even Bo, Burr, and Oates sat tamed at the table. The healthy glow to Oates's eyes confirmed Trigg's suspicion that he'd been the doc's other customer. Trigg's stomach gave a lurch, and he two-stepped quicker to join the ranks.

"Here we are." Mrs. Hudge whisked through the door, two large bowls overhead. "Oh, Mr. Gentry, so glad you've recovered."

The bowls hit the hardwood table. Dumplings and mashed potatoes. He'd hit the culinary jackpot. Once Hocum grunted his prayer, the men were off to passing to the right, heaping piles of food on each plate. If this kept up, Trigg would feel like himself in no time. And, golly, did he want to get back to normal.

He'd let the aromatic healing food settle and then take a walk to build his strength. Maybe tomorrow he'd get Buck out. His horse needed some fresh air and exercise same as he. He'd have to be fit to continue this journey.

His eyes shot down the table at his brother. Bodine's eyes were bloodshot and his face pale as he struggled to chew and swallow. Trigg gave a sigh. From the looks of Bo's green gills, the doc would be back around soon.

And finding Ivalee would once more be on hold.

Chapter Seventeen

O dette gripped her arm. "The buggy is ready."

Cora scurried beside her smaller cousin as they exited the back door. She fingered the large lemon peel ball tucked in the pocket of her extravagant dress. For some reason, she couldn't leave it behind today. "Are you sure it is all right with Aunt Josephine?"

Her cousin dismissed her with a wave. "Yes, yes. She's up talking gibberish to Madame Gerard. Perhaps they are planning more pineapple dresses for you, no?"

Cora's lips twitched as Lyon assisted her inside the carriage. More pineapple dresses indeed. As if she would need more than one. Jumping Jehosiphats. She didn't even need one. "Where are we going?"

"It is a surprise."

An unpleasant sensation washed through her as she eyed the glassed-in pinery. The driver climbed to the front and off the carriage went. To wherever.

The carriage wasn't the same petite two seater she'd ridden in from the wharf. This one, no less opulent with its ivory cushioned seats, possessed more seating with the two benches facing one another. They were completely enclosed, easily passing the scenery without passersby realizing the occupants. Was this Odette's plan?

Her cousin seemed to be quite pleased with herself, sitting so content next to Cora, her gloved hands resting demurely in her lap. Silly. They were merely driving or visiting. Isn't that what she'd done for the last two weeks? Driven around, calling on Odette's socialite friends?

But her heart sank as they turned towards the left. Wasn't this heading back to the center of town? Aunt Josephine had mentioned several times about avoiding the downtown area, preferring instead for the merchants to visit the home. Cora forced her hands into her lap, copying Odette's regal set of her chin.

Cora recognized a few buildings. They were nearing the docks. "Odette, where exactly are we going?"

Odette turned flashing eyes on her. Her cousin seemed an odd mixture of a headstrong, gentile woman. "You were right the other night. Remember how we talked about not being matched with strangers or tedious fellows who hold no interest to us?"

Uh-oh. Yes, shortly after Cora had discovered that Odette's secret infatuation had been none other than Wilkinson Dunbar. And in the heat of the moment, she too, had proclaimed a secret flame.

Had she really declared Trigg Gentry as the man she hankered after? How her heart was nearly breaking as Father strove to push the middle-aged Mr. Thomas on her as a suitor? What a fool she was, confiding in Odette. Cora clenched her gloved hands.

"Yes, but Odette—"

A finger raised in Cora's face along with a refined tilt of Odette's head. "Now, now, Cora. We must be true to ourselves. You were completely correct when you proclaimed that Mother should indeed accept a perfect gentleman as Wilkinson. He hasn't sprouted horns or grown speckled feathers. And even so, both of those are quite accepted in our house."

Goodness. Odette had taken their private conversation of mutual hopes and dreams and had run with it. What would Aunt Josephine and Uncle Calvin do when they realized their only daughter had willfully mapped out her own future?

"Mother embraces the barnyard and her illogical pineapples, why would she not embrace her only daughter's bien-aimé."

Given the seriousness, Cora's voice came out a bit breathy. "Bien-aimé?"

"Beloved."

Perhaps Odette was more like Aunt Josephine than she thought. It seemed she had only traded the forced marriage drama at home for her cousin's. Without the carefree enjoyment of playing baseball with her nieces and nephews. She stuck her hand into her pocket and pulled out the lemon peel ball. If it wasn't for her unwanted suitor waiting at home, she might shuck this fancy gown and head for Indiana.

"Do you know anything about the sport of baseball? It's quite interesting, and if we head back to your house, I can show you how to play catch…"

The look on Odette's face froze the rest of the words in Cora's throat. Her cousin's widened eyes went from her face to the ball Cora clutched in her hands. Odette sniffed. "One eccentric in my world is more than enough, thank you."

So much for trying to change the subject. Cora stifled a sigh and shoved the ball into her pocket. They turned onto Market Street, and after a few blocks, slowed. Cora leaned forward to glance out the window at the sound of a piano tinkling. Odette shuffled to the other bench, leaned forward, and placed her hand upon the door's open window. A soft expectant expression rested across her features. The carriage came to a stop on the side of the road.

Clearly they waited for someone. "Odette?"

"There he is."

Cora swung back to catch the person of her cousin's interest. Wilkinson Dunbar stepped smartly down the front steps of a large weathered house. H. Hudge was the name splayed near the door. Cora had no time to contemplate what that must mean when he was there, entering the carriage. Odette wreathed in smiles, and Wilkinson had eyes for no other than her. He settled on the bench next to Odette and lifted her gloved hand and pressed his lips against it, his eyes never leaving hers.

"I could hardly wait for this moment," he breathed.

Good gravy. She was their chaperone. That's why Odette had insisted she come.

"I counted down each second," Odette smiled, clutching his hands. Then it seemed she remembered the third occupant. "Wilkinson, this is my cousin, Cora Taggart. But then, I believe you've already met."

He nodded briefly to her but turned back to stare adoringly at Odette.

"Nice to see you again." Cora nibbled her lip. She might as well be a tassel hanging from the curtains for all the mind they paid her.

Wilkinson leaned forward and whispered something in Odette's ear. Cora rolled her eyes. "I'm going to get some fresh air."

Odette gave a quick nod and leaned forward to whisper back to her companion. Cora clambered out and down the floating stairway before the driver could assist and strode around the back of the carriage. Which was worse, sitting in a buggy of lovers cooing or standing on the side of a busy road?

She flicked her gaze about. The buildings in this area needed some upkeep, if she were comparing it to her Aunt's opulent home. They stood in stark contrast to the piano music which now began to float towards her again. A few notes went sour and then the tune picked up again. It seemed to be coming from the H. Hudge home.

Nothing like getting a closer to listen. With care, she circumvented the busy thoroughfare to the other side of the street. Here a brick sidewalk trailed the road. As she drew nearer the home, the music grew louder as did the mistakes. She'd listened to Odette play several times. Her fingers ran up and down the lengthy keyboard without a mistake, twining the most difficult pieces with ease.

But the version she heard now seemed quite heavy and mottled with errors. She could barely make out the tune which seemed to be the same that Odette had played for her. Fur Elise by Beethoven, her cousin had told her. It had become a favorite of Cora's. As she strolled ever so slowly, her mind fixated on the music. Even with its missteps, the composition was still enjoyable.

A movement caught her eye at the corner of the house.

"Cora? I mean…Miss Taggart?"

She started and stared hard at the man. "Trigg?"

His grin and dazzling blue eyes looped her into a world quite unlike the surroundings. The piano music had slowed into a different tune as she approached.

"What are you doing here?"

As they drew closer, his smile grew softer, his eyes gentled with…pleasure? Suddenly Cora was very aware that their demeanor towards each other much resembled the secret lovers inside the carriage. A small laugh trickled out.

"I'm staying here for the time being." He gestured to the home behind him.

She blinked, trying to dispel the atmosphere that seemed to only include him and the soft piano music. "Oh, I see. But what about…your sister?"

He grimaced. "Yes, well. The trip has been on hold. I've just come through some sort of nasty bug as well as my traveling companions. But don't worry. The doctor assured me I'm quite recovered."

"Oh, I am so sorry." The paleness on his cheeks verified his words.

Trigg glanced to the busy road. "Why, it seems you just appeared from nowhere."

A breathy laugh popped from her. "No, not really. My cousin's carriage is there, across the street."

"Come," he tucked her hand into the crook of his hand, "do you have a few minutes to sit?"

Why did it seem she couldn't quite catch her breath? "I—" Cora swung her head toward the carriage. "Perhaps just a moment."

The grin he gave her filled her with a thousand shimmering shivers. A particularly sour note stopped all music, and Trigg grimaced. He winked and leaned forward with a loud whisper. "Mrs. Hudge's piano playing leaves a lot to be desired."

Despite herself, she giggled. As he led her up the porch towards the worn bench, the music began again in a simpler hymn.

"Not exactly home, but the grub's good."

"How long are you here?"

He shrugged. "Another one of my party's ill now."

"Oh, no. That's terrible. It's not..." Her eyes tried to say what she couldn't voice.

He grinned. "Not according to Dr. Hendricks. Stomach bug. A nasty one at that."

A sigh slipped from her as she settled against the back of the bench. Only then did she realize Trigg's leg firmly pressed against hers. Heat climbed her neck.

The man next to her studied her face. She dropped her gaze to the dilapidated porch and then at the traffic. "Busy road."

"Hmmm. I hadn't noticed."

She turned her eyes to him. "How could you not?"

"I have a gorgeous blonde with the greenest eyes I've ever seen sitting next to me, and you ask me that?"

Oh. Cora turned her head to let the bonnet block his probing eyes as her face became a blazing furnace.

"Cora."

She drew in a breath and glanced at him. "Yes?"

He smiled. "I just wanted to see you blush."

"Oh." She set her attention on a green hack pulled by a shiny ebony horse. It trotted by at quite a clip.

"I thought I'd never see you again."

She tugged her eyes from the disappearing buggy. "I thought the same."

"When will you be returning back to New Albany?"

"Not for some time. Probably in the early fall."

He nodded, watching the traffic clop by. "I'm not sure I can put you from my mind, Cora Taggart."

A gasp drew his gaze. *Nor I you.* Although she couldn't be so bold as to whisper the words, she felt sure her eyes conveyed their meaning.

"I'd like to call on you. Would your father allow that?"

Cora blinked. Would he? Heaker Thomas's face intruded. "I'm not sure. You would have to…consult him."

"Then I shall."

Her mouth parted as they searched one another's eyes.

"I know it's not proper, but I'd like nothing better than to kiss you." His cheeks stiffened. "But I dare not, given I've been sick. And, of course, I haven't spoken with your father."

She needed to change the subject and fast. For despite propriety, she wanted very much to feel his lips on hers. Pulling the ball from her pocket she shoved it into his hands. "You asked about it on the steamer. Here it is."

He grinned and quirked a brow as if he understood her abrupt change of subject. His big hands turning the ball drew her attention. Rough, well-formed hands. The same that had clutched her hand in a kiss.

"It's a fine baseball."

Her face burned like a fireplace in a winter snowstorm. He must think her a fool. "Do you think Mrs. Dixon is right about it being improper for a woman to participate in such things?"

His mouth twisted, his eyes alight with humor. "Cora, I'd like nothing better than to have a catch with you. I think it sounds like a most enjoyable activity."

Her mouth parted. His blue eyes, lit with humor and something else, seemed to vacuum her into a place where only she and he existed. And no matter what she tried, she couldn't break the spell.

"Cora." Her cousin's voice broke the seal of her fixation from Trigg's magnetic blue eyes. Oh, yes, Odette. She and Wilkinson had emerged from the carriage.

The pair scurried through the traffic and hurried up the walk. Odette's eyes flicked to the shabby exterior of the home. "What are you doing here?"

Cora bolted upright. "I...I, uh this is Trigg Gentry."

A grin vined across Odette's face. She curtsied, still gripping Wilkinson's arm. "How do you do? This is Wilkinson Dunbar, my intended."

With a nod, Trigg grinned. "We've met, actually. And how's your sister?"

"Well, thank you."

"Oh, how delicious. Cora never told me that you were still in the city." Odette pulled a card from her pocket and held it out to him. "But since you are, we cordially invite you to our Pineapple Cotillion."

Trigg took the invitation with a puzzled glance at Cora. "Oh, sorry. This is my cousin, Odette Glenridge."

"We'd be most pleased to have you attend. I know Cora would be delighted."

Cora widened her eyes at her cousin's audacity.

Trigg's chuckle met her ears. "I'd be most delighted as well, although I doubt I will be able to attend."

Her body literally drooped in disappointment which drew his eyes. "It's not that I don't want to come. But I have a duty to locate my sister."

She nodded. "I understand."

Wilkinson cleared his throat. "As much as I'd like to continue visiting, I must get in and see if Mrs. Hudge is pleased with the tuning. Then I must part."

Odette's face fell. "Must you? So soon?"

"Yes, my love."

Cora stole a glance at Trigg who was openly staring at her in a sad sort of way. "I guess we need to leave."

"If you get another chance, you know where I am." He winked.

"And you as well," she nodded toward the invitation in his hand.

Oh, how she wished she didn't have to leave. Is this how Aleena felt when she'd first realized her feelings for Abel? Had Father felt so tied up when he'd first laid eyes on Mama?

Trigg gripped Cora's hands and pressed her lemon peel ball back into her hands. He set his large warm hands around hers. "Until our next meeting. Plan on a rousing game of catch."

She nodded, gave a soft smile, and then hurried after Odette who had drawn away on the sidewalk for a few last whispers for Wilkinson's ears only. Cora slipped the ball into her pocket and fluttered her fingers goodbye at Trigg, her heart squeezing ever so painfully.

"Come, Cora, we must be going." Odette wiped at the moisture collecting in her eyes. She wrapped her arm in Cora's as they picked their way across the street. Both of them turned and gave one last wave, Odette, throwing a kiss as well. Lyon handed them up into the carriage, and both she and Odette gave forlorn sighs as they fell onto the carriage bench.

"I wish someday that I never have to part from him," Odette whispered, closing her eyes.

Cora blinked. Was it any wonder she wished the same about Trigg?

Chapter Eighteen

Odette remained calm only a moment before she shifted herself to the opposite bench and peered at Cora. She smoothed down the pleats in the olive Basque jacket with her lacy-gloved hands. "Now, what I need to do is find a gentleman, a discreet one, from which to borrow a silk frock coat. Let's see, a pair of lovely checkered trousers would be handsome as well. And lastly, a cravat. Loosely tied. Not horizontal. I'm afraid Father would throw him out for that alone."

Cora blinked. "What do you mean? Did you invite Wilkinson to our get-together?"

"Cotillion, Cora. The Pineapple Cotillion. And yes, I did." A wicked glint sparkled in her eyes.

"Is that allowed?"

Her cousin sniffed. "I refused to be escorted by Alfred. Mother must understand the way of love. And how better to select my own beau? But he must be properly dressed."

"He seemed quite presentable the way he was."

Odette's eyes grew round. "Oh, Cora. Dear country Cora. He was wearing daywear. For working. That would never be acceptable next to our evening wear at the Cotillion. Even if we are covered in pineapples."

Her companion leaned back on the cushioned bench, tapping her lips with one gloved finger, as her cousin took in the passing scenery. "But who? If only I could enlist Madame Girard's help without alerting Mother."

The late spring breeze wafted into the enclosed cabin, cooling Cora's heated face. She glanced out the window. At home, she'd be looking at fields of freshly planted corn and beans. But here, house after house passed by. This place was so foreign. Perhaps she was an unsophisticated soul as well as a misfit. Her list of undesirable qualities seemed to be growing rather than shrinking.

And this gathering seemed to be so pretentious. So...high-society. Cora had been so confident she could don the persona of a cultured lady. But it was becoming obvious she didn't fit in here either. And not just for her tomboy ways or her height, for Aunt Josephine stood nearly as tall as she. No, for her country ways.

At this rate, Cora would never find a place where she felt accepted. And maybe...that was okay. After all, her aunt wore pineapples on her head, spouted French, and decorated her home with enormous sculptures. Odette, refined and prim, lived in a house where chickens and goats meandered in and out of the house. Trigg, tall, strong, and...handsome had a sister who'd run away. Everyone seemed to have something unconventional going on in their lives. Everyone. *Trigg*...no. She refused to contemplate how at ease she'd felt in his presence. It was like...coming home after a long absence. She shook the thoughts away. There were more immediate things to attend to.

Cora took a deep breath and peered at her cousin squarely. Country or not, she still had abilities. And good or bad, she would use them to help Odette. "I suppose I might be able to help."

Her cousin leaned forward, interest live in her eyes. "What do you mean? I know you sew, but are you a seamstress?"

Cora shrugged. "Not really. I generally make women's clothing, but I think I could figure something out. Especially if I had a suitcoat for a pattern."

Odette clapped her hands, making no sound but small dull thuds. "Excellent. Could you accomplish it all in the few coming weeks?"

"I think so."

A smile stretched across Odette's face. "If you could do it, Cora, you would indeed be my heroine, and I, forever in your debt."

Oh, great-grandma's grasshoppers. What had she gotten herself into now?

That evening Uncle Calvin sat at the head of the gleaming table. Cora mutely ate some sort of flaked fish as Aunt Josephine dramatized the entryway for the cotillion. Her uncle had only graced the dinner table twice since she'd come nearly three weeks prior. He wore a bored, indulgent expression with a small quirk at the left side of his mouth. Not an overly handsome man with his paunchy belly and silver hair that encircled the balding top like an Olympic wreath of yore.

But his eyes were sharp and his countenance full of restraint and perseverance, which Cora suspected were qualities of great need when dealing with Aunt Josephine. Perhaps this was why Uncle Calvin seemed to always be traveling for business.

"We shall open the doors, quartet music floating throughout the room, announcing each arrival at the door. An archway woven in ivy and lace, interspersed with baby's breath, crowned by my pineapple reproduction, will frame the door as each party-goer enters. Lyon will announce, he has such a beautiful intonation, plus his French is *exquis*." She kissed her fingers here, and let them bloom open toward the ceiling. "The room will be draped in yellow silk as it complements the main color of green and blends in with the golden pineapples embossed on the wallpaper. And lastly, baby's breath will fill the room which will be lightened with hundreds of candles on every surface."

At this Uncle Calvin sniffed, then drolled, "We have gas chandeliers, Darling."

"Ah, yes, but they don't lend the romantic aura I so wish to create." Aunt Josephine batted her long eyelashes which suspiciously appeared false.

"Quite a fire hazard, my dear."

Aunt Josephine's smile grew tight. "Then we will have extra staff circulating to be sure nothing becomes too overheated."

"Mmm."

Cora wasn't sure if Uncle Calvin appreciated his rather bland soup or was acquiescing to the pressure of Aunt Josephine's demands.

"Now, Cora. I do so wish you had the opportunity to invite one of your acquaintances, being as it is, somewhat, your debutante appearance into the world. A little late, perhaps, but I am sure, here in St. Louis, you will catch the eye of a suitable gentleman."

The servants floated about, removing soup bowls and replacing them with the main course of roasted lamb. Had Mother been corresponding with Aunt Josephine about her lack of suitors? Had Heaker Thomas entered the conversation amongst the sisters? Ugh. Trigg's handsome face blossomed in her mind as Cora stuck her soup spoon in the bowl. Lille, Johnny-on-the-spot, pulled it away. "Actually there is someone."

Odette's eyes swelled and her head shimmied in small shakes.

Cora's eyes pivoted from her cousin's clear warning to first, her aunt, and then, her uncle. She forced a pause, forking a small mouthful of the odd meat into her mouth. *Confound it, think of something.* Her attempt to stall enough to force her earlier statement into oblivion failed, as her aunt and uncle continued to stare at her, their brows slightly elevated. Ahhh. "Well, of course…I have…Odette. And that is the only one I need."

Maybe it did sound a little forced, trite even. Cora turned a warm smile on her cousin across the table.

"Oh, yes, Mother. Cora and I have become grand friends."

My, Odette was good. It came out so nice and convincing. Aunt Josephine barely paused before she launched into the next Pineapple Cotillion topic of consideration.

"Then, we will conduct tours of the Glenridge Pinery. Once those conclude, we will have the grand slicing. That's where you come in, Dearest."

"Hmmm."

Tasty lamb or noncommittal grunt of dissatisfaction? Again, hard to tell.

"Once our guests have seen the delicacy of the ripened yellow fruit, the servants will come on cue with silver trays ladened with luscious chunks of pineapple speared through with the most adorable tiny sterling oyster forks. I specially ordered them with little carved pineapple designs, monogrammed of course."

"Hmmm."

Cora almost let out a snicker. Her gaffe was all but forgotten. And forks with pineapples? How else could they possibly be shaped?

"We can't linger too long—" Bo's cheeks puffed out as he hung on to his horse's saddle. He pressed his hand against his mouth once more as another heave came. Then, giving up the fight, he turned away and spewed the contents of his stomach on the ground. Bourbon coming up had to burn more than it went down.

"Bo, be reasonable. Oates and I were sick for a week. You need rest."

His brother came up for air, buffalo robe undisturbed. Perhaps it had melded to his body. "Nonsense, Brother. I'm made of tougher stuff than that."

Trigg shut his eyes for a moment to stem rolling them. Oates and Burr stood by the barn, mounts saddled, but uncertainty outlined their shoulders. He shifted his gaze back to Bodine's pale face. The man had regurgitated for two days and the thin set of his cheeks belied his health claims.

"Don't need to wait on my account." Bo grabbed the saddle horn and flung his leg over in slow motion.

With a shrug, Trigg slung his head at the two cohorts to mount, and he stepped in the stirrup. By the time he'd boarded, Bo had set a pace down the driveway, leaning precariously against the neck of his mount.

But three days later, after disembarking from their St. Louis packet at Muscatine, Iowa, Bo had quite recovered his jaunty air. Though that should have cheered Trigg, and he supposed it did, dealing with the scallywag made him hesitate to appreciate Bo's good health. They cut out from Muscatine after a few inquiries and then put in two hard days of riding.

When they finally stopped for the night, all the long, miserable days and nights had put Trigg in a right cantankerous mood. He loosened the saddle from Buck and heaved it to the ground. His gaze cut to the saddle bag. What he wouldn't give to be back on Mrs. Hudge's porch sparking with Cora.

He reached down and slid the fancy envelope from the saddle bag. Turning his back to the three behind him setting up camp, Trigg pulled the lacy invitation out in the near darkness.

Flint and steel scraped behind him and with the fire flare, Trigg could just make out her name in fancy calligraphy. Somehow, holding the invitation brought Cora just a little closer. Wouldn't it be fine to spin her around a polished ballroom floor? Or better yet, cozy up in a private corner where they could—

A bump and a meaty hand snatched the fancy page from Trigg's hand. Bo's laughter echoed as his brother bounded away. Trigg spun.

"What do we have here?" His brother wedged between the two lackeys. "Looks like Triggey's been holding out on us."

The three of them broke into snickers. Yep. Sure made it hard not to wish his brother's belligerence was toned down with a little dash of flu weakness. "Give it back."

Bo flared a gaping smile. "Been holding back on me, old boy? Swanky paper, and oh, looky here. Done got yourself invited to a debutante ball."

Burr and Oates stuffed their faces with pemmican near the campfire, but paused long enough to guffaw.

"Durn if it ain't getting too close to the fire. Shame if it got all burned up." Learing, Bo held the missive over the flames.

Trigg made a lurch for it, but Bo tugged it back with a churlish laugh. "Not so fast. Wait. You know what? I bet this came from that fine thing we saw on the steamer. Who knew my little brother could woo the ladies?"

Chapter Nineteen

Cora stared at the inside of the jacket and blew her bangs up. Holy comoly, tailoring a man's suit coat would be her undoing. The exact measurements, the turning of the sleeve, the lapels. All of it was proving quite a challenge. And Odette wanted it as soon as possible so Wilkinson could try it on and allow for alterations. Cora wandered out of the huge closet where she hid her creation and collapsed on the canopied bed, arms above her head.

From an ornate frame hanging on the wall, the imitation *Mona Lisa* peered at her. She was of no help. Cora sat up and glared at the blanket-covered blob in the corner. That thing would surely offer no consolation. It would merely continue to frighten the bejeebers out of her when Cora failed to remember the huge, imposing thing's presence in the corner.

Her gaze traveled to the unique writing desk, a glass case where the faux French Crown Jewels rested. Tempted as she was to try on the famous imitation, the case was locked. Besides, how would that help get Wilkinson's jacket finished?

If she could ever manage to assemble the garment, would it look hokey? Would it look like some misfit country girl with a flair for sewing had pieced it together with puckers and misstitched seams? She gave a groan. What would Aunt Josephine say? What if Madame Girard got wind of it? Cora closed her eyes and rubbed her face with open palms, then paused to cover her face. Why had she promised to do this?

What had Abel said? *Soak up all the world while you're there.* Yes, that was it. Well, if soaking up all she could was hiding in a closet, trying to sew a man's dinner jacket, she had arrived. She sat up and glanced out the window.

A beautiful carriage of shining black glided by, pulled by a pair of strutting palomino horses. She'd been here long enough to know that was the Jorgansons, five houses down. Mrs. Jorganson and her three daughters went calling on Mondays. Cora hadn't done much more than visit a few neighbors, usher farm animals out of the house, and scheme with her cousin. And when not scheming, Odette was either cloistered in her room or gone.

Cora sighed and rose. Enough dinner jacket for now. She wanted to get out. She *needed* to. And Lord willing, she would. She collected her shawl and her matching hat but left the lemon peel ball tucked in a drawer.

Trigg always tugged at her memory when she let herself be removed from the responsibility of outfitting Wilkinson. He hadn't stopped at the house. She hadn't heard anything from him in over a week. Perhaps he had wandered on to the next stop in search of his sister. She paused a moment to pray for him.

She opened her door to relative silence with distant chatters echoing down the hall. Madame Girard and Aunt Josephine. Not another fitting? Or more tablecloths or draping cloths or ceiling draping or uniforms for the servants. Should she alert her aunt of her plans or just try to arrange for a carriage on her own?

She tiptoed down the hallway, voices growing louder and louder yet muffled behind the sealed sewing room door. Well, perhaps the closed door was a blessing. She paused and backtracked to Odette's room. Being accompanied was proper. She knocked softly. A few moments ticked by before her cousin peeked through a small crack in the door.

"Oh, it's you."

Cora smiled. "I thought to get out and take a carriage ride. Do you think that's possible?"

"Most assuredly. And an excellent idea."

Odette disappeared for a moment and reappeared with a fitted jacket, matching her muted blue skirt and cream blouse.

"Do you think we should tell your mother?"

An ever-so-slight sneer danced across Odette's fine features and then it was gone. "No, no sense in pulling her from her plans with Madame Girard."

Her cousin swept breezily from the room yet walked a little more lightly as she passed the sewing room. Cora followed her down the stairs with nary a sound.

"I know just where we'll go." A small smile tucked the corner of Odette's mouth.

Once they reached the carriage house and notified the servants of their intentions, the men and boys scurried about to ready the horses. It struck Cora that perhaps it would have been better to have made more definite plans to avoid the help hustling about to the commands of Odette.

But her cousin seemed quite unconcerned as she entered the pinery. Cora had visited the hothouse several times to see the spiky plants growing in rich black soil in careful rows. Several had crowns of fruit in various sizes resting on the pinnacle center. Several servants circulated the arboretum. They were hushed, speaking in whispers, as if their very intense tranquility would insure the maximum amount of ripe pineapples for the cotillion.

Through the pinery windows, the same enclosed carriage they had used the other day appeared in the driveway, harnessed to the two matching bay horses. Odette waved at her from the doorway and Cora hurried toward her.

"Are you ready for an adventure?" Odette's voice sounded like a child's on Christmas morn.

Cora sighed, reminding herself that she could be cooped up in the sewing closet. She settled against the cushions and stared at her cousin seated across from her. Perhaps they would pass H. Hudge house. "Of course. Ummm. Where are we going?"

A falsely demure smile met Cora's gaze. The carriage turned left, a clear indication they were on their way downtown. Cora glanced quickly to the right to catch sight of the Lucases' farm fields in the distance. Lucas Place, the newest addition on the west side of town, would soon be adding more elegant homes and pushing away the quiet rural edge of town. But for now, the familiarity of the fields sent a dizzying wave of homesickness through her.

"We're going to pay a call to a downtown establishment."

The calm in her cousin's posture, hands quietly resting in her lap, would be believable if it weren't for the dancing devilish light in her cousin's eyes.

Cora stuffed down the nagging nudge of Aunt Josephine's constant reminders, with her fears of disease, of avoiding downtown. But where had Cora's bold adventuresome nature gone? The baseball-playing seamstress of old?

Cora glanced at her fine white gloves and glowing purple satin dress, each of the many ruffles trimmed in black. A gift from Aunt Josephine. As well as the sizable black touring hat covered in purple feathers. At least no giant pineapple rested on her headwear. Never in a thousand years would Cora have chosen such a creation. Nor the colors. She looked with envy at Odette, who always appeared in muted hues, well fitted, without the massive flowing ruffles. Even her hat was delicate, perched on her head like a fine apple blossom.

Well, it was obvious where her old self had vamoosed. Beneath layers of her unfamiliar surroundings and billowing piles of garish satin.

"Have I ever explained the sport of baseball?" It was out of Cora's mouth before she could squelch it. Surprise and then disapproval crossed her cousin's face.

"Whatever are you speaking of, Cora?"

No sense hiding it now. "Baseball. It's a game. I showed you my lemon peel ball."

"Oh, yes. That. Wherever did you get such a notion?"

"My brother saw a game in New York once. The Knickerbocker team...." The horror on her cousin's face stopped her.

"Cora, that's quite uncouth. Why, I don't believe any proper gentleman would be involved in such a thing let alone a lady."

So talking her into a game of toss was out of the question. A rigorous session of catch would have chased away the city cobwebs that seemed to tighten around her. At least Trigg had appeared interested. What a lovely thought. Pitching with Trigg, showing him those things dear to her heart, her mitt, how she could slide into base to avoid a tag. My, if Odette could get a glance at her thoughts, she'd likely pucker up quite a sour-lemon face. Cora tightened her lips to avoid the smirk that tugged at her mouth.

Odette turned her head to watch the passing scenery, and Cora followed suit. She wasn't in a summer field with a bat in her hand, Trigg flipping the lemon-peel ball, grinning that lopsided grin, a spark of fascination in his eye. No matter how much she wished it were true. Besides, home meant dealing with Father and Mr. Thomas.

She gave a small sigh so as not to attract her cousin's attention. At least it was a perfect day to get out and about. Early summer had put on her brightest sun, highlighting the beautiful new leaves on the trees lining the street and the blossoms near the homes. A cascade of tiny pink roses covered a picket fence of a particularly neat bungalow.

But the traffic was ungodly. How on earth Odette and her family could stand the constant hubbub of the city was a mystery to her. The crowds thickened, the dust and smoke clouding the air, and the surroundings turned commercial. Before long, they had pulled near the curb on Fourth Street. Musical Depot. 56 North Fourth Street.

"We're here."

Odette's announcement seemed to carry a note of breathy pleasure. Cora's brow puckered. What could her cousin be up to?

With the aid of the footman, Cora swished from the carriage cabin behind Odette. Her cousin wasted no time and entered the store. A bell at the top of the door proclaimed their entry.

The showroom was huge. Gleaming pianos and harpsicords took up a large percentage of the floor space. A number of large-bellied stringed instruments were featured to the right, sizes varying from hand-held to large floor models. Wind instruments hung on a far wall, both wooden and brass. Surprisingly, their sizes varied greatly as well. Cora had just started to make out a plethora of percussion instruments toward the back when a man approached.

"Ah, ladies. For what do I owe such a pleasure?"

Wilkinson, dressed in a day suit of charcoal grey, sported a lighter gray ascot at his neck. Although, he had only eyes for Odette.

"We were out for a bit of fresh air this morning. And I could think of nowhere else I'd like to visit." Odette took a step forward just as Wilkinson did. He grasped her hands as if the pair had heard a silent waltz start up from the instruments around them.

Cora cleared her throat and Odette stepped away. "Forgive me, Cora. I thought you'd be intrigued to see Wilkinson's place of work."

Or for Odette to see Wilkinson? "It's lovely. I've never seen such a large establishment or so many musical instruments."

"Wilkinson can play nearly all of them." Odette's words came in a rush, a tinge of color high on her cheeks.

"Odette, Darling. You exaggerate."

Her cousin patted his clasped hands. "Please, play something for us."

He looked around, the expanse void of customers. "Very well."

Wilkinson steered Odette through the bulky pianos and harpsicords. Cora followed behind. They stopped at a huge shining piano the size of a small room. Grotrian-Steinweg embossed the panel above the glimmering keys.

"This is my favorite. An import of Germany, although they just set up shop in Manhattan under Steinway. It's not only the most expensive on the floor, it's the finest in quality of sound as well."

Wilkinson seated himself as if millions of people sat at the edge of their seats in breathless anticipation of the notes to come. He rested his right hand upon the top as he settled his left onto the bass keys. Then his right fluttered down and the musical interlude ensued.

Cora was no connoisseur of music, but she instantly recognized not only the beauty in the richness of the sound, but in the talent of the man who fingered the ivory keys with a ferocity that took her breath. Some minutes went by, the notes spinning nearly out of control and then slowing ever so slightly, then tumbled into a dramatic ending.

Odette clapped in joy with an adoring sigh. She leaned towards Cora and whispered, "Franz Liszt, 'La Campanella.'"

No sooner had she finished her words when Wilkinson launched into the next selection. This one started with a loud rumble of keys and rarely let up, perhaps only slightly in degree of loudness. How his fingers flitted over the keys in such speed made Cora's mouth drop. Wilkinson's body language mimicked the gyrations of the music, his head jerking with the bold pounding of the keys, until at last the music slowed and dropped in volume. Wilkinson tipped his head back as the song ended.

"Bravo, Wilkinson." Odette turned in glee to Cora. "Robert Schumann's 'Toccata in C Major, Opus 7.'"

But Wilkinson only paused a moment before he launched into yet another. This one light and flaring from high keys to low, much more calming than the last although the speed of Wilkinson's fingers never slowed except at the very tail of the piece.

"Fabuleux, magnifique!" Odette waxed French in her eagerness to bestow praise. "Frédéric Chopin's 'Etude in G-sharp Minor, Opus 25; number 6.'"

Cora also found herself clapping as Wilkinson stood, a sheepish grin upon his face and a sheen of sweat at his brow.

"You're too kind." He eyed the keys in length, as if in regret, before he stepped away.

The bell on the doorway sounded, and an older man in a black day suit stepped in. The way his gaze flicked about the room indicated a fellow employee rather than a customer.

"Excuse me." Wilkinson left them and threaded his way to the front.

"That's his father." Odette whispered behind a gloved hand.

Ahhh. The two men conversed as they strolled to the back of the store and then disappeared behind a door.

Odette spun, eyes alight. "Well? What did you think?"

Cora's gaze returned to the piano, eyes taking in the instrument that only moments before had poured out a depth of deeply emotional music. "I think this piano is absolutely lovely, if you're thinking of purchas—"

"Not the piano, Silly," she giggled. "Wilkinson. We have such elevated dreams of him playing a solo part or a concerto with a backdrop of an orchestra. Perhaps one day he may even play abroad."

"Oh, how exciting."

Odette nodded. "I'll go check on him. I wonder what's taking so long."

Her cousin hustled toward the back of the store. Cora plucked a single note on the magnificent instrument in front of her. The one note seemed out of place in a place so full of silence. Much like herself. And not just in her hometown. A bit of dismal melancholy wrapped around her, and she hugged herself, seeking a bit of comfort.

She wandered from one instrument to another, admiring the different wood and details carved into some. Then amongst the cellos she strummed one string, enjoying its deep timbre.

The drums sat in imposing silence and Cora dared thrum one. And while the sparkling cymbal called to her to test its brashing brilliance, she veered away toward the door where Odette had disappeared.

Cora paced a few minutes more, her gaze going to the store front windows lit by the cheerful spring sun and dancing across the lids of the pianos to the door. Where was Odette?

With a deep breath, Cora turned the marble doorknob and slipped through. It was dimmer here, with a hall of doorways and a warehouse of sorts through the door in the back, cracked open.

She glanced from side to side at the closed doorways until she came to the warehouse. Inside, large crates and boxes occupied nearly every spot within the dimly lit space. A dingy place indeed next to the brilliant showroom up front.

A murmur of voices led her to weave between the boxes to the left, the light growing ever dimmer as she went. Against the concrete wall in a quiet corner, Wilkinson and Odette stood, interwoven in a passionate kiss.

Cora spun and tiptoed back the way she'd come. Glory. Odette was risking her reputation indeed, to kiss a man so blatantly. So intimately. A man not her husband. Why, she would never—

Trigg's handsome face stopped all thought. An immense longing swelled in her chest. Her lashes fluttered closed, and she let go a long exhale through pursed lips. What would it be like to lose oneself in a kiss with a beloved?

Suddenly, she wished more than life that she and Trigg were tucked back in a concealed alcove. Interwoven, blatant...intimate. And then she knew. She, like Odette, would gladly risk it all.

For Trigg.

Chapter Twenty

Trigg squinted and blinked. He was dreaming surely. Another wave of agony shut his eyes quick. Cool wetness touched his head, and he sucked in a breath and then let out a sigh.

"Trigg?"

His eyes snapped open. There she was again. Alive. His own baby sister. The world swirled for a moment. Her concerned features floated into his vision. Two braided pigtails fell on either side of her face. A leather headband encircled her head and feathers and strings of beads hung from the strap. His fluttering eyelids blocked the view for a moment, and then he forced his eyes back open. He glanced down. Buckskin covered her in a type of fringed dress. His head kept repeating over and over that it was her, but the woman who knelt beside him looked more Indian than Ivalee.

"Is it really you?"

A smile met his eyes. "Yes, it's me."

"How...how..."

The coolness returned to his head. "Shhh. Here now. Settle down. You need to rest."

What a strange turn of events. Not in his oddest dreams would Ivalee ever be comforting him. The tomboy of the family had never paused long enough to nurse anyone. Snatches of her traipsing about the Kentucky countryside on a mule lit his battered memory.

Perhaps he was just dreaming for this reality seemed much too fuzzy. Too warped. Yes. A dream... His eyes defied his weak mental command to stay open, and his eyelids slid closed.

Dark met his eyes when next they opened. Crickets serenaded somewhere close by but not too close. To his right a banked fire glowed only red, deep under the ash. The smell of smoke intermixed with the smell of dried grass. And although pain still had him nailed to the pallet below him, he rose above it in full consciousness. A coyote howled in the distance.

He turned his head and peered through the dimness. Lumps covered in animal skins on the other side of the fire indicated other people lay there. But the muted light made it impossible to recognize who might be there. One head, perhaps two? He shifted slightly, bringing a spank of fresh pain shimming down from his head through his ribs. Both arms seemed to function now. But squeezing and opening his fists ate up all his strength reserves. So for now, he allowed himself to slip back into sleep.

The light woke him a third time. Shuffling indicated someone drew near. His bones ached still, but not to the screaming extent they had the day before. Without thought, a heavy sigh escaped, and Trigg struggled to sit up. Hands touched his shoulders, and he slung his head back to discover who it might be.

"Ivalee. You're not just a dream."

A laugh. "No, dear brother. I'm quite real."

Trigg raised his hand and brushed the feathers hanging from her headband. "How?"

She pressed him back to the pallet and swabbed something cool to his brow. "This is my home now."

"What home?"

Ivalee pressed a wooden cup to his mouth. He drank deeply, the fresh cool water reviving his inner parts. He lay back with a gasp of satisfaction.

"You must listen, Brother. This is my home, here with the Meskwaki. I am a bride—"

Trigg snapped to a sitting position throwing his hands to his head in pain. He tensed his shoulders, gripping his head. He gritted his teeth a moment, his eyes squeezed shut to block the waves of torture that thundered to his brain. "Ivalee, no..."

His kid sister pushed him back to the pallet none too gently, and he yielded, weak as a newborn colt.

"Didn't I tell you to listen? I'm married. I live among the Meskwaki Indians. My husband is here, Rowtag."

Trigg shut his eyes to calm the rising ire. Getting worked up would only amplify the pain pulsing through his skull. Then he blinked his eyes open and studied the rushes that encompassed the structure he lay within.

Ivalee called the foreign name again, slightly louder, and the den darkened for a moment. Above him appeared a stern, distinctly Indian, face, deceptively older, but quite capable of doing a great deal of damage to Trigg. Especially now, in his feebleness. He studied the character in his fringed buckskin, loose black hair affixed only with a leather band.

After a struggle, Trigg pushed himself up and with Ivalee's help, stood. A most unenjoyable experience, but he refused to meet the Indian lying on his back. Trigg towered over the man, but his smaller size did not belie Rowtag's wiry strength. His face contained harsh angles and a prominent, finely chiseled nose. Perhaps he struck Ivalee as handsome, rugged maybe. Exotic, most certainly. Even though compact, Trigg could see ferocity in his dark eyes that would more than make up for his size.

A gentleness touched the native man's face as he glanced to Ivalee. "Ihkwe·wa, mi·čiwa."

Ivalee nodded, her eyes straying to Trigg who jutted out his chin.

"My woman. You no take." The fierceness in Rowtag's eyes thickened.

Trigg glanced to the small opening in the straw matted house. Rowtag murmured to Ivalee who turned and bent to exit the enclosure. Outside, numerous others just like this man camped nearby. Quite a band to contend with alone. What choice did he have?

"How'd you find her?"

His sister dipped through the doorway once again, carrying a basket. "He saved me, actually. You might be surprised to know that the new state of Iowa is quite cold in late February."

Trigg grunted. Standing, squared up, quickly sapped his energy.

"Sit, dear brother. There's no one needing rescued now." She seated herself near his pallet which she patted.

Nothing sounded better at the moment. Sitting down proved to be as great a struggle as standing.

"Here. Rowtag reminded me you needed some food. Then, you can ask me questions all day if you'd like."

"You're too young to be here. To be married."

A snort lit from Ivalee. "Father gave his blessing."

"Father?"

A wry smile lit her face as Rowtag settled behind the fire, crossing his arms in vigilant stance. "Yes. We located him."

"Where?"

"Eldora, of course. But then, you knew that. It's why you are here."

He stuffed the meat from the bowl into his mouth. It had a gamey, strangely spiced taste, but edible. "Yes. At least that is where I think we were headed."

Her eyes widened. "We?"

"Bo and I. Oh, and a couple of his cohorts."

"Bo." She turned and muttered some unintelligible words to the Indian man behind her, gesturing toward the door. He merely nodded.

She gave a small sigh. "He won't leave until he is sure you aren't here to swipe me."

Trigg eyed the stoic Indian. "Smart man."

"Did you think I would settle for less? I know you don't like it, but he's my husband and I love him. He's Meskwaki. And so am I, now." Ivalee passed the wooden cup to Trigg once more. "By the way, he understands what you're saying. His English is pretty good."

"Obviously." He took a good swallow. Already he felt better. "Perhaps you better explain a little more thoroughly."

She shrugged. "You know, I left in early February on Eclipse—"

"My best jack, I recall."

Irritation clambered across his sister's pretty face. "Are we going to argue about your donkeys or do you want to listen?"

Trigg shoved a piece of strange vegetable into his mouth.

"My mission was to find Father. But I found a blizzard instead. Rowtag found me and nursed me back to health."

"I have no doubt." He shot the Indian a squinted stare.

"Trigg. There was nothing inappropriate in it. He moved me to his mother's wickiup and I recovered. He was one of the few who could speak English. The Meskwaki live here in secret. Most of the tribe have been relocated to Kansas. But they are planning to return. Or at least, hopefully. Then, we, the Meskwaki will have a permanent home in Iowa."

Trigg raised an eyebrow.

"Right. Back to my story. Rowtag scouted the area and located Father. He was already packed and ready to move on. I guess the gold rush in Eldora didn't pan out."

"Now there's a surprise. Where'd he go?"

"California."

He blew out a breath. "Little late for that one, isn't he?"

Ivalee stirred the food. "Who knows? He had gold fever bad. And by that time, I had no desire to accompany him. I only wanted to stay with Rowtag."

His sister turned a glowing smile toward the bronzed-skinned man keeping watch. A flicker of softness lit her husband's eyes.

"You're too young for this," Trigg growled.

Her head swung round. "Am I? Not hardly, Trigg. You know full well I could be hitched back in Kentucky by now."

She had a point.

"Besides, I'm sixteen and old enough. And Father gave his blessing."

Trigg's brain throbbed. He'd skipped right over thinking about her birthday in his rush to get here. It must have been nigh on a fortnight ago. He brushed a shaky hand through his hair. Even if he wanted to do something, he had no strength to follow it through.

His sister laid a hand to his face and their eyes connected. "I won't leave, Trigg. I belong here. If you take me back, I'll run away again."

"Rowtag no let leave." The Indian stepped closer with his declaration, fists tightened at his sides, the cords at his neck bulging.

Trigg growled a sigh. "Keep your shirt on. I'm not taking her anywhere."

He eased back into a lying position on his pallet. Wasn't it obvious? Trigg wasn't taking anyone anywhere at this point. Not even himself. "Where's my horse?"

Ivalee grinned. "He's being taken care of. Slightly lame from your foolish run through the dark. But Rowtag says he'll recover."

With a nod Trigg shut his eyes. "Has Father already left?"

"Yes. Several weeks back." She covered him with a skin and patted him. "Get some rest. Then we can explore some more. All is well."

All is well. All is well. The words repeated in his head as he drifted back to sleep. It didn't matter if it were true or not. He would have to accept it. Ivalee had made her choice.

The next day Trigg managed to leave the wickiup and stroll through the small collection of grass huts, low slung to the ground to avoid detection. The looks he received bid him unwelcome but tolerated, for Ivalee's sake. Or rather, Lomasi, which was what the Meskwaki called her, meaning pretty flower. And Rowtag? His meant fire. Trigg could see the smoldering of the man's soul in his eyes. Especially in defense of Ivalee.

The Indian people seemed to accept Ivalee as their own. She fit right in with her tomboy spirit and her proud ways. And it was entirely apparent she was smitten with Rowtag. She settled next to the women weaving the dried grasses into baskets, stirring the cooking pots, and chasing the infants crawling in the dust.

Strangely, a sense of calm fell on Trigg. He'd come thundering into the state of Iowa, looking to rescue and battle anyone who'd taken or hurt Ivalee, and yet found she was quite happy and prosperous. She looked up at him from her spot near the fire, her hair braided much like the other women. The only difference being her light skin and blue eyes. Ivalee smiled.

Rowtag sidled up to him. He swept a hand over his face. "Woman, beauty. Wîpekothiwa."

Trigg turned a puzzled face to him. Rowtag jabbed two fingers towards his eyes. Ahhh. "Blue. Her eyes are blue."

A ghost of a grin swept the Indian's features. He grunted. "Blue. Yes, blue. Much beauty."

Again Rowtag turned to stare at Ivalee. His sister didn't seem to be the only one besotted.

With a hand to the smaller man's shoulder, Trigg grinned. "You take care of Ivalee?"

Rowtag thumped his chest with a fist, his face intense. "I die for woman."

That's all he could ask for. Trigg pounded the man's shoulder, falling into Rowtag's vernacular. "Yes, you good man. Take care of her. You husband."

A stern nod from the Meskwaki man assured his message had gone through. Trigg tucked his hands in his pockets. He would stay a few more days. And then, he'd head back east. He pointed to the grass. "Blue?"

The Indian actually grinned. "No. Ashkipakethiwa."

"Yes. Green. I look for ash...kipake...thiwa."

Rowtag jabbed two fingers at Trigg's eyes. "Your woman?"

Nothing wrong with his new brother-in-law's smarts. "Yes. My woman."

Chapter Twenty-One

"**L**ille, more candelabras." Aunt Josephine flicked her hands at the servant.

Cora's eyes grew huge. Candles covered every surface of the huge parlor and dining area where the cotillion would be held. How did her aunt think she needed more? And where would she put them?

Cora trailed the servant to the butler's pantry. Aunt Josephine bustled about like a frenzied rabid raccoon, scurrying from one task to another, squealing commands, flapping her arms in hurried exasperation, her eyes in a shiny glazed-over glare. The poor servants wouldn't have the energy to serve anyone this evening if she kept it up. This get-together had gotten out of control.

Lille said nothing as she snatched two silver candelabras and handed them to Cora while she picked up two more. Lyon appeared behind her to manhandle two large floor candelabras from the closet. Surely, her aunt had gone mad at last.

They arrived back to the main room and Aunt Josephine commanded and pointed with hyper precision. Cora placed hers on the mantle amongst crystal bowls filled with other candles. Truly the room would be aflame.

She peered around at the spacious parlor. Most of the furniture had been situated against the walls to allow the guests to roam about freely. Any unnecessary furniture, although not anything spouting a pineapple, had been banished to the third floor. White organdy and lace swags adorned the stairway wrapped in ivy and baby's breath. A few yellow buttercups were woven into the creation.

Outside, the men were in mid-stream building an impromptu arbor, square built with corner posts draped in the same gauzy material, gathered with yellow bows. A wooden floor for dancing was taking shape in the center. Smack dab in the front lawn. The idea had popped into Aunt Josephine's head a week back. Right after she'd decided the string quartet would set up shop on the far end of the porch, floor to ceiling windows opened to allow the music to travel wherever the guests strolled.

Yellow taffeta covered the ceiling in puffs, conducive to keeping the noise level down. At least according to Aunt Josephine. Two new servants shuffled by her, and she realized she'd frozen in the middle of the parlor. Her aunt had brought in a dozen new servants to decorate and serve for the evening's extravaganza. Cora let out a sigh and moved to the stairway. She'd been busy since the break of dawn. To her eyes, it was way past ready, but she was sure her aunt would not agree.

She glanced up the stairway. A rest from the bustle would be nice. Lyon passed through the room carrying two more silver floor candelabras to set up on the porch. Or rather, the veranda as Aunt Josephine called it.

With quick feet Cora climbed the stairs. Veranda, cotillion, pinery, extravaganza. Her vocabulary had certainly expanded. Aleena would be pleased. At the top of the balcony, she watched the servants bustle about, and a spasm of homesickness welled up her spine. Oh, for the comfort of home and homey things. Everyday country things.

"Abel, I'm trying to soak it all in, but I miss everyone so dreadfully," she whispered to herself. But the pall of her forced courtship brought a lump to her throat. The excitement of going home would be ruined. She couldn't help but compare her cousin's passionate relationship with Wilkinson to the tepid, reluctant one she would begin with Heaker Thomas.

Would she ever feel that same all-consuming ardor for a man she could barely stand to court? She tried to imagine kissing Heaker the way Odette had kissed Wilkinson in the dim warehouse corner. But every time she tried to visualize it, Trigg became the man who wrapped her in a fervent kiss. Oh, my. Oh, heavens.

She was in love with Trigg.

Cora backed away, dashing moisture from the corner of her eye. How could this have happened so quickly? Trying to return home to follow her father's will had now become impossible. And how would her parents accept a strange man over their choice of a suitor? She moaned and clutched at her throat. Then she scurried to her room and closed the door.

A few hours later, a tiny knock sounded, and Cora peeped out. "Oh, Odette. Come in."

"No, no. I just wanted to let you know that I'm going to Wilkinson's store. I'm planning on dressing there so he and I can arrive and be announced together."

A gasp escaped Cora. "You mean I'll have to do this alone?"

A ripple of regret filtered across her cousin's face. "I do apologize. But I must let Mother know that Edgar is not for me. Hopefully arriving as a couple, she will accept Wilkinson's request to court me."

"I see."

Odette tilted her head. "What's wrong?"

Cora shook her head and turned to pace her room, stopping to stroke the pineapple creation that hung from a hook on the armoire. "Nothing. I'm fine."

Odette's small feet beat a staccato across the floor. Her cousin's hand tugged at her arm, forcing Cora to turn. The tears on Cora's face widened her cousin's eyes.

"'Tis love, no?"

Cora nodded. Odette enclosed her in a hug and Cora rested her head upon her cousin's.

"Chin up. Who knows that he won't return?"

Cora forced a smile to her lips. "Perhaps you're right."

"Of course I am. Keep hope alive." Odette winked at her play on Cora's middle name.

"But meanwhile," Cora tugged her hanky from her sleeve and dabbed her eyes. "I don't know how to be a debutante. What do I do?"

Odette gave a demure smile. "You'll do nothing. Mother will send a servant to help you dress. She'll do your hair. Then you'll wait in your room until all the guests have arrived and have been announced. When the music stops, a servant will alert you, and you will step to the balcony where Lyon will announce you. It's as simple as that."

Where she will proceed to stumble down the stairs in a series of cartwheels, legs sprawling, pineapples flying. "Odette..."

Her cousin patted her hand with her gloved one. "You'll do fine. I'll be here. Don't worry."

Weren't those the famous last words? "I..."

But Odette had already trodden to the doorway, and with a wave, she disappeared.

Lille appeared an hour later. Thank goodness it was the quiet little maid. Somehow she trusted the petite girl with compassionate eyes. The green pineapple dress slipped on without a hitch over the mounds of ruffled crinolines. Despite the tremendous width of the skirt, it swayed nicely when she walked.

Then Lille attacked her hair. The woman was a wonder. She pinned and tucked until a cascade of strawberry blonde curls tumbled from the crown of her head down her back.

"Oh, my." Cora could hardly breathe when the woman finished. "I've never looked so fancy. Thank you, Miss Lille. Thank you so much."

The servant merely nodded, but a glint of pleasure shone from her eyes. "Now, miss. Make-up."

Make-up? Never in Cora's life had she worn any. Her plain face transformed into a stranger, a debutante with her powdered face, rosy cheeks, and a slight hint of lampblack lining her eyes. Lastly, Lille applied the rouge to her lips topped with a shiny balm. Cora caught her breath. She looked like a queen. If only Trigg could see her now.

"It won't be long, Miss." The maid nodded to her and went to stand watch at the door. The cheery string quartet's music drifted up the stairs. The servant motioned to her. "They have just begun Mozart's *Eine Kleine Nachtmusik*. That is your cue."

The perky music echoed louder up the stairs. Yes, she remembered. Yesterday a stately gentleman had come and played the tune upon his violin. Nerves danced down her body, and she let out a puff of air as she walked the hallway toward the balcony. The dramatic beginning of the song crescendoed into a much slower, muted section and the string quartet dropped the volume.

Cora stepped to the edge. The room was literally overflowing with candles, giving the room a soft romantic feel. The gas chandelier also glowed, putting her in the perfect light for all to see. Her heart fell to her feet. Cora took small wisps of breaths to try to cover her nervousness How she wished this were her wedding day with Trigg waiting on the landing below.

But it was Lyon who stood at the bottom of the stairway in a black tails. And instead of her family, strangers gathered in the room below, at the doors, and the open windows. Her eyes lit on a vaguely familiar figure dressed in a silk mourning dress. Widow Dixon and Elizabeth Rogers stood near the fireplace next to several others, whom Cora could only guess to be the Cantrells, their hosts. The plague had followed Cora here, even to this place.

"Mademoiselle Cora Hope Taggart, niece of Monsieur Calvin and Madame Josephine Glenridge." Lyon's deep voice boomed, making best use of his faux French accent. A smattering of applause skittered around the room. Uncle Calvin mounted the stairs to escort her safely to the landing. Thank goodness. Her face flamed red-hot by the time she'd gained the lowest step.

Couples floated by, greeting her by name and introducing themselves as Cora clung to her uncle. Then Uncle Calvin escorted her around to the available men. To her astonishment, they kissed her gloved hand and bowed, some with looks slightly less than honorable. She blushed, curtsied, and attempted not to jumble up the common words of "nice to meet you," and "thank you for coming," while trying to toss in a few, "enchantés," when Aunt Josephine stepped closer.

Cora caught sight of Odette on Wilkinson's arm near the hors d'oeuvre table. His dinner jacket looked quite impressive, even if she was the only one who noticed. Still, it wasn't something she was anxious to do again anytime soon. She smiled at her uncle and released his elbow, training her sight on Odette. At least she knew her. But a gentleman, Mr. Giles, perhaps, clutched her arm.

"May I sign your dance card first, my lady?"

Her mind stalled. Dance lessons had occupied her previous week. "Uh...of course."

Her new escort smiled, of the yellow-teeth sort, and led her off. He stood just shy of her height and wasn't horrible to look at. Still, between remembering the dance steps and her nervousness, it was difficult to enjoy the waltz.

A sense of accomplishment fell on her as the last notes of the minuet finished. But the sense of ease didn't last long as a line of eligible bachelors swarmed her for the next dance. The room dimmed as the gas chandelier was extinguished, throwing the room into a more intimate atmosphere.

"Miss Taggart." Her current dance partner nodded and took her into his arms, slightly too near. He was a looker, and a devilish glint sparked from the corner of his blue eyes. At least Mr. Rathford was her height. Still, he wasn't Trigg.

She gave a tremulous smile. Conversation was out as she counted out her steps.

"Will you be long with the Glenridges?"

Cora misstepped trying to work out an answer to fit between the waltz steps. "A few more weeks."

"How glorious. I'd be glad to show you about town, if you so desire. Just you...and I." His brows jumped suggestively.

Oh, my. Unchaperoned? She cleared her throat. "Have you ever played baseball?"

Her handsome partner seemed a bit taken back. "No, I don't believe I'm familiar with it."

Drat. Why had that tumbled from her mouth? Again. "Oh."

"Perhaps we could walk the grounds, and you could explain it to me." He gave a disarming smile, giving Cora the impression that wasn't the only thing in his thoughts.

"No, I believe..." The music stopped. Funny how the songs often just ended on a couple of notes. She applauded and resisted the pull of Mr. Rathford's fingers on her arm. But she need not have worried. The next dance partner had stepped up. Nearly a head shorter than she was, with a shock of red hair.

"Dance, Miss Taggart? I believe it's my turn." He grinned ear to ear. "I'm Earl Fortithe, remember?"

She hadn't. But she was relieved Rathford's fingers slipped from her arm. Away she went, swirling about the room. Despite his small stature, he seemed most confident in his steps and was easy to follow. He whirled her right out the door, down the few steps onto the wooden dance floor outside. She couldn't help but giggle as they spun around the squared gazebo among the other couples.

As soon as the music came to an abrupt close, a blond took the redhead's place, with a smooth-planed face, hair on the longish side. Another one with a wolfish gleam in his eyes. She blinked and took in a soothing breath.

"Miss Taggart? I'm Charles Charvelt, but I'm sure you recall me. I'd count it a privilege if you call me Charles."

She fanned her face and blinked at his forwardness. At least he was taller than she. But even that didn't make up for his poor manners. "Perhaps we could get a drink before we dance?"

263

He gave a thin-lipped smile, bowed, and indicated she should precede him. She settled on one of the wrought iron lawn chairs near the edge of the arbor. Her new escort disappeared through the crowd and appeared moments later with drinks in both hands. He settled next to her. Mr. Guiles? No, Charvelt. Except he preferred Charles. Oh, yes. How had she forgotten?

"Thank you so much."

"You are most welcome." He took a sip and settled his eyes upon her. "It gives us a chance to talk. Is this your first trip to St. Louis?"

"Yes. It is."

A lazy smile stretched across his face. "And does our fair city measure up to New Albany?"

My, he had done his homework. "It's different."

"Different in a good way, I hope?"

His perusal intensified and Cora squirmed. "Mmm-hmmm."

"You look quite stunning in your dress, may I say." His eyes dropped and settled somewhere just south of her chin before settling back on her face. His eyebrow quirked. "I do indeed like mature women."

Cora's gulp of punch turned into a choke. Mature? Feathered falcons. How was one to take such a comment? She jumped up, trying to keep herself from dumping her drink on her dress.

Charles stepped closer and rubbed his hands up and down her upper arms. "There, there, my dear. Have you quite recovered?"

"Please, I need a moment." She shoved the drink into his hands and strode toward the house with him hot on her heels. He wasn't going to let go easily. She threaded through the parlor, the dining hall, and the back hallway to the water closet and shut the door. Thankfully the room was spacious. She paced. Somehow she needed to avoid Charles. After several deep breaths and a check at her woeful expression in the mirror, she deemed herself ready for the onslaught once more.

She slipped from the room, when the coast appeared clear, and continued down the opposite end of the hallway, coming instead to the library which then led to the stairwell. The string quartet started up another selection. Cora took the opportunity to pass through the door and hurry outside.

Cora wandered toward the driveway, away from the impromptu dance floor, glancing about for the nosey, intrusive Charles. Carriages lined the space three across and overflowed out into the street. She pressed her hand to her heart. As exhilarating as it was to be whisked from one partner to another and gentlemen showing an inordinate amount of interest in her, she needed a moment to collect herself.

Going upstairs to her room was out of the question. All eyes would witness her escape. Including Charles. So she made her way toward the backyard. She glimpsed a group of party goers following a servant to inspect the pinery. To avoid any more new dance partners, Cora hunkered down, watching through a carriage window.

The group sashayed into the glassed-in arboretum, and Cora scurried for the carriage house. Inside was quiet and hushed. Ah.

Just the place. She treaded down the immaculate stable area, petting each animal and whispering a greeting, just to settle herself.

She spent longer with the goat, Shev. At least that is what she called her, since Cora couldn't seem to catch the French phrasing of her name. The young spotted nanny hunted for treats in her pockets and bleated in frustration when none appeared.

"Hush, silly thing. I'm a debutante tonight. I have no time for goat snacks. I don't even have pockets." She gave a small giggle and shoved the eager animal back into its stall. La Chèvre danced on her back legs, resting her front hooves on the top of the door, bleating in disapproval at being left.

Cora tiptoed to the hen house, hoping to hush the stubborn little goat by disappearing. But the place was locked up tight. No stray hens to grace the house tonight. Poor La Poulette.

Voices echoed to her, louder now. The group touring the pinery must be returning to the house. Cora stayed hidden away and then slipped behind the building.

She took a deep breath and settled against the back of the carriage house. This was no good. Was she embracing all life had for her this night? No. Even Abel would be ashamed of her hiding in the darkness, frittering away her night of her own debutante cotillion.

Still, being back home amongst familiar surroundings and people would be preferred. Yearned for, actually. She swung around the building and made her way up the driveway. A shadowed gentleman made his way towards her. Oh, no. Not Charles. But the man had seen her, so ditching him again was out of the question. She sighed and treaded closer. She might as well accept the evening for what it was.

Moonlight slipped through the trees, illuminating the man's features. Her breath caught. It wasn't Charles at all. She gave a soft coo of surprise and rushed towards the figure. A shaft of light illuminated that charming smile as it curved upward, those eyes deep in the night.

With a gasp, she whispered his name. "Trigg?"

Chapter Twenty-Two

Trigg's grin widened. "Am I late?"

She took a full inhale. Glory hallelujah, hiding in the barn didn't sound as tempting as it had earlier. "Maybe a little. But I don't mind."

His gaze swept over her. "Bet your dance card is full up already."

A giggle popped from her as she handed it to him. With a twist of his lips and a sparkle to his eye, he slipped it in his back pocket. "Shame you lost it. Guess I'll have to fill in."

"I don't think I mind a bit." Her eyes raked his form dressed in solid black evening wear. He'd never looked so handsome. "You look very nice."

A chuckle broke from him. He yanked the sleeves of his suit coat. "I'm sure I don't measure up to the high society, but at least I tried.

With a brazen flair she fingered his lapel and then pressed it into place. "I wouldn't have minded if you'd shown up in your work clothes. Oh, I should have asked. Did you find your sister?"

He nodded. "I did. Married."

Her mouth popped open. "How is that possible?"

The music paused for a moment before another slow tempo began. He took her hand in his. "I guess when you find the one, there's no need to waste time."

Cora's breath snagged at the husky tone in his voice.

"I've missed you." Trigg pressed a kiss to her hand.

A short satisfied sigh broke from her lips. "Oh?"

He stroked her cheek with his fingers, his face closing in on hers. "I thought maybe I'd never see you again."

His carefree smile faded, but a deep fervor flared in his eyes. "And now that you're here, I'm not sure I'll do things proper."

His words didn't really register. Her eyes shifted from his lips to his eyes. Ever so gently, his mouth brushed hers. She clenched his hand, breathless for want of more.

"Trigg?"

"Cora?"

"Could you kiss me proper?"

In a wink his lips met hers again. Not in some breathy brush, but in a deep soul-searching question. Cora lifted her hands, ran them up his lapels to the back of his neck. The warmth there cascaded through her fingers caressing the hair at his nape. Inwardly she soared. Never had she felt so alive, so wanted. His hands slipped to her back and drew her nearer, sculpting the curve of her back to his shape.

She could feel reality slipping away, losing control. With a gasp she drew back and broke the bonds of his embrace. Trigg's face looked as stunned as she felt. For a moment she just stood and breathed. "I…think we should stop."

Trigg took a hesitant step forward. "I probably should apologize, but…I can't. I want to court you, Cora Taggart. And when I get back to New Albany, I'm going to speak to your father about it."

With a blink she stepped forward. "Truly?"

A slow grin slinked across his face. "Truly. If you'll have me."

She stepped closer and took his big hand in both of hers. "I would like that very much."

"Perhaps, for the safety of your reputation, we should join the festivities?" He winked and pressed her hand into the crook of his elbow.

She tilted her chin just a touch to gaze at him as he guided her through the parked carriages. Her insides still shuddered with the passion of the kiss. Just being with him, on his arm, sent a buzz of excitement through her. She understood what Odette must have felt that day in the piano shop.

Around the corner, the dance floor appeared, lit by dozens of candles under the stars, music floating up from the suited players. People milled about in a slow waltz. It struck her as the loveliest place she'd ever been. And suddenly, she wanted to be nowhere else but here, on Trigg's arm.

He leaned toward her ear. "I'll warn you up front. I'm not much of a dancer."

Dizzy with delight, she managed a soft grin and whispered back, "Me neither."

Yet with sure hands he laid his right hand to her waist and clasped her hand with his left. Their eyes connected, their bodies swaying and whirling. So much promise rested there in his eyes she could barely breathe.

و~

Trigg couldn't take his eyes from the green flames of Cora's gaze. It took a great deal of control not to hurry her from the dance floor to revisit that kiss. Her lithe body drifted with his lead, not too close, yet too far away. He longed to draw her near, press against her, outline her body with his one more time.

But he knew he needed to tend things correctly. She would be under her aunt and uncle's care, and he had no wish to upset his future plans of sparking with her. It would take some patience, and some travel. Bliss and Roe would help at the farm until he could make Cora his own.

At the close of the song, a bell sounded from inside. The dancers around them meandered to the front door and the large open windows. Reluctantly, he drew his escort with the flow, even though he could barely pull his eyes from her face.

Inside, a woman stood on the stair landing. She wore the most comical hat with a pineapple smack dab in the center. The same fruit danced across the woman's entire dress. In her hands she cradled a real pineapple, ripened to a golden hue. Next to her stood a rotund balding man with an incredibly apathetic look upon his face. However, the woman's face flushed, her eyes sparkling in glee. Could this pair be Cora's aunt and uncle?

"Welcome one and all." The woman in the ridiculous hat raised her hands. "As you all know, it is a wondrous night of celebration which my husband and I wish to make an annual tradition. The Glenridge Pineapple Cotillion."

A smattering of applause circulated the crowded room. A familiar superfluous stream of laughter drew his gaze to two women near the fireplace. The exact pair he and Cora had played cat and mouse with on the steamer. He blinked and leaned into his companion. "Is that—"

A giggle met his ears. "Unfortunately yes. But we are skilled in dodging, aren't we?"

A rumble lit his chest. "Absolutely."

It was only then than he noticed the tiny green pineapples that dotted his lovely companion's dress. Wasn't this Cora's debutante event? Questions bubbled, yet died a quick death as the woman in the hat continued her speech.

"The Glenridge Pinery knows no equals to it distinguished design and efficiency. And we, of course, choose the most precious soil to propagate the most delectable and heavenly fruit known to man. We've seen great success in past years. But, I am proud to

272

announce that we have produced a record amount of this fruit this year. You might say, we've been fruitful."

Here the woman paused and chuckles circled the room.

"When you taste it, you'll agree that it is indeed a delicacy like no other. And our dear friends and acquaints, we wish to share our abundance of this amazing fruit with all of you. People of St. Louis and beyond, we give you—the pineapple. Lyon, bring the trays!"

Trigg peeked through the last window, having the advantage of his height, and saw at least a dozen servants entering from the far side of the vast rooms. Silver trays with small chunks of yellow fruit covered the surface. Dainty silver forks stood erect from each hunk of fruit.

A servant soon circumvented the porch area and both Cora and he grasped a fork from the serving tray. Cora grinned and tapped his fruit with hers in a salute. Chuckling with her, he popped the morsel into his mouth. Indeed, the juicy sweetness rivaled no other he'd ever had.

"Delicious." Cora exclaimed, eyebrows rising in surprise.

He nodded.

People drifted about, and the quartet began a low tune.

"Come. You should meet my family."

Cora tugged his hand along behind her through the door as it cleared. The couple on the landing had disappeared, but his companion wove her way through the dancing crowd until she met up with her cousin on Wilkinson's arm.

"You remember my cousin, Odette? And of course, Wilkinson."

Trigg nodded and shook Wilkinson's hand. "Good to see you again."

"Nice to see you were able to attend, Mr. Gentry." Odette smiled, flinging up a brow and a sly glance at Cora. "I'm sure my cousin is thrilled you are here."

Cora's face took on a pink hue and she shot Odette a look. "I was going to introduce him to Aunt Josephine and Uncle Calvin."

"I believe Mother stepped into the library with Father. She's concerned there isn't enough pineapple." Odette rolled her eyes. "Pineapples will be the death of me yet."

Cora giggled and motioned Trigg to follow her. She threaded through the crowd to a back hallway, dim without the candlelight. At the end of the long hall she opened the door into a spacious library, lit only by the light of the moon.

"Oh, dear. I guess they've already left." She spun with a stumble and found herself back in Trigg's arms. Echoes of the party rumbled about them. "Oh."

Trigg grinned, tightening his grip. "Don't worry your pretty head about it. I don't mind."

Pretty? He thought her pretty? Even if she were, how did that detract from all of her other unsavory qualities? She stared at him, mouth parted in wonder. He was so handsome and debonair, with that teasing half-smile on his face. The fire in his eyes.

Finally, her doubts came blurting out. "But…why, Trigg? You heard Widow Dixon's words. I'm considered a misfit. I'm too tall, an old maid, and I like playing baseball—"

"You also use gentleman's horses for desks, drop heirloom bookmarks, and you sputter like an angry hen when you feel you've been wronged—"

Cora threw her hands wide. "Then why?"

Trigg stepped closer in the shadowy room. "Because I can't look away from your green eyes. You're feisty, practical, and I love your sense of humor. And I can't stop thinking what you'd look like with your blonde hair down. And what it would be like if your last name were Gentry."

Her gasp made him chuckle.

She pulled her hands from him and stepped away, splaying her hands at her throat. Then, she whirled to pace as the moonlight followed her lithe movements.

"Maybe I shouldn't have alluded to that last part. Just yet."

Cora paused her anxious movements and froze. "Father said when I return, I'm to consider a local man."

Now that wasn't welcomed. "Is that right?"

She nodded, fussing with the shining curls at the nape of her neck. "Yes. Not because I want to. But because he needs a wife and I'm nineteen. That's old to have never been married, don't you think?"

"I think I want to know what your opinion is of this fella." He advanced slowly.

"Well, he wants someone for his children and—"

He turned her toward him and ran his hands down her arms, causing her to look up. "No, Cora. Not what he wants. What do you want?"

Their breaths intermingled. The wafting scent of roses intermixed with her skin made him almost forget his question. Surely, it was hard to keep his hands off her.

"I...want to marry for love."

A smile danced at the corner of his lips. He smoothed a stray hair behind her ear, and she closed her eyes for just a moment. "Do you love him?"

"No."

Trigg's smile widened. "Do you think you could love—"

"Help! Help!" The screaming voice halted all conversation.

Cora pulled from him and hurried to the door. Trigg trailed right on her heels. Up on the stairway landing now, Trigg could see several people making a circle around a portly gray-haired lady in the center of the parlor. Horror spread across her chubby face as her fingers fumbled about her neck.

"I've been robbed, I say. My diamond necklace is gone."

"Halt the music."

Trigg could only gather this heavy-set man was Uncle Calvin. "Anyone see any jewels lying about?"

Another squeal lit the room. A thin middle-aged woman rubbed her neckline. "My pearls. They're missing as well."

"Everyone check. They could have fallen."

The woman in the pineapple hat grew pale as she approached the mantel. "My golden pineapple. It's not here. Calvin, the golden pineapple is gone!"

Screams suddenly erupted on the far side of the room. Flames from an overturned candle lit the silky tablecloth and licked its way up the wall, scorching the velvet pineapple imprints as it climbed.

Chaos ensued. Servants rushed to the kitchen, the cotillion guests rushed for the open door and the wide windows. A bucket brigade started with Uncle Calvin at the forefront. Cora clutched at Trigg's suitcoat.

"Let's get you out." He gathered her to him and wedged his way through the crowd. As they pushed through, a large figure disappeared into the crush of carriages. A very familiar figure usually dressed in a buffalo skin. *Bo.*

Trigg hurried Cora across the front lawn to the edge of the street near the wrought iron fence where many stood, mostly women. His eyes strained to see up the street where he suspected Bo would go. He leaned down and pecked Cora's cheek.

"Listen to me, Cora. I have to leave."

"What?" Her startled, frightened eyes nearly undid him.

"I must. I may have—"

"Cora!" Odette rushed toward them and embraced her, sobbing.

He rubbed Cora's back to catch her eyes. "I'll be back."

Trigg wasted no time locating his horse near the carriage house, and dodging the exiting vehicles, he turned his horse toward the street.

Cora stared at the man's face so close to her own and gave a small sigh. "I've already told you several times. Trigg Gentry is not a thief."

The small-built lieutenant from the St. Louis Department of Police straightened, checked his pocket timepiece, and looked across the bright library at her uncle. Even with the windows cracked, any breeze had little effect on the summer heat. Even as early in the morning as it was. The four other officers in the room stirred restlessly. The acrid smell of smoke still hung heavily in the air despite the door being sealed.

Uncle Calvin stepped out from behind his large mahogany desk, fastened his hands behind his back, and strolled toward her chair. "You must understand the urgency of these questions, Cora. This thief not only escaped with handfuls of expensive jewelry, but my safe was completely emptied as well."

He swiped a handkerchief across his forehead and she nodded, chewing her lip.

Another officer scanned a notepad. "It appears, after a full investigation, that this Mr. Gentry didn't act alone. We believe one diverted the crowd's attention while the other or perhaps two others, ransacked the house safe."

The tall lieutenant with the handlebar mustache shot an ominous glare at the officer, obviously sub-ranked by his attire. And his leaking of information. Information that couldn't possibly be true. Trigg couldn't have used her as a diversion in such a scheme. Could...he?

"We only need a means to detain him, Miss Taggart. He was the only one of the invited guests who arrived unannounced without an invitation. Therefore, he is our prime suspect."

Frustration and fear mingled in her chest. "But I told you. My cousin and I did extend an invitation."

What more could she say? She'd told them everything she knew multiple times, her faith in Trigg never wavering. He'd been so sincere. So trustworthy. And with her the whole time.

Yet, she wanted to ask the officers why they hadn't questioned Wilkinson or Odette. True, he'd possessed his invitation while Trigg had come without his. Still, he hadn't been among the people her aunt had initially invited. For the first time since leaving home, she wished Aleena were here. She would know how to handle this difficult situation.

"Very well, Miss Taggart. We will be in touch if we have any more questions." Lieutenant Mobly nodded.

She nodded and rose from the stiff chair near the fireplace and made her way through the sea of officers. Now what? Cora pinched the door closed on her thoughts. The smell jumped out stronger here. She wove her way to the left instead of heading for the servants' stairway, now, the temporary household stairway. Through the dining area, a boarded-up barrier hid the damage of the fire. The smell of smoke hung thickly in the air.

But Cora knew what it looked like without seeing it. Horrible black burn marks ran up the far corner and across the ceiling. The material burned very quickly. By some miracle the servants and men had managed to pull the ceiling cloth down and douse the walls with buckets of water. And while the structure had been saved, Aunt Josephine had collapsed, confined to her bed. It hadn't helped when the whole fiasco had hit the papers the next day. Fire. Robbery. Embarrassment.

And she? She would pack and hop a steamer for home on her uncle's recommendation. Hoping for a chance to hear Trigg's explanation would not happen.

For despite his promise, he had not come back.

Chapter Twenty-Three

Well, it was over. Her grand adventure. The return steamer journey had been a grim three days. A trip she couldn't help but compare to the one she'd enjoyed with Trigg at her side. The glaring, painful, and very obvious difference brought moisture to her eyes. But, at least the first leg of her journey home was over.

Cora rubbed her fingers across the bookmark in her sleeve as she waited for the luggage to be loaded on the Concord stagecoach. She'd read the words of her grandmother over and over. They offered a snippet of comfort.

"No, no, my good man. I'll be carrying this duffle myself."

A rather thick gentleman with graying hair patted the brown case as the lads threw the luggage up to be strapped to the stagecoach roof. Cora turned away. What had once been an exciting adventure on the crowded carriage only loomed as a long harsh day to Miles's house. Dunkirk stood by to make sure she got properly loaded but would not be accompanying her. Bartholomew would be floored that she'd traveled the last section of this journey alone. Not even imagining the outraged look on her brother's staid face cheered her.

What did she expect? Every thought and feeling had a funeral pall to it since the fire. Since Trigg had kissed her. And disappeared. Now, she would go home and marry Heaker Thomas and raise his children. In a loveless marriage.

"Thank you, Mr. Dunkirk. For all you've done."

The man merely bobbed a slight nod, perhaps a glimmer of regret in his eye.

Cora blinked back the grinding disappointment and boarded first, heading to the back window seat. At least she could get some air as well a day's supply of dust. The man with the duffle settled in front of her. The rest of the passengers crammed every cranny, and she waved briefly at Dunkirk as the stagecoach jerked forward.

Four hours of dust later, they made their stop at *Log Inn* to take on fresh horses and to allow the passengers to eat. Cora sat with an older couple and resisted their desire to chat. Although the food was good, she was exhausted. Now going on two weeks since the cotillion, she hadn't managed a full night's sleep since.

Once loaded back inside the stagecoach, Cora set her head against the padding of the stagecoach wall. Bartholomew would have plenty to say about napping in public. Yet, her eyes couldn't stay open. Lack of sleep and a full stomach soon had her drifting into a fitful sleep.

Gunfire and the tipping stagecoach startled her from sleep. Passengers clutched the frame of the vehicle with panic written plainly on their faces.

Cora wiped the grime from her eyes. "What's happening?"

The elder woman next to her gripped her hand. "We're being chased."

Another sound of gunfire had all of them ducking their heads. Cora peeked out her window and saw three men on horseback coming full speed. The woman beside her pulled her to the floor where they huddled in a mass of frantic passengers.

The stagecoach picked up speed until nothing but a roar peppered with gunshots filled Cora's ears. Then the entire vehicle tipped. Everyone screamed. Suddenly they were tumbling about the cabin, at last stopping on its side. Cora moaned, having a heavy body on top of her and wiggling people below her.

The silence was deafening. The coach tipped slowly up and then crashed back onto its four wheels. Cora slammed against the far wall near her seat. The passengers groaned and attempted to regain their seats.

A huge whiskered head poked in, sporting a rifle. "Everyone. Get out."

Quiet gasps followed as the nine passengers lumbered from the aging Concord. Cora, the last to disembark, tailed the older couple. Everyone lined up along the stagecoach facing the three men. Wearing a thick buffalo skin, the biggest man, a riotous dark beard peaking around his mask, aimed his gun at the gentleman with the duffle. Cora gasped. Even with half his face concealed, she recognized the outlaw. It was the same man who'd accompanied Trigg on the steamer.

"Turn that over to my men." He jerked his head for one of his men to snatch it away.

"Oh, dear, no. I do believe this is quite inappropriate. I protest, sir. In every way. 'Tis robbery—"

The well-dressed man stepped forward to battle for his small leather case. A tussle ensued between him and a smaller, masked member of the gang. Everyone else shrank back

The bearded man barked. "Get out of the way, Oates."

The men parted and a deafening blast felled the protesting man, who slid to the ground, gasping and bleeding against the coach.

"Run!" was all Cora heard and her quivering legs obeyed.

She ducked around the back of the coach and headed for the trees. The older couple moved faster than she ever thought they could and ducked behind a thicket of overgrown bushes.

Cora kept running. To where, she had no clue. Gunshots sounded behind her and she froze. She'd gone so far that the area was fully shaded. Where to hide? What to do?

Roy had shimmied up Mama's apple tree. Yes. A tree. A huge maple stood center from her with a branch so low, a tall girl could shimmy up with little difficulty. Cora raced for the branch, hearing footsteps thumping ever closer. With a leap she grasped the large limb and scampered her booted feet up the bark. Fear pushed her on, climbing higher and higher.

Nearing the top, the thick middle branch thinned and Cora could feel the movements and the creak of the tree as a light breeze rippled through the leaves.

She clutched the center branch, standing upright on another below. Glancing down, she could only see the ground in a few spots. But what she did see scared the beejeebers out of her. Her grandmother's bookmark lay at the base of the maple, marking her spot as clear as day.

She closed her eyes and pressed her face against the ripples of the gray trunk. They would find her. Like Hansel and Gretel she'd marked her spot. Her blasted irresponsibility would be her undoing.

A creak of saddle leather froze her. Trying to control her breathing, the smell of bark in her nose, she glanced down. A familiar head stood right below the tree blocking the bookmark. The face turned up until he linked eyes with her.

Trigg!

As quick as a glance, he moved away from the trunk. Gruff voices drifted up. The plethora of summer leaves filtered every other word. She strained to hear.

"—looking for you—know what's—gunshots from—"

Trigg's voice. Then the voice she'd heard from the bearded man tightened her muscles.

"—doing my job—you—a man with a—"

The voices drifted away and Cora sucked air into her lungs. Had Trigg led the man away? The same man that had interrupted her midnight chat with Trigg on the St. Louis steamer? Did Trigg know this man? Worse yet, was he involved with him?

Cora pondered these to avoid thinking of her current circumstances. But after clinging to the tree for a good twenty minutes without being found, she knew she would have to climb back down. A treacherous thought as shock had stove up her limbs.

As quietly and carefully as possible, she slid her way down the maple. With one last jump, she fell to her knees on the ground with a grunt. Her head whipped around, but no one seemed near. She stood, searching for her bookmark. But it was gone.

Brushing the dirt from her navy skirt, she pondered what to do next. A lone rider came through the trees at a rush. Cora gasped and slid behind the large trunk. She was caught now.

A soft voice carried through the woods. "Cora."

Trigg. She peeked around the trunk, ready to scurry away. But it was him, alone, and she wanted to collapse in relief. He rode next to her on his splotched horse and dismounted.

"Come on," he grabbed her hand and tugged her forward. Without explanation he plopped her on his horse. Then he swung up behind her. His arms encircled her, and he grabbed the reins with one hand.

She swiveled her head. "What's going on, Trigg?"

"I'm taking you home."

"But a man's been shot."

He kicked the painted pony and it shot off. Trigg put his lips near her ear. "I need to get you out of here."

"But where have you been?" Her words left her as an offering to the wind, for Trigg kicked his mount into a gallop. He leaned against her to keep them both seated, one firm arm around her middle.

At last they slowed as they neared town.

"Which way to your house?"

"Past town, north." When he hesitated, she pointed the way. The pace stayed steady until she recognized Miles's fields. "We're almost there."

Trigg stopped on the side of the road and dismounted. He wove to the edge of the woods and entered.

Enough silence. "Trigg, we have to talk."

But he neither acknowledged or slowed.

"Trigg."

With a deep sigh, he stopped and turned. "I need to get you to a safe place."

"My brother's house is right through that field."

He approached and lifted her down.

She shoved from him. "What just happened, Trigg Gentry? I want some answers and I want to know now."

He shook his head. "I can't really explain because I don't know myself."

Cora poked him with her finger. "You told me you would return to my aunt's house in St. Louis. And you never did."

The horse stomped as if aggravated with the volume of voices. Trigg put a hand to the back of his neck. "I know. I'm sorry, Cora. But when things went missing at your fancy shindig, I saw my brother leaving your aunt and uncle's house, a place he had no business being. I had to follow him. He might have been responsible for the missing jewelry."

Her mouth dropped open. "Your...brother?"

"Yes. The bearded guy. At the stagecoach."

She stepped back, hand to her heart. "Your brother shot that man with the duffle."

"Did you see it?"

"Yes, I saw it! I stood ten feet from it," she spat.

Her companion drew his hat off and rubbed a hand through his hair.

"And not only that, my uncle's safe was broken into the night of the cotillion. Everything was taken."

Silence stretched between them as Trigg fiddled with the saddle and fastened the saddlebags.

"That's it. You have nothing to say?"

"What is there to say? I'm not involved in this. But I think my brother is in deep."

The doubt she felt must have rippled across her face for he stepped nearer. "You've got to believe me, Cora."

"Then we should have notified to the authorities," she huffed, crossing her arms.

He shook his head. "No. My priority was to get you safely to your destination."

"But Trigg—"

He held up a hand. "You've got to trust me. I'm going to drop you off at the house and then I have to find Bo."

"What? Why?"

Trigg encircled her waist with his hands, ready to deposit her back in the saddle.

She gripped his hands. "Wait."

They stood, his hands on her waist and her hands on his. The intimacy came crashing through the shock of the previous hour and she stared deep and long into his blue eyes. When her voice came, it was hushed and broken. "Don't leave me, Trigg. Not like this."

He groaned and instead of lifting her to the saddle, he tugged her into his embrace. Tears licked at Cora's eyes. If he went back, he might be arrested. Or killed.

Trigg's breath sent quivering sensations down her neck. "I have to. For now."

"You didn't come back last time."

A hum from Trigg's mouth made her wish he would stay right where he was. "You didn't give me much time."

His hands roamed the curves of her back, and he drew away to gaze at her. "I will find you, Cora. Believe me. I'll get this all cleared up and I'll come for you."

He stepped back and pulled the treasured bookmark from his pocket. "Here. I found it under the tree."

Cora pressed his hand away. "No, you keep it. You can return it when you come back for me."

Trigg nodded, and stuffed the bit of cloth into the pocket of his brown cotton britches. "Deal. I'll get this all cleared up and I'll come for you."

A tear drifted down her cheek. "Promise?"

His arms pulled her close and tightened around her as his lips descended once more. It didn't make sense. All the unexplained events in the last two weeks. Her anger at him for not returning. It all disappeared when his mouth touched hers. A thousand dreams danced over her skin when he deepened the kiss, pulling her ever closer.

The kiss ended and he reached a hand up to stroke her cheek. "A promise sealed with a kiss. Cora Taggart, I'll be back, looking to make you my bride."

"I'm already yours."

Trigg lifted her to the horse, gazing at her. "I love you, Cora."

A gasp leaped from her breast. "I think I must love you, too. I can barely stand the thought of you leaving. It's breaking my heart."

He mounted the horse behind her, wrapped his arms around her, and pressed a kiss to her neck.

"Don't worry. I'll be back as soon as I can."

Trigg nudged the horse forward and at the edge of the empty yard, he dismounted, gave Cora one last kiss, and then rode away.

He disappeared through the brush and she swiped her tear-stained face. How would she ever be able to wait, not knowing if Trigg's own brother had killed him in cold blood? With a sob she turned and rushed for the house.

Chapter Twenty-Four

Trigg settled around the small campfire just north of Evansville. Poor Buck was spent, and he didn't want to ruin his best horse. After trailing Bo for two weeks, he deserved some rest. Trigg grunted. So did he. He was bone-saddled tired.

Besides, he needed a few idle moments to think. His brother's trail had gone cold. Where would Bodine hole up? Had any of them been apprehended? After checking the robbery site, there was no hint besides a blood-stained puddle to direct him one way or another. And galloping in asking questions was foolhardy.

Bottom line, where would Bo go? What would he do if he were hiding? Trigg spat into the fire just to listen to the sizzle. He'd go somewhere comfortable. Somewhere where he knew the lay of the land like the back of his hand. That way his stalkers would be at a disadvantage. Then it hit him.

Home.

That's where Bo would go. He hadn't been home in years, but it hadn't changed in the years he'd been gone. He knew the area. Free food. Free lodging. Bliss and Roe would be so glad to see him on the onset. They wouldn't be curious enough to ask if he was running from the law.

Bliss and Roe.

His thoughts stuttered to a stop. How far would Bo go to protect himself? Would his brother place his own siblings in danger? As much as he wanted to believe Bodine would never do that, Trigg had to be realistic. It was a very real possibility. So, tonight, he'd rest. Tomorrow, he'd run Buck into the ground to protect Bliss and Roe.

Trigg stood and scraped dirt over the flames. He couldn't afford to be detected by a curious passerby in the area. There was too much at stake. He checked on his mount and rolled out the bedroll.

But, armed with a plan and tucked in for the night didn't halt Trigg's ruminations. Bo had hidden his surprise well at Trigg's appearance when he'd shown up under Cora's hiding tree. But there had been something troubling in his brother's eyes.

Guilt? Yes, perhaps. Danger? Most likely. Hadn't there been earlier signs Bo had left the rails? Trigg had always had his doubts. Bo claiming to be a bounty hunter had smacked false. One would have to have some sort of moral spine to be able to apprehend hardened criminals on the run. His brother seemed to lack a set of good principles even as a young child. He seemed determined to discover how many ways he could put a hurt on Trigg without exposing himself.

How long had this thievery been going on? Sure, his activity at the track seemed shady. But weren't most of the folks pressed around that track greedily lusting after a way to earn money the quick and easy way?

But there had been more. Departing from the Evansville steamer had brought the authorities because of a theft. The same at St. Louis. A ruckus had ensued which had brought in the officers. He sat up. Exactly how deep was Bo in this lifestyle? And hadn't Cora told him he'd shot a man point blank?

He pulled the bookmark from his pocket and rubbed it between his fingers. His good luck piece. No. Cora's promise token of his return. And he must return, for his future lay with Cora. His true love. His life.

"Dear God, protect me. Help me do what needs doing," he breathed the prayer as he poked the talisman into his pocket.

A thorn tore the tender skin on Cora's thumb. She pressed the bloody spot to her mouth and tears bit her eyes. The scrubby last picking of the heat-weary blackberry bush wasn't worth it anyway. Nothing but an attempt to escape the confines of the house.

Her belongings had arrived shortly after her return, via a small detachment of deputies. And they had plenty of questions. Which brought on even more outraged questions from Bartholomew and concerned glances from Miles and Beulah.

Whether the heat of the altercation or the actual August heat had brought on the stifling atmosphere in the house, Cora couldn't tell. She suspected both. So she'd confined herself to outside chores. Like picking late berries that weren't worth the time.

"Cora."

She turned. Miles loped along the cornfield toward her. Cora set her bucket down and pressed a hanky to her thumb.

Miles, tall, tanned, and blond as the sun from working outside all summer, pulled a wry grin as he approached. "Hiding are we?"

A grin tugged at her own cheek. "Honestly?"

Her favorite brother stopped in front of her and crossed his arms. "Cora, haven't we always been?"

She shrugged and grabbed up her bucket.

"Come on." He waved her over to a nearby copse of trees and stomped down the tall weeds surrounding a huge tulip tree growing gleefully straight towards the sun. Miles indicated the flat spot. "Sit."

They sat in silence for a few moments. It fed Cora's bruised soul. She leaned back against the lumpy bark. But the quiet didn't last long enough.

"Thorn poke you?"

"Yep."

A chuckle came from her brother. "Aleena wouldn't approve of that word."

Cora merely blinked. She was past caring.

"You love him, don't you? This Trigg Gentry."

She sighed. He hadn't wasted any time. "Yes."

"My. A yes with a sigh. You've got it bad." He paused a moment to cross his big booted feet. "You worried about this robbery thing?"

"I'm afraid for Trigg."

He nodded and then pointed. "Look, a bluebird."

How prophetic. Blue described her emotions perfectly. The quick little bird paused only a moment on a nearby branch. Then darted away. Just like her joy of discovering love. Here one day and gone the next. Now her love-sick heart drooped in sorrow.

"Did you read the newspaper? The man shot at the stagecoach died. They trailed the shooter and captured one of the thieves. Apparently injured and not expected to recover. I guess a stagecoach passenger had leaped on one of them and knifed him."

Cora appreciated the update. In a way. Bartholomew had been hiding the *Daily Clarion* in hopes of keeping Cora protected from the current news. Overhearing gossip at church, however, was impossible to block totally.

"The shooter is Trigg's brother. I'm not sure that helps his cause of innocence."

Miles grunted his assent. "True. Yet sometimes brothers fight worse than anyone."

Her hope plummeted to a new low. What would happen when Trigg caught up with his evil brother?

"But hey, I'm sure that's not the case for Trigg."

He must have realized the impact of his words and wanted to retract them. A sniff escaped Cora, and Miles handed her his clean handkerchief. His big arm surrounded her shoulders and pulled her to him. "Aw, Cora. I didn't mean to worry you."

"No, it's okay. He promised he'd come back. I just need to wait."

He pulled her into his arms and whispered in her ear. "And trust. And hope."

She nodded against his shirt. Yes. God, she needed the last one most of all. What Cora Hope Taggart needed most was divine hope.

The smell of Bliss's fried chicken tickled his nose as he pressed into the back of the barn. Even at this distance, the aroma found its way into the outer building. Thankfully the structure was empty. None of the mules would give him away with their noisy affection. Two extra horses in the corral told him two extra someones occupied the house. On closer inspection, he recognized Bo's bay horse and Oates's black. Burr must have been the one who'd been injured and captured. Word circulated that he most likely would not survive.

He was home. But not comfortable. He'd like nothing better than to belly up to Bliss's chicken and greet his brothers. A bit of a homecoming, it was. But he couldn't chance it. Bo wasn't just family. He was a criminal.

Buck, ground tied, chomped grass about a half mile back. Probably a foolish decision, because there would be no quick getaway unless he jumped on one of his breeding mares. And he wasn't going to leave Bliss and Roe alone.

Speak of the devil, Bliss, dressed in sunny yellow, stepped out the back door, her purpose-driven step aimed toward the hand pump. How to get her attention without letting everyone know he was here was the trick. He watched her pump a bucket full of fresh water which made his throat ache. Sure would taste good after the stale canteen liquid. She stood and pressed her hands to her back, looking out toward the corrals of mules. Now or never.

He kept his eye on her through the crack of the door and pushed. If he remembered right, yep, right about now. The blamed rusted hinge let out a loud squeak. Right on time. Bliss' hands fell to her side. He pushed it again. His sister looked toward the house first before setting out hesitantly toward the barn.

One last push caused her step to falter. Great. One too many. Now she was spooked. He glanced through the crack at the house. He'd have to be more obvious. He tugged his hat from his head and poked it out the door and quickly back in.

Bliss glanced back once, still hesitating. *Please Bliss. Don't go to the house.* Finally she tread closer.

"Hello? Is anyone there?"

There was no way she'd continue to the barn without knowing it was safe. He'd have to risk it. He stuck his head out, finger to his mouth, and then motioned her towards him. With quick feet she hurried closer and slid through the crack.

"Trigg! You're back. Bo and—"

He pressed a hand to her mouth. "Shhhh. I know. I'm trailing them."

Puzzlement rippled across her forehead. "Why? I mean the Oates guy is kind of unnerving, but..."

"Bo's big trouble."

In the dim of the barn, her blue eyes grew round. "What do you mean?"

"Robbery, murder."

The bucket dropped. Her gasp coupled with her hands that flew to her mouth told Trigg Bo hadn't had a good old heart-to-heart chat with them. Not even close.

"Murder? How can this be? He's our brother."

Trigg shrugged. "All I know is, we have to help the authorities round them up. Last I heard, they had few leads. Burr might spill the beans, but I doubt it. I think they're in pretty deep."

"Burr?"

"Bo had two buddies. One was captured. I guess he was knifed, and they caught up with him. I figure he's in jail or busy dying. Bo don't mind sacrificing him as long as his gizzard is safe."

Bliss stood for a few minutes before her face opened in realization. "You mean that stagecoach robbery north of Evansville?"

Trigg nodded. "The same."

His sister pressed a hand to her breast and paced away, trying to absorb. Then she spun. "What are we going to do?"

Trigg bent and took a double handful of water from Bliss's abandoned bucket and drank. Then he swiped his mouth. "I need you to get Roe to the barn. Don't let anyone know I'm here. Then, excuse yourself. The two of you go to the sheriff's department. I'll stay here and keep them treed."

Bliss shook her head with vigor. "I won't leave you. Bo will be suspicious if we both disappear. And you might need me."

Like a hole in the head. Trigg let a rush of breath escape. She did have a point, though. The both of them disappearing would signal Bo that something was up.

"Fine. We'll send Roe. Make some excuse. Some plausible excuse. Now, tell me where they are and what they've been doing."

Bliss whispered the day's activities of Bo and Oates until Trigg finally pushed her toward the door. He thrust the bucket in her hand. She'd already been gone way too long.

"Fine. Get back. Act normal. Somehow alert Roe I'm here and send him out."

She nodded and slipped through the door.

Thirty minutes later Roe appeared in the barn. Trigg slid out of his hiding spot in the corn crib. After the briefest of hugs and whispered concerns and plans, Roe caught their best mare and trotted off for town.

Trigg checked his gun and gathered rope. Now to sneak into the house.

❧

Sallie pitched a heavy stick into the sluggish Patoka River. Cora clutched Wiley to herself and kept a firm grip on Bess's hand to keep them away from the water's edge. The river had grown low in the dry summer heat. Soon September would come and the days would grow mellower. She looked forward to it. That and... Cora pressed a cheek to Wiley's blond head. Thinking about Trigg would only make her sad.

"Good job, Sallie. Now, let's settle over here and have a little snack."

The child came obediently, her face radiant from being able to traipse through the countryside. Bartholomew and Eleanor had borrowed Miles's wagon to look for a house near Princeton. Thus the child had been left in Cora's care. As always. Cora had become the permanent nursemaid. And if Trigg never returned, her father would marry her off to old Mr. Thomas to continue her nursemaid duties.

Bartholomew had announced he'd decided to put down roots and work as an accountant. This new excitement had done a lot to squash the shock of the tumultuous robbery scene and Cora's lone arrival at the house.

Still, she knew once everything settled and Bartholomew opened his business near the Princeton Courthouse on Main, talk would resume. Then she'd be on her way home. Where Trigg could not find her. A place where Father would insist she give Heaker Thomas a chance to court and marry her.

She set little Wiley down and encouraged the girls to sit on some squashed dried foxtails. From her bulging pockets she pulled out apples, and three sets of eager hands reached for the sweet treat. She stretched her legs out long and fanned her skirt out. After the long walk the children seemed content to work their young teeth into the firm apples and yank at the grass around them. Wiley drooled more than he accomplished any bites. Cora smiled and wiped away the mess with her hanky.

Quick stomping steps brought Cora to her feet. Miles appeared, a strained, but hopeful look on his face.

"We've got to get the kids back." Her brother gave a hesitant grin. "It's Beulah's time. The baby's coming."

Chapter Twenty-Five

I wait for the Lord, My soul doth wait, and in his word do I hope.

Cora's bookmark verse hammered Trigg's brain as he flattened against the back of the house. Through the bedroom window, he could just make out voices. From the volume, it indicated they were still finishing Bliss's fried chicken. Trigg's stomach growled audibly as if the mere smell had angered it. The hardtack and jerky had been too long ago and too meager.

He ignored the belly pangs and gritted his teeth. One good jump would plant his hungry stomach on the window sill. The trick was to make it a silent leap. More difficult than it sounded.

Trigg laid his rifle and rope inside the window just to the right. Then, slowly he elevated his body with his arms on the sill and negotiated his head into the opening. Smothering a grunt he wiggled the rest of his body inside.

His parents' room. Bed made, dusted as if Pa would return any moment. The door hung open to aid in ventilating the hot August air out of the house. Now to remember the trail of loose squeaky boards. That would have Bo and Oates on high alert by the time he stepped into the kitchen.

He navigated with caution, reaching the doorway. A loud snap indicated someone had left the house. He pulled up his rifle.

Bliss appeared, eyes widening at the barrel of his gun.

Trigg yanked it down. "What are you doing?"

"They just walked out."

He strode through the parlor into the kitchen. "Why'd you let them go, Bliss?"

She pulled on his arm before he could follow. "Don't, Trigg. It's two against one. The authorities will be here soon. It'll be much better odds.

He shook her off. "Don't you know how serious this is? I need to detain them."

Bliss clutched at him. "No. Bo is loaded for bear. All gruff and twitchy. He's sure to shoot first and ask questions later. At least wait and let them reach the trees. You can trail them more safely."

"You're not making sense. Are they leaving?"

She nodded. "Said they had more business to do."

"Business?" He set the safety back on his gun. Wait? She had a point. He could keep the element of surprise if he waited for them to disappear into the woods. He groaned when he saw the direction they took. West. Straight towards Buck.

"I can't stay, Bliss. They'll find my horse and then they'll know I'm here. We're all in danger if he thinks I'm out to capture him."

Trigg waited until the barn blocked his departure. Then he eased through the door. Looking back at Bliss he said, "I know it's hot. But lock the doors. Don't let Bo or Oates in. Promise me."

She nodded and he took off for the corral. Most of the mares had young donkey colts at their sides. Stirring up too much of a ruckus would garner Bo's attention. He decided to sideswipe the thought of getting a mount. He started running along the fence row hoping that would block his movements.

Winded, he made it to the woods. He could see Buck ahead in a small clearing. Perfect. He'd managed to avoid Bo. Trigg crept slowly and clutched the horse's reins. He closed his eyes in gratefulness and stroked the animal's neck. Now to follow Bo.

A metal click made Trigg's eyes pop open.

To his right his brother, still mounted, grinned. "So we meet again, little brother. Seems I can't shake you. But I ain't got time for games today, old Triggy."

Bo's rifle was aimed dead center. Trigg stepped out in the open and spread his arms. "Fine. You want to shoot down your own brother in cold blood. Go ahead. But you and me both know they're coming for you."

A laugh greeted him like gravel to the face. "That so?"

"You've been stealing all along, haven't you? Those steamer robberies. Then you grabbed the jewelry at that fancy party. Broke into the safe of Cora's uncle, too. You even shot that stagecoach passenger, didn't you?"

Bo mumbled and Oates dismounted. That couldn't be good. "Here's the deal, little brother. Oates is gonna tie you to that tree over there and we'll be on our way. I've tolerated you long enough. We've got some serious riding to do, and I don't need my little brother tagging along."

Trigg pulled the gun up and oscillated between the two men.

Bo dismounted. "Don't be stupid, kid. I don't want to kill you."

Trigg backed away. If he could get to the trees, he might escape. But Oates circled round behind, making it impossible to keep his eyes on both men. Buck whinnied and danced around.

"Put the gun down." Bo still advanced.

Suddenly a crack sounded and pain exploded in Trigg's shoulder. He hit the ground on his face, the agony taking his breath.

An expletive exploded from Bo. "You idjit. You done shot him."

"Didn't you hear him? The sheriff's on his way."

Trigg swam in and out of consciousness. He felt himself being pulled against the ground, a rough piece of cloth shoved in the bleeding hole at his shoulder. He cried out and banged his head on a tree trunk. His last conscious thought was of the two of them mounting and riding away.

Heat. Oppressive heat. Trigg ran his hand across the pain in his right shoulder, and white-hot stars flashed behind his eyelids. He sucked in a lungful of air to rouse himself, but it only stained the pain stars red. He groaned and flicked his eyes open. A circular metal object floated close to his face. A gun barrel.

"You are under arrest for robbery and murder."

He blinked and focused on the face behind the barrel. Sweat dripped down a shaky thin face. Older man. Fear live in his eyes.

"Get the gun outa my face before you blow it off," Trigg gritted. "Do I look like I'm fit to escape?"

The gun lowered which gave Trigg a glance of the other two young deputies, faces alight with morbid glee.

The oldest one, bewhiskered with one limp eye barked at his two companions, "Untie him, raise him up, get him on the horse."

Oh, this was not good. Before he prepared himself for the pain, they lifted him. A cry of anguish wrung from him. Everything misted into a haze. "Wait."

He must have gone unconscious for a moment as everything grew still. Trigg cracked his eyes open. "Where you taking me?"

"To jail, Compadre."

Trigg squeezed his eyes shut. "You do that, I'll be near dead before we get there."

That seemed to quiet his captors.

Then a grunt. "Get him on that horse."

So death. Trigg staggered between the two, wishing the one on the right would quit yanking up on his arm. They set his foot into the stirrup and shouldered him somewhere. By the time he'd fought his way out of unconsciousness, his face was planted in Buck's mane. Trigg turned his face and resisted the impulse to push himself up. He wasn't sure he could stay conscious if he did.

The next sane thought Trigg had he was lying in his parents' bed, blinking at the ceiling. The curtains were drawn, making the room dim. Someone moved about nearby.

"Trigg?" A woman's face appeared, pinched in worry. Bliss.

His sisters waking him from unconsciousness was becoming a habit.

"Doc's on his way. There's a deputy still here." Bliss pressed her lips together in a grimace. "They say you're under arrest."

He nodded, ignoring the dull pain in his shoulder. "This isn't exactly how I planned this."

"What are we going to do?"

His first impulse was to shrug, but he nixed that and closed his eyes instead. "Nothing. The law is involved now. I'm shot. Not much I can do."

Her eyes flicked toward the red handkerchief covering his wound. "How did it happen? Did Bo..."

"Naw. Although he did have me in his crosshairs. Oates shot me from behind."

Her gasp caught his attention. Poor Bliss. Always thought the best of folks.

"But why? Why would he do such a thing?"

Tiredness swept over him and his eyes grew heavy. "They're on the wrong side of the law, Bliss. They'll do anything to stay free."

Bliss nodded, tears shimmering in her eyes. She squeezed out a rag and laid it on his head. "Sleep now. You'll need your strength."

She sniffed and whispered, "I'll need your strength."

❦❧

Cora grimaced as Beulah's hand dug into her arm. Then, the contraction passed. Her sister-in-law's face went deathly pale between contractions as she gasped for air.

Dagum, where was Miles with the doctor? He'd left on a horse eons ago. The three children entertained themselves in the front yard which scared Cora to death. Hopefully, Sallie was old enough to keep the two younger ones out of trouble.

Cora slipped from the room to glance out the window. Yes, so far so good. Sallie had them ringing the rosie. She hurried back into the bedroom. Beulah went stiff as another contraction took hold of her. Cora hurried to her side.

Once it passed, a jingling sound caught Cora's attention. Someone had arrived. Thank God. Beulah's eyes drew to hers.

Cora gave what she hoped was an encouraging smile. "See? It must be the doctor."

Beulah's face relaxed a moment. "Good. Retta told me the second one would come fast."

But when Cora pulled the curtain to the side, it was only Bartholomew and Eleanor. Cora scurried toward the door. The wagon stopped near the house. Bartholomew first surveyed the children and then shot an accusatory glance toward her. But Cora beat him to the punch.

"I'm glad you're home. Beulah is having her baby. Bartholomew, watch the kids. Eleanor, come and help me."

Not waiting to see what her older brother thought of her commands, she rushed toward the sound of the low moan. Beulah, in mid-contraction. When she relaxed, Cora pressed a cup of cool water to her lips.

"Is the doctor here?"

Cora loathed to tell her the truth. "Not yet. It's Barth and Eleanor."

"You may have to deliver my baby, Cora. It's close."

Thunderation. She might have to deliver her new little niece or nephew. Cora adjusted the pillow under the small woman's body. At least she had Eleanor. She wouldn't have to deliver a baby alone. A small sound at the door drew her attention. Her sister-in-law stood there, pale as bread dough.

"Eleanor?

The woman spun and ran from the room.

Great, just great. "I'll be back."

At Beulah's nod she followed her sister-in-law's trail and found her seated on the porch steps, hugging herself. The children, oblivious to the situation, ran about the yard in joy. Cora put a hand to Eleanor's shoulder.

"I need you."

The woman clutched at the fabric at her throat. "I…can't."

Cora fixed a hand to her hip and scowled at her.

Her eyes went wide, her hands wringing. "It's blood and such. I've never had a strong stomach for it."

A sigh squeezed from Cora.

"But Bartholomew went to get the neighbor lady, Retta. She'll be of some help. And I'll watch the children. I'm sure the doctor won't be much…longer." Eleanor turned her head away.

Fine. Cora whispered a quick prayer. If she were Beulah's last line of defense, so be it. She stomped back into the house, set water to boil, and joined her sister-in-law for the appearance of her next niece or nephew.

Beulah's moan grew more pronounced. "Help me, Cora. It's coming."

And surely it was. Her sister-in-law's cries became more insistent as she clutched at the sheets. Cora tried to remember everything her brothers had done when new calves and foals had arrived. It couldn't be much different, right?

Cora slipped a thick sheet under Beulah. Soon the head bulged and slipped out. Cora grasped the tiny bloody head, waiting for Beulah to push again.

"The baby is almost here, Beulah. You can do it. Just a few more pushes."

The small woman seemed almost spent, gasping for air, drooping from exhaustion. But the contractions wouldn't slow now. Beulah bore down once more.

"Oh, dear, dear Lord, help me," Cora whispered. "Help Beulah."

With a small twist, the child's body fell into Cora's hands. Trying to still her trembling, she wiped off the small baby. As she rubbed, the child sucked in her first bit of air and then another.

"Is my baby girl well?" Beulah whispered.

A loud squall burst from the babe and her skin turned bright red, flailing her tiny limbs.

Cora giggled. "Oh, yes. She's perfect."

The doctor shuffled through the door at that moment, threw his black medical bag to the floor and hurried forward.

"Looks like you've got everything under control." The dark-haired man chuckled. "Congratulations, Mrs. Taggart. You have a girl."

Beulah gave a soft smile, her sweaty head resting against the pillow. "I knew all along."

He made quick work of severing the umbilical cord and delivering the afterbirth. Cora fetched the water and gave a quick sponge bath to the squirmy newcomer with Beulah gazing in adoration.

Once she bundled the baby, she pressed her into Beulah's waiting arms. Her sister-in-law cooed to her new daughter and stroked her skin. Cora followed the doctor's directions and made the room tidy again. Soon Miles, large and anxious nosed into the room. He took a knee next the bed, kissed his wife's forehead, and peeled back the blanket from the babe's face.

Cora smiled and eased toward the door to slip from the room.

"Wait, Cora." Beulah's voice floated softly across the room.

"Yes? Do you need something?" Cora paused at the foot of the bed.

Beulah glanced to her husband, love radiating from her face. "We want to call her Hope, after you."

A slow sob rose up Cora's throat. "Really? Oh, my. I'm so…honored."

"I believe," Beulah smiled, "everybody needs a little hope."

Chapter Twenty-Six

Hopeless.

That covered his situation to a T. Doc had removed the bullet and patched him up, but he was still weak as a child. He sat up in the bed and swung his legs to the floor. The deputy sitting in the chair across the room shifted. Oh, yeah. Then there was him. The guard. The sheriff had deemed Trigg to be extradited to St. Louis as soon as he healed enough to travel.

He rotated his right shoulder slightly. Pain shot through his body. It would be awhile before he was totally well, but not long before he mended enough to head to St. Louis.

And then there was Cora. Waiting. Hoping.

What to do? He glanced out the window where a slight breeze had sucked the lacy curtains out the opening. He could slip out. But then what? He had no idea where to start looking for Bo. Trigg suspected the deputies were trailing his brother, but he had no real proof. Lips were sealed to his constant questions over the last couple of days.

Being related to Bodine had become quite a drawback. Still, he knew his brother like no other. The sooner this was solved, the sooner he could return to Cora.

West, west. Where would Bo be going west? His brain snagged on an old cabin deep in the wood to the west of the house. The ancient structure had been the original home site of his maternal great grandfather. Just a rough-cut cabin. He and Bo had frequented it many times as boys. But it had been years since he'd been to it. The old thing had probably been swallowed up in brambles and vines by this point. But if it still stood, it proved to be a great hideout.

Trigg glanced around. They'd taken his rifle. And where was Buck? Could he get him saddled and headed out before he was discovered?

He would take his chances.

Trigg eased into a standing position. The guard, arms cross, hat-covered head back, grunted in his sleep. Trigg slipped his arms through his shirt sleeves, grimacing and holding back a cry of pain on the right side. He eyed the deputy's gun that hung from his holster. That was out of the question. Right now, he had to shimmy through that window without tearing open his shoulder.

He tossed his boots through the opening. Then, using only his left hand, he wiggled through the opening feet first. Trigg landed and rolled out into a sitting position. He paused a moment, his face pinching against the blinding pain. That had cost him. Once in a standing position, he thrust his feet into the boots.

Pain was a constant companion as he angled toward the corral. Buck grazed with the jacks and nickered when he saw him. The obedient horse followed him when Trigg opened the gate, and he led him into the barn.

Inside the dusty interior, Trigg ran a hand over his mount's neck. "Hey, old boy. You needing to stretch your legs, too, huh?'

After locating the blanket and the saddle on the saddle tree, Trigg carried them toward his horse. Before long he had Buck tacked up and ready to go. He strode to the feed room and stuck his hand down low in a barrel of corn. Near the bottom he located the canvas-covered handle of his grandfather's Colt revolver. He tugged the package free of the grain.

The gun had suffered little since Trigg had hidden it here a few years back. It was the one thing he didn't want to see Bo get his big hands on. Now, it would be most helpful. If he could get it dirt free enough to shoot.

On the highest shelf, he pulled down a box of ammo. Blowing and rubbing the weapon made it gleam once again. Trigg shoved in five .28 caliber bullets and filtered the rest into his pocket. Only time would tell if the old gun would fire correctly. He shoved it down his back into the waistband of his pants.

Agony accompanied Trigg's swing up into the saddle, and he paused a moment to grit his teeth. Then he guided his horse out the back door. A few glances at the house behind him told Trigg the guard still snoozed beside his empty bed. He heeled Buck with his boots. The sooner he disappeared into the woods, the better.

A warmth on his right shoulder made him peek beneath his shirt. A small red stain bled through on the surface of the bandage. Trigg didn't have long to complete his task.

He'd only gone a couple of miles before he pulled up. This time, he wouldn't leave Buck behind. The back forty acres had thick woods surrounding it. The cabin would be all but consumed by the thick foliage. Trigg dismounted and stepped lightly through the deep undergrowth, avoiding anything that might snap to give his location away.

A huge vine-covered lump with a huge bramble bush had to be the old cabin. Trigg stopped behind a collection of small saplings to watch. They wouldn't be making a fire. And it was blue-blazing hot. What would they be doing?

He bid Buck to stay and Trigg crept up, hunching low to avoid being seen through the busted out windows. The vegetation made it impossible to wedge up close enough to peek through the windows, so Trigg positioned himself on the far corner. He poked his head around to where the front door had originally been.

A low groan snagged his attention and Trigg froze.

"Yep. You had to be stupid, didn't you?"

A low voice drifted to Trigg's ears. Oates?

"Think you could cheat me, huh? Didn't think I'd defend myself, did ya? Guess you didn't see I back shot your brother." A short laugh followed.

Trigg ducked and crawled beneath the window. That brought the pain alive in his shoulder. Sweat broke out on his forehead. Finally, he shuffled next to the door. Vines had been cut and pulled from the front.

Another groan of pain came from inside. Had they seen him? Were they putting on some kind of ruse to trick him?

"Now, all I need to know is where you stashed the rest of the dough. Tell me, and maybe I'll let that brother of yours know where you are."

Trigg flattened against the old house. Oates appeared to be right next to the opening. With his attention on recovering the hidden funds, it was prime time to burst through and find out what was going on.

Trepidation fed extra strength to Trigg's muscles as he pulled the gun from his belt with his left hand and rushed the door. Inside the dim area, he charged at the only standing person in the room. Sensing the upraised hand held a gun, he slung his arm against Oates and a gunshot ripped toward the ceiling. The force of Trigg's attack knocked them both to the dirt floor. Oates grunted as Trigg landed on top of him.

Trigg locked his right forearm underneath Oates's chin and pounded the man's arm into the ground with his left. Oates's hand let go of the gun handle and the weapon skittered across the ground.

Oates growled and thumped Trigg on the chest. A pulsating shot of pain rippled through his body. Trigg pressed his lips together and popped Oates with the bottom of his Colt and then jumped away from him. He took two steps back and held the gun up, clicking the hammer in a deathly threat.

"Don't make me pay you back a bullet, Oates." Trigg snarled. "Hands up, where I can see them."

Wooziness made Trigg blink. He'd shoot him in the leg before he'd wrestle him again. His shoulder couldn't take the strain. He glanced in the far corner. His brother lay there motionless.

Trigg motioned with his head. "What's up with Bo?"

A moan punctuated a single word from the downed big man in the corner. "Knifed."

Keeping his Colt revolver trained on Oates, he said, "Go sit next to my brother and don't move. Got it? Oh, and move slow. My finger itches."

Oates stepped backwards, hands up, his lanky frame easing across the small cabin. Once he'd slid to the floor against the far wall, Trigg fetched Oates's gun. He lowered his old gun and shoved it into his belt. Then he checked the cylinder of the new gun. Loaded for bear with five remaining bullets. He clicked it back in place. Good. This Colt Navy .36 caliber was definitely more dependable than the aging revolver he'd rescued from the corn drum.

He strode toward Bo, keeping his new gun trained on Oates while he visually checked over his brother. His face appeared red and a thick trail of blood caked from above his right hip. Trigg knelt and worked the matted shirt loose. Bo groaned as he loosed the fabric. A gaping belly wound oozed blood.

A cold chill ran through Trigg. Whether the shiver came from his own bleeding wound or the seriousness of Bo's, he wasn't sure. He pulled the Navy up and aimed it at Oates. "What happened?"

The hollow-cheeked man shrugged. "Live by the gun, die by the knife."

Waxing poetic? Trigg cocked the hammer. "Whose knife?"

"He cheated me."

"Out of what?"

Behind him five men burst in, guns drawn. The feeble rays that permeated the room were enough to highlight the sheriff's and deputies' badges clear enough.

"You're all under arrest. Drop the gun."

Trigg set the safety and dropped the gun to the dust.

The short sheriff motioned with the end of his rifle. "And the other one."

Reluctantly, Trigg pulled the old Colt from his waist band and set it with the other. The men rushed forward with handcuffs and had both Trigg and Oates secured in a few moments. Outside they loaded both men on their horses and tied them to the deputies' mounts.

Next, four of them hauled Bo from the confines of the cabin and flopped him over the last horse and tied him secure. Trigg supposed he should have pleaded for more mercy as they manhandled Bo, but he was in enough trouble as it was. And Bodine had made his bed.

After a long tromp into town, the sheriff locked Trigg in a cell. Oates went into the next one while a resident yelled obscenities at them from the last. Bo never made it through the doors of the sheriff's office.

Trigg sat on the brick bed covered with a thin mattress as the sheriff sealed the trap door to the downstairs. Trigg's shoulder throbbed with waves of agony. But the clang of metal sliding through the lock brought even more misery than his injury.

The bright future he'd envisioned with Cora died a quick, cruel death.

♥∞♥

Cora sat in the rocker in Beulah's living room as Wiley toddled about. Bartholomew and Eleanor had left to finalize the purchase of a home in Princeton and Miles had gone back to the fields. At least Beulah was getting some rest.

The fresh face of the one-week-old infant fired all kinds of wild hopes in Cora's thoughts. Some day she would have a tiny one to care for. Trigg's child. Her face flared hot, but her current companions didn't seem to mind. Wiley flung the soft cotton blanket to the floor and cuddled up in it. His gentle personality, so like Beulah's, lended to a happy, content boy whose eyes drifted closed.

She wanted to let out a laugh, but the sleeping infant in her lap kept her from it. Wiley had put himself to bed. Beulah had mentioned he did that in earlier conversations, and now she was a witness.

Longing tore through her breast. Yes. A boy and a girl, in her own home would seem the best dream she could conjure. Surely Trigg had found his brother by now.

Fear cut longing in half. Bo had murdered a fellow passenger. Was Trigg safe? A man that could kill and rob didn't seem likely to have respect for his own brother. A brother who didn't agree with his lifestyle. A brother who loved him enough to search for him.

A whispered prayer passed Cora's lips and a tear trailed her cheek. She sniffed. He could be on his way back here even as she rocked baby Hope. Yes, she would wait.

The door burst open, waking Wiley from his nap. He sent out a wail and Miles scooped him up.

Cora rose, alarmed by the set of his jaw and the sadness in his eyes.

He held up a telegram. "Grandmother's dead. She passed this morning."

Sorrow lowered Cora back into the rocker. Tears of grief now joined her tears of fear.

The next week disappeared in a flurry of activity. Packing, journeying home, the funeral, the appalling grief that blanketed everything and everyone. Miles and Beulah hadn't come because of the new baby, but the rest of the family, nieces and nephews included, gathered around for a lunch outside the church. Mother, in her black gown, scurried around to help even though the other ladies insisted she let them serve. Being active had always helped in times of turmoil or distress.

And now Cora wandered to the gravesite once more on the other side of the church. The low murmurs of church folks and a few peals of laughter ushered her quickly around the corner of the church. She rested her back against the white-washed wall and scanned the cemetery headstones. At least Grandma Prescott had chosen a delightful summer day to be buried.

Green burst from every direction in vibrant health, reaching for the bright blue sky. Except for the overturned soil atop grandmother's grave. She'd lived a good life. Survived a great deal of disappointments and heartbreaks. And she still managed to find hope. Grandmother had triumphed in her life, her family, and her belief in the Lord. As Pastor Weaver said, she'd loosed her chains of sickness and was now reaping the benefits of her heavenly reward.

Cora rubbed her throat and held back tears. If only she could seek Grandmother's advice on heartbreaks right now. She could use a good dose of her stored-up wisdom.

For in the few weeks, once the grieving time had ended, Heaker Thomas would come calling. And unless Trigg showed up soon, more heartbreak seemed destined for her already shredded heart.

Chapter Twenty-Seven

C ora paused at the base of the stairway, gripping the leather mitt and lemon peel baseball. Surely playing pitch with the nieces and nephews would help to pass the time and drive away the doldrums.

Mother's voice floated to her as clear as the summer day, trickling from the kitchen. Cora froze in her tracks.

"He's too old. You know that." Utensils jingled in the background. Undoubtedly, Mother was clearing the dish rack.

"She's not been the same Cora since she's been back. Heaker may not be her age, but I can vouch for his character. She'll come to see this decision is for the best." Her father's quiet voice stilled her mother for only a moment.

"He does have impeccable character, Will. I'm not arguing that. What I am concerned about is Cora. There's nearly twenty years between them. She's but a child next to him."

Cora took a gulp full of air as she clenched the ball inside the leather glove. Her fate being decided without her.

"Jennie, she'll be twenty. Heaker's a fine man. A fine man. He'll take care of her. He'll love her. And she'll learn to be happy."

Mercy. The man was almost her whole lifetime older. How could her parents do this to her? And what about Trigg? How could she wait for the man she loved while courting another?

Her mother cleared her throat. "Learn to be happy? What kind of future is that?"

"Your very own mother, God rest her soul, can attest to such a marriage. She told you how happy she was, didn't she? Your parents started out in a marriage of convenience and they made it work. She might not have been happy at the beginning, but it turned out fine."

Cora slumped against the wall. Why hadn't she told them about Trigg? Because it didn't seem real. The cotillion in St. Louis, his rescue. It all seemed like a dream. Except for the fire and the murder, that is. Boy meets girl, boy rescues girl. Unfortunately, boy disappears had been the ending.

That was it. She would march right in the kitchen and tell them all about Trigg. How she loved him. And Trigg loved her. How she refused to court Mr. Thomas. Then—

"Besides," her father's voice continued, "as much as I hate to point out, Jennie, no one's ever asked to court her."

Except Trigg. And he hadn't even had time to ask her father if he could. But before that? No one. Ever. Too-Tall Taggart had batted a zero. With a muffled sob in her throat, she spun, and quietly let herself out the front door. Heart heavy, she pressed the glove and ball on the porch rocker.

Sadness set wheels to her feet, and she scurried down the road toward town. If only she could get away before anyone from her family could see her. Or stop her.

Once she reached the edge of town, she slowed and took a breath. Now that she'd arrived, she really had no agenda. Just to get away. To get a breath. To think. Lament. That was all. Cora turned on the outer skirts of New Albany toward the neighborhood where her family usually shopped and did business. It was familiar and offered a shred of comfort.

Ah. Miss McGarlee's fabric shop. It stood like an oasis beckoning her. Even if she couldn't express her feelings to anyone, she could lose herself in textile. She scrambled toward the door. A huge framed man strode across the street, but she ignored him, focusing on her destination. Until his bulk stepped in her way.

Heaker Thomas.

"Howdy, Miss Taggart." He nodded and offered up a slight quirk of his mouth.

A sad attempt at a smile perhaps? She nodded, breathless from her speedy gait.

He stared at her, eyes deep from what? Nervousness? Embarrassment? Eagerness? Cora wasn't sure. And she didn't want to find out.

Mr. Thomas shoved his meaty hands behind the bib of a filthy leather apron. He must have run to meet her straight from his blacksmith shop across the street. She continued to blink at him, and he chewed the thick moustache hair near his mouth. Wrinkles surrounded his eyes. His face could be described as pleasant, she supposed. Slightly too short. But while he wasn't an ogre, he was indeed, old. At least older.

"Is there something you wanted?" Cora could stand the silence no more.

He shuffled. "Reckon I'll meet up with you this Saturday. Your pa said it was fine to stop by."

Cora could feel her chin start to quiver. Now was not the time to discuss her first call from a man she couldn't have less interest for. She nodded. "Excuse me, please."

She slid between him and Miss McGarlee's shop window and flew to the door. The bell chimed as she rushed in. Thankfully the place was empty. Cora bustled to the back, behind the long rolls of fabric that stood almost as tall as she. A peek between the textile assured her Mr. Thomas had moseyed back to smithing.

Without ceremony, she sat upon a low storage box tucked behind the rolls of fabric. She wiped her face with a shaking hand. Dear heavens. How would she ever get through a call from that man when her heart belonged to Trigg? Dag blasted. Everything was out of sorts.

"Hello?"

Miss McGarlee shuffled about the store. Cora dropped her head down and eyed the worn, wooden floor. It was a shame the shop owner had fixed that doggone bell. Hovering here in the back corner was a terribly great spot for hiding from the world. At least from her parents and Mr. Thomas. Yet, it would only be a matter of moments before...

Small feet appeared in Cora's vision.

"Why Cora, wee lass. 'Twas ye that rang the bell."

She just couldn't meet the older woman's eyes. Not yet. Not now. Tears swam, blurring her vision. The old gal plopped down on the wooden chest next to her. Her gentle voice undoing the last of her resolve not to bawl.

"What is it, Lass? What ails ye today?"

Fingers urged her face up.

"Och. Tears on a bright, bonny day? Tell ol' Miss McGarlee what ails ye."

Cora only shook her head and closed her eyes.

A snort burst from the elder woman. "Man trouble, I'll be a-betting. Come along. A spot of tea always gets to the bottom of it, ye know."

Like a whimpering puppy, Cora allowed Miss McGarlee to tug her by the hand into the back room and up the stairs to a spartan living area. They passed by four metal headless mannequins and over to a small woven rug in front of a burgundy camelback sofa and a padded patterned chair near an empty fireplace.

But Miss McGarlee didn't stop until she reached a small wooden table with two ladder back chairs near a compact kitchen area. With a tiny stove. She settled Cora at the table and placed a kettle on to heat.

The wide woman took the chair opposite her and patted her hand. "Now, out with it. Heartbreaks come a dime a dozen and are best remedied by sharin' the load. What's the trouble, Lass?"

At this point, there was no holding back. Like a cork popped from a bottle, Cora unleased the whole horrible tale, St. Louis, the fire, the stagecoach tragedy, the impending courtship, and lastly Trigg.

"And have ye told yer parents about this Trigg lad? Perhaps they'd feel differently if they be aknowin'."

Cora shook her head. "He hasn't come back. What if he never returns? Maybe it was just a fanciful dream. Like some Cinderella tale."

"Nonsense. I'm sure yer folks would be understanding of the circumstances."

Miss McGarlee pressed a scented hanky into Cora's hand. Blurting and sipping the Irish tea had made Cora feel a slight bit better. But it didn't solve her problems.

"The Lord has a funny way of working these things out, Girly. You've got to trust."

She nodded. Something she had told herself for the last several weeks. But maintaining her hope was easier said than done. Cora rose. "Thank you for the tea. I really should be getting home. It's nearing the dinner hour, and I always help Mama."

Miss McGarlee nodded and rose on her thin legs and waddled toward the door. "And rightly so. You're a jewel, ye are."

Reaching the bottom stair, Cora caught sight of the back door. "May I take this way?"

"Och, Darling. Use the front door. Hold yer head up high and march right out there, I say. Surely, but don't you be a-worrying. 'Twill all work out. You'll be seein'."

The bell rang at that moment, and Miss McGarlee snorted again and hiked toward the front, greeting the new patron.

Seeing Mr. Thomas rush over to her again wouldn't be good on her patched-up heart. No, best to slip out the back. Her wounded heart couldn't take much more.

With a glance toward the front she whispered. "Sorry. I just…can't."

Cora slipped through the back door and set a good pace for home.

ॐ

Weeks had dragged by since Trigg had been detained in Henderson County's brick jail. Now, having been transferred, he cooled his feet in the large cell in St. Louis, awaiting a trial. Sharing the small room with five other degenerates hadn't been on Trigg's list of things he needed to do. But at least his shoulder had healed during the long wait.

A prison guard passed by. Trigg stuck his hand out. "You promised to get me paper and a pencil."

"Keep your shirt on." The solid prison guard grunted and shifted down the hallway. The man had been unmoved by his pleas for writing equipment. He had to get a note to Cora. Who knew what the woman must be thinking? And the trial loomed off in the distance.

A shoving match started behind him over one of the hammocks, and Trigg slid down the farthest corner and sat on the floor. How he wished he were back at the farm with Bliss and Roe. He'd be planning a new homestead for Cora and himself. Instead he was contemplating being incarcerated as an accomplice.

If he could only go back to the point of guiding Cora safely home. He would have stayed. Met her family. Cleared his name. Asked her father for her hand. But no. He'd been stupid to chase after Bodine. Shoot, he'd been stupid from the beginning when he sought him out. He knew Bo was bad news. But, if he hadn't gone to New Albany, he would've never met Cora. And he couldn't take that back.

"Here. All I could find." The jailer shoved a wad of papers and a rough stub of a rectangular pencil at him through the bars.

Trigg stared at the pile and his mouth popped open. A pure treasure trove. He gripped the bars and yelled at the disappearing jailer. "Thanks. I owe you."

He filtered through the crumpled pages. Most of them had scrawls across the back, but he didn't mind. Three pages. First, he'd pen one to Cora. Then to Bliss and Roe. The last one would be to his grandmother. She deserved to know about Ivalee. And Bo.

Ignoring the tussle behind him, he turned and sat crossed-legged, knees to the wall. He flattened the first page and tucked the other two into his sock. A prayer crossed his lips in a whispered fashion to keep the numbskulls from noticing him. He would fight to the death for these three slips of paper.

He paused before he tacked on to his breathed prayer, "And please, Lord Jesus, get me out of this mess."

Cora stared at the crinkled, smudgy envelope in her hand. Aleena stood next to her tapping her foot on the wooden walkway outside the post office.

"I will ask one more time, Cora Hope Taggart." Her sister's face had tightened into a stern mask. "Who is Trigg Gentry?"

"He's a…man."

Aleena narrowed her eyes. "Obviously. If you're not going to be any more cooperative, give me the letter."

Rebelliousness roared in Cora's chest. "Why?"

"Because you're too young to be entertaining letters from strange men." Her sister swiped at her hand to snatch it.

But Cora stepped back. "Too young? Mama and Papa are pushing me to court a forty-year-old man, and you're saying I'm too young?"

"Nevertheless, it's my duty as your married sister to protect you. Hand it over."

Anger wove through the defiance swelling in Cora's chest. And indignation. She stretched up to her full height, towering over her shorter sister. "Good gravy, Aleena. This is not some stranger. I don't want to be protected from the man I love."

Her sister's mouth fell open and her eyes popped wide. For the first time in Cora's life, her elder sister had no words.

"Furthermore," Cora added, her voice quivering only a little, "I have a right to any and all mail without your interference. As much as you'd like to keep me as a little ten-year-old child, I'm not. I am a full grown woman who will soon see my twentieth birthday, fully able to make sound decisions of my own."

Aleena shook her head as if to clear it. "How…when?"

Cora let a nervous giggle pop out. "Here, actually. Then later en route to St. Louis, and lastly, at the cotillion." She stuck the envelope into her pocket and snapped her chin up. "Now, I'm going to run to Miss McGarlee's to purchase some thread."

Without waiting for her sister's reply, Cora scooted down the walk at a swift pace. The bell on the door made Miss McGarlee look up, but she was fully engaged with cutting pink cotton for a woman with two daughters.

Perfect. She made her way through the maze of tables to her wooden chest perch behind the tall rolls of fabric stacked on a wooden table. Once seated she pulled the envelope from her pocket.

Dearest Cora,

I am truly sorry I've let you down. Going after Bo was the worst mistake I could have ever made. Please don't be shocked, but I am in jail in St. Louis. I'm awaiting a trial, where I hope they will find me innocent of any charges.

Because I am innocent, Cora. And even if no one believes me, please, I pray you do.

My fate awaits me at the trial. Bo and Oates are in custody as well, but I have no word of them. They did tell me Burr is dead.

I have to be honest with you, my sweet. There is no guarantee that I will be released. I may be indicted as an accomplice to the crimes that were committed. You know what that will mean.

Therefore, Cora, I must release you. I can't take advantage of your promise to wait for me when I have no idea what will happen. My love for you remains, deeper than ever. But I know your life must go on, regardless of what happens to me.

All my love,

Trigg

Tears bit her eyes as her grandmother's bookmark fell into her lap.

Chapter Twenty-Eight

"Y ou will not, under any circumstances, Cora, return to St. Louis." Her usual calm father delivered the blow in a low voice.

Cora swiped her tears and stared at him. Miss McGarlee had been wrong. They didn't understand. They still thought of her as a child unable to make decisions for herself. And now Trigg would be alone through his incarceration, his trial.

"But I love him," she stuttered.

A gentle light returned to her father's eyes. "My daughter. I'm trying to protect you. Such an ordeal could take weeks, months."

"I could stay with Aunt Josephine."

Her mother, seated next to her at the kitchen table grasped her hand and squeezed gently. "But it's your reputation at stake, Cora. This man is a prisoner—*a prisoner.*"

"He's innocent."

Her father's tall frame paced the room before turning slowly. "Nevertheless, he is awaiting trial. There are serious charges against him. Surely you can understand our concern. Once more, we've never even met this man."

Abel peered at her from across the room. Sympathy resided there, but clearly he sided with her parents. "Maybe just wait a few weeks to see what comes of it?"

She stood and shook her head. "I will obey you, Father, because it is right. I live here, under your roof. But you all are wrong to think that Trigg could ever do such a horrible thing. He will come. And when he comes, I want you to promise me you will hear him out."

Her father nodded his head. "I can do that. If he's released of all charges."

Cora swallowed. "I ask permission to write to him."

Her father looked toward her mother who nodded before he replied. "Very well. But you must remember, Cora. If he is convicted of anything, this relationship is over. Do you understand?"

She nodded.

"Meanwhile, Mr. Thomas will be joining us for dinner this weekend. And you will be cordial, I trust?"

Anger simmered below the surface, but Cora managed to keep a lid on it. They didn't believe her. They thought of Trigg as a criminal. So on marched the plans for her to be courted by Mr.

Thomas. It was one thing to challenge Aleena. She could not deny her parents. Her voice came out a bit clipped. "Yes, sir."

A sadness rippled over her father's face, but she hardened herself to it. If he would not trust her, he would not receive her glowing adoration for his decision. She would endure it and wait. And hope. *Everybody needs a little hope.* Beulah's words sent a shred of comfort through her soul. It was the best she could do.

However, that choice lost its snap by the time Mr. Thomas stared her down from across the table on Saturday night. Clearly, this man entertained serious ideas of their courtship. And the matter of Trigg had been tucked away into the secrets for the Taggarts' knowledge only.

"So, Heak. How's business in town?"

The man pulled his attention from Cora to address her father. She gave a small sigh of relief as she flipped the slice of ham over. Her ability to enjoy the food had disappeared as soon as Mr. Thomas's muscled body had cleared the doorway.

"It's good. Can't complain."

And that was the fifth four-word answer of the hour from their visitor. She licked her lips and stared at the mound of mashed potatoes. Excusing herself would be unacceptable. She had promised to be pleasant, and she would grind her teeth to dust to accomplish that.

She stuck her hand into her pocket of her best pink dress and rubbed the bookmark hiding there. Her mind quoted the verse to give her courage and strength. *I wait for the Lord, my soul doth wait, and in his word do I hope.*

Yes.

"Miss Taggart, a walk?"

Four words of frustration. She pushed away her plate and rose. She would be obedient to a fault but she didn't have to like it. "Of course."

She cut a glance to Abel before she skirted the table.

"But you haven't finished eating yet, Cora," her mother intoned.

Pausing near the door, she answered. "I've had quite enough, Mother, thank you."

Her mother blinked at the double meaning, and Cora followed her companion to the door. The lingering heat of mid-September hung on every tired leaf, even as the day approached the evening hour. The heat alone justified the space Cora maintained between them. The silence stretched as he twisted his hat in his huge hand.

Finally he broke it. "Nice weather we're having."

Cora was caught between bursting out laughing and rolling her eyes at the four measured words. Two could play that game. "Maybe a bit hot."

He looked at her then. His dark eyes spoke volumes. All the awkwardness there crowded out Cora's next thought. Pain seemed wedged right in with the uneasiness in his eyes. Really, she should pity him. The poor man only strove to find a mother for his little ones, his youngest chronically ill. It would be a difficult situation. A lonesome mission. She sighed, understanding dawning on her heart. He was a good man, but not her man.

"And how are your girls?"

His face brightened. "They're getting along fine."

Cora allowed a small smile. He did love his children. That was admirable, if nothing else. Her thoughts centered on his youngest, a child she'd never laid eyes on. "And little Tupie?"

And just like that, the glow on his face vanished. Something like dread took its place, and he looked away.

Mr. Thomas shrugged, the muscles of a hammer-swinging blacksmith rippling beneath his yellow shirt. "She needs much prayer."

Yes. If Cora could do nothing else, she would pray. Pound on heaven's door for Mr. Thomas's youngest while she prayed for Trigg Gentry.

Her companion stopped, and she paused, looking askance. An indecipherable expression filtered across his bearded face.

"I should head home."

"Of course," she murmured, thankful the uncomfortable encounter would soon be over. "I'll let my family know. I'm sure you're anxious about the girls."

He nodded. "Thanks for the meal."

And just like that, a man who sought to court her jumped into his wagon, and disappeared down the lane. She had escaped. At least for today.

৩০০৩

By October, Trigg set his foot on the cement walk outside the St. Louis Courthouse. At last, a free man. Bodine had gotten him into this mess, and his testimony had gotten him out. Bo and Oates had not been so lucky. They were convicted and being extradited to Indiana to stand another robbery charge and murder. And at least part of the stolen items had been recovered.

He sucked in a lungful of fresh early autumn air. He patted Cora's letters in his breast pocket. She'd been his champion from the very beginning. Promised to wait, no matter how long. Yet, the nagging thought of a distant suitor dug at him. If it wasn't too late, he had somewhere to be.

Boarding a steamer took no time. But the journey dragged excruciatingly. Top of his list? He'd stop to talk with Grandmother even though his gut pushed him to rush to Cora. His kin had a right to know about Bo.

After two days of floating the Ohio, Trigg sat on Buck staring at his grandmother's formidable mansion. He rode up the lane, nodded to the servant who took charge of his horse, and strode to the back door.

Fibby's welcoming face greeted him warmly. "Mr. Trigg, done been a good year seeing as we's done welcomed you twice now. Get on in here."

He grinned and clutched his hat until she pulled it from his grip.

The big woman's eyes rounded out as she leaned forward to whisper. "Yer grandmother's not been the same since ya left. Don't much get around. Stays in her room most all the time."

Trigg's face scrunched. Odd. He'd thought his grandmother had been pounded from wrought iron. "I see."

"Miss Ruth," Fibby ducked her head into the shadowed hallway. "Gots company."

The same delicate servant stepped into the room, merely flicking Fibby a glance rather than answer.

Miss Ruth motioned to the hall. "This way."

Trigg wove his way through the familiar passage and arrived in the parlor. His eyes swept the room and settled on the large mural above the fireplace. The droll painting of his grandmother and grandfather with his mother as a small child had been replaced with the full family shot, showing his mother and father as young parents.

Bodine, probably the same age as mother in the previous portrait, looked young and innocent. A stab of remorse shot through Trigg to think what had become of his brother's life as he, as the small child stood there gazing back at him, his whole life ahead of him. Trigg was positioned beside his older brother and Roe, a baby, lay nestled in Mother's arms. Bliss and Ivalee were but sparkles in his parents' eyes. There had been no more visits to the grandparents after this frozen glimpse of time.

"Mrs. Graves will be here shortly." Miss Ruth disappeared after a bob.

He nodded and stood to study the painting that had been absent on his last visit. His mother, still young with her life choices ahead of her, stood with her hand upon Father's arm. Father had that gleam of adventure in his eye, his shyster ways only beginning to suction the life from his young wife and family.

His mother smiled, a soft but tenacious look in her eye. Yes, that would be her undoing. Ivalee had the same gleam in her eye.

But perhaps she'd landed a more deserving husband despite what regular folks would say.

She was beautiful, his mother. He couldn't deny her charming looks. Dark hair, bright, almost silver eyes. And although he didn't think of himself as particularly handsome, he'd inherited much of her features. From the point in the painting, not much more than a year or two, Father would abandon the family and run about the country full of exaggerated dreams of success and freedom.

A man who now chased his dreams of gold while his children toiled to keep the homestead. And, by George, Trigg would make the farm a success. He'd promised himself a long time ago he'd not be the man his father was. That he would be there to take care of his family. He would pay off the land, marry Cora, and work with Bliss and Roe to pay back any and all of his father's debts.

He spun toward the noise behind him. Grandmother stood at the door, dressed in black. And although her clothing was the color of wrought iron, the thin pale face bespoke suddenly of frailty.

She floated across the room and sat in her usual throne chair adjacent to the sofa. "Please be seated."

He nodded and reclined on the brown sofa. He would get right to business. No time to waste. "I thought it important—"

Grandmother held up her hand and he stuttered to a stop, a bit confused. Surely, she wouldn't call for refreshments. Getting to Cora as soon as possible was of the utmost importance.

"I must divulge something, Triggley." She paused and closed her eyes for a moment. "I've received some correspondence from Ivalee…"

Her face seemed to fade to a shade of chalk, and she pressed a hand to her breast before she continued. "And a connection in St. Louis sent me a wire of the happenings there."

"So you know?"

She rested the paper-thin hands in her lap, pulling herself erect. "Yes."

Well, what much else could be said? He went to rise. "I guess that's all I had to say."

"Please."

The word seemed to rip from his grandmother. As if the word scraped her throat as it exited. Trigg settled back on the sofa.

"The Lord has impressed upon me the last fifty years, a difficult lesson." Those silver eyes of hers pressed into his. "And it is this. You can't force people to become whom you want them to be. Ivalee's married to a savage. Bodine's a criminal. Your father's a gold digger. And my daughter's...dead."

Trigg worked hard to keep his face at an impasse. Grandmother had never been so blunt.

She rose, elegant even in a moment of straightforwardness and turned to stare at the photo. "So, Triggley. I feel that I must do what I can to help my future descendants who seem to be pursuing the nobleness of life." She spun and peered at him. "Therefore, if you or Bliss or Rowland have retained any debts for your farm or from your father's reckless squandering, I wish to satisfy such debts and assist you in any forthcoming endeavors."

He jumped to his feet. "I can't let you do that."

"Why ever not? How will you sustain a wife and family if you are mired in liability? For one thing, no woman would endure to have you."

"The woman I love will have me regardless." He lifted his chin and eyed her with determination.

She stepped forward. "Is that so? You've picked a particular female?"

Trigg gritted his teeth. "I have."

Grandmother's left eyebrow rose a fraction. "Please tell me more. Sit, sit. I'm greatly encouraged."

Although his grandmother swished back to her seat, he continued to stand. "You're suddenly interested in my farm and my choice for a wife? After all these years?"

"Yes, Trigg. I was…wrong."

Grandmother never called him Trigg. He sat. Did her eyes look slightly misty?

"This…" an uncharacteristic pause made Trigg lean forward, "estrangement is not your grandfather's fault. The man thrives on working the day away. It was I. My pride. But now…" she smiled softly, sadly, "I feel my family slipping away. My own life is beginning to decline. And I realize how remiss I've been not to have been more of a support to my own child and grandchildren. I regret it. Deeply. I wish to…make amends. If you would let me."

She pulled a hanky from her sleeve and dabbed at her face. "Please, tell me of this…woman you wish to wife."

After a moment's hesitation, he began. He told her about Cora, of her beauty, her fiery spirit, and her endless faith in his innocence. How they had met and danced and how she was now, still waiting for him to arrive. His grandmother soaked it all in, as if she really had reformed and actually cared.

When he finished, she reached over and patted his hand. "You have chosen well. And you will start your life debt free. And if you require anything else, it will be done."

When he started to protest, she held up her hand. "Not just for you. But for Bliss and Rowland as well. And if you so desire, I wish to offer the mansion as a location for the wedding."

Trigg swallowed and glanced around the stuffy room.

"I will spare no expense. Perhaps planning for the wedding will cheer myself as well."

"I'll let Cora know. If she'll still have me."

They both rose. She stepped closer and clasped his hand in her bony ones. "From what you've expressed to me, I have no doubt she will."

Trigg glanced at their hands. Never in his memory could he ever remember grandmother touching him. "Thank you."

"Please call again and keep me abreast of your plans." She rose on tiptoe and pecked him on the cheek. Then she pressed her cheek against his and whispered, "I love you."

She whisked away before he had a chance to return the sentiment. Miss Ruth stood near his elbow suddenly, and he shut his mouth that had been hanging open. The servant handed him his hat, and he hurried to the back door.

"You come back now, Mr. Trigg." Fibby scurried up behind him as he strode through the door.

He paused, his hand on the doorknob. "You know, Fibby, I think I will be back. Very soon. I'll be toting sticky buns that I promised myself to bring you. But first, I've got a woman to propose to."

Chapter Twenty-Nine

Under the maples in the side yard, Father carried on an animated conversation with Mr. Thomas. It was obvious that Papa liked him. And Mr. Thomas spoke more with him than he'd ever uttered to Cora. But still, he seemed to be a man of few words and deep thoughts. With a few skipped weeks between, this was only his third visit. Thankfully, the word hadn't circulated yet that they were courting. However, Cora knew if Trigg did not return soon, the word would soon be out.

The day had dawned bright for a family dinner. The last warm days before the chill of late fall wedged in, beamed bright with hope, the perfect weather. She'd dressed in her best frock, a blue and beautiful as the robin-egg sky, at the insistence of her mother. It brought out the green in her eyes. Azure. Miss McGarlee had insisted the color made her hair into spun gold. How she wished Trigg could see her decked in her best dress.

The kids' tables were crowded with chattering children, and the adult table buzzed with conversation. Soon the days would get too cool, and they'd be forced to move the clan inside where everyone would be stepping on one another.

Cora leaned back, thankful she didn't have to carry on a conversation by herself with Mr. Thomas. He was deeply engaged with the men at the table. Cora sipped her soup as her father and her intended started a discussion on the changes in the state's school system. Abel along with her brother Everett, had joined in the conversation of the newly organized township schools. She felt a little guilty, yet thankful, that she hadn't had to even make small talk.

For a man in a hurry to have a wife, Mr. Thomas didn't seem to be in a rush. They had a short stroll one minute, and then he'd sat around outside under the trees conversing with her family the next. Either Tupie had been unwell or he'd had work to do at his blacksmith shop. Nevertheless, the visits had been few and far between. But she dreaded to think what today would bring.

Jimmie, fully mended from his broken leg, slipped to her side to whisper, "How about a game of catch?"

So excited he was fully mended, she wanted to grab him up in a hug. Jimmie would no doubt not want any of her slathering of love. Too babyish for him.

Also, she didn't want to pull away the men's attention either. If she were careful, she could slip away and none of them would even realize her absence. She fingered the napkin in her lap and glanced toward the gentlemen. Then she leaned over and whispered. "I'll get the mitt and ball. Meet me in the front yard."

She rose and pressed the napkin to the table. Was it horrible that she looked more forward to playing catch with her nephew than spending time with the man trying to court her? No. It just reiterated her love for Trigg. No one could take his spot in her heart.

What was happening with the trial? The last letter she'd received from him indicated the trial should have already occurred. However, there was no word on its outcome. No news was good news? She hoped the old adage rang true.

She skipped up the stairs and pulled the mitt wrapped around the lemon peel ball from the bottom drawer. For a moment she scanned the room, slapping the ball into the mitt over and over. Too soon spring would come and she'd see her twentieth birthday. Tarnation, if she didn't marry, Widow Dixon would fuel the gossip pots with more proof that she was destined to be a dried-up old onion-skin maid. Like Miss McGarlee even though the older woman seemed to be quite happy in her lot.

Yes. If Trigg never returned, perhaps this was God's plan for her life. For she feared once true love passed her by, it would be impossible to replace. Yes, it would be absolutely impossible to fill the gaping hole in her heart.

She glanced to the window and thought of marrying someone like Mr. Thomas. An older man, whose main concern was caring for his girls. She could be useful there, she supposed. But it would be a life of drudgery in a loveless marriage.

Cora shook the dark thoughts away and scurried toward the front door. Jimmie met her with a huge grin, the sun glancing off his snowy blond hair. He slapped the center of his homemade mitt that Abel had made for his son. She tossed the ball to him, and he fired it back. The rest of Cora's Double N Herd nosed in, begging to play. Jimmie's brow furrowed, unwilling to share with the other nieces and nephews. Soon an argument ensued and Roy took off with the ball. All the nieces and nephews chased after him. Cora stood alone in the middle of the yard.

"There you are," Aleena appeared at the corner of the house, her voice carrying a hint of disapproval. "Mr. Thomas has been looking everywhere for you."

He must not be too gifted at hide and seek then. Cora stemmed a smile. "I was just playing with the kids."

"Don't forget. He's here to see you." Aleena crossed her arms in a tight knot.

How could she forget?

"Go sit on the porch swing. I'll corral the kids and send Mr. Thomas to you."

As usual. Her family directed her life. With a sigh and a muttered grunt, Cora nodded and acquiesced. She shuffled up the steps and perched on the swing. Maybe she deserved this. Maybe she *was* childish.

No. Suddenly, she knew it just wasn't true. Yes, she was too tall and often too headstrong. And yes, she loved to baseball and her nieces and nephews to distraction. But, deep down, she didn't feel like an adolescent at all. Her aching heart reminded her every moment that she'd grown into a woman. A woman in love, pining for her soul mate who may or may not ever appear in her life again. With a sniff, she flapped the mitt open and closed, punching a fist into it until her other hand stung.

A large figure caught her attention as it rounded the corner. Mr. Thomas. She shoved her mitt-covered left hand under her leg and sat up straighter.

He offered a small smile as he climbed the stairs. His black pants carried particles of Aleena's best rolls. "Mind if I sit?"

Not the four word thing again. She wasn't sure she could endure it. Nothing like a lie when a soul couldn't be truthful. "No. That's fine."

She shrank away as he sat. The man slung a sledge for a living, and his upper body strength and width were a testament to his occupation. Father should have made this swing a tad wider.

"Nice day we're having."

"Uh-huh."

Jimmie came flying around the corner. "I got the ball back, Cora. Catch."

The lemon peel ball flew with great accuracy, and Cora whipped her mitt from under her leg and snatched the flying orb for a clean catch. Mr. Thomas's hand was there too and nearly knocked it from her grip.

His face opened in shock. "I thought it was going to hit you. I didn't realize you'd catch it."

She shrugged. "It's a game we play."

Her nephew's eyes grew huge. "Ope, sorry. I forgot."

The child disappeared in a flash. Aleena would tan his hide if she found out he'd interrupted the sparking on the front porch. Cora sighed and wedged herself farther away from the thick body next to her. Blast. How she wished she could spring from the swing and call out after Jimmie for a game of catch.

She felt Mr. Thomas's gaze. Cora lifted her eyes to his, and he stared long and hard. Heat rushed to her face. How foolish she must appear to him. She looked away.

"Cora?"

Something in his tone made her return her eyes to his. His whiskers seem to stick out in all directions.

His brow puckered. "I think it's time to talk."

She gulped and ran her fingers over the lemon peel ball.

"You know I'm quite a bit older than you."

Cora nodded.

"I've got five girls that need a mama."

Jiminy Christmas, here it was. He was going to skip the courting all together and just propose. Dear, Lord in heaven. What could she possibly say? By all that was good and holy, she couldn't marry Heaker Thomas, a man nearly twice her age. A man she had no interest in. She clutched the ball as her only comfort.

"But I don't think this is working."

Her mouth dropped open and she searched his bearded face. "What?"

Mr. Thomas grew still. "I think there's too much age between us. And if I'm honest, I don't think you're that interested."

Oh, my. She rubbed her tongue against the back of her teeth, eyeing him. She blurted, "I'm so sorry."

"No need to apologize. I understand." He gave a tired smile. "God's plans are better than ours."

He stood and headed for the steps. Then he turned. "No hard feelings between us?"

She rose and followed him. "Of course not."

He nodded. "I'll go speak to your father about it. Goodbye, Cora."

And just like that, he strode around the corner and disappeared.

Hallelujah. She'd been delivered. Praise Jesus, she wouldn't have to marry a man and leap into a ready-made family. Cora meandered toward the front steps. She hesitated at the top step and chewed her lip. So…this was her lot.

Cora leaned against the porch post. Surprisingly, a sadness washed over her. Not because of Mr. Thomas's departure and cancellation of courtship plans. But because she'd be alone now. Even her unwanted suitor's sporadic visits had brought some sort of comfort in the fact that someone had thought her worthy to be courted. Sort of. It had made her feel a little less of a misfit.

She settled on the steps, picking at the laces of the lemon peel ball. A few minutes later, Mr. Thomas appeared and walked toward his waiting wagon parked under a canopy of oaks. He didn't seem to be in a hurry and a whistle could be heard as he walked. He climbed into the wagon seat and threw up a wave as he steered the horse toward the road. Cora lifted a hand in reply.

So it was over.

The scent of mother's roses near the porch perfumed the air, reminding her that life was still sweet and full of God's blessings. She inhaled deeply. Yes, she would go back to her sewing. Perhaps she would offer to help Miss McGarlee at the shop. From the looks of the fabric piles back in Cora's hiding corner, the older woman could use some assistance.

Cora took another deep breath and stretched, a prayer of thankfulness on her lips. She popped up and spun to enter the house. With her hand on the knob, a creak of saddle leather made her pause.

Was Mr. Thomas coming back? Had he forgotten something? Jumping catfish, had he changed his mind? Fear licked a fire through her as she turned. A lone rider appeared from the road. A tall, slim rider. She knew this person, didn't she? Hope rippled through her as she stepped closer to the edge of the porch steps. The man lifted his head and a grin spliced across his face. That dear, dear face.

Trigg!

He'd come. He'd come for her! The mitt and ball fell with a thunk to the porch. She thundered down the steps and took off running. By the time she reached him, he'd swung off the saddle, and she flew into his arms.

His laughter mingled with her tears as he swung her around and around until she was dizzy. By the time he'd set her down, they were both laughing with joy. But awed silence replaced the laughter when his eyes met hers.

"You're here." She peered at his silver-blue eyes lined with tiredness.

His eyes flamed with desire. "Yes. I'm here for my bride."

She inhaled a shaky breath as his lips came down on hers, crushing in neediness, gentle in love. Cora clutched him to her as if he might vanish into thin air, giving herself like never before. Passion flared like a torch between them. Her heart soared as he deepened the kiss and pulled her even tighter.

Finally he broke away and his hungry eyes swept her face. "You're even more beautiful than I remembered."

Cora yanked at his lapels. "Don't ever leave me again."

"I don't plan on it."

A laugh of pure joy tumbled from her. Then she gasped. "The trial. What happened?"

He grinned. "Obviously, I'm free." Then his face grew sober. "My brother confessed I had nothing to do with any of it. He'd never been much of a brother, but he did what he could to set me free. I'll ever be grateful for that."

"Oh, that's wonderful."

He nodded. "Not so wonderful for Bo."

"I'm sorry, Trigg."

"You reap what you sow." He ran his hands over her back and pressed another quick kiss to her lips. "But I want to talk of other plans."

He brushed the flyaway hairs behind her ear. "I love you and I want the whole world to know. And I thought of nothing else but marrying you and starting our life together. Cora Hope Taggart, will you marry me?"

"I love you too, Trigg Gentry. And yes, I will marry you."

He tugged her into his arms again and sealed the promise with a hungry kiss. The noise of children giggling brought them apart. Near the edge of the house stood most of Cora's nieces and nephews, staring, grinning, and making kissing noises.

She giggled and shot a glanced toward Trigg. "Welcome to the family."

A burst of laughter erupted from him. "I reckon the one I need to see first then is your father."

The seriousness dampened some of Cora's glee, but she nodded, grabbed Trigg's hand and waded through the sea of children. Trigg greeted the kids and patted their blond heads. The adults had already left their seats and were on their way to see what the excitement was all about when Cora pulled Trigg forward.

Introductions went around and at last, Trigg stood toe to toe with Papa. Same height. Same suspicious stare. Cora worried her lips as the two of them wandered off toward the barn. Abel threw his arm around Cora and squeezed.

"Don't you worry, little one. I think there might be a wedding in your future after all."

"Abel," Aleena admonished her husband.

"Ah, Lovely," Abel reached up to massage his wife's shoulder. "You remember what it was like. Young love."

The gaze between the two of them turned tender, a side of Aleena that Cora seldom saw. Her sister broke the romantic trance with her husband and turned to study Cora.

Her sister stepped forward and took Cora's hands. "I know I've been hard on you. Perhaps too hard. But, I've always wanted you to be happy, Cora. I've had you in my prayers so much in the last months, I don't think I've drawn a breath that your name wasn't upon my lips."

Phoebe, Cora's other sister drew near, tears upon her lashes. "Me, too."

Ada, her sister-in-law, also came forward and they formed a circle about her. They laid their hands upon her, and Aleena began to pray, lifting up Cora's future to the Lord. Tears poured down Cora's face at the love and support of her family. They were aggravating, intrusive, and bossy, but she knew they loved her. When Aleena whispered an amen, they ended with a hug, a happy crying group. When they broke apart, Trigg and her father were striding toward them.

"I think this is a day of celebration," Papa announced, his hand upon Trigg's shoulder. "For today, I've agreed to give Cora's hand in marriage to Trigg Gentry."

Her family clapped, and she went forward and grasped Trigg's hands. She had waited and trusted God with her future. And she would go forth with life, full of hope, knowing God's plans would sustain her through the darkest days. The square peg had finally journeyed to her proper spot.

Together, Cora and Trigg, with God's leading, would begin their journey to their future path framed in everlasting hope.

Chapter Thirty

Cora gasped as she stepped from the carriage festooned in white silk and holly. Trigg's grandmother's mansion was truly decked in the holiday spirit with a wedding flair. Silk bunting lined the elaborate porch between the two spires. Potted poinsettias lined the walk and continued up the steps. The dim lighting of late December showcased the candles winking merrily across the porch railing. When she'd caught her breath, she grasped the bouquet of red roses in her hand and ran her fingers along the seam of her elegant green velvet dress.

Her wedding just seven days before Christmas. How fitting. A season of salvation. Trigg had saved her from a life of a loveless marriage, and Christmas would commemorate the Christ Child's birth, who came to save everyone from the curse of sin. Truly it would be a season of great celebration for the rest of Cora's days.

Her father appeared at the door and strode toward her. God bless the man. His face told of the emotions battling within him as he contemplated his youngest on the day of her wedding.

His jaw clenched as he pressed her hand in the crook of his elbow. "I am not sure, Cora dear, that I'm quite willing to part with you."

Even all the nervousness of the day didn't squelch her grin. "You can visit us anytime you'd like. Kentucky isn't that far."

He drew her to a stop and faced her. His eyes narrowed with intensity. "Are you happy, Cora? Truly happy?"

Tears pricked at her eyes and she clutched her father's arms. Suddenly emotion swelled her throat. She whispered, "Yes, Papa. Very happy."

With a nod, he hugged her tight. "Then I have no choice but to escort you to your man. But if you ever need us…"

"I know. You'll be right here."

They paused beneath the mistletoe hanging in the doorway, and her father bent to kiss her cheek. Then he whisked her through the door and down the aisle between two sets of chairs filled with people in the huge parlor. Her large family had spilled over onto the groom's side. But Trigg's grandmother, grandfather, plus Bliss and Roe didn't seem to mind.

Even Aunt Josephine and Odette, on the arm of Wilkinson, had made the journey to her special celebration. Odette pressed a hanky to a tear that trickled down her cheek and gave Cora a tremulous smile. Her cousin now planned her own wedding in a few more months. It seemed both of them would, at last, marry for love.

The guests packed into the room turned expectant eyes upon her as she swept to the front. Toward the groom. Cora blanked out the people and the quartet in the corner playing some sort of deeply moving music and focused on Trigg. He pumped his fists as she approached, and his eyes all but ate her alive. If she hadn't been in front of a room full of guests, she would have giggled at his eagerness.

Once her father kissed her cheek and passed her over to Trigg, a feeling of rightness washed over her. This is where she belonged. On Trigg's arm, by his side. Loving him, supporting him, sharing her life's journey with him for decades and beyond. At last, Cora was not too tall, nor too tomboyish, nor too childish, nor anything else. She had found her home, and God willing, she would stay there, part of Trigg himself.

The ceremony floated along with Cora in an almost incredulous trance. Good gravy, she wanted to pinch herself to make sure it was for real. As the pastor finished up the vows, the quartet kicked in with *Fur Elise*. Trigg moved forward and lowered his head to hers. The kiss was short and sweet but held promise of much more to come. The heat in his eyes bespoke the same.

And then they turned to their family and friends, being announced as Mr. and Mrs. Trigg Gentry. Amidst the rice, the couple scurried through the rows of people and hurried through the door. The same decorated carriage she'd arrived in awaited to whisk them away for a getaway at a nearby cabin on the Ohio River.

Cora hugged her family and wiped her tears. Happy tears. Trigg wrapped an arm around the stiff elegant elderly lady he'd introduced as his grandmother and pecked her cheek. Amongst the well-wishes, they tread the brick walk through the iron gate to the carriage.

Once they settled on the bench seat, she and Trigg waved to the wedding guests scattered about the yard. He pulled her gently into his arms and pressed a kiss against her lips that stole her breath. Then, he trailed a row of kisses to her ear.

"You are beautiful, Mrs. Gentry," he whispered, nibbling her earlobe.

Her face scalded and a giggle escaped. "Oh, my sir. You're being quite forward."

Trigg bounced his eyebrows. "You haven't seen anything yet, my wife."

Warmth rippled from her cheeks to her toes, the heat between them thwarting the near freezing temperature of the carriage's interior. She leaned forward and touched her lips to his, more than willing to venture beyond with the love of her life. Finally, the waiting was over.

And as the horse's hoof beats marked each step further down the path, amidst the couple's sighs and kisses of love and passion, Cora and Trigg's great journey of hope had just begun. No longer a misfit, Cora was indeed, well fit. To a man named Trigg Gentry.

About the Author

When Peggy Trotter's not crafting or DIY-ing, she's immersed in a story scene of some sort, always pushing toward that sigh-worthy, happily-ever-after ending. Two kids, two in-law-kids, and three grandchildren (and one on the way), the delight her life, as well as her Batman of 36 years whose cape is much worn from rescuing his wife from one scrape or another.

Winner of the prestigious ACFW Genesis Award in 2014, she flip-flops from historical to contemporary to suspense, but always inspirational. But ultimately, it's always about Ransomed-Ever-After Fiction. Incredible characters and storylines reveal God's guiding providence and unending love.

My Note to You!

I pray you enjoyed *The Misfit Bride*, that it gave you clean, inspirational entertainment or even helped you on your own life journey. Being in that place of waiting like Cora is a difficult place to rest. But most of all, I wanted to stress the fact that nobody~NOBODY is an outcast to God, no matter how weird, broken, or odd you might think you are, or are made to feel by others. ***God loves you***. He sent his own Son, Jesus, to save each and every soul. Every person is precious in His sight. So precious, He died to save each wayward soul.

I love my readers and enjoy interacting with all of you. Please join me on my websites and sign up for my newsletter to get information on my next books. Oh, and there's always prizes!

Links:

peggytrotter.com

peggytrotter.blogspot.com

diamondsinfiction.blogspot.com

Twitter: https://twitter.com/Peggy_Trotter

Facebook: https://www.facebook.com/PeggyTrotterAuthor

Goodreads:

https://www.goodreads.com/author/show/13778873.Peggy_Trotter

Amazon Author's Profile Page:

amazon.com/author/peggytrotter.com

Instagram: https://www.instagram.com/peggy_trotter_author/

Pinterest: https://www.pinterest.com/PeggyTrotterAuthor/

LinkedIn: https://www.linkedin.com/in/peggy-trotter-44a29b95/

BookBub: https://www.bookbub.com/authors/peggy-trotter

MeWe: mewe.com/i/peggytrotter

Parler: https://parler.com/profile/PeggyTrotterAuthor

Usa.life: https://usa.life/PeggyTrotterAuthor

Gab: https://gab.com/PeggyTrotterAuthor

Don't miss the second installment of the Society of Outcasts Series *The Lowborn Lady* releasing 12/1/21. Keep reading for the blurb and the first chapter sample.

The Lowborn Lady
Society of Outcasts
Book Two

Rhapsody Hastings finds herself in the arms of ruffian Cavanaugh Blackledge when her carriage breaks down on a dark country road. Wedding him stills the scandal of the late night tryst while soothing the guilt she holds of her first husband's untimely death. So, she accepts the arrangement as her own personal penance. Yet, an unexpected mission wakens her dead heart. But it's a costly gamble. A high society lady shouldn't be involved in such dangerous, illegal conspiracies.

Using his new marriage to shield his clandestine operations proves to be an unanticipated godsend for Cav. And how could he not appreciate the fetching Rhapsody's presence, creating the perfect buffer when he must face his former true love, now his smug brother's wife.

But their artificial life turns ugly when information surfaces, putting both his and Rhapsody's covert efforts in jeopardy. Secrets reveal more secrets, but the skeleton in Rhapsody's closet may not only undo her, it may make them both very dead.

Chapter One

Remember ladies. Grace...at all costs.

Miss Potter's finishing school mantra berated Rhapsody Hasting's brain while the hand of her dead husband weighed on her shoulder. Rhapsody tightened her grip on the armchair to repress the instinctual recoil. Surely the woman who'd dispensed such wisdom had never—never sat for a mourning portrait.

Rhapsody shifted her chin slightly, bringing his pale rigor mortis paw into her peripheral vision.

"Mrs. Hastings, please move your head a bit to the right. And here," the brown tweed-coated man appeared from beneath a black sheet shielding the back of the camera, "if you could reach up with your right hand and lay it over his."

No, nothing gleaned from Miss Potter's Ladies Etiquette and Finishing School had prepared her for this. Mindful of the twitch that tended to pulsate below her left eye, Rhapsody tensed her jaw. Miss Potter intruded into her thoughts again.

A true lady never reveals any distress or disappointment. Your countenance remains unimpassioned, imprisoning all the uncouth lowly desires of the commoner. Rhapsody, still that tic near your eye. Miss Potter would snap her waspish figure to attention in front of her, making sure the terrible malady had been controlled. *Always remember ladies. You are to be graceful, elegant, and refined. Sacrificing everything for dignity.*

"'Yes, Miss Potter.'" All girls replied in low controlled tones. Too loud and one earned a wooden spoon to the head.

Reality pressed the fog of childhood away. The brown-tweed coat approached her. The best photographer in the city, she'd been told. He grasped her wrist most unwelcomely and directed it toward the lifeless claw. "If you could just clasp this area of your husband's hand, it would make such a…fine picture."

In other words, make the dead appear alive. The photographer pressed her fingers against the dead-cold, stiff hand. Rhapsody blinked only once. But revulsion still burned an acid trail up her throat.

"Right here, Mrs. Hastings. Lovely."

The photographer's platform pole exploded, bringing a burst of light into the air. Rhapsody wasted no time dropping Devlin's stiff cold extremity and shrugging from beneath him to a standing position. She brought her wrist to her nose, inhaling the smelling salts in the hanky tucked in her sleeve.

"Brilliant. Now, I will leave Mr. Hastings in the stand for group photos. I believe the rest of the family are to assemble soon?"

"No, please remove him." She couldn't get to the door fast enough.

"Ma'am?"

A hesitation and a slight turn at the door brought her husband's accusatory stare into her eyes. Her breath hitched. She pressed a palm to her throat. "No. Remove him immediately and return him to the casket."

She spun to avoid any more dialogue and headed toward the gleaming cherry stairway. *Feet progress slowly, grasp the rail with firm yet gentle pressure, slight hitch to the skirt, chin averted, but not up.* Miss Potter's voice nagged away. Right now Rhapsody loathed this lesson. Better to scurry up the stairs, slam the door, and never reappear. Again. Ever.

But she directed her delicate shoes to promenade to her room, toward the master at the end of the lengthy hallway. Eight bedrooms. She'd insisted. Why, Rhapsody had stipulated every item. Specially crafted, delivered, no cost considered for perfection. The small hallway table she passed came from France. Worth a small fortune. The ivory statue, *Genteel Lady in Garden* rested atop the unique table. Carved from the ivory of Africa, the figurine had traveled the great Atlantic Ocean to adorn this specific location.

She paused beside the lady, swathed in a beautiful frozen robe, clutching a flower to her nose. A surge swelled inside Rhapsody's breast, and it was all she could do not to swat the French-made table down the stairway and watch the ivory figure explode into a million shards.

Instead, Miss Potter returned. *If you must, stab your nails into your palms. But you shall squelch all emotion. A lady of class never allows it to be shown.*

Her hands clenched. The proper way, only allowing the pinky and ring finger to dig while leaving the others lax. All appeared calm. She jabbed her nails into her soft flesh and strolled to the last door on the left. Yes, she had insisted on the left with its ornate door and crystal doorknob.

Once inside she pushed the solid slab closed and turned the skeleton key. How to escape the next twenty-four hours was beyond her. She inched forward, grabbed one of the four columns of the ridiculously huge four-poster bed and pressed her cheek to the cool mahogany.

After a few deep breaths, drawn short by the overly tight corset, she settled on the edge of the ruffled bedspread. Then she decided to stand. It proved much more difficult to breathe sitting down.

A knock sounded at the door. "Who is it?"

Had her voice always been so harsh and demanding?

"Maid, Ma'am."

"Go away. I have no use for you now."

Silence.

Rhapsody's gaze met the daguerreotype of Devlin and herself hanging near the door. Much different time and much different circumstances. She rose and plucked it from the wall. Even from a still photo his stare shamed her soul. She stomped to the desk near the window to thrust the castigating image into the drawer. Another knock, sharper and insistent.

"Rhapsody. Open this door."

Mother. The one who insisted on niceties rarely followed them herself. Rhapsody's reluctant feet slipped across the Oriental rug. She twisted the key in the lock and the massive door opened with a rush.

"Your presence is required downstairs. Family photos."

"I'm feeling under the weather."

Her mother's eyes narrowed. "Of course you are. Laying your husband to rest is an unpleasant, but necessary task. Come."

The family matriarch rotated her imposing black hoop skirt and brushed through the doorway, her freshly coifed hair stiff with fine breeding. Her mother turned at the door. "Five minutes, no more."

Irritation. Rhapsody used her old trick and tightened the muscles running to her ears, causing them to move only slightly. It always produced a soft rushing sound that she imagined as her temper, simmering. Anything to relieve tension. "Send Lissy up."

Her mother blinked and nodded once, like always, and disappeared like a ghoul. Rhapsody rushed forward to shut the door. She gripped the crystal knob and closed her eyes. How? How could she draw this torture to an end? The shallow breaths she panted inspired inspiration.

At the tentative knock, Rhapsody whipped the door open, earning a flash of Lissy's eyes glowing in her dark face.

"Yes, Mum?"

"I need tightening." Rhapsody stepped back and allowed the servant to enter and eased the door closed.

She turned and gripped the post once more.

"Mum?"

Rhapsody spun and slung her hands to her hips. "What is it, Lissy? I'm needed downstairs without delay."

The obedient servant nodded, her little dust cap bobbing as she curtsied. "I done strung you to twenty this morning."

"And?"

Again the whites of the woman's eyes bugged as she looked left then right. "Well, that's the tightest you ever gone."

"I want nineteen and a half. Or possibly nineteen. I need to look my best for my husband today."

Lissy blinked a quick succession of flutters, but nodded. Rhapsody once again set herself against the pole while the woman undid the buttons down the back of her black satin dress.

"Lock the door first."

More hesitation from the seasoned maid.

"Now."

"Yes, Mum."

Rhapsody took the last deep breath she was liable to have for the rest of the day as the lock tumbled into place behind her. Then the maid resumed, yanking and pulling. Moisture popped out along Rhapsody's brow.

"Mum, I can't—"

"Tighter!"

A foot landed against her backside as the sturdy maid tugged. Rhapsody tried to relax and allow the stays to pull her smaller, but it was a battle of pain. At last the corset held and Lissy let go. Rhapsody rested against the column for just a moment, taking silent puffs of air through her nose. She pushed away and stood. "Now, my hair."

The broad servant nodded and hurried to the dressing table. A rush of fogginess crept into Rhapsody's vision, and she clutched a hand to the post. "No, you imbecile. I can't sit."

"Yes, Mum."

The woman rushed behind her and adjusted the curls at her nape. A crisp knock brought everything to a halt.

"Rhapsody. Come."

Lissy hustled to the door and turned the key. The portly maid opened the door with an odd, perhaps sympathetic, look on her wide face.

"Mum—"

Rhapsody held up a finger. "Speak when spoken to, Lissy."

The black woman nodded and cast her gaze to the floor. Rhapsody glided past. Indeed, this was perfect. A shadowy mist threatening her vision pulsated to the beat of her runaway heart. She grasped the rail with new meaning. It was her only means to safely reach the bottom of the stairway. Chin up, face emptied of the agony she carried not only beneath her corset, but in her heart.

Ah, the family milled about the entryway and spilled into the drawing room where Devlin still stiffly stood. Hesitating at the bottom of the stairs, she took several shallow breaths. With her husband's dead mocking gaze upon her, the darkness closed in around her.

What splendid timing. Her knees buckled and the finely woven carpet runner rose up to greet her. Her left eye gave a slight twitch. Sorry, Mother. Family picture time was over. The room disappeared into a hazy, distorted blur.

Rhapsody jerked from the pungent smell of salts and fluttered her eyes open. A circle of faces hovered above her including mother, Lissy, looking guilty, and father, with a worried crease across his brow. So, they'd placed her on the fainting couch in the downstairs guest room. How apropos.

The tin-type ceiling glared at her. Someone spoke, but she only heard her memories. "Tin ceilings are meant only for parlors or kitchens, I believe. Much too extravagant for the entire home." Gertrude Smidely had assured her outside the church house one hot morning.

Rhapsody had been draped in her sky-blue day dress. The large hoop, multiple crinolines, and the daring dip beneath her chin garnered the attention of every male in the congregation. She remembered giving a snide tinkle of laughter. "Perhaps, but Devlin will deny me nothing."

Nothing. Except his very presence.

Someone slapped her hand.

"Rhapsody, dear, are you well?"

Again, Mother. Little had she cared a mere twenty minutes earlier. Or had it been longer than that? Had they conducted the funeral? Buried her husband in the cold spring ground?

Rhapsody struggled to sit up. But Father, and her accessory to the crime, her corset, pressed her down.

"Lissy, run get a cold cloth." Motherly tones. Stiff and disapproving.

"Dear girl, answer me. Can you speak?"

Darling Father. At least a smidgen of sympathy had found its way into his voice.

"Yes."

The neat salt and pepper beard parted to allow a gentle smile. He looked older today.

Mother straightened. "Never mind, Lissy. Let's get her into the parlor."

Father also rose. "You can't be serious, Minerva. She's only just awakened."

But Mother whisked away, gathering the distant male relatives of the family to carry the entire couch into what Mother called the parlor. Rhapsody ignored the men lifting her couch and the sputtering of her father while stilling her tongue. She'd personally made sure the room was larger than a parlor. Therefore clearly, it could only be christened a drawing room.

"Here, here. Set her next to Devlin." Mother's voice carried a slight twinge of enjoyment, carefully veiled. How she did love to be in charge.

"No. Stop." A family photo of her on a fainting couch, reclining like some saloon wench? Indeed not. "Set me down. Immediately."

Her cousins acquiesced and lowered the chaise near the door.

Mother leaned over her. "My dear. You're revived. Irvin, Gotwald, grasp her arms. Perhaps we can have a decent family photo after all."

Her two distant cousins clamped her elbows and drew her from the couch. Once standing the dizziness threatened again. But since Mother seemed so insistent on these photos, even fainting dead away would not change the woman's mind.

Her two bodyguards remained at her side as Mother and the photographer placed everyone in their places. The men all but carried Rhapsody toward her upright, deceased husband, his blank stare encompassing the entire room and denouncing her at the same time. She squeezed her eyes shut until they had rotated her away from his accusatory stare.

"And now, stand here, Mrs. Hastings. Men can you back her up, right against her husband? That's it. Perfect."

Perfect? Her back now rested against her spouse's rigid dead body. But thankfully, the photographer did not insist on crooking his hand around her arm. Still, she leaned away. It would serve her right if they'd wrap Devlin's arm around her neck, and he suddenly roused from his lifeless pose to squeeze the life from her.

"We need to be in haste. I feel my daughter is still quite unwell." Father, her knight.

"Yes, yes, of course. All eyes here." The photographer leaned behind the camera and pointed to the circular lens on the front.

Rhapsody lifted her chin, set her teeth, and pulled her ears back. The rushing sound simmered inside her head as the flash exploded once more. Then, a slight indention convulsed in record pace below her left eye. Miss Potter would be horrified. Nevertheless, a slight satisfied sigh escaped Rhapsody's lips. This unpleasantness would soon be over.

As unconsciousness rose up in a black fog, she hoped above all hopes she would never awaken. For in reality, she envied Devlin. He had the pleasure of physical death while she remained nothing more than a walking cadaver.

"Pleasssse…"

The word exhaled from her as she crumpled to the floor.